Sacred Space

Sacred Space

edited by Marsha Rowe

Library of Congress Catalog Card Number : 92-60149

British Library Cataloguing in Publication Data
A catalogue record for this book is available from the British Library

Copyright © 1992 the individual contributors
Copyright for 'Kate' by Thomas Keneally © Serpentine Publishing Pty. Ltd. 1992
Introduction copyright © 1992 Marsha Rowe
Volume copyright © 1992 Serpent's Tail

First published 1992 by
Serpent's Tail, 4 Blackstock Mews, London N4
and 401 West Broadway #2, New York, NY 10012

Typeset in 11/14pt Bembo by Contour Typesetters,
Southall, London
Printed in Great Britain by Cox & Wyman Ltd.,
of Reading, Berkshire

Contents

Introduction

In my youth I liked to climb the stout Japanese maple which grew outside our front door and sit on a favourite branch. I took a book with me, and read. If I looked up I could see the sky, blue and distant. If I looked down, I sometimes saw people passing on the path below. A canopy of fluttery leaves protected me from the sun. I could not move about, for fear of falling off the branch, nor was I comfortable, because there was nothing to lean against. I sat, feet dangling, in freedom and seclusion. No one could make demands on me, I had no duties to fulfil, nor people to satisfy. In contemplation, my soul drifted.

I did not realize then that the tree was the symbol of connection. Its branches reach towards the heavens, its roots delve into the underworld, making it the marker of consecrated ground, a symbol of place, of belonging. The planting of the tree, the setting of the pillar, the balancing of the flagpole, these are the placements that divide the world of the cosmos – the ordered and the known – from the un-world of disorder and chaos.

Reading was essentially part of this communion, in which I was taken out of myself into a netherspace that reduced my own world to a speck. It was sacred, an act of holy purpose almost, because it bestowed upon me a sense of my own humanity, a discrete sense of self, through the imagination. Without it I became emptied and devitalized. By taking me beyond my world, it gave me back myself.

In a secular age, that great marker of difference – the tree of life – seems to have fallen. In our pluralistic society, there is no longer a mighty supernatural tree, no one God, no singular mark of transcendence.

When I left Australia, I discovered that for the exile, the immigrant, the wanderer, the tree's symbolic fall can be swift and painful, tearing away the inner skin of the soul, the transparency of one's own background, family, beliefs, national identity. Once-imagined worlds become the void at one's own feet. There is nothing to stand on but the community in which one finds oneself, with its own values, different ways of relating and going about life. 'Mine was the incognito of a phantom,' wrote Simone de Beauvoir, confronted by the otherness of America, 'I felt invisible to every look.'*

The spirit of the exile may wish for more of the day-by-day stuff and will seek not to be other to the surrounding life. It may never again be enmeshed in any particular place, but there may be anchor points. For years I made little altars of objects in each room that I lived in. I arranged pots, flowers, favourite books, pictures, into a world-in-miniature, a meditative bonsai space, that resonated with the kaleidoscope of different selves I was juggling at the time.

In the European secular tradition, the space that is sacred is art. It is through art that the human spirit transcends its limited 'material confines', as Salman Rushdie has put it.

To seek transcendence through art alone may leave the spirit weightless, floating free.

In this anthology each writer gives a different view of the sacred in a secular age. The transcendence that they describe is in the reshaping of the language or signs by which it has been previously understood. These include cultural patterns of relationship, symbols of national identity, of gender, and religious moral codes.

There is a confidence in these stories that suggests that a new sense of sacred space is being realized. These writers are strongly and intelligently aware that any old mumbo-jumbo will not do, and that the space for the sacred is necessarily conflictual, fascinating, nourishing, its discourse wide open to radical discussion and debate.

In some contributions the space of the sacred is all-embracing. It is a city or a town – civic space. Sacred space then appears as a political landscape. It includes the citizens and their relationship with each other, as well as the architecture.

Rosalind Belben observes the village heritage within the lives of city dwellers in Rumania. It alerts her to a pattern of relationships that is lost in Britain. She writes of Berlin as it was when still divided by its wall. It was an artifical atrium to the West, but it was also an oasis of culture, where it was safe to walk at night.

To the European, the Australian landscape is an 'emptiness' because it is bereft of small villages. In Australia this notion of countryside is inappropriate. Two stories in *Sacred Space* are set in Australia and one in the United States and each plays against the ancient European opposition between town and country.

In Thomas Keneally's story the heroine, Kate, seeks alleviation and a vision by travelling to remote areas with a farmer named Gus and a kangaroo and an emu rescued from a Tableau Vivant of the Australian Coat of Arms. Kate is a rich woman, who has lost both her children. She throws piety to the winds, and has sought transcendence in childhood through a scandalous uncle, a priest. Gus suggests also a Koori vision of the land as sacred map, dissolving the division of outside and inside.

SACRED SPACE

Drusilla Modjeska describes an abandoned farm in an Australian valley as a lost paradise, dreamlike and unsustainable. Contrasted by other scenes, of occupants past and present, an image emerges of a land where reality and illusion blur into each other, and of possibilities for a different future, neither romantic nor utopian, for an Australian culture born of many but not yet there. Instead there's a dance of reflections, nothing fixed except the movement of change itself.

'Civilization' as inside space, expanding and encroaching on 'wilderness', the outside space, is satirized by Jonathan Lerner. When his character Eliot flies into Miami and observes the sprawling city, he is unaware that he is about to confront his own nostalgic fantasies and pretensions, and that the outside space – the Everglades – holds the sacred key.

In 'Bathtime', Jenny Diski homes in on the sanctity of the bathroom's private space. Is a bath just a mundane bath, or is it a re-birth?

Juan Goytisolo evokes the mystic passion of the dervish seeker of truth Jalal al-Din al-Rumi, the poet who wrote of his ecstatic love of another dervish. The sacred art of the dervishes cannot, Goytisolo argues, be reduced to aesthetic spectacle without losing the transcendent quality of the dance itself.

Jean Binta Breeze's story claims the sacred for the most fundamental act of possession, a piece of land, a space for a life.

In my story the character adopts the colour blue as a mantra. She imagines that by searching to understand the history of the colour, which is also the colour of the planet, she will overcome her alienation. Something or someone continually threatens to break in on her obsession.

In a secular age, the spirit is perhaps more conservative,

harking back to earlier certainties. It is interesting to see how this is resisted. Lucy Goodison sets her archaeologist heroine brooding on the past. Before the Grand Narrative of Western History had even begun, with no stories written down, and only the design of artefacts and the modelled curves of an empty vessel to go on, she seems to tilt backwards into the sacred territory of matter.

The Western concept of life as a journey is different from the Eastern concept of life as a way. One celebrates the triumph of the individual, the other celebrates the dissolution of the individual. Yet in both cultures there are places that individuals set apart as special, that become infused with meaning. They may be actual places that witnessed some private rite of passage; they may be public, and historically recognized, such as Ayer's Rock in Australia or Stonehenge in Britain, whose sacredness is fought over by different groups, each claiming ownership; or it may be music, or an event, that is not personal but social.

Two immense natural rock formations that are the sites of myth are described by David Craig. Gibraltar, and its opposite, Abyla, form the two great pillars rent apart by Hercules, gateway to the Mediterranean. The space between two rocks was in itself symbolic, and their shapes intimately related to the myths projected onto them. The Cailleach in Scotland is a Celtic earth mother, grand and grim. She is coupled with another, across the loch. Such mighty paired rocks became the mother and father of stories.

Marsha Rowe

*Simone de Beauvoir: *America Day by Day*

A Little Piece of Land, Lord!

Jean Binta Breeze

'Take the shoes from off your feet, for the ground on
which you walk is holy ground.'

I would like to tell you the story of Cousin Eva. She is an
ordinary woman, has led an exemplary and ordinary life,
quite common in its details to many other women of her age.
An old woman from the peasantry possessing a love of her land
and her people, but has never been able to place her feet on a
little piece of land that she could develop in her way and know
she would never have to leave again. She represents a people
without economic power trying to claim their own. The land
they have cleared, tilled, seeded, watered and tended into a
garden, but can still be moved off at a moment's notice. But let
me stop analysing and simply tell you her story, and maybe,
just maybe, we will see how a people's need to control their
own space comes from individual need for sacred space. So . . .
to Cousin Eva. . . .

'One, two, tree, bwoy,
mi an yuh a spree bwoy,
come mek we pull togedda, bwoy'

The chant went on and on, punctuated by the grunts of
the men. Each time they got to the last line, they lifted the

small wooden house a little further on to the back of the truck.

Cousin Eva sat, her arms protecting a large wicker basket, the kind usually used to carry yams. It was covered with a clean tablecloth she had sewn herself from some white patterned material that Mass Beddie's daughter had given her last Christmas on a visit from America. Cousin Eva was very proud of that tablecloth. Everyone had said it was good material for a church dress, but Cousin Eva knew she would look like a walking window. She had sewn it how she wanted, peering over it in the evening light, her thimble glinting as her fingers moved. There had been a few pieces left over which she had folded neatly and packed into one side of the basket for, God spare her life, she was going to make a frilly curtain for the window when the house was settled on the piece of land.

> 'One, two, tree, bwoy,
> mi an yuh a spree bwoy,
> come mek we pull togedda, bwoy'

With a last gigantic lift, muscles straining, stomachs taut and glistening with sweat, the men finally eased the house off the concrete blocks which had been firmly pounded into the earth to support the house. It wasn't wise building a proper foundation until you were sure how long you could stay.

Cousin Eva had had her fill of family land. Her husband, Mass Abel, God bless his soul, had built their house on family land in Miles gully, but when he passed on, his family had started all kinds of quarrel and argument about it. Since Mass Abel did not leave a title and Cousin Eva wasn't the warring kind, she had paid some men to move the house a little further up the road to a spot that Mass Sonny was renting her.

Well, the little field of gungo that she planted each year with a few yams to keep her going was mashed down in the heavy rains two years ago. Last year, cows had run loose in her field and ruined the crop again. Mass Sonny wasn't much better off than her and had wanted his money for the land. There was nothing Cousin Eva could do but ask the church brothers to move her again.

That time she had been very hopeful. A distant cousin who owned a sizeable yam field and did quite well out of rearing chickens, had offered her a house spot in exchange for weeding in the field and cooking for the men on work days. She had managed that for about a year until the arthritis had played up so bad, she couldn't manage climbing up and down the hills.

Cousin Eva wasn't the begging kind and, after all, you couldn't expect a man, cousin or not, to give you land for free, not in these times. She might be poor but she was brought up with her pride and not even arthritis was going to make her lose her dignity. So, she prayed hard and did what she could selling a little callaloo she grew in the backyard, knowing quite well that the Lord helped those who helped themselves. Then, one day, Mass Sony's own pigs came in and rooted it all up. There was no one she could cry to but the Lord.

That time He really seemed to answer. A letter came to the post office from Mass Abel's one son in foreign land. He had stopped sending the regular postal order after Mass Abel died. No one could blame him for that. He wasn't Cousin Eva's son. She didn't have any children for Mass Abel, in fact, didn't have any children at all. Something, must be the Lord, pricked him to send the fifty pounds. She knew from the amount that she wouldn't be hearing from him for a while. But, God bless his soul, he had remembered when she most needed it.

This time she decided to make a clean move and arranged a

reasonable deal with Blue who drove the Bedward truck for boss man. If you knew the driver well, you could always make a deal on the side. It was how poor people got backra to work for them so the exploitation wouldn't be strictly one way.

Cousin Eva knew that she had been a decent, hardworking citizen in her country for nearly sixty years now, and she wasn't going to die in poorhouse. If they could pay to keep her there, then she was sure they wouldn't mind if she occupied a piece of government land. If the government owned the land, then it belonged to the people. Cousin Eva was sure she was the people and was always thinking it was such a shame to see good land lying idle when so many people had none.

'One, two, tree, bwoy' and the house was on the back of Blue's truck on its way to what was now called 'Capture lan' in Cascade. Cousin Eva was sitting in her chair inside it looking out the window as they bounced along the country road for two miles or so.

She didn't know what put the thought in her mind, maybe she was getting stupid in her old age, but as they drove along, she couldn't help wishing that she could live in a house that kept moving just like this. She could see different sights everytime she looked out the window. That would be a good way to spend her last few years after living in one village for so long. After all, if you had to keep moving house so much, you could very well keep on moving, house and all.

> 'One, two, tree, bwoy,
> mi an yuh a spree bwoy,
> come mek we pull togedda bwoy'

The house was now firmly settled on new concrete blocks. As time passed, the foundation would be strengthened. The men eased back, lifting caps, wiping brows. Surveying their work with pride, they smiled at each other in celebration of their strength and turned to Cousin Eva for the best part of the proceedings.

She already had the bottle of white rum out of the basket and was wiping the cups clean of any dust from the travel. Cousin Eva wasn't a drinking woman but she had grown up with hardworking men and understood the need for a fiery rum every now and then. She supposed Blue and the other men were a lot more regular, but they were good men.

Blue broke the seal of the bottle and poured a few drops in front of the door to the house. 'May only good spirits visit yuh!' With deep belly laughs and slaps on each other's shoulders, the bottle was passed round.

Wiping away the grim expression that always comes with the fire of swallowing rum, Blue picked up Cousin Eva's basket and placed it ceremoniously inside the house. He didn't want to see the tears of thanksgiving in her eyes.

'Time to go back to Massa wuk.'

That evening, as the moon rose, Cousin Eva watched it from her chair by the window, her Bible on her lap.

She reached a hand inside her bosom and pulled out a knotted handkerchief. Opening it out on the table, she separated the money into different piles. She knew what each was for. A good vegetable garden to eat from, she could sell the excess at the local market. Some chickens, and a fence to protect them, a good fence. She couldn't stand to lose another crop. Then a good stove. She could bake and sell lunches to the children from the big school nearby.

Slowly bending, she removed her shoes. Favouring her right knee, she knelt by the chair.

'Tank yuh, Lord, tank yuh, a likkle piece a lan, tank yuh, Lord!'

The Privilege of Orpheus
Rosalind Belben

Rumania broke the heart as East Germany never could and never did. Perhaps it was the blue of the sky, or the warm smell of city and earth, left by the Romans. Or the radiant look of the flowers in the Cişmigiu Gardens and the screwed-up pieces of pork on the plate. Perhaps it was Rumanians.

In East Berlin the ignoble feeling that the people of the DDR were somehow themselves responsible for the heaviness in the air was hard to shake away. In Bucharest a *gaiety* was palpable, and it was ravishing, it came as a relief; although the closed faces were all around, and life was a good deal more sombre.

It was easy to descend from the capitalist clouds of the West and be very stupid. Nevertheless, to step from West Berlin into East Berlin remained one of the more extraordinary journeys in the world, so long as the way back was open.

I was even fond of the wall, it loomed out of the mist, accompanying me on walks; it was to be met everywhere, across lakes and rivers, canals and fields, in the street, in the woods, an old friend. It kept the wild boar in and chaos out. I saw it in snow, in baking heat, unadorned.

I hoped I would live to see the wall come down.

West Berlin was unique, of course. Its life was ephemeral, perpetually; destined to vanish almost in a night, when distant friends, not understanding, were to be shocked that I should mourn it. To them I might say: it made one think of a village. It let humans be. It gave them space. The uncrowded village of two million could be anarchic and unconventional, or docile and clean. It was stuffed with what are known as art treasures. Smart places were within ten minutes on the S-Bahn of deep forest. One could sail and swim, still can. I, a woman, could walk home at one or two in the morning through the middle of West Berlin carrying my handbag. All the pleasures of capitalism were shut in this island and some of the distressing things didn't flourish so. It was quiet, some found it too quiet. But it was not at all provincial; to me, it had the flush of an animal on heat.

East Berlin on the other hand had seen too many tom-cats. There the quiet was painful, and one felt sorry.

The sense of sorrow was complicated for those who didn't feel comfortable in, or with, the West.

I flew from Schönefeld with a Rumanian general, three staff officers and an old lady from the coldest village in the Carpathians. We faced each other across tables. To show his disregard for his own safety the general wouldn't do up his seat belt. He was bulky, if the Interflug aeroplane had turned over he would have squashed us and broken our necks. But he talked to the old lady, who was dressed as a peasant, without any sign of condescension. He chatted in this friendly manner because the old lady could well have been his mother, in England such a reason would have prevented his noticing her. One of the staff officers asked in German after my husband, he made a face when I asked after his wife. He chose kindly to explain to me how one used the metro – he gave me his map of it – in Bucharest and glowed when he spoke of Ceauşescu, whose real achievement the metro was. On the tarmac at Otopeni the military party was met with delicate kisses by three more officers. The uniforms were tin-pot, I thought. In the terminal building, where I was trapped for three hours, a man bent gracefully over a woman's hand.

It was very slow: it's *Rumania*, a Rumanian mother said, torn by nostalgia and tears of exasperation, to her western child.

In my bed big black fleas leapt a foot when the sheet was drawn back. I was taking Amoxycillin, great thousand-milligram pills, for an abscess. If I'd realized I tasted nasty and it gave me immunity I'd have rationed it out for the whole of my stay. But the fleas bit me at the end.

They were in the good room. In the first, the dirty towels at the hand-basin had sent me down to reception. A Swiss tourist was in a voice of bitter misery querying the exchange rate. He tramped off. I mentioned the towels. The man and the woman at the desk turned closed faces to me. The housekeeper was summoned. I slid a packet of Kent cigarettes towards the man receptionist. His hand whipped over it and it vanished, his lids flew up and he smiled. I had watched this done at the airport. He had an endearing smile. Before I reached the lift and the housekeeper with the clean towels on her arm, he called me. He would put me in another room. He gave me a double room with a private bathroom and a kind of balcony. It marked me out, to all who worked in the hotel, as someone who understood, as someone who hadn't come empty-handed, stupid and cross to Rumania.

Kent cigarettes, and it had to be Kent, were vital. It is unlikely the people one gave them to would have smoked them.

The reception desk had a brass-lined hole in it, through which keys should have been dropped. I didn't see it. I pushed mine across the top, others did the same. On the last evening I went out to supper and when I came back I found someone had been in my room. Florian couldn't find the key and the housekeeper, that same housekeeper although there were at

15

least two, let me in. She and I gaped at the mess together . . .
The visitor had used nearly all my soap, it was a soggy blur on
the edge of the bath, the bathroom floor was in puddles, my
towels sat weakly on it. He had hung his leather jacket on a
chair, and his bag was propped beside it. He had tossed – bitten
– or slept on both the beds, and mauled the old television set,
not knowing the programmes hadn't yet started. He had hung
my nightie on a hanger in the wardrobe and tipped my
padlocked shoulder-bag over and over. The housekeeper went
away to fetch sheets and the fellow turned up at the door. He
was Turkish and he spoke some German. His bag and leather
jacket were by now at the reception desk; why on earth hadn't
it dawned on him they'd made a mistake with the rooms, I
asked him, very scathingly. I marched him downstairs. He's a
Turk, the housekeeper said, sinking onto a chair in my room
and lighting a cigarette, he said to Florian he thought it not
unusual that the room should have a nightdress in it, he
thought the hotel had provided you, the Turkish boys are quite
simple. But the hotel had run out of linen, I'd have to wrap the
pillow in a sheet. There was a football match, a difficult night.
I started to laugh, I gave her a packet of Kent and she
embraced me. He didn't take a thing, I said. They are honest,
the housekeeper said. She looked tired. That a hotel
housekeeper should sink down in my room and light a
cigarette struck me as a little quaint and I was flattered. Her
sweetness of expression had been searing, and her musical
voice.

All Bucharest took me for Bulgarian.

In my blue cotton jacket, bought for its lack of labels, with
my dark hair and ruddy cheeks, I was not as faceless as I'd
planned; but it did, it was fine, being Bulgarian. In East
Berlin a scarf knotted behind the head separated me from the
West and in queues in bookshops East Germans mumbled

companionably to me or saw me as someone straight from the potato fields. But Bucharest was rather chic.

Rumanians could be sour with tourists who didn't understand. They have, or had, abundantly, a thing which is recognized all over Eastern Europe. In Rumanian, it might be described as *candoare*. A purity, of spirit perhaps. An innocence; a simplicity. But that is misleading. They could speak to their fellow human beings stripped of the cling-film we cover ourselves in. They looked each other directly in the eye and spoke, to strangers as to friends, without pretension, without clutter. I suppose I have a fairly direct look, and people responded, in Bucharest, to something in my face; yet it was a long-forgotten skill, antediluvian, which I was quite exercised to summon. I was intoxicated.

It was one of the first things in East Germany to disappear, it is said; and the sense of togetherness has gone. Eleven months after the wall had fallen I noticed people were tending not to meet each other in the eye at all. But there it was surely not so pronounced.

In Hungary, in Czechoslovakia, in Rumania, it may still be taken for granted: *there is that, we have that*, they say. Whatever it is, not really describable.

In Rumania, I felt, it would stay intact even whilst a person was doing something brutal to his fellow. That was a puzzle. The purity, then, was not related to goodness or darkness. It was more primitive.

In my room, there was in the padlocked shoulder-bag, along with the Kent, the wherewithal to make a parcel, German brown paper and German string, coffee and German biscuits, Swiss chocolate. It used to be forbidden, bringing a parcel into Rumania; but in pieces it was permitted. I had the address in my head. Before I could pack up the parcel, which wouldn't have fitted whole into the bag, I had to find the post office, it wasn't where it was on the map. I found what I thought was a post office. Rumanian packing paper was more difficult, the only paper on sale was purple and, though thick, not stout. The brown would be too remarkable, I decided . . . until I found myself waiting one morning in a bookshop for the deliveries to be unwrapped. Printers had brown paper. So I wrapped the special biscuits and chocolate and coffee in the German paper, lining it with sheets of the Rumanian newspaper *Scînteia*, a visible fringe of that showing, and a printed date. Whether these precautions were necessary or not, I didn't know. Nor whether the biscuits, not in a proper cardboard box, would break. I set off. The post office was not a post office. I was forced to ask. I had walked past the real post office several times without seeing it. But one didn't send parcels from inside the post office. I fumbled in my mind with the Rumanian, wondering if I'd been told to go to the third door from the corner or the fourth. It was the fourth. I had to fill out a form. I was unprepared for that. I had carefully not enclosed a letter, I had now to write the sender's address on the parcel and to produce a weight and a value and a description of contents. I was lucky. The woman clerk and I were alone, she was smiling, she knew without my telling her what the contents were and supplied the right word: *alimentară*. A look of acute and astonishing anxiety crossed her face when I hovered, hesitated . . . room, she'd said, room. But it was only that I'd forgotten my room number. Otherwise all seemed normal. I pulled a bar of German chocolate from my pocket. Please, I said. She broke into wider smiles. She hoped very much she'd see me sometime again. I began to enjoy myself. So long as no harm came to the friend's old father to whom the parcel went . . .

How did one tell where the risks lay . . . The couple in the dumps at the restaurant table who pleaded with me, once they'd gathered I was English from West Berlin, to accept an invitation to their apartment, did they not *know* it was proscribed, it was illegal, that even our conversation should be reported in writing, in detail . . . I couldn't accept because I was going to Sinaia, and I, with my cynicism, saw they looked on me more as a potential friend in the West who would send terribly-needed parcels; like awed ducklings who've landed a fish; he a construction worker . . . we were close to Ceauşescu's monstrosity; and she . . . her job I didn't discover. The husband wanted my digital watch, he leaned back and ached for it. The wife if she'd noticed would have censured this, his expression said.

People chatted to me irrepressibly. Footballers, in Bucharest for the match, who came by chance and then on purpose in the hotel to which I was farmed out for lunch to sit by me at my table, and who picked the slugs from my lettuce and waved them under the waiter's nose, football players, four young men, with long glossy locks, who would choose to sit by a middle-aged Bulgarian from England and out of the corners of their mouths talk of politics. The dining room was full of ordinary Rumanians.

Or the professor of sociology and his acquaintance, both tight, who discussed at length at the supper table – there was nowhere else for me to go to sit, the place I'd chosen was jammed – which of them wanted me the more and which should take himself off; before, disconcerted by my chuckling, addressing me in French. Nobody spoke Bulgarian. Or the girl student of mathematics of whom I asked directions, walking me a fair distance back to my hotel, which I'd lost; in the hope of a correspondence scribbling down her address – her country friend recoiled – right under the scowl of the hotel's Securitate spy. She lived in a *bloc*, I remember. Prudent or for her sake paranoid, I didn't keep her slip of torn notebook. The small boy, dancing beside me for sweets in the Cişmigiu Gardens; some tall policeman leaning against a wall at the railway station; a peasant woman with a red roan sausage, a dignified old man in the street near the Herăstrău Park; they all bent on me that amused, curious, uncomplicated glance of complicity in my private meanderings around Bucharest.

But I often remember strangers with peculiar intensity, abroad. It wasn't that.

The waiter, in that hotel where I had my lunches, was quite desperate to change money. I had no dollars, I had hundred-mark notes, and I couldn't see, since he was offering four times the official rate, how I'd use up a hundred marks in lei. I took pity on him. He brought me a large bundle of hundred-lei notes rolled in a white napkin. I put it in my lap and didn't look at it at once. I laughed secretly. He was very grateful, fetching me coffee when there was coffee, the better food, keeping an eye on me from far off after I was mysteriously shunted out of his direct domain. He would open his jacket or touch the inner pocket, hasty to flap it as though he were hot when people stared at him oddly. He would sail past me, hissing supplication, he needed to change more, but I had to shake my head. I also felt a shiver of fear. Within hours of our transaction, one of the un-Kented receptionists had asked with a drawbridge face for my passport. It wasn't given back to me for twenty-four hours. Someone had forgotten to re-stamp the visa. Shivers of fear were groundless. Changing money in the street might be illegal but it was all part of the economy, nobody was going to harass me, nobody was going to bother.

In Eastern Europe one at last understood one's own insignificance. I saw, too, that for me the flicker of fear came as a bonus, a novelty, more amusing than wondering on a London pavement whether it's a mugger the running footsteps herald or a rapist. Unused to having to telephone from the street, to knobs of poor bread and screwed-up pork, and a guard on the tongue, to the pyramids of tinned red vegetables in the shop windows and the queues for milk, to times when bread was gone, any fruit, for months coffee, to moonlit streets, to the general spectacle, I was drenched in adrenalin. In Rumania, at least, more bizarre than the DDR, in extremis, more child-like and more defiant, far friendlier, and more, perhaps, perilous, one's interest could be caught, one's face bright.

It could be fun to be stranded in some distant spot when the trains suddenly pulled up, even to walk in a Bucharest swirling in dust, to trip over rubble, to trip over the swathes of destruction of some grim reaper, to eat, relieved there was food at all, what food the restaurant offered, to have no choice, to go into the metro and see no hoardings, no blasts of advertising, to goggle at television which mocked the intelligence to an elevated degree, be exhorted to admire two sinister little figures, big tractors and scenes of singing and the sunflower harvest. Fun to find, with tears of joy, in this desolating landscape, the old world.

I must always have wanted to be alone in a large museum, to have the whole thing to myself.

An invisible person reached the room ahead of me to turn on the light, and as soon as I'd opened the next door the light behind me was extinguished. I knew it was a person, I spotted her when she was slow; and she'd set me off in the right direction at the start.

She ran round behind, saving the electricity: I waded confidently into these great pools of darkness which I couldn't actually see.

There are several collections in the History Museum. The major attached to the general on my flight knew the one I'd visit above all, in a place stuffed with Roman and Dacian treasure, would be that of the presents given to Ceauşescu by foreign potentates. I stuck my heels in. The grumpy woman at the ticket kiosk knew I'd want to visit it. The policemen in the main hall watching her knew that too. I was sent up the stairs to it, even without the right ticket, and I had to shake my head and tramp down. Perhaps it was permanently lit.

So I was alone in Prehistory.

Rumania is rich in things dug up or found.

The man cudgels his brow whilst the woman squats. They are a famous couple, because they are so very early, and because of the so very early maker's art. The name given to the two of them is *Gînditorul*, The Thinker. One could have held them, tiny, black and eloquent, in the palm of one's hand.

In the Calea Victoriei, children in uniform were singing patriotic dirges from which the words *our dear Nicolae Ceauşescu* often escaped sweetly into the air.

Where the Calea Victoriei sloped down to meet the river, the Dîmbroviţa in its concrete bed ready at the next earthquake to flood the metro beneath, there stood the building in which good friends of mine had lived. Never once in our conversations in Berlin had I grasped that they'd been given a prime view of Ceauşescu's vast construction site, that they'd had to look at it on waking. Beyond the farther bank of the little Dîmbroviţa it rolled upwards, muddy and churned, roaring, on the graves of pretty streets, with the new, unfinished Acropolis saddled to it and a small church tugged to its rim. Of that quarter of Bucharest gone, of such taste in architecture, I was sure they'd spoken; of how Ceauşescu would at a whim order storeys knocked off, the silhouette caught in the cock of his hands; of hearing the bulldozers, the cranes, all night. But not of being forced to watch.

Bucharest had still some beauty left.

To the exiled East Europeans, or to East European

intellectuals, it was no surprise, that a lid had been kept on nationalism, and that it would when the lid was blown be busy scrambling out; together with other isms of somewhat less charm. They understood long before we did. In Rumania, children who learnt not to talk, almost before they could talk, not to repeat at school what they heard said in private at home, those children also learnt a version of history more verifiably distorted than ours is. Grown-ups may not have believed a word of it, but without public discussion, without a public conscience, nothing challenged old ideas and prejudice could thrive. A particularly repulsive element of the Rumanian press encouraged the latter then and, unabashed, hasn't saved its breath since. What the exiles had to learn quickly and what those left behind are probably, I'm afraid, scrambling to assimilate, is that we in the West don't kiss hands, our manners *and our manner* have toddled on.

For those of us whose nostalgia for a gentler, less rude world was still a memory, there was, in tormented Rumania, a museum to visit.

One could return to the West haunted by that intent expression in people's eyes; haunted by our own loss.

They could communicate with their fellows with unforced directness, and without – for selling themselves didn't arise – self-consciousness, *not*, I think, because they were people all in similar trouble pitted against the tragedy; rather, because that was how they had for centuries communicated, *as once had we*. Without the fending of anyone off.

The Stalinist system had preserved a way of being, a phenomenon of human nature, to us obsolete if not in us extinct, within the more or less sealed borders of an all-too-human disaster of a state.

The closed faces, functionaries, customs officials, police-men, hotel receptionists, those too, the surprise of hearing a word or two in their own language from a foreigner sprang some trap in them wide. I could speak a little Rumanian. The look said: I am your fellow, no matter how I treat you it is not forgotten. How one puts a value on it I'm not sure.

How does one value the priceless Gînditor; *The Thinker*, seated, dignified, cudgelling his brain while his wife squats in her lowly position on the ground. And the wife, how does one value her: should one ask why she hasn't clapped her hand to her own brow; or assume that she scorned to compete.

If, in the West, it was, and is, long forgotten . . . well, startled in the winter of '89, emotional about their freedom, and smug, and then, it seems, scandalized too, we haven't been of a mind to fuss over curious relics of behaviour there we barely recognize; or to search for moral good. More of a mind to trample and instruct.

I misinterpreted the major's metro map, I found myself surfacing and no connecting line to the Garǎ de Nord. I asked the middle-aged man in a suit who happened to be beside me on the steps. The line wasn't finished, it was planned . . . A man in working clothes and an astrakhan hat heard our conversation and stopped, he was going to the Garǎ de Nord, he would take me, by tram. The tram stop was nearby but one couldn't point it out, better if I simply followed him. The middle-aged man said he would fetch his car, better if he drove me in the car. They spoke with some heat. Very well, go with this gentleman, said the middle-aged man. You will be quite all right, quite, he said wistfully. I walked beside the man in the labourer's astrakhan hat. He told me he came from the country, the land. I told him I did too. He pointed to a swathe cut through the houses; the dwellings, since washing hung where the rubble ended. The metro, he said. He had five children, during the week he laboured in Bucharest. While we were waiting at the tram stop I noticed the middle-aged man drive past us, squinting carefully in our direction, then satisfied. In the tram my new friend punched both ends of his ticket, for I had none.

. . . And if all seemed to have it, that which constituted *candoare*, the malign and the benign, the hooligans and the heroes, the liars, maybe what I, foolish, differently innocent, interpreted as sweetness, as something primitive, was nothing more than an uncomplicated smile. But I don't think so.

All these ways of being, frozen by communism . . . or nurtured . . . for decades; and now probably doomed, along with the habit of reading . . .

I stood at a window. It was one of those rare days when little rolls of spicy minced meat were for sale at a stall in front of the baker's shop next door. Behind the window sat rows of women at antiquated typewriters. Their clients bowed their heads or leaned forward, an elbow on the typist's desk, urgently. One client was crying. From a typewriter towards the back wall a long document poured, from another a letter. One typist listened, bored. Her client it was who wept. By the door, a queue of three had formed.

One has to say, perhaps, it is now of no value at all, it's a positive handicap, in our . . . civilized, decent democracies. Yet it remains precious. A gift, almost sacred, one might think, if one's faith, or lack of it, lies in man.

In the Cişmigiu gardens, with a bad cold, sneezing and coughing, I set off to walk to the farther end, more or less diagonally. The paths were lined with chairs on which people sat, their faces turned to the sun. Almost every chair was occupied. They looked at me mildly, without staring in the basilisk manner of the West. The chairs petered out and the dancing boy, cajoling me to disgorge *bomboane*, sweets, took their place. I had sweets in my shirt pocket. The boy, who waved and grinned when I glanced back, became smaller. I walked on steadily. I could see the upper halves of houses and buildings above the trees and knew I'd crossed the diagnonal, I had only to go on until I reached the gate. I studied the map. It was a longer walk than I'd thought, much longer. I stumped and sneezed past more people on chairs, another stretch of lake or pond. It was Easter, 1988. It was warm. I was hot. The gate was in sight, I went out of the park and took my bearings. I was going to the Gară de Nord again. It was odd, another swathe for the metro. But it was some other site, greater by far, framed at the end of a side-street. I hadn't known there was a building project of that size in this part of Bucharest. The neo-Romanesque arches of Ceauşescu's palace, clad in scaffolding, floating, from my viewpoint, above the dwellings of the mortals, with shock I recognised it. I was in the Bulevard Gheorghe Gheorghiu-Dej. I was facing in the opposite direction to that in which I should have been. I had walked in a figure of eight, from one end of the park to the other, passing without recognition the gate I'd come in at. I abaondoned my purpose and went towards the Dîmbroviţa and the metro station Izvor – it means spring, the watery kind – and that hallucinatory wasteland.

Rumania showed off the communist system at its most grotesque; in full, rotten flower. To anyone with a sense of history, Eastern Europe offered one of the great sights of the twentieth century. It was our privilege to enter this Hadean world; or not to, out of principle.

To certain of those who've led, in the West, staid lives, maybe there was, in the surreptitious, a thrill; in the changing of money on the black market; in ferrying packets of Kent across a counter; in flitting among the shadows of an unlit street, especially if it's a street of noble edifices in the heart of a capital city; in being aware that one had, in all this, rubbed up against the innocuous cheek of a geniunely sinister state.

One tasted the privations of Berlin for an afternoon; or those of Bucharest for a week; and took aspirin to Warsaw. It was political tourism. One didn't set off for Rumania in the dead of winter and share the electricity cuts, one didn't try to read by a light bulb of ordained wattage; in difficulties, one could wave one's passport, be booted out unscathed.

In Rumania, it seemed, one was visiting shades in some torment. There was, as in East Berlin, a sense of voyeuristic guilt. Yet all those people who spent hours in the Checkpoint Charlie Museum, were they ghoulish . . . I didn't think so. It *is* morally possible to recognize courage and the human spirit.

One might travel to the East believing communism to be an evil. One might go on a pilgrimage to Lenin's tomb. Human foibles had brought a not so contemptible ideal to its knees. Or on business. One might go by accident, on a package tour, to ski or swim or sit in the sun. One might go out of curiosity, or to look at art treasures. Or, not in the mood to see the *modus vivendi* of the West – its propagandists soon to appear disagreeably triumphal – as a lot less vulnerable to abuse.

One might go wistfully; helpless and woolly.

That salutary lesson, whichever of those salutary lessons it was we fancied was ours, there was no doubting the force of it.

As for Rumania . . . Rumania, in trouble, was also rather wonderful, as England will never be, I feel, again.

It had been plain, since the first evening in the hotel, with the Kent, that I was a human being. Two of the women on my floor who cleaned kept an eye out for me and would, so long as the other wasn't watching, run ahead of me and stand on one leg by the fleas, asking if I needed directions to a zoo, or the botanical gardens, and glinting at me, anxious; they were sure I'd want to go to a zoo. One scolded me: she had to wear trousers, because there were no stockings or tights and hers all were laddered. I'd brought no tights. Each tried hard to give me the impression it was she who did the room. But they had inevitably to work in pairs. There was a third, whom I liked. One afternoon I asked her why a policeman was fidgeting by a door in the lane below my balcony. He'd been there for hours. Scaffolding had been put up. It would have tempted a western thief from the pavement. Then the policeman had come. Maybe his purpose was to stop the thief. The building was to be painted and to have its cornices repaired. She dragged me down the stairs to the reception desk. Florian would tell me why there was a policeman in the street. Florian said it wasn't at all on account of the scaffolding. It didn't matter, whether there was a policeman in the street or not. His expression was one of chagrin. He was embarrassed, I thought, that I should assume the stationing of a policeman outside a hotel in Rumania had special significance. The imaginations of foreigners were too fertile, or overwrought. She dragged me up the stairs. I was to show her. On which side of the hotel was it . . . where was he, the policeman. She suddenly opened a door; an ordinary, numbered door in the corridor. Inside, it wasn't ordinary. You can see through the window, she said, taking no notice. The room was full of beds, seven or eight in a room of modest size; blue with smoke, and quiet. On each bed at least two willowy, youthful figures were sitting. Someone leant with an elbow on the sill and in that split second puffed a cloud into the air. They turned their pallid faces towards us.

Kate
Thomas Keneally

Come for a walk, Kate? he asked.

A clear evening under an immense sky. A few streaks of white vapour on the horizon. He walked towards the only hill you could see from the farmhouse. This was a knob of stone, a rare bump left over in the flatness by some old play of forces. – This is very hard rock, Gus told her, pushing against the surface, out of whose crevices trees grew in postures of great determination.

Gus pointed to a long dent at the base of this stone plug. It reminded her of something from her adolescent travels: the sort of indentation the carriage wheels of the Romans had made in the cobbled streets of Pompeii. It looked equally historic. She was tired and her head, still full of holy white fabric, did not at first take in what she was looking at. But the rut ran all along the stone plinth of Gus's only mountain.

Gus said, See there's a water hole amongst the rocks here on the far side.

There was a sort of academic reproof in his voice.

– Only in good seasons, of course. That's when kangaroo come here to drink. Imagine, Kate, how long it took to make this dent in the rock? How many kangaroos it took, travelling in file, to make this rut? I reckon it took thousands of years to make this little road. That's millions of generations . . .

He loved the idea of it.

She looked around and Chifley was considering her. He had

followed in a random sort of way. He didn't seem as impressed with the indentation in the stone as Gus was.

– See, said Gus, it means buggerall to him. I bring him to places like this and it doesn't trigger anything. I'm the one who gets excited. You know, thinking how many kangaroos it took. The does following the bucks. The young men kangaroos with their eyes on the does, sly-like. Not ready to make a move yet.

A laugh broke out of him. He was a little abashed at its lack of control.

– He *did* go chasing after does once, but he was too young and an old grey beat him up. He did it a second time. And he was still a little too young. He could do it now and be a success. But he doesn't. He's sticking round as if he wants to look after me in bloody old age.

The not-so-Reverend Frank had, dear bookbuyer, on first coming from Ireland, served out here in this sparse diocese around the Darling River. I remark on that not because I mean to force your hand, to use the news in any creaky, coincidental way. We've had enough of that in this account. I mention it almost for its own sake, and for its bearing on white vestments.

On the Soldier Settler verandah, where Gus sat reconstructing an old rifle the Soldier Settler had left behind as useless, Kate remembered sitting up to dinner tables in her childhood, staying there long enough to make the adults forget she was there, or slipping down off the chair and camping amongst the legs of guests and parents, in their adult musk, part animality, part dry cleaning fluid. And then Uncle Frank would begin tales of his youth in the diocese of Wilcannia-Forbes. He would have been exemplary here, though perhaps he must have desired some of the squatters' wives. As he reasoned with them in the confessional before Mass at some far off church or even on someone's sheep station, he must have thought with usual male vanity, I could make her a happy woman.

But those were his celibate days. The seminary and the Ten Commandments still cast a shadow over him, and he was pure and fresh-faced. Yet quick to punt at country race meetings, on the dirt racecourses (rainfall wasn't adequate for turf) where the Abo jockeys and their crooked trainers had the races all arranged but where God too had a hand, as Uncle Frank believed, in the placings, and an influence amidst the clouds of dust.

Under the table, Kate became recipient to Uncle Frank's mysterious tales of his first bush diocese.

So Father Tim Brady, parish priest of Wilcannia some time after the birth of Christ and before the birth of rock'n'roll! While the bush was still innocent and full of Gus-like battlers. Brady dies, twelve thousand miles from his brother's farm in Offaly, Republic of Eire. Priests come from all over the enormous see to watch Tim into the Australian earth. The bishop, Kieran McDonagh, drives all the way from Forbes with his curate-secretary. By the time the priests all get there, the nuns have had to close the casket, but they tell Tim Brady's arriving brethren that Father Brady had looked tranquil and had died well.

So there's the coffin in the big church of Wilcannia. In the nineteenth century when wool was worth so much in Liverpool and Huddersfield, when paddlesteamers took Wilcannia's fleece away down the Lachlan and the Darling to the sea, it had seemed that there would be nothing but growth and growth on this distant river. But by the time Tim Brady's corpse sat surrounded by his brother priests, the Sisters of Mercy, and his parishioners, Wilcannia's church was already too big for a shrinking town.

Frank O'Brien and his friend Michael Cassidy file with all the others past Tim Brady's closed coffin, and Mike Cassidy whispers. You know, Frank, I wouldn't be so sure Tim's in there. I think he might have run away to New Zealand with a woman. He was never one for the washing. Tim, and I've never known him to smell so good.

Tim is taken out to the graveyard and put beneath the alkaline-streaked alien sod – if he'd died earlier they could have fitted him into the churchyard, but it was full up by now with nineteenth and early twentieth century Irish clerics. After the interment, the bishop and all the priests come back for the mother of wakes at Tim's enormous and empty presbytery. They do not get together frequently, so that even death must provide a social pretext. And would you believe it, it starts raining? The drought ends. The flood comes. The Sisters of Mercy maintain that this is due to Tim Brady's intercession before the throne of God, though if he had such power with the Deity he had kept it something of a secret from his bishop and his fellow priests.

In country where the yearly rainfall is eight inches, they get *that* by breakfast the next morning. The town is utterly cut off. The sanitary truck cannot get through to take the full can (which Uncle Frank describes in his telling at table as *heavy with the wastes of mourners*) away.

By the second morning His Lordship Kieran, Bishop of Wilcannia-Forbes and of Neapolis Trojanos *in partibus infidelium* (the Bishop's phantom diocese in infidel Turkey) appears at the table and thunders at his clergy.

– You boys are going to have to do something about that shit can. A man's balls are dragging in it.

It gave an electric excitement to the young Kate Gaffney to be told that a bishop spake thus. That was the special scatological merit of Uncle Frank's tale for her. She would sit rocking beneath the table, while hilarity jerked the knees of all those around her.

The memory of the white vestments of the *Missa de Angelis* was sustained in Uncle Frank's old diocese by the grown and bereaved Kate, hidden in a forgotten farmhouse on marginal land. *In partibus infidelium.*

The beds were made now in the room off the kitchen, the old stove creaked and ticked with heat, a family of possums having been driven from the chimney where they must have nested for thirty or forty years.

Outside, Chifley and Menzies prowl without intent a cold, electrically radiant blue night. While in that small room off the kitchen, the two iron frame beds are jammed close together, which suits the fellow travellers' need for warmth. Fully clothed in the darkness, they find they have huddled close, each to the inner rim of his bed.

The air outside seems to chime with cold, and in these cold-to-the-core conditions Kate is to receive the final revelation concerning Chifley and the dreams of flight and air. In the dark, holding onto her frankly in a way which they have both agreed to consider good manners, Gus begins to talk about an old blackfeller who'd worked for his father. At first it seems a casual story. Folklore. An effort to charm.

But from the earliest words, at the speaking of one word in particular: *language*, Kate understands straightaway that it will be a grievous tale, more than Gus knows.

As gently and breathily told by Gus:

– The old feller said how the gift to talk had been out there, on the plain, a separate animal, looking for an owner or a friend or something. All the others were scared of it, because they thought it was a dangerous beast, a troublemaker, a real meat eater.

– So there was a sort of committee made to decide who was going to get stuck with language. And someone said, some animal, some totem creature, Give it to the humans. They're vain and they're stupid, and they'll like it.

– The animal chosen by all the others, said Gus, to persuade the humans to take on the talking business was the kangaroo.

This story on the edge of drowsiness and the possibility of drowsy caresses wakes Kate up fully. It is that she knows now in an instant what Chifley's placid intensity meant. It was a kind of persuasion. It was the urging of language upon her. At once she begins weeping.

– What's the problem, Kate?

He is panicked and presses her shoulder to find out.

What she most bitterly hates is to find herself stuck with language now, in the rump of her life, when it is a futile implement. She understands now the transaction behind the Chifley dreams, and so the viciousness of dumping talk upon her. Though she knows she will still exult in him, she has an awful, rankling, bitter sense that he owes her more still, and better.

– What is it, what is it?

The way he pushes against her shoulders, which he has never seen bared, about whose scarring he is ignorant, will lead by degrees and ultimately to gentler touches still.

She is pacified. It's no use arguing the matter. The panic at owning tongues subsides. Gus's arm goes all the way across her for warmth's sake. He desires her too, but that is no excuse in his book for intruding upon her. He is an antiquity of vanished values, poor Gus, and artless in a way unknown elsewhere.

Not properly asleep, she beholds the remote ghost of her own desire in the room, substantial enough, together with Gus's more robust animal presence. She wishes she could be absorbed in that wordless urgency. But it stands off a little way from her yet. It is just as well. The thing has to happen by degrees, by random caresses. Gus would not be able otherwise to accept the shame.

They needed to heat their bathwater on the fuel stove. Ruminating on the language trick, Kate did it, taking a long time over it, and then ultimately bathing herself. She saw how her hips had expanded – they were now what people called ample. But she wanted more dimpling of fat around the inside of her thighs. She hadn't yet achieved the amplitude of Connie Murchison's cook Shirley. She washed her genitals and felt the unfamiliar blood in them. Like a postcard from a distant place, she thought. Because of that she came out dressed only in her worse-for-wear bra and a blouse on her shoulders, and a slip which had once been cream and had turned yellow from washing with rough soap. Gus said with fear, Aren't you going to put something warmer on?

When they put out the storm lantern, he held her as usual but tentatively, from behind. To let him know that all was permitted, she reached behind her, one-handed, and stroked as best she could – not flesh but the hard fabric of old army pants. Soon she felt and was pleased by his solidity. She helped him raise the yellowed slip and he entered her with that grate-fulness which is the better part of the male spirit.

More time for recollection than she'd been permitted in Myambagh, or had permitted herself.

The memory arose of how at one time Bernie Astor's office had been employed a little oddly to conduct American astronauts on a tour of Australia. The Australian tracking station at Tidbinbilla had been their only link as they crossed the earth's southwestern corner; the city of Perth had kept all its lights on till the small hours to provide a navigational fix!

The astronauts had been sent by NASA to thank a friendly nation.

One was a Christian of fundamentalist tendencies, and the other was a wild technocrat reasonably assured that Australia's pleasant women would be anxious to reach out to the flesh he had carried to the moon and back. At first Kate was repelled by him, but when he discovered that Kate was not one of those who wanted the astral experience which was his to offer, he took it with an unexpected style and settled down to become a mere companion.

So that one night, drinking late, she had been able to raise with him the friendly, hackneyed question. Had he learned anything of God in space?

She asked him because by now she expected from him a novel answer. He had already disproved the accusation that spacemen were homunculi. He had told her, for instance, that he hated the jungle training and suffered a childhood phobia of insects. When dumped with the others north of the Panama Canal in rotting rainforest where they were expected to live off the land, he had become ill when served iguana, and had huddled on a muddy slope watching the mulch of leaves beyond the door of his pup tent for fear that they might disclose a spider or a scorpion.

His frankness about his refusal as a certified superman to countenance lizard meat had gone together with his brotherly acceptance of Kate's rebuff to generate a kind of friendship. So, both their brains tinted with whisky, she could raise with him the question of space and the ultimate principle.

The astronaut grew sombre and said he – like the fundamentalist who had already gone soberly to bed – believed in the Incarnation of Jesus Christ.

She looked for a twitching of his joker's lips but there was none. So he believed in the Incarnation. How strange he'd say it just like that! Raging at his own reflection in a mirror behind the bar. Real Hound of Heaven stuff; wrestling with divinities. And playing out his startling argument.

– God was made flesh in Judaea, said the astronaut. God made Jewish in fact. Imagine. I believe it. I wish I didn't. It has what you could call important implications for my lifestyle and my future . . . I realized in my spaceship – really had it come home to me – that we, the earth, the race . . . we're a suburb. A little corner. A cul-de-sac.

– It is therefore in my opinion obscene to be stuck with the idea that the only intelligent life in the universe is here, here in this deadend street. What I believe is . . . Christ has been throughout the universe, to many, many constellations. Otherwise there's no sense. Okay, that's number one.

– Number two. Number two: our idea of aesthetics and of what is noble in the body of a man or a woman is based on gravity. Gravity makes us. Gravity made Marilyn Monroe. Gravity made Jesus Christ. If we lived on a planet where the gravity was 1.5, Christ would be four and a half feet tall and have an enormous flat brow to stand the extra pressure. Marilyn Monroe would be four foot two and her ankles would be seven inches through, and we would still think that was damn marvellous. Because gravity would've given us our idea of beauty as well.

– But imagine (continued the astronaut to the now enthralled Kate Gaffney). Imagine a planet where the gravity was three, Christ and Venus would be hunched over, they would drag their forepaws along the earth. And again we, made by that same gravity, would think they were beautiful, worth dying for, worth our souls. And then a planet with gravity eight! Christ and Venus would be serpents or multipedes, and *he* still would have died to wash us in his blood and we would still have wanted *her*.

She remembered the nature of the awe she and the astronaut had shared then. Reverence for the serpentine Messiah. The vision of the serpentine Venus. It took much headshaking to rid the imagination of these images.

The Kate who made love to Gus knew she was Kate from a planet of gravity two. Her skull had been pressed flat by the weight of events. She had turned herself by will into a Venus from an alternate planet. She had let the gravity of Murchison's Railway Hotel thicken her. Yet Gus clearly came from a similar planet, because entering her and caressing her from behind, his mouth near her ear, he writhed and jerked with cries of praise.

As Chifley had had one or two great and foredoomed glandular adventures, Kate imagined – but she may have been wrong – that this was a rare excursion for Gus's body. In tune with this belief, Kate herself felt certain waters breaking and flowing inside her. She approved of it all distantly, a Maharani approving of the coming of the monsoons.

Flung with abandon across the frost outside, Chifley waited, owing her something for the pain of language, even for the millilitres of painful breath, the ounces of broken words Gus uttered against her ear.

But though Chifley had the lungs and sinews, he couldn't provide everything. Towards the edge of sleep, she said, Would you let me go to Mass?

– What do you mean, *let*?

– I want to take the truck if you'll let me. I want to go to Mass in Bourke or Wilcannia.

– Bloody long way to go to Mass, Kate, he said.

He was very wary with his affection now the frenzy had ended. Again, being proud, loth to offend or presume.

– But it's okay by me, he added then.

– And if I meet Burnside, I might sign. Just for peace. But I wouldn't let him follow me back here. This place wouldn't be found or anything . . .

– Your business, Kate.

Amongst the dwindled numbers of devout in Bourke, she attended the Mass. The church in Wilcannia where Mick Cassidy had cast aspersions on the then and forever late Tim Brady was, as Gus had persuaded her, too far to go, so Bourke must serve.

The cast of the rite:

The Catholic doctor and his placid wife and handsome and mannerly country children.

The Catholic lawyer who looked Lebanese, and his young freckled-Irish spouse.

The elderly women, and the runty little men called Kelly or Mahony who had worked on cattle and sheep stations and retired in town, wearing everywhere, perhaps even to the bathroom, the sweat-glutted Akubras they had worn in their days of labour.

And although the congregation was smaller than the Irish monsignors who had built this church would have ever foreseen, it was in some ways as if nothing had changed since Uncle Frank had been a cleric of this diocese. The young priest could have been a bygone not-so-Reverend Frank. Though Frank and the others had come to Australia because there were too many devout for even the native Australians to supply the sacerdodal need. Whereas this lad was here because no one cared anymore, because Madonna had acted and Jack Nicholson had slickly taken the souls of the young. The crass but complex world would in the end distract even the country doctor's wholesome children.

KATE

The priest was wearing green vestments, for that was the season of the year.

She sat through the Mass and numbly through the sermon. The young priest had been to some elocution teacher who had taught him to hone the final consonants of words. She listened to the shape of his words and imagined where he came from. The standard green lane in mid-Eire? A pub in Meath? Or judging by the burr, a pub in Derry.

Numbly she took communion from one of the town's remaining nuns. Not a galleon of a nun, full habited in the manner of the year when Tim Brady had perished in this diocese. A nun in a calf-length dress. A modern woman.

At the end the priest with the sharp-honed words blessed them in English. Divesting himself of his green chasuble at the altar, he made for the front of the church to intercept his departing parishioners and peck some of the women on the cheek. Such Protestant folksiness wouldn't have characterized the wrath-of-God, I-might-shake-your-hand-but-God-will-still-damn-you Irishmen of Uncle Frank's youth.

Only a few aged faithful, dissenting from the folksy handshaking and kissing in progress outside, stayed behind to make their private devotions. Kate stayed with them. She could hear the young priest being genial around the doors of family vehicles, sticking a head in to rib one of the children on intelligence from the parents. He seemed so remote that the world – at least the world as it existed in Bourke – was tearing him further and further out into the secular streets. His green vestment lay barely remembered on a chair.

Kate left by a side door. She passed the graves of monsignors called Cullen and Fitzergerald and entered the sacristy from the outer door. The smell of Uncle Frank and all the others was there. The highly scrubbed and beeswax scent of the catechism. The smell of Uncle Frank's soft hands on race day. Long before he thought of applying them to Mrs Kearney's whippet body.

There were long, brown varnished drawers with brass brackets to hold a label. *Albs. Tunicles. Surplices and Stoles. Chasubles.* Two drawers of chasubles.

She pulled out the lower of the two. Red and black assailed her eyes. Blood and desolation and burnt offerings; martyrdom and loss. She kicked this drawer shut with her shoe. She was affronted by even the chance idea that the black of the Mass of the adult dead applied to her case.

A new drawer. With the green and yellow, there were two sets of white – a modern silken chasuble, made for the weather, and a heavy brocaded and braided one built without reference to Bourke's mean summer temperatures. She pulled this one out. She inspected it, felt its texture, and then folded it to herself, against her breasts. The young priest appeared in the sacristy doorway coming from the church, carrying his green chasuble of today's Mass, but not as intimately as she carried the white.

He was surprised, but he said pleasantly, Is there anything I can do for you, madam?

Kate walked towards him. Yes, she said. These white vestments . . .

– The heavy set, he said, still pleasant and willing to humour. Probably eighty years old, that one.

She hit him in the stomach with all her force twice and then ran away, clasping the thing to her. The churchyard rang with the Jansenist disapproval of dead monsignors. The street was empty though except for peppermint trees. All the faithful had vanished.

She did not wish to have to explain to Gus what the vestmen
for the *Missa de Angelis* was doing in his truck. It sat beside he
on the front seat and she felt it one-handed and was satisfie
Ultimately, she was pleased to encounter an irrigation cana
well before the turnoff to Gus's place. She laid the whit
chasuble down into the water, and it floated away like a
august living thing.

– That's it, she said reassuringly, standing on the edge of th
canal, on the limitless bottom of a once inland sea. It was we
known from the classroom: two hundred million years too lat
the English gentleman Charles Sturt came with certainty t
find a sea that had so long stopped lapping, and had foun
instead the harshest light off white objects and been blinde
instead of bathed.

She inspected her hands with which she had taken the win
out of the Lord's anointed. She did not know why she'd done
to that poor, jovial man.

Back in the truck, she drove home on spidery trails amongs
the stringybarks to the Soldier Settler ruin, and went inside t
sit by the stove and listen to Gus's quiet enquiries.

Gus turned on the radio news in the still afternoon as the
sat content, with her morning's work done, he with h
veneration of her and the old rifle to work on.

The radio said:

– Well known racing identity, the Reverend Franc
O'Brien, was arrested in the early hours of this morning at
hotel in Ermington, Sydney.

Letting an unwise yelp loose, Kate saw that Gus had notice
nothing. She composed herself. She knew the name of th
hotel after all. *The Partridge and Grapes*. A massive barn of a
Aussie hotel to carry such a cosy name. Mrs Kearney's hote

– Also arrested was an associate of Father O'Brien's, Mr
Fiona Kearney. Father O'Brien and Mrs Kearney are arraigne

with taxation fraud, illegal gaming, and with violations of the Federal Telecommunications Act. Mrs Kearney and Father O'Brien between them have interests in at least ten Sydney hotels, of which Mrs Kearney is nominee. Mrs Kearney is the widow of well known East Sydney alderman, Mick Kearney, who at the time of his death was a witness before the enquiry into illegal gaming. The Reverend Francis O'Brien was suspended from duty by His Eminence, Cardinal Fogarty, Archbishop of Sydney, in November 1988, at a time when the Reverend O'Brien's connections with starting price book-making were revealed before the Independent Commission into Corruption.

Morosely gratified Fogarty, who had managed to move in on Uncle Frank before the police did. Though there was no sense to it, she felt something like fury at the righteousness of His Eminence Fogarty.

Gus heard all this newsreading static too but knew nothing of what it meant. Chifley, beneath the stringybark, heard it and gazed at the verandah.

– There, she believed he placidly said. The gift of sodding language. Keep the bastard.

– Thanks a lot, said Kate.

At least the radio was too prim to say what Kate knew in her blood: that Uncle Frank was dragged half naked from the same bed as half naked Mrs Kearney. Neither of them beauties, Frank in his tousled plumpness, she angular and her face blurred. As she had heard someone, probably a friend of the Kozinskis, say, If he was going to break his vows, you'd think he'd get better value than Fiona Kearney.

What is required of me now? she wondered. Whatever it was, there wasn't any chance she would provide it. The not-so-Reverend Frank was not dependent on her favours.

The bottle the shocked young fireman had pressed into her hands.

– Reached inside the door, but this was all there was. All I could get before everything went. Sorry. Sorry.

Even in prison, Uncle Frank would be Uncle Frank, a god who would know where the bottle was. In a cupboard at Mrs Kearney's at Ermington at the worst. In a cupboard at *his* house in Abbotsford. It wouldn't be right to ask him now, burdened as he was.

Just the same, she wondered should she write to him? Not that he needed it? He would have the best of counsel. His ten hotels would pay for it. His tax evaded earnings. If not that, his loyal brother-in-law James Gaffney, or his tame mortician O'Toole.

Thomas Keneally's story comes from his novel, *Woman of the Inner Sea* (Hodder & Stoughton, 1992).

Bath Time
Jenny Diski

Eventually, everything had fined down to a single dream. It was this: a bath. But no ordinary bath. It was the perfect bath Meg wanted, the one she had been waiting for, building up to by degrees, as it seemed to her now.

It was perfectly simple, really. She wanted to spend a whole day in the bath. To go to sleep the night before knowing that the next day was her bath day and wake in the morning and remember that her waking hours were to be exclusively devoted to it.

Easy, some might think, but not so easy, actually. It required the right bathroom, and a hot water system that could keep the bath at the right temperature for as long as necessary. It meant a day when there were no interruptions; no phone calls, no doorbells, no appointments, guaranteed solitude. Not impossible conditions, either singly or combined. There were probably thousands of people – more, hundreds of thousands maybe – who had, or could create, the right circumstances. But, for one reason or another, Meg had never managed to get all the circumstances needed for the day-long bath to come together.

The day-long bath was a notion that had come to her more than eighteen years ago, but which she had never been able to put into action because unless everything was right, there was no point. And *every*thing had never been right at the same time.

The size of the bathroom was not a factor. Meg was

perfectly happy in small rooms; unused space tended to make her anxious. The bathroom she had as a child was perfectly adequate, she remembered, though no larger, in the tiny two-roomed flat, than it had to be to contain the bath, washbasin and toilet. It was clean, neat, and although she couldn't actually visualize the walls, she supposed that they must have been a bathroom sort of colour, pale pink or eau de nil. Not to her present taste, but she didn't think she'd have minded as a child. The actual suite, as they say, she was certain was white. Baths and toilets didn't come in any other colour, then, unless you were a starlet or a duchess. Still, satisfactory, as a physical environment, as it was, when she remembered that first bathroom, it was with fear. She always saw herself sprinting from it, dragging her knickers up from around her knees as she ran, while the waterfall rush of the cistern filling up threatened to engulf her from behind. It was always essential to get out as fast as possible after she'd pulled the chain – yes, it was a proper chain, hanging from the raised cistern. She always left the door open, of course, to facilitate her escape, once the time had come when her parents insisted that the toilet had to be flushed.

Water had scared her, then. She used to wake nights screaming, and when her mother arrived would tell her that she was afraid of drowning in a flood. It did no good for her mother to point out that it wasn't raining, there was no flood, and that even if there had been, Meg was not at risk in her bedroom on the fifth floor of a block of flats in the middle of London. The flushing of the toilet seemed to Meg a premonition of rising waters breaking down the brick walls, seeping, then surging, through cracks in the window frames, and overwhelming her. She was aware from a very young age, for no reason she could now fathom, of the lethal power of massed, fast moving water.

The only other thing she remembered distinctly about the first bathroom was that her mother always poured disinfectant into the bath when she ran it for her daughter. She could see the bottle of Dettol upended in her mother's hand and the brownish orange liquid hitting the clear bathwater in a thin stream, instantly clouding it. It seemed like a magician's trick, or later, when she heard the story at school, the miracle of Christ changing water to wine. But she wondered also what germs she carried that her mother battled against. Dirt was dangerous, of course, there was no doubt about that. Her mother cleaned the flat and washed clothes and herself with a vigour that plainly was keeping something terrible at bay. Illness, the plague, perhaps, but that wasn't really it – her mother had no understanding of the virus theory of disease, colds came from wet feet, flu a willed perversity on the part of her daughter to make cleaning activities next to impossible – Mrs Tucker was keeping dirt away, which she called germs, because it was *bad* and threatened the fabric of *niceness* which it seemed to be her job to maintain against all the odds. She put Dettol in her own bath, as well as her daughter's and complained each morning, her face heavy with disgust, about Meg's father's casual attitude to cleanliness.

'He never washes in the morning above his elbows,' she would say, hissing almost, at the horror of it, as she scrubbed vigorously between her legs at the washbasin. 'I'd rub myself away if I could, keeping clean. He only has a bath at the weekend because I nag him. Filthy pig.'

Mrs Tucker had had an impoverished childhood, deprived of everything, as she told Meg, including the luxury of a bath and hot running water. The germs, Meg came to understand, were mainly to be found in that area that her mother paid so much attention to in the morning. Her mother stood naked at the basin, her legs apart and washed down there was if her life depended on it, while Meg sat in a foot and a half of opaque, pungent water watching. She concluded it was from that place between her legs that the dirt originated and where the Dettol was supposed to do its germ assassinating work. Meg wanted bubble baths and creamy soap like she'd seen on the television, but always it was milky, sharp smelling water and coal tar soap, and every nook and cranny to be washed so that when she called her mother to tell her she'd finished she could answer each element of the litany – 'Have you washed your. . . . . .' (the list included all the cracks and crevices that might be passed over by a haphazard washer) – with a truthful, 'Yes'.

Leaving home had been no hardship, she'd had enough of her mother's scrubbing of things and herself, enough of her father's tight-faced loathing of everything his wife and his miserably small, clean home represented. She went with a light heart to teacher training college and the flat she would share with four other students. Then, the world was full of promise.

The bathroom however was a disappointment. Well, hardly a disappointment, only to be expected, really. The flat was soon covered with cheap and cheerful things to negate the unaltered fifties drab. She and her flatmates flung colourful bedspreads over dull moquette, put up posters of the Beatles and other heroes of the hour as they gradually became available in the dawning light of youth culture, and lashed out on a set of stripy mugs to drink their instant coffee out of. There wasn't much that could be done about the bathroom. That one *was* eau de nil (though pock-marked by patches where age and damp had flaked off the paint), and by now Meg minded. The lino was icy and cracked, wind whistled in from a broken corner of the window, and there was no kind of heating. But there was, as her mother would have pointed out, a bath and hot running water. At least, it was sometimes hot, and it did run, though so slowly you could write the best part of an essay while waiting for it to fill even a third full. It was a huge cast iron bath with claw legs, of the kind that later would become much sought after, but this one was chipped and caused the already lukewarm water to chill almost as soon as it finished falling from the chrome swan's neck of the immersion heater tap. The water heater made such terrible, threatening noises, clanking and burbling that Meg and her friends would turn it on at arm's length as the pilot light whooshed the flames into action, and then run for their lives back upstairs to their room, just in case, this time, it really did explode.

But none of this was unusual. It was what student's digs were like, what most people's homes were like. Things changed very slowly. And for Meg and her friends it was part of the fun of being independent at last. Waking up in the morning, dashing down to the bathroom, freezing feet, freezing water, a quick memorial swish with the toothbrush, it was all as they expected, and fun with it. Meg hadn't developed the notion of the day-long bath at that point in her life, but she could, and did, make some changes. For one thing, she bathed only once a week, like everyone else (and like her filthy pig of a father) because no one could afford to feed the meter for more baths than that on a small student grant. But she did set aside enough money to buy herself a bar of Imperial Leather soap and one squashy plastic container a week of vividly coloured bubble bath. Nothing fancy, but she was prepared to risk her life with the immersion heater for long enough to cut the corner of the sachet and watch as the squeezed liquid turned the water blue, or green or pink, and, even in the slow stream of the immersion heated water, began to form bubbles quite as luxurious looking as the advertisements.

She lay, or tried to lie (the bath being too big and slippery), for as long as the bubbles lasted – which wasn't long – in spite of the rapidly chilling water. It was a hint, at least, of baths that might be to come, just as a passionate grope curtailed by the early arrival home of a flatmate, was an embryonic taster of long, languorous hours of love, once the circumstances made it possible. Whatever discomfort Meg and her friends put up with, it was with the unspoken assumption that their lives would develop, financially and socially, to the point where things would be just right and comfortable with it. But for now, at least there were no more Dettol baths.

Meg couldn't, however, remember that bath with much affection. It was where, in her last year at college, the mess that resulted from the bath (made extra hot with kettles of boiling water), the bottle of gin, and the dubious, but, as it turned out, effective pills, came away from her. She hadn't been very pregnant, no more than a particularly heavy period left her and turned the water pink and mucky, but, relieved though she was her head reeled at the sight of what was supposed to become a baby swirling away, in a livid, turbulent whirlpool, down the plughole. She wished then, quietly to herself as her friends helped her out and dried her off, that she had a bottle of Dettol.

Over the next few years of being a student and a probation teacher, there were several more, only gradually improving, bathrooms of a similar kind. The only really notable one – the one out of the lot of them which remained in her mind's eye – was as dingy and unwelcoming as all the rest, although it was enhanced by having one wall covered with mirror-like paper and a couple of posters of Jimi Hendrix that had curled at the edges from the damp. But it was where Meg learned not to hate washing her hair. Then, her hair was long, flowing, as it was supposed to do, like heavy rippling liquid down her shoulders to the soft, equally flowing lines to tie-dyed Indian cotton, full sleeved blouses and long skirts. It was an endless business washing and drying her hair. Sometimes it would take Meg a fortnight to build up the necessity to the point where it was unavoidable. The bath did have a rubber hose attachment that could be pushed on to the tap, but crouching, bare topped in the cold bathroom was a dismal business, until the day she washed her hair while under the influence of LSD.

Waterfalls poured down on her upside down head, tiny drops of wet light, fragmenting into colours of minute and jewelled brilliance so that her saturated hair twinkled messages like psychedelic stars in a multistranded universe. The feel of foaming shampoo squeezing through her fingers was an indescribable, unearthly sensation. When she rubbed her hair dry, the colours that had sparkled in the droplets of water jiggled inside her head as if her brain was a kaleidoscope, and the smooth wet strands were a beaded curtain that swished aside and let in shafts of light like a cubist painting. All in all, a thoroughly excellent experience, and although she never washed her hair on acid again, the memory remained.

That was the same bathroom where Doc used to shoot up, and where, as Meg sat on the edge of the bath, watching him perform his ritual, he told her one day, after the H had hit, that he had found an incredible cottage in Sussex they could share with another couple he knew, and what about getting out of London and the hassle of everything? It was near enough for him to get his supplies – the other couple were both addicts – and they could organize enough stuff between them to keep everything sweet. Meg, who did not use heroin, but who often washed out his syringes for him in a curious kind of transformation of domesticity, appropriate to the time, stared at Doc. For a second, she imagined a cottage bathroom, roses on the wall, wooden towel rails, a pretty chintz curtain, a deep grained oak window ledge with scented things for bath and body. Then, as she visualized it, she saw it littered with used syringes, smears of blood inside the transparent tubes and spots of it congealing on the tip of the needle.

'No, I'm not going,' she said.

Doc said nothing, but rolling down his sleeve, walked out of the bathroom, packed his small leather suitcase, took his books from Meg's shelf, leaving curious gaps, and left. She never saw him again.

With the passing of flower laden peace, Meg's life took a turn towards the more conventionally domestic. Marriage to Peter, who, like Meg herself, had also only been passing through a period of dissolution, provided a new bathroom. An entirely new bathroom. New walls, new floors, new ceilings, new everything. They bought a derelict house, and with the aid of a council grant – a piece of lost history, if ever there was – Meg and Peter carved a bathroom out of a large unused cellar, just in time for the arrival of the baby.

It was the largest bathroom of Meg's life, square and roomy and designed for living in as much as for cleanliness. Either Meg or Peter would lie in the bath with the new baby beached, like a small, gurgling whale, on their chest, while the other parent sat in a wicker chair chatting about their day – Peter teaching, Meg indulging herself full time in baby care – or reading snippets of the newspaper aloud. And when Florence was asleep in her cot, there was enough room on the floor of their bathroom for Peter and Meg to make love on a towel, after soaping each other in the cramped but friendly bath.

Since the entire house had to be renovated, the grant – decent though it was – had to stretch as thin as strudel pastry.

Living and bedrooms got priority and were finished; white walls, bookshelves, brightly painted furniture in the baby's room, stripped pine everywhere else. But the kitty was empty just at the time when the bathroom was ready to decorate. The bath and everything was there, plumbed in and working, the walls were smooth and pink with Peter's remarkably effective plastering skills, but there was no paint on the walls, no covering on the cement floor, and, because it didn't seem important, no door or doorframe in the empty rectangle prepared for them.

No one minded. Certainly not the baby, who had no history of bathrooms, and not Peter or Meg. It was, in fact, the best bathroom Meg had ever had. It was warm, with *two* radiators as she had insisted, it was clean, and the water ran from the taps fast and hot. The lack of a door didn't present a problem. After a few months of nappy changing, cleaning up baby vomit and scrubbing dried pulped food from the kitchen chairs and floor, privacy didn't seem an issue. It certainly wasn't an issue worth going into the red for. It was true that when the grannies came to visit they complained, and other people, wishing to appear laid back, took to whistling while they had a shit, but Peter and Meg weren't bothered enough to do anything about it.

But it was then that Meg thought about the day-long bath and realized, best bathroom of her life though it was, it was not possible. It was very rare for an ordinary bath to be uninterrupted by Peter popping in to chat, or ask what they were having for dinner. Even when Peter was at work, Florence would come crawling and beaming through the unfinished doorway, or worse, remain silent, forcing Meg to get out of the bath every ten minutes to make sure she was still playing quietly with her crayons in her bedroom. Moreover, hot though the water was, there was no chance of keeping it that way for the hours she fantasized, because it took a whole tank to fill the bath, and then it was at least an hour before the water was hot again. Just not the right conditions, though Meg did develop her concept of bathtime. In her mind now, there were two kinds of bath: the working bath, where she soaped and scrubbed, washed her hair, shaved her legs. The business-like bath. The other kind had nothing to do with being clean. It was about lying submerged to the chin in scented, oiled water whose heat seeped through her skin and into the very marrow of her bones. Warmth was the point of this kind of bath, a warmth that didn't seem available anywhere else; not in Peter's arms, not in the baby heat of Florence against her breast. It was a private, solitary stoking of her fires, and one she began to wish she could prolong beyond the social needs of her husband and child.

But when Florence was eight, the bathroom plaster had lost its bright pinkness and the cracks (Peter being a good, but not professional plasterer) had become too big not to notice. The lack of a door suddenly became something of a problem, although it took a while for Meg to understand this. Peter had always disappeared into the bathroom on a Sunday with a pile of colour supplements, but now he started to announce his visit.

'I'm going to the loo,' he'd say.

Meg was faintly surprised at first, because it didn't need saying, but she gradually realized that what he meant was, 'leave me alone, don't come wandering in and start reading one of the papers on the floor and discuss interesting recipes you come across.' His announcement about visiting the loo was the same was bolting the door, had there been one. Meg shrugged and kept away after being snapped at several times.

'Do you mind!'

But then she noticed that for some weeks, or was it months,

she had been bathing after Peter had gone to bed at night, only getting out once she was sure he was fast asleep. Neither of them could say, 'I want a door on the bathroom,' because it was obvious that it would be tantamount to saying, 'I want a divorce.'

The next bathroom *was* painted. It was white and had perfectly acceptable greyish vinyl tiles on the floor. It was the most civilized bathroom of her life. Small, efficiently designed, and when had she ever had an actual bathroom cabinet to keep – not Dettol – make-up, cotton wool, TCP and burn ointment neat and out of sight? The flat was big enough for just the two of them, Meg and Florence, and was a typical newly converted, square, paper-thin walled series of boxes, but it looked nice enough. But the day-long bath was still out of reach, not just because she could not solve the problem of keeping the water hot, but because the idea of having the bathroom to herself for an entire day, or even an entire hour, was laughable.

Between the ages of ten to fourteen, Florence made the bathroom her very own, as much her territory as her bedroom. It seemed a necessary part of her development. The mirror, the make-up (Meg's), bath oil, shaving foam, razors, scissors, tweezers, became essential adjuncts to Florence's daily life. Meg would try to point out that the bathroom was shared, and that her make-up was not, but Florence's need for self-definition caused her memory to blank on the subject. Meg got used to using the bathroom in those odd moments when Florence had vacated it, collecting damp towels that had been strewn on the floor, saving lidless pots of creams and open wands of mascara from drying out before she could run her bath.

During the day she worked, back at teaching, being a single

parent and therefore unable to afford the luxury of choosing poverty and daytime access to her bathroom rather than earning a living. And although Florence spent every other weekend with her father, Meg still didn't have the bathroom to herself, because that was the only private time she and Jack had together for unfettered love-making, what with the thinness of the walls and the compactness of the space. She didn't feel she could tell him he couldn't come round on alternate weekends because she wanted the bathroom to herself.

Eventually, however, Jack had receded into amiable friendship, and Florence left home, successfully reared, disappearing into university life and travelling vacations. All the years of gazing at herself in the mirror, trying on alternative faces, different eyebrow shapes and lip outlines had, astonishingly, turned her into an elegant but thoughtful person clearly on her way to becoming a committed and successful lawyer. The day she announced that she was sharing a large house near her college with some friends, Meg put the flat on the market.

She looked at numerous properties, but she could not make the estate agent understand that she meant what she said when she asked to see a flat in need of total redecoration. He assumed a woman of her age would want something nicer, but she explained that she had very special plans and could not afford to dismantle something that was already in place to put in what she wanted. But, the estate agent explained, for the money she had, she could get a decent place with everything in good order even if it wasn't exactly the order she wanted.

'But I've got very special plans,' Meg explained again, patiently.

Eventually, with some distaste, the estate agent showed her a flat that was near-derelict in a dingy road of dreary terraced houses.

'I can get you something much better,' he kept saying as they creaked up the stairs, Meg taking care not to catch her heels in the holes in the filth encrusted carpet.

But it was just what she was looking for. The house had been left empty for several years as the owner, hoping for a property company hungry for an investment, found himself stuck in the downward spiralling house market of the late eighties. Eventually, he put each of the two flats on the market at a price which meant, even though Meg sold her flat at a loss, there was some money left over.

Not much, not enough to repair and renovate the flat into something decent and comfortable to live in, but enough for what she wanted to do.

'I'll take it,' she said.

The estate agent shrugged, happy enough to get any kind of sale, the way things were.

Meg was not gifted with practical skills. The amount of money she had to spend on the flat was small, but it was enough to employ a builder to do what she wanted. She found one in a local paper and showed him the job.

He walked around the flat, digging his heel professionally into soft spots in the bare floorboards, and pressing his palm against ugly stains on the wall, muttering 'Dry rot, here,' and 'Damp, I'm afraid.'

'Don't worry about that,' Meg said, steering him past the uninhabitable rooms.

He noticed, in one of them, a made-up mattress on the floorboards, and a metal clothing rail.

'You're living in this place?' he asked. 'In this condition? Haven't you got anyone you could stay with until the work's done?'

Meg was ahead of him and had reached her destination.

'Here. This is what I want sorted out.'

She handed him the sheaf of papers she was carrying.

'I want it done exactly like this.'

The builder looked at the drawings. They weren't professional, but they explained well enough, and in minute detail what the customer wanted.

'Yeah, OK. This looks fine. And what about the rest of the flat?'

'A boiler. Just a boiler.'

'Central heating, you mean?'

'Just a boiler,' Meg said again. 'There's no need for radiators.'

The builder stared at her.

'All right, then. Now, the rest of the flat.'

'That's all. The bathroom and the boiler. That's what I want done. That's all I've got the money to do.'

'You can't live like this,' he said, and concentrated hard on the specification she'd handed him. 'You know, you could do this much more cheaply and there'd be enough left to get the basics done on the rest of the flat. You've got to have a kitchen, and the bathroom and living aren't habitable.'

'I want the bathroom done *exactly* as I've explained.'

The builder was about to argue and opened his mouth, but then thought better of it. This one was a crazy he decided, and a job was a job, especially these days. He shrugged.

'You're the boss, mate,' he said. 'When do you want me to start?'

It had taken six weeks to level the floor, put in a damp proof course, strip and replaster the walls, find a bath of exactly the required length and build it in, plumb in the other fittings and decorate to the client's requirements. The longest job was the tiling – from floor to ceiling with four inch glazed white tiles, and six inch white ceramic tiles on the floor. It wasn't a large space, but the tiler, near desperate towards the end of the job, worked out it had taken four thousand and seventy three to cover the walls. He started on the floor with the light heart of a Cinderella who had only a few more beans to pick up before she could go to the ball. Then the fittings were put up. These were minimal. One chrome towel rail, a glass shelf above the washbasin and another running the length of the bath. The small window was reglazed and the frame and ceiling were painted with four coats – no, three would not do, Meg had insisted to the painter – of white eggshell. Then the new boiler was installed – a boiler that harked back to the old immersion heaters of Meg's past. It heated water directly from the mains as it was drawn through to the taps, needing no storage tanks. Meg, at last, had a good, constant flow of hot water to top up a cooling bath.

The bathroom was finished just in time for the Christmas holidays. Florence was off to North Africa with a boyfriend and Meg announced to friends on the verge of inviting her to Christmas lunch that she was going away, too. There was very little money left, but she had costed the bathroom with great care, so there was enough for the final essentials. She did not, of course, mend the doorbell that didn't ring when pressed (indeed, with the aid of the builder's tools, she unscrewed the knocker that the builders – her only visitors – used to gain entry). Nor did she use any of her precious funds installing a telephone.

Meg spent the first days of the holidays buying white towels, a variety of astonishingly expensive French designer foaming bath oils, and a chrome rack to place across the bath that had a place for soap, flannels, *and* a book stand attached with a small chrome tray next to it just the right size to hold a wine glass.

Then, when everything was in place, she took the time to stand in the doorway – with a door and a lock – and inspect her new bathroom. Behind her, and to each side, the rest of the flat remained as derelict as the day she had bought it, but she didn't notice, or care. She stared into the bright bathroom and her eyes almost ached with its gleaming whiteness. It was, for all the time and money lavished on it, quite sparse. There was nothing in it except white tiles, a carefully folded white towel and the white bath, washbasin and sink. The rest of the fittings were silvered chrome and glass. Meg had ditched her make-up – she had thrown away everything from her previous bathrooms. There was a square edged black bottle of scented bath oil and some discreet pots containing face packs and washing grains on one end of the long glass shelf above the tiled wall side of the bath, and a neat pile of books on the other.

New bars of plain white soap waited on the bath tray and the washbasin. There was a white electric toothbrush and a dispenser of toothpaste, from which she had taken off the label, so that it too was plain white on the glass shelf over the basin. Meg surveyed this bathroom of hers that she had made, and found it good.

It was Christmas Eve, and Meg sat in the old chair she had brought from her previous flat, in her empty living room with peeling walls, eating a takeaway from the Chinese place round the corner. Tomorrow would be the loveliest day of her life. She listened to the boiler humming quietly to itself, in constant readiness to produce however much hot water was required. Nice. Something really special to look forward to. How many people had lived their lives up to the point Meg had reached and could say that they were about to fulfil their great ambition? Only a few, she suspected, among the millions, who would look back at the end and wonder how they had missed their moment. Meg's moment had come. Tomorrow she would have the Christmas Day of her life. You only had to know what it was you really wanted, she told herself, wrapped in her duvet in the freezing, desolate room, with the smile of a cat savouring the prospect of tomorrow's bowl of cream.

The Whirling Dervishes

Juan Goytisolo

Translated by Peter Bush

I was snow, your rays melted me;
the ground soaked me up; mist of the spirit
I rise up to the sun.

Mawlana, *The Diwan of Shams Tabrizi*

Despite the numerous testimonies collected by his relatives and disciples – by his son Sultan Walad, by Ahmet Aflaki and Sepashalar – and the scrutiny of modern writers, Mohamed Iqbal, Reynold Nicolson, John Arberry, Eva de Mitray-Meyerovitch, Mehmet Onder and Michel Random, the life of Jalal al-din Rumi, better known as Mawlana, is still graced by a legend fashioned from myth and reality. The handsome Green Dome that stands out sharply from Konya's slender minarets as startling as a mirage, shelters beneath its conical roof of Turkish tiles the remains of one of the world's greatest mystics, comparable in importance to Eckhart, to Hallax or Ibn Arabi, to John of the Cross or Teresa of Avila. The author of the famous lines

Come, whoever you may be, come
Infidel, pagan or idolater, come!
Our door is not there to discourage
Though I perjure a hundred times, come!

THE WHIRLING DERVISHES

Whether Farsi, Turkish or Greek,
Learn the language of those who have none!

was born sometime between 1190 and 1200 in the now defunct city of Balkh within the boundaries of Afghanistan. His father, Baha ud-din Walad is from a family of theologians and his religious and philosophical teachings earn him the honorary title of Wise among the Wise. Nevertheless, some *ulamas* who envy the power he wields in the town disagree with his interpretations and accuse him of undermining the sultan's power. Baha ud-din is hurt and writes these lines to the monarch: 'Armies, thrones, treasures, the mortal things of this earth, belong to kings. We are dervishes and need neither land nor sovereign power. We shall continue our journey pure in soul and shall leave the sultan his wealth and vassals.' He leaves Balkh in 1220, and shortly afterwards the Mongols destroy the town and the entire kingdom of Khurasan. 'I leave God to go to God,' Baha ud-din Walad will say on hearing the bad tidings. 'I come from nowhere and am going nowhere.' The small caravan of refugees flees before the armies of Genghis Khan, heads westwards across Persia and Mesopotamia and takes temporary shelter in Syria. There Baha ud-din visits the famous mystic from Murcia, Ibn Arabi, who, so the story goes, see Mawlana respectfully following his father down the street, and exclaims: 'Miracle of God, an ocean walking after a lake!' When Baha ud-din and his followers have made their pilgrimage to Mecca, they settle in the city of Karaman, to the south of Anatolia, where young Mawlana is married. In 1229, the Seleucid sultan of Konya, a great patron of the sciences and poetry, invites Baha and his family to come to his kingdom and generously places one of his schools, or *madrasas*, at his disposition.

Mongol devastation and bloodletting had produced panic

and created in the countries under threat an atmosphere of profound spiritual anguish, fertile ground for the development of mystical ideas. Sufis, preachers, philosophers, and wandering dervishes were welcomed by the religiously tolerant Seleucids. The town of Konya was a forum in which doctrine was disputed by both orthodox Sunnites and Sufis of different schools, a place of fruitful freedom enjoyed by Shiites, Christians and Jews alike. For two years Baha ud-din worked unhindered as a theologian and preacher. Upon his death, Mawlana succeeded him as head of the *madrasa*. He made the journey again to Aleppo and Damascus and met poets and sages and then returned to Konya where he devoted himself to the study of literature, law and science, began to write sermons and study Greek philosophy until he was known as a prestigious *ulama*, preacher and mufti. When his first wife died, the mother of his first born, Sultan Walad, and of Ala ud-din Chelebi, he married Kerra Hatun and had two more children. He was the spiritual leader of his community, famous for his sermons and *fatwas*, respected by monarchs and the people; the career of Mawlana – literally, *Our Lord* – seems set firmly on course when suddenly it is disrupted by an unexpected incident that radically alters his life.

Mawlana meets Shams Tabrizi and the meeting sweeps away his body of knowledge, his certain truths: like volcanic lava it carries all swirling before it. Through the many versions related by his disciples it is possible to see the event of 29 November 1244, 'the union of the two oceans', in a rich profusion of detail. According to one disciple, Shams the dervish bursts into the *madrasa*, throws Mawlana's books into a water container and responds to the owner's criticism by taking them out one by one, each perfectly dry, as if they have not suffered from their immersion: another relates how, while Mawlana is expounding his teachings to a group of novitiates,

Shams enters the room and points at a pile of manuscripts and asks, 'What is this?' 'You know not,' Mawlana replies. Suddenly the volumes blaze into flames, and it is Mawlana who exclaims, 'What is this?', and the intruder who replies, 'You know not,' before he disappears. In a less fantastic account, Mawlana is riding his donkey to the bazaar, when a hirsute, ragged dervish, his eyes like fiery embers, seizes the donkey by the reins to which he clings tightly between naked arms. He blurts out two questions of a mystical nature. Mawlana replies and then falls delirious. Once he has come to, he takes Shams' hand, leads him to the *madrasa* and shuts them both in a cell for forty days.

Mawlana has discovered love. As Sultan Walad, his first son, later says, 'God allowed Shams to show himself uniquely to him . . . No one else had been worthy of such a vision. After waiting so long, Mawlana saw Sham's face; his secrets were diaphanously revealed. He saw he who cannot be seen, he heard what no one had ever heard from human lips . . . He fell in love and was annihilated.' To describe this experience of death and transfiguration Mawlana writes simply: 'I was raw, I was cooked, I was consumed.' The two mystics finally come out of their seclusion, which has been watched over by the young Sultan Walad, and go to the inauguration of a *madrasa*, where Malwana is to speak. Curiosity and envy centre on Shams. While the wise and the worthy argue over which honorary place corresponds to them, the dervish crouches in the corner where the shoes are piled. Mawlana calmly pronounces: the wise men will sit on the couch, the mystics on the cushions and the man in love next to his friend. To the amazement of those present he goes over to the side of Shams Tabrizi, whom from that moment on he will call 'My Lord.' 'Love orders the universe,' Mawlana says, 'we are atoms, it is the ocean and we are mere drops of water.' Mediator and incarnation of occult Understanding, the dervish sets Mawlana on fire. He establishes him in his library, welcomes him into the heart of his family, offers him the hand of an adoptive daughter, dedicates countless poems to him. Shams wrenches him from spiritual lethargy; he is the avatar for the unknowable deity. Mawlana has seen God in his wild, thorny form, which is how his cry of 'Oh Shams, oh my God!' should be interpreted. He scandalizes the Islamic dogmatists by playing on Shams' name, meaning sun in Arabic – and writes: 'The sun of Shams' face, glory of Tabriz, shines on nothing mortal without making it eternal.' Mawlana abandons his sermons and *fatwas*, neglects his pupils, absorbs himself in mystical discussion, scorns all wordly respect and consideration. Mehmet Onder tells how the dervish, perhaps influenced by the concealed ethics of the transgressors or *malamatiya*, subjects Mawlana to a harsh test: to put an end to his pride he tells him to go and buy wine in the market. When Mawlana obeys and is publicly ridiculed, he throws the flask away and embraces him, moved by the manner of his greatness. Shams initiates his friend into the dance of the dervishes and the envious mutter, 'Who is this Shams who has snatched our master from us, and deprived us of his presence?' Is he a magician, an infidel, a heretic? Why has he led Mawlana astray, away from his studies, his piety and knowledge? The day Shams' wife suddenly dies, the gossip becomes poisonous: only Shams can be responsible for the young girl's death. The dervish, a target of hatred and lies, leaves Konya on 15 February 1246, without warning Mawlana, and disappears.

When Mawlana discovered Shams had gone, he fell into a state of collapse. He took refuge in poetry and began to compose his *Mystic Odes* or the *Diwan of Shams Tabrizi*. He desires only that his departed lover reappear: if love is madness, he resolves to be a madman among the wise. He sends messengers out to look for him as he writes: 'I am afraid to visit the places where you walk, fearful of those who love you/Day and night you live in my breath;/to see you I look at myself in the mirror' 'Body laid waste', 'a thirsty traveller', 'a lonely recluse amid the ruins', he calls after, entreats his friend, when he hears he is in Syria, travels in vain to Damascus, and sends him servants and gifts. Back in Konya, inconsolable, he writes impassioned poems; entranced by mystic love, he dances hour after hour with the whirling dervishes. Sultan Walad, Mawlana's first born, makes a fresh attempt to find Shams. Guided by a beautiful dream he is successful. Walad prostrates himself at Sham's feet, gives him his horse, urges him to return. He tells him how the slanderers who include his younger brother, Ala ud-din Chelebi, have repented: the whole city anxiously awaits him. Shams relents, and the two mystics are reunited before the gates of Konya to popular acclaim and in the presence of the nobility. His hagiographers have recorded conflicting versions: some say Mawlana goes to greet his beloved and, as in their initiatory encounter, grasps the reins of Shams' mount, Aflaki and other disciples say Mawlana falls thunder-struck from his horse and returns to the *madrasa* in the dervish's embrace, where they dance the *sama* in celebration. Between the 8 May and 5 December 1247, Shams stays by Malwana in perfect, mystical communion. In those months, the Sufi master writes some of the most beautiful compositions in his extensive, often challenging poetry dedicated to his friend's dazzling, solar presence: 'Object of my drunkenness,/syllable on my tongue:/ without you, the planets are a prison;/don't sleep yet, wait.' The orthodox believers led, some say, by Mawlana's second son, are scandalized by the poetry's intimate tone, and plot Shams' death. On the night of December 5 they set an ambush for him, and now he vanishes for ever. Whether knifed to death by the conspirators or thrown down a well, his eclipse has remained a mystery that no-one has unravelled to this day . . . Some think that Shams' corpse was exhumed and buried in Mawlana's mausoleum years after the latter's death; however, Mehmet Onder recently discovered some remains hidden beneath the burial place in the mosque dedicated to Shams in the centre of Konya. Whatever the truth may be, for centuries the dervish's sudden end has charged the magnetic power of his legend.

Mawlana's grief overwhelms him. Dressed in mourning, he can only find consolation in the *sama*, surrounded by dervishes and musicians. 'Separation', writes his son Sultan Walad, 'left him beside himself; love turned him head over heels. Once a sage and mufti, he became a poet; an ascetic, he was now drunk on love . . . Night and day he danced the *sama*, circling over the ground, spinning like the firmament. His mournful cries reached the Throne; both great and small heard his laments . . . He gave money to the musicians, and gave away all he possessed. For never a moment was he without dance or *sama* until no one was left to chant, all were silenced and worn out, unmoved by gold and gifts. All sick and weary, and without wine, in a haze of intoxication.' Although Mawlana, from whom the truth was piously hidden, does not see Shams again, he finds him thanks to the luminous path of poetry within himself. Once consummated, he shares with him the brilliance of 'words of substance', as José Angel Valente writes of John of the Cross: 'Although far from him tangibly/without body and soul we are an identical light./ look at him, if you wish; look at me, if you want/ seeker!, I am he and he is I . . . Since I am he, what else could you be seeking?/I am he, yet I speak of myself./I surely watch out for myself.' After the experience of being *emptied* by the *Mystic Odes*, Mawlana signed his poetry with Shams' name: there is no difference between them; the lost dervish speaks through him. Converted into a symbol of divine love, his absence proves the reality of the world and has the power of re-incarnation.

In 1249 another anagnorisis again wounds the poet with a shaft of light. One afternoon, after leaving his house, Mawlana crosses the goldsmiths' district and suddenly hears the beating of hammers shaping the metal. He catches the rhythm of the tools; the music transforms pain into ecstasy. He casts off his cloak, closes his eyes, turns towards the sweet harmony of the tapping, rests his head on his right shoulder and listens to the secret language of the metal-beater. The planets dancing around the sun gradually fuse with the thudding heart in his breast. Mawlana swings himself round, and as artisans and passers-by jostle to see him, one of the goldsmiths orders his apprentices to quicken their pace, to strike louder, louder till, losing all restraint he rushes over to dance with him. The gold merchant, though illiterate, imposes himself with the grace of possession. Henceforth it is he who comforts Mawlana in his cruel separation from Shams. Having surrendered body and soul to the way of *extinction*, Salah ud-din Zarkub, the gold-beater, renounces his worldly goods, shelters in the calm of the *madrasa* and becomes the poet's *new sun*, the one he calls Master among Masters and immortalizes in his poems.

'Dance lightly, oh, Sufis, weave your ethereal circles!' Once more Mawlana lives intensely: Shams has reappeared in the countenance of the humble goldsmith. As before he binds him to his own family by marrying his loyal first son to Salah ud-din's daughter. The two men live in close union for ten years. If Shams' defects – his coarseness, fits of anger, liking for wine and other open defiance of religious law – had charged his opponents' spite to the point of causing his death, it is now the craftsman's rudimentary education that becomes the target of their hostility. Envy and gossip, and failed assassination attempts do not however disturb the peace enjoyed by the two mystics, for them whom only 'he who dies before dying really lives'. When Salah ud-din expires in 1258, Mawlana organizes his funeral with all the hullabaloo of a wedding, carrying his corpse shoulder high as far as the tomb to the sound of flutes and kettledrums. Later, the master of Konya finds the light yet again in the person of Hasan ad-din Chelebi, a dervish belonging to his own brotherhood and fully versed in Sufi texts, to whom the poet dictates the six volumes of his *Masnavi*, an epic work encompassing all the different stages of his spiritual journey. Mawlana himself dies on 17 December 1273. As described by Aflaki in his colourful exposition of the master's deeds and words, 'they had scarcely brought out his corpse on a stretcher than nobles and the people bared their heads; men, women and children, everyone came: the tumult of their voices sounded like the Resurrection. Everyone cried, and most of the men shouted and rent their clothes until they were almost naked. Members of different communities and nations had come together – Christians, Jews, Turks, Arabs, Greeks – each with their own holy book. In accordance with their customs, each repeated verses from the Psalms, the Pentateuch and the Gospels . . . readers of the Koran read beautiful *suras*, the muezzins melodiously chanted the prayer of the resurrection, twenty groups of musicians recited songs and poems composed by Mawlana.' And so the poet's desires were fulfilled, when he anticipated the attitude of his followers in the course of his last journey; *joyful*; *cheerful*; *drunken*; applauding his final meeting with the Beloved. The *wedding night* of the great mystic has been celebrated ever since on the anniversary of his death, and a crowd of *mawlawis* and admirers come from throughout the world, gather to worship in his tomb, in the famous mausoleum built within the precinct of the *madrasa*.

2

None of Mawlana's extensive, beguiling work, both in verse and prose, has been translated into Spanish; but any reader who is interested but ignorant of Farsi like myself, can consult the English translations by Reynold A. Nicholson and John Arberry, whose scrupulous faithfulness to the text does not deny the occasional successful poetic intuition. The mystic's works have been translated into Turkish, Arabic, German and other languages, and have been the subject of numerous studies, glosses and commentaries, among which, as one might expect, the Hispanic contribution is conspicuously absent.

The nature of the lasting fascination of the *Mystic Odes*, the *Masnavi* and *Fîhi-mâ-fîhi* is complex, many-sided. As their interpreters have emphasized, the contemporary reader can only wonder at the visionary gifts that allowed him to divine, long before Copernicus and recent discoveries of physics and astronomy, the Earth as part of the solar system, the number of the planets or the way each atom reproduces in miniature the whole of the cosmos. The dervishes' drunken whirl is the constant, dizzy round of the new stars:

> Oh, come, daylight, the atoms are dancing!
> The souls plunged into ecstasy are dancing!
> I'll whisper to you where the *sama* is going.
> All the atoms of the air and the desert
> you must understand, seem numbed.
> Happy or sad, each atom
> falls in love with the truly ineffable sun.

The poet's daring images of the soul's path to perfection, are close to those later formulated by other mystics like John of the Cross or Teresa of Avila; the open, ecumenical nature of his doctrine is a bridge that spans different cultures and epochs, unexpectedly drawing us nearer to him. The order of the dervishes was inspired by his life and writing, their definitive rules were written down by his son, and prescribe the rites of the dervishes exactly as they have reached us today, establishing for its members a framework of free thought, which without fanaticism, without breaking Islamic doctrine, seeks to find expression in the emptying of the inner self or ego through a combination of prayer, music and dance. The lapping of water, strains on the flute, whispering hum of silence, shaped the peace of the *madrasas* in the times of Mawlana: in the reign of the Seleucid sultans the insane were cured by the gentle harmonies of violins and flutes. The *mawlawis* do not accept the existence of insurmountable barriers between sects and religions, travel around in groups preaching poverty by example, scorning the symbols and attributes of worldly power. "Be slaves, move over the ground like horses," the master said. "Don't try to raise yourself up on the shoulders of the people like a corpse being carried to the cemetery." Although Mawlana's ambiguous language of love and extraordinary spiritual openness clashed with the dogmatism of some *ulamas*, his orthodoxy is not unworthy of the great mystic and jurist, Al Ghazali, whose work reconciles Sufism with strict faithfulness to religious law. 'In step to two rhythms,' Mawlana wrote, 'I place one foot firmly on the law while the other roams freely over the seventy-two nations [of the world].' Certain passages from the *Masnavi* seem to display a remarkably perceptive evolutionary conception of the universe: 'Man passed from the kingdom of the inorganic to the vegetable, without recalling his previous condition. When he reached the animal stage, he forgot he had been a flute . . . Later he reached the human condition, yet forgot his tender years. When he changes again, he will transcend his present state.' But Mawlana attributes to *cosmic ascension* the nature of the spiritual itinerary or mental peregrinations of the Sufi masters: penetrate the ocean of divine love, 'in which your drop is transformed into sea.'

Although the doctrine of the mystic of Konya is no longer disputed by his compatriots, the words and actions of its initiator arouse in contrast suspicion and criticism. Shams' often eccentric behaviour, described by his own disciples, seems to expel him to the antipodes of sanctity. He is bad-tempered and violent, he treats Mawlana roughly, he does not hide his fondness for gambling and is often rude to those who loved him best. His attitude seems incomprehensible until it is related to the *malatiya* with its singular conception of the many paths to perfection. The spiritual lineage of the dervishes, just like the famous *kalandari*, whose Syrian-Christian origins have been established by Marijan Molé, rejects the good works and authority of pious, strict behaviour. The virtues of the *malamati* should be secret, and, in order better to hide them, he openly practises all that denies them. By challenging conventional orthodoxy and public opinion, he draws nothing but scorn and censure upon himself, tames the pride in his soul, sacrifices appearances to the purity of his heart. Like the *malamati*, Shams showed off his scepticism, he scorned prayers and rituals and when questioned by his followers, had the nerve to declare: 'Rosary, religion and convent are the law for ascetics; talismans, scepticism and taverns are the law for lovers.' As Random, Leconte and other scholars have pointed out, the dervish who inspired Mawlana probably belonged to one of the brotherhoods which for centuries have travelled the Islamic world practising the dance, preaching poverty and abstinence, and sometimes professing an external amorality that made them popular with the people and the uneducated, deliberately outside the bounds of the religious establishment.

If nomadism, a notion of a journey that is both internal and external, is one of the keys of those who chose, like the light-footed, roaming Sufi, to fuse love and knowledge, the original meaning of the *sama* has not been entirely elucidated and is still the object of conflicting opinions. According to Molé it was practised by the primitive communities of Anatolia, Syria and Mesopotamia and must then have been spread through the Islamic world by alchemists and magicians, as a symbiosis of pagan love and mystical experience: its adepts would resort to the presence of youths whose lithe forms reflected divine beauty and brought on ecstasy. This custom, fiercely criticized by the enemies of Sufism – as was their use of opium, hashish and other drugs that induce trances and oneiric flights – was finally condemned by the devotees themselves as spurious and alien to their spiritual quest. The status of the *sama* was debated in a proliferation of religious literature over two centuries. Their adversaries accused the dervishes of hypocrisy, paganism and concupiscence; their prayers, someone humorously commented, did not go further than the tips of their moustaches. But the work of Abu Hamid al Ghazali, whose brother was a famous Sufi poet and passionate defender of the *sama*, prescribed the criteria for the ceremony's performance and endorsed its legality. In his 'Revival of the Religious Sciences' he examines in detail the rites of the dance and the relationship of the dances to the progress or stations of the soul, excluding anyone who is immature, the impure, the impressionable, anyone who might tear off their clothes and be unable to control hysterical outbursts. However, in spite of that, promiscuity, the presence of youths, drug taking and other rigorously proscribed activities would continue among groups of dervishes scornful of orthodoxy. When the traveller from Tangier, Ibn Battuta, visits Iraq he describes in his *Rihla* a dance session in which the participants walk through flames and bite off the heads of snakes.

Nothing could be more alien than this fervour to the deep mystical meaning of the *sama* conceived by the master of Konya. The circular dance, as was shown by Shams was the true symbolic axis of his doctrine. The divine intoxication to which it aspires mirrors the order of the universe, the gyrations of the world and of the planets. Life, time, stars rotate in a perpetual dance: to commune with them you join in the *sama*. 'Why cling to the earth like a green plant?/Aren't your movements the key to grace?' Only he who chooses the way of union will be able to discern the secrets of nature. To become light, the lover must be reduced to shadow; before the illumination sought by the spirit, darkness is infidelity:

> Our intoxication does not need wine,
> nor our assembly lutes or harps.
> Without orchestra or flute, wine-pourer or ephebe,
> we shall get drunk and elated, inebriated friends!

The *sama* was described by Sultan Walad and later discussed and elucidated by his descendants. The *Treatise on the Mawlawi ceremony*, by Mehmet Chelebi, the major reference for all scholars includes a beautiful invocation of its mystical substance:

> A moth enraptured by his light
> night and day, insanely, I burn away
> A wolfhound at his door,
> I am loved by the world.

Over time, the congregation of the *Mawlawis* gained in power and riches what it lost in authentic simplicity. From the eighteenth century, the Chelebis enthroned the Ottoman monarchs, and were privileged to present the sultan with his sword. After spreading throughout the vast empire, they suffered from its degeneration, and, three years after the abolition of the caliphate, the father of the new Turkey would abolish the order of the *Mawlawis* and all its brotherhoods and monasteries.

3

The arrival in Konya after the journey across the scorched, abandoned meseta landscape is a real pleasure. One leaves behind the images and impressions of the capital created by Ataturk: severe, imposing buildings, Prussian rigidity, pedestrians and traffic veiled in mist, restrained bustle, a feeble sun, cold, sharp edges. Snapshots from two days of walking the streets: silhouettes in threadbare coats appearing and disappearing in the haze, unshaven faces, piratical expressions, brusque gestures, extinguished cigarettes hanging from lips, masticating jaws, struggle for survival, human steamroller, savage devouring of sandwiches, rough virile beauty, hard features, shadowy eyebrows, bushy profusion of moustaches. Like Bursa or Edirne, Mawlana's adoptive town offers the curious traveller a variety of monuments as splendid as those of Istanbul. On my second visit to the city I easily found my way about and returned unhurried to the places that seduced me years ago: the forest of columns in the sober Arab mosque of Ala ud-din, now being fully restored; the great *madrasa* of Karatay, its dome open to the night's gleaming constellations through a central cupola, to the delight of any novitiates, keen astronomers and astrologers; the *madrasa* of the Slender Minaret, also erected by the Seleucids, whose blue enamelled tower was struck by lightning, and especially the mosque and convent of the order of the whirling dervishes which has now been turned into a museum, the resting-place for the remains of the founder and his family. The organizers of the commemoration of Malwana encouraged me to explore places linked to the poet's life, to go on an excursion to Karaman, where Malwana lived during adolescence, and to visit one of the mosques where there was once a monastery belonging to his order, its tiny cells open to the public.

The present status of the dervishes in Turkey is ambiguous. The *tarikas* (brotherhoods) and *tekkes* (convents) were abolished sixty years ago: officially they do not exist. Conscious of the *mawlawi* legacy, the leaders of the new lay state are nevertheless striving to preserve its cultural dimension: the dervishes of Istanbul and Konya comprise two music and dance groups whose ritual attracts devotees of the *sama* from numerous countries, and for this reason they are often sent abroad as a showcase of the artistic riches of Turkey. So the *mawlawi* ceremony survives in this ever fascinating but somewhat mediated form, and forces anyone who knows the life and work of Malwana to ask himself and others a number of questions, doesn't the reduction of ascetic experience to a purely aesthetic act undermine to some extent the premises on which the *sama* is based, the mystic glow of its fire, the vertiginous, intimate fusion of knowledge and love? Doesn't the initiatory value of the dance perhaps fade when it is turned into a spectacle, into a cultural export, a tourist asset? Do those who now practise the *sama* preserve Sufi ideals, or do they merely perform gestures and rites like professional actors?

From my conversations with the dervishes in Konya and my observation of the Mawlawi ceremony held in the old convent at Galata I have not been able to reach any conclusions, confronted as I was by two contradictory experiences and by the use of a double language ridden with reservations and assumptions. Accepted as a legacy from the past and exploited as a tourist image, some dervishes unwillingly agree to being ascribed to folklore, preferring that to outright censorship. The annual anniversaries of the *wedding night* of the great mystic, and cultural exchanges with Europe and the United States gives them a chance to meet and unleash their Sufi inclinations without infringing the law. The popular fervour aroused by Mawlana – the devotees who on cold December days go and pray in his mausoleum, stretch out their hands in accordance with the norms of Islam, then hold them delicately to their faces as if to spread around the grace and virtue they have received – shows without a shadow of doubt that his spiritual influence has persisted.

The *mawlawís* I talked to in the dressing-rooms of the Konya sports stadium, where they were getting ready for their dance, declared unequivocally that, although they did not live in a separate community or practise celibacy, they felt that they were dervishes within themselves and tried to adapt their morality and behaviour to Mawlana's precepts and teachings. As I was to discover, not all the members of the association which sponsors their performances share this same philosophy or their generous spirit: the attempts by my companion, the photographer Coskun Aral, to organize the *sama* in a more suitable setting were forestalled by the association's impossible economic demands. However, whether commercialized or not, the *mawlawí* ceremony survives: any fortunate spectator experiences in turn the happiness, entrancement and surrender that, according to the Sufi poets and masters, overpower even those who are mere eye-witnesses.

The ritual of stripping off civilian suits and slipping on the habit – the white blouse, waistcoat and bell-shaped skirt, the coloured sash the dervishes use to bind themselves together, the cotton robe they wrap majestically round themselves, and finally the ochre fur cylinder higher than a Cossack hat or the hood of a Holy Week penitent – follows a liturgy that at times evokes that of bullfighters: adults and novitiates kiss their caps before putting them on: they become self-engrossed, alien to all around, or talk quietly with friends and followers who have come to greet them. Among the visitors, they tell me, is Ahmet Ohzan, a famous actor and singer who has just given up his career in order to become a Sufi.

The Konya *tarika* still directed by the Chelebis descending from Mawlana, is made up of singers and musicians, the old *chij*, or master from Istanbul, and twenty-six dervishes aged between 13 and 55: the adult cloak is black, but two youths wear a blue one and the youngest is in green. Some of the faces of the dervishes, while they were waiting on their benches, unaware I am looking at them, have a rough, disturbing beauty. Workers, traders or artisans have been subtly transformed into something different: the austere habit of the brotherhood endows them with an emblematic glow: it seems suddenly to give them a halo, an irresistible impression of pride, rigour and calm.

By the time I wrench myself from this spectacle and slip on to the ugly basketball court where the *sama* is going to be performed, singers and musicians have already gathered in the area opposite their master's sheep skin, which, though tiny, solitary and pathetic, points, of necessity, to the *quibla*, in the absence of the octagonal room, with its pulpit or *mimbar*, and the recess or *mihrab* traditionally decorated with stalactites.

4

As I was to witness the following day in Istanbul, the Konya *sama* is enacted with slight variations in accordance with a centuries-old rite. The dervishes enter the room opposite the spot where the master will stand, move forward very slowly in single file and line up to the right of the entrance next to the balustrade or barrier separating them from the audience. The white of their tunics symbolizes the shroud; the black cape they wrap around themselves, the tomb; the brown cylindrical hat, the stela or funeral column that crowns gravestones in Ottoman cemeteries. The *chij* – his hat tied with a turban – walks behind them and heads towards the skin or mat opposite the musicians. Masters and dervishes, solemnly greet each other with a nod of the head, then settle down on the floor, absorbed in meditation. The session (*muqâbala*) begins with the chanting of prayers: *suratas* from the Koran, poems by Mawlana, a special oration for the prophet. Suddenly, a singer, in the purest of voices, intones the praises to Mohamed, written by Wallal ad-din Rumi himself, a stately chant, austere yet dazzling. The lead flautist improvises a melody on his *ney*, and the other musicians join in the prelude, anticipating the short signal to begin, a tap from the old man. Immediately, the dervishes respond loudly, lower their heads to the ground, rise up in unison and, led by the guide or *samazán*, bow in turn to the master before circling once, twice, thrice, round the court in an anti-clockwise direction. At the end of these circumvolutions, the *chij* stands up, steps a few paces forward to the left (point one) of the sheep skin, gives a hint of a bow and, without losing sight of the skin, finally stands to its right (point two). The guide then walks to point one once occupied by the master, exchanges a greeting, and both embark, in slow cadences, on the previous whirling movement around the court. In turn, the dervishes imitate their expressions and gestures: move from point one to two, bow to each other, and form a silent chain behind them until the circle is closed. The wheel girates three more times: after the last turn, the dervishes return to their places,, and the old man, to his skin or mat. To the Sufis, these rotations symbolize the stations on the path that leads the immature soul to the bliss of knowledge and annihilation.

Flautist, musician and singers strike up again, and with the exception of the *samazán* the dervishes suddenly throw off their capes, keeping only their white habits and cylindrical hats. The guide goes to point one his right hand resting on his left shoulder, and vice versa. He respectfully kisses the master's hand and, after receiving his silent acknowledgement, steps to his right, inside the circumference from which he must direct the bi-orbicular movement of the whirling dance. One after another, their hands crossed over their shoulders, the dervishes greet the old man, seem to be set free from their invisible chains, stretch out their arms right palm upward, left palm downward, lean their heads to the right and begin to dance.

Although already seen in dozens of drawings, engravings and photos, the *sama* of the Konya dervishes arouses a sense of creative fulfilment, one to be compared only to that ephemeral power of the act of writing when it unexpectedly accedes to a state of grace: a vertiginous round, a drunken dance, a feathery lightness. The dervishes spin like tops, their tunics forming Saturn's rings, the white whirling folds turning into levitation. Following the guide's directions, they join one or another of the orbits of the planets, go from equinox to solstice, winter to summer: skies, stars, earthly elements evolve as weightless as an atom, their ebb and flow that of souls subject to the universal pull of the sun. The flute or trumpet blast of resurrection has dragged them from their tombs: the mystic *journey* of the dervishes goes, according to the Sufis, from the east of being to the west of non-being, from the west of non-being to the east of God. Vortex, immersion, drain, the dance annihilates illusory existence, allegorizes the stages of ascent to dispossession.

It is not my intention to set out the wealth of interpretations and complex symbolism of the *sama* but to point to the artistic mastery and the emotion it communicates to the spectator. The whirling movement of the dervishes brooks no comparison with other dances: nothing could be further from it than the stylized drama of Spanish flamenco or the genteel perfection of ballet. The dervish surrenders to inebriation with ineffable lightness, his hands languish like withered petals, eyes turn blind, floating head hangs as if drowned in the ethereal air. Snowflake, planet or atom, he delicately gyrates around himself, in silent orbit around the absent sun.

Obeying the music's rhythm the dance is broken off three times, when the master greets the dervishes and invites them to continue to rotate. When, to the notes of a gentle flute, he in turn joins the circle, the Sufi's inner communion is consummated: the ceremony is nearing its end. Whirling dervishes return to their seats and don once more the black capes they had cast off. After a fresh reading of the Koran, the prayer in honour of the prophet and chanting of the Fatiha, the master bows his head still more, and, followed by hieratic dervishes, majestically abandons the hall.

5

The famous *tekke* or Mevlevihanese in the present Museum of

Classical Literature in Istanbul, situated at the top end of the unruly alley that cuts down through the district of Galata, zigzagging past its tower, the old Sephardic synagogue and the bustle and colour of the street with flat-roofed houses, finally spilling out into the chaotic hubbub of the Karokoy bridge and the quaysides of the Bosphorus, comprises an octagonal room with a pulpit and *mihrab*, columns with Corinthian and Ionic capitals, carved wooden banisters and a circular level with shuttered windows, one of the balconies of which, opposite the *quibla*, is traditionally occupied by the musicians during the *sama*.

The session I attend, together with a select, cultured bourgeois audience, a vestige of Francophile Constantinople, is in two parts: a concert of Sufi music and a performance by the dervishes. Instrumentalists and musicians first occupy the centre of the room: the extraordinary virtuosity of the flautists, the players of lutes, violin or kettle drums allows one to appreciate in a proper setting the spare beauty of the melody and predisposes one to hear Mawlana's poetry. In turn, sometimes in chorus, the singers modulate their bell-like voices, and happiness, or, rather ecstasy, overcomes the listener. The Sufi concert reaches an intense degree of austere, naked purity. Their liturgy pursues ascesis and sublimation, distils and equips the spirit for mental immersion in the dance.

But the Istanbul dervishes do not make the same impression as the Konya ones: their haste or ineptitude as they reach towards that ethereal state of abandonment and dispossession of the self required by the *sama* proves in my eyes their immaturity and lack of preparation. Apart from their guide, whose lead to the whirling dervishes, impelling them from one orbit to another, is proud, stirring and delicate, the group's members are like actors who do not live the ceremony from within: for some mysterious reason they lack grace and magnetism.

Is it the fault of the dervishes or of my exhaustion after a long, tiring journey? After leaving the *tekke*, I return to my hotel and re-read Mawlana. 'He who sees and he who is seen,' he tells me, 'become one within yourself.' A fortnight later as I write these lines, I am still unsure of my judgement or of the accuracy of my vision.

Shadow on Blue
Marsha Rowe

Language was one-track. Tanya was commuting but never arriving, never going home. She saw a house island, a dreamy figure, blue's indeterminacy without edge or surround, a blue lake in a black hole. The track stopped there. She got off.

Yves Klein was twenty when he lay on the Côte d'Azur staring up at the sky, and raised his arm to sign his name. 'The blue sky, my first art work,' he said. At his exhibition in 1958 visitors were offered a blue cocktail. All who drank it urinated blue for a week. 'The blood of the body of sensibility is blue,' said Klein. He was the blue messiah. He did not want his hands messy. He stood in the Galérie Internationale d'Art Contemporain, in formal dress, and gestured. Three naked women appeared before a Parisian audience, smeared their bodies with deep blue paint and pressed themselves against sheets of paper. Klein said, 'I could continue to maintain a precise distance from my creation and still dominate its execution. In this way I stayed clean.' In 1960 he patented International Klein Blue, a dry, rich, deathly colour between cobalt and ultramarine.

Twenty years later Tanya stood in the Musée National d'Art Moderne in Paris gazing at Klein's *L'Arbre, Grande Eponge Bleue (SE71) 1962*, at the crevices and hollows of the sponge in which blue dripped like velvet. It was a brain soaked in electricity. In front of *Monochrome IKB 3*, she looked at blue until she saw nothing. She fell in love. When they were first exhibited, Klein's monochromes of blue were hung out from the wall. She read in a catalogue that he wanted them to 'invade', to impregnate the space of the observer. Klein had once flown from a window, was photographed, anyway, so that he seemed to fly, into the Eden of space. Tanya imagined his leap into infinity. For Klein, 'Blue was the last veil over the face of the void. I have made an exhibition,' he said 'and I think I may have to die for it.'[1]

Klein was insomniac, driven by amphetamines and by an urgent desire to fix his blue pigment without murdering the colour. He soaked sponges in polyester resins. He wore no protective mask. Aged thirty-four, he died. He identified with Christ.

'I bet I can make you say black.'

'Can you?' Tanya ran her hand along the railing and looked out at the North Sea.

'What colour is the sky?' Phoebe asked.

'Blue', said Tanya. Children always paint the sky blue and the sky was still blue that first evening in Whitby, the night before Saul arrived, though later in the holiday it rained every day.

'I told you I could make you say blue.' Phoebe pranced ahead of her on the promontary.

'You said you could make me say black.'

'I told you I could make you say black.' Phoebe ran in triumph out along the wooden pier towards the fishermen and the lighthouse.

Their cottage was in the old part of town, below the ruins of the Abbey on the cliff. Later that night, when Tanya had walked Phoebe back from the pier, and after they had watched the gulls resting in a chimney in the old fisherman's yard, and eaten and gone to bed, Tanya was woken by a loud, sucking thwang. She turned on the light. She saw that her bedroom door had swung open. She left the bed and checked the spiral stairway, the living room below, and then the attic above where Phoebe was sleeping. Nothing was disturbed. Back in her room she pushed open the window. During the day there would have been the screeching of the herring gulls, but now there was nothing, not a sound, not a breath of wind, only the sour, lingering smell of low tide and dead fish.

The next morning Phoebe was thrilled when Tanya told her that Whitby was the original setting for Dracula. Tanya took a photo of Phoebe lying in an open limestone grave in the Abbey grounds. Phoebe thought that the Abbey was Dracula's place, and the grave must have been a part of the story. The sun was in Phoebe's eyes, and she was squinting in the photo, so that afterwards it didn't look quite as funny as it had seemed at the time.

Tanya lived with Saul in an old stone house in the north of England, and sometimes, glancing with a frown at the dipped grey sky of the north, felt homesick for Sydney Harbour and the high blue radiance of the southern sky. Her room was on the top floor and she kept it warm with a coal fire. Sometimes she slept with Saul on the floor beneath, in his room next to Phoebe's. At night she heard the owls hoot, and the wind's wuthering at new year, and the cold traced lightly over her hands, and her shoulders seemed weightless. In the mornings she was surprised by the lace curtains of frost on the window, the tracery of white moss on the path outside, the late roses crystallized and the holly leaves embroidered in silver.

She painted the walls and the floorboards of her room white. In that white world, she sat cross-legged, leaned back against a dusty pink cushion near the fire, and meditated for twenty minutes each morning. She chose blue as her focus, not for any particular reason, simply because she wanted to decide for herself what sign to use.

First, blue appeared as a lake. At its centre floated a weatherboard house, flanked by a verandah on which a figure stood draped in a kimono, her torso turned slightly one way, head the other, with that artlessly contrived grace common to a million porcelain figurines sold in tourist shops. She was light as a ghost, and silent. The blue lake was the space that invaginates, that cradles, backs up, contains, without which there was nothing.

When spring came she had been meditating for half a year, but she felt darkness come over her. The feeling stayed with her for three days and nights. She had lived through crises before and knew what it was like to be overcome by nervous exhaustion or too many drugs, when she had to withdraw from the world and rest. During those times she would take to her bed for a day and it seemed to her that she crept up into a cranial burrow where she hung, dark and shivering, wide-eyed, until her anxiety passed and she returned to her usual self.

This time she showed no outward sign of being disturbed. Neither Saul nor Phoebe seemed to notice that she was preoccupied. She slept, and went about her life in the normal way but she was frightened. She watched everything around her rather carefully, as if the world might vanish at any moment. Everything seemed miasmic. She wasn't sure how she could come out of the darkness.

After three days and nights she woke feeling better. She continued to meditate. The blue that she imagined seemed to spill away from all meaning, flood into an ocean where she could dive then float, face turned to the sun, forever in and out. But blue was also the world outside of her, which had a blue sky and a blue sea and people who spoke language with the word blue in it. Blue, she recalled, was for boys. True blue she had to discover for herself.

Once blue did not exist. In the beginning, there was light and dark, the poles of what we now know as the spectrum. Between them was warmth, like the sun or like fire. Hues had no names. In the Homeric epics, the word *leukos* translates as 'white', though it signifies brightness, and *melas* translates as 'black' though it's more likely to signify darkness. In many languages it has been found that words for white and black are always the first to be coined, with red coming third, and blue last.

'To be like the plumage of the bulbul bird' or 'to be like the egg of a fern-owl' are two of the ways by which the M'bay language designates different shades of blue by analogy, because it has no word for blue. Gaelic also has no word for blue. Instead, there are phrases like 'the colour of a rough sea' or 'windy sky', fifty or so attributes of the land, sea, sky roped in for the picking. Homer had no specific word for the colour blue. He too used composites, like *ioeides*, 'looking like the violet'. He used a word, *kuaneos*, which may have meant the blue pigment indigo, and thus an association of blueness, yet it is as often used as a substitute for *melas* (black), and may have only meant depth, or dark.

Plato's spectrum had three primary colours, the white, the black, and the red. To this he added *lampron*, meaning 'the bright'. In his system, other colours were curious mixtures of these. Thus, white mixed with *lampron*, and 'falling into' deep black produced another term, *kuanoun*, the deep blue of indigo, but still this was not blue as a colour-in-itself. Aristotle's use of yet another word, *kuanous*, was the first to come close to an abstract sense of blue. He used it to describe the colour of the sea depths. And it bordered on black. In one passage of the *De Coloribus*, he used a different but related term, *kuanos*, and seems to have summoned this blueness for the sky: 'air seen close at hand appears to have no colour . . . but when seen in a deep mass it appears to have a colour like *kuanos* . . . This again is the result of its rarity, for where light fails the air lets darkness through.'

Outside someone kicked a can down the street. Tanya was in Saul's room, wondering whether or not she should live with Saul and his daughter, Phoebe. She walked to the mantelpiece, looked at the print of a Cézanne watercolour of Mont Ste Victoire leaning against the wall behind Saul's usual clutter of biros, screwed up balls of old tobacco, a child's toy cow, his Russian coke bottle, a light bulb stuck in a flower pot. The picture looked like a cloud of blue turning into a mountain. Winds of colour twisted into trees and spread over the plain in the foreground. She could not hold onto the perspective. She fled from blue tree to blue shadow to blue mountain. She dived under yellow streaks, floated along green, surfaced at mauve where the blue met the orange. She stepped back to the middle of the room, tripping on a pile of dirty clothes on the rug. She looked again at the print and then around the room, at the white curtains pulled across the window, the tall white cupboard by the door and the map of the world pinned above Saul's bed, and saw no maelstrom of colour. Again she looked at the print and saw that it was simultaneously whole and pulling apart. She sat on the bed and wrote a note for Saul to tell him that she had decided that yes, she would move in. She asked Saul to ring her, and said that she had been admiring his Cézanne print and understood why it was his favourite, adding, 'substance reduced to the dance of shadows becomes manifold,' without having a clue what she meant.

Woad Plant. Engraving. 1752.

Blue's European history starts with woad. Woad was the Celtic blue. Extracted from the plant, *isatis tinctoria*, woad has been traced back to an iron-age site in Denmark, and to an Anglo-Saxon pot from Somersham, England. Caesar confronted Britons body-painted in woad and the word Britain itself is supposed to have come from Prettanoi, the Greek version of the Celtic Pritaini, or 'painted ones'. It is also possible that the Britons, like the Northern European tribes, wore woollen trousers dyed with woad – body clinging garments branded barbaric, and banned by the Romans.

(Although Tanya read later a newspaper account that questioned woad's early history. Researchers working on the body of the sacrificial Lindow Man, discovered preserved in a bog in 1984, announced that the blue on the mummified body came not from woad but from the copper carbonates, malachite and azurite. She also found a report suggesting that woad was not grown extensively in Europe until after it was introduced by the Moors into Spain in the 11th century.)

The 13th century was the century of blue, a period of celebration which established royal blue, the festive blues, the heraldic blues and the moral virtues of blue – constancy and loyalty – alongside the duller peasant and workaday blues. These blues came from woad, which was a gross feeder and exhausted the land. Its cultivation required constant care. To extract the dye from the leaves of the woad entailed fermentation which gave off thick, nauseous fumes. Elizabeth I banned woad dyeing from her vicinity. At the end of the process the woad was collected into compacted balls of dried powder. These were then dissolved in the dye vat, where urine often provided the necessary alkaline agent. The dyeing was mysterious and indirect, the blue colour emerging only after the cloth was dipped. Oxidization – exposure to air – brought the colour to life. In Coventry, famous for its blue, the people complained that the woad dyers kept the flower of the vat (the strongest, freshest extract) for their own use. It was only with the Reformation that blue became deep sombre, uniform, Puritanical. (Wool to be dyed black had to be dyed blue first.) Woad was of enormous economic importance, grown mainly in northern Germany and in southern France, where it was called *pastel*. In addition to dyeing, it was mixed with calcium carbonate into sticks of chalk for design drawing, hence the term pastels. Blue becomes, always, the marker, the definer.

One evening after Tanya moved in with Saul, she clipped his Cézanne print behind glass and put it on a high shelf in the kitchen next to a blue and white bowl that she had bought on holiday with Saul in Spain. She filled the bowl with oranges and stood back to admire it. Phoebe was watching from the doorway and asked her for an orange. Tanya reached for one and accidentally knocked the bowl onto the floor, scattering the oranges. The Cézanne print crashed down after it. Half the glass stayed clipped to the print, the rest shattered amongst the bowl's broken pieces. The oranges rolled under the table. Tanya did not replace the glass or the bowl, and the print went back into Saul's room.

When light enters the human eye, it is received by the rods and cones of the retina where it is converted into electrical pulses and carried by the nervous system to the brain. The retina is an outgrowth of the brain. At the centre of the retina is the fovea, densely packed with light sensitive cones. There are only three types of cones by which we perceive all the colours and shades of the spectrum. At the centre of the fovea lies the 'area centralis', the most sophisticated region of the retina, which picks up on form and detail. Here there are no blue sensitive cones and when the eye tries to converge on something blue, it misses. When you see a blue painting the odds are you can't focus on it.

Tanya was surprised when she came across a reference to blue as spiritual, not long after she started to meditate, in Christopher Isherwood's *A Single Man*. She'd never thought, when she chose blue, that, at all.

Shortly afterwards she came across another, quite different meaning, one that she rather liked, in Violette Leduc's description of Nathalie Sarraute's smoking Gauloise after Gauloise, 'The blue of that packet was more real than nature,' she read, 'and she smoked with total conviction.'[2] That was more like it. Addictive blue, dislocated, utopian, and safer than faith.

Blue had led her astray from the meditator's goal of achieving single-pointed awareness, a mind disciplined to tranquillity, free of attachment to emotion, feeling, ideas. She accepted that blue was her obsession. She was pursuing blue's history. When she visualized the lake she imagined that she told the silent, solitary figure on the verandah what she found.

It was a time of intense dreams. One night she dreamed of Sydney Harbour. In the dream she saw a monster with sleepy eyes drag its clumsy arms up over the side of a ferry. The passengers screamed. The sun was shining on the blue water. Someone lopped off the arms of the monster and it slid back into the blue depths.

When she woke she thought about her childhood, and the harbour. Once when she was going into town on the ferry with her mother, she walked outside onto the upper deck and saw a large white bird resting on the seat. She went in and told her mother, and the other passengers went out to look. Was it an albatross, they asked each other? It was too big to be a seagull. Was it wounded? Tanya thought it was an omen, but of what?

She would spend hours down at the wharf where the ferry docked. She watched yellow tails browsing in the seaweed, or leather jackets swimming past the mussel and barnacle encrusted pylons, but mostly she just looked at the water itself, turquoise or emerald near the wharf, ultramarine further out. She thought the water was an oracle and waited for it, too, to speak. The passengers would come off the ferry and say, 'Hello Tanya. Nice day.'

At home Tanya's mother used to shout 'come and look', and she would join her mother at the window of their flat to watch the arrival of a great white passenger liner, or a grey aircraft carrier, a tanker, a submarine, amidst the yachts, tugs and fishing boats that filled the harbour. When Tanya left Sydney, it was on one of those passenger liners. She thought she would feel some sort of resolution, sailing away on a great white ship, but she felt nothing.

INDIGOFERA *scapo recto, foliorum pinis ovatis ad apicem obtusis late virentibus, florum spicis erectis, floribus sparsis, leguminibus teretibus pendulis incurvis, subhirsutis.*

Blue's conjugation with darkness rather than with brightness was part of early Christian tradition. The writings attributed to Dionysius the Areopagite, of the 5th century, popular in the Middle Ages, talked of the 'intangible and invisible darkness . . . that light which is unapproachable because it so far exceeds the visible light.' It was comparable to Moses' sojourn in 'the darkness where God was'. In some early church mosaics and manuscripts, Christ's mandala is dark at the centre, lighter at the edge, and in two tones of blue.

In the New Testament the blue tassels of the shawl that Moses purposefully wears as a reminder to God and prayer were likely to have been dyed with indigo, a dye from the plant *indigofera tinctoria* (of the same genus as woad, yet up to thirty times more potent). To the Romans and Greeks, the origin of indigo was a mystery. It was used as a paint rather than as a dye, and thought to be some sort of base compound since the pigment came from India via Egypt (hence indigo, from the Greek *indikon* meaning Indian dye) compacted into rough blocks with indigo's characteristic coppery sheen. The Indian word *nil*, for indigo and for blue, passed into Arabic and the Egyptian *Nil el biahr* means 'the blue river' – to us, the Nile. Indigo dyed bands sewn on Egyptian mummy wrappings date back to 2,500 BC.

The aristocratic dye of the ancients was purple. It came from Murex, a tiny sea mollusc, used as far back in time as Minoan Crete. Its colouring agent – indigotin – was, however, the same as that of indigo and woad. It was a mark of status, supremacy and charisma. During the dyeing process, the colour progressed, moving from yellow-green to blue-green, through blue and red, to violet.

Of the three hundred or more species of the indigo plant, seventeen are native to Australia, but the aboriginal people dyed no blue, used no indigo.

Indigo was ranked with the spices when the Portuguese first imported it along with tea, coffee, chocolate. In England, the introduction of indigo dye met with no resistance but on the Continent a battle between woad and indigo continued for centuries. In the 16th century imperial regulations in Frankfort-on-Main damned indigo as 'the recently discovered injurious and fraudulent, devouring and corrosive colour', and prohibited the use of it as the 'devil's colour'.[3] A century later the King of France introduced the death penalty for its use.

The East India trade included *indiennes*, Indian hand-painted textiles. The vogue for *indiennes* was as insatiable as that for the blue and white Ming porcelain, first seen in Europe also at the beginning of the 17th century. The transfiguration of the Chinese motifs into chinoiserie, the willow pattern, the blue birds, the tragic lovers, rivalled the fashion for *indiennes*, and made the eventual triumph of indigo inevitable.

The blue motif was a matter of life and death. Cobalt blue, the blue used for the porcelain, for Bristol glass, was called after the *kobolds* or goblins thought to be in the German mines, that made the miners ill. The first European cloth direct-dyed with an indigo pattern like the *indiennes* used pencil or English blue, and depended on arsenic, an injurious process not superseded until the end of the 18th century by fayence blue.

The history of indigo is the history of slavery. From the middle of the 17th century, the British and French owned indigo plantations in Georgia, Louisiana and Virginia, and the

West Indies. At its height, the indigo trade was more valuable than that of cotton. In 17th century Jamaica the French had sixty indigo plantations. A century later they had over three

thousand, by which time the French ban against indigo had been lifted and indigo patterned resist-dyeing techniques had been mechanized. The vapours from the dye preparation baths were odious and nauseating, and work on the plantations was particularly arduous. Many slaves died young. The slave revolt in San Domingo in 1795, and the French Revolution, ended France's trade in indigo. After the War of Independence, Britain could no longer exploit its American colonies and rapidly expanded its established indigo plantations in India, gaining a virtual worldwide monopoly.

The schoolgirl in blue. A thing of the past. Tanya hated her blue school uniform which did not fade. Didn't it make her look sallow, yellow like the yellow peril, the Australian Other, and the dark truth of Australian history?

Her father had hated blue. He never wore blue shirts, and avoided – like the plague – looking like a blue collar worker. He wore white overalls at work, which he changed into once inside the factory. Mum washed his overalls. She used postwar washing powders with optical brighteners to absorb ultra-violet. Re-emitted as blue light they made the fabric appear whiter than white. Mum taught her to sew. When Tanya left school, she liked a certain deep blue and made a shirt dress of deep blue viyella. She was proud of the French seams and the double shirt yoke and collar.

Janey had blue eyes. Janey had once shouted 'bluestocking' when Tanya wouldn't visit because she wanted to do her homework. Tanya remembered the luxurious sadness when she and Janey played *Blue Moon* over and over on the record player. She lay on the couch and Janey slumped in an armchair with her hands between her thighs. It was always at Janey's, in the basement sitting room with the nylon curtains that kept the room shrouded in half-light. Janey's father gave her sherry and liked it when she laughed at his jokes but her own father called Janey a guttersnipe, which showed what a snob he was. When the best friends fought about it, Janey shouted at Tanya that at least she, Janey, was clean, meaning that Tanya was dirty, and anyway Tanya couldn't dance and had no personality, not like her, Janey, with the bright chatter and the bright blue eyes.

Tanya, as a child, spoke not of her own thoughts or feelings. What if she now, after months of meditation on blue, tried to galvanize blue's speech? The ecstacy of blue that was active and aspiring, that sought to sublimate the tedium of the body's boundaries in a quest for perfection. But the body? She ran towards blue's pleasure, fucked inside blue's streaming eroticism, unseeing of the upward, written blue that inscribed her. She refused to think of the blue pencil that censors, the blue movie of pornography, the blue light of the police station. Blue pulled her away from the bed she lay in. Blue was inside her. Blue was not her fantasy.

The blind cannot see darkness. To come out of darkness, is not to see, suddenly, brightness, but to move within a spectral blur until shape and form are gradually apprehended. Emerging from her three days' dissipation in darkness, Tanya walked in the garden. She turned round and round under a cold, crystalline, northern sky. No mother-of-god warmed her atheist's heart, no blue-robed lady reigned in a nook of memory. As a child she was frequently warned off the idolatrous saints which she was told littered the Roman Catholic church. No such craven images were accepted by the clean-spirited Church of Englanders attending St Augustine's where the venerable magnolias grew taller than telegraph poles, and the grass was kept down by two roaming sheep. But one Easter, Tanya's favourite Sunday School teacher, the one with the short-hair-framed-heart-shaped face, handed each of them a book mark on which she had painted a blue and pink watercolour of a winged, angelic figure. Tanya wanted to kneel piteously to kiss it. After the lesson she slipped the cherished bookmark between the pages of her Bible while she mouthed the words of a hymn in a fever of grateful sentiment as highly wrought as the stained glass windows on the church walls.

Intensely blue stained glass seems to approach the spectator. In the High Gothic cathedrals which sprang up in France in the 12th century, blue glass predominated. At Chartres its deep register acted as a screen against rather than a transmitter of, *lux*, the divine origin of light. Its preciousness was likened to *saphirus*, the sacred stone, which did not refer to the gemstone, sapphire, but to the deep opaque blue of lapis lazuli. This scale of values was to change completely in the 13th century. The Virgin, already worshipped as the Immaculate Mother, had been crowned Queen of Heaven and of love by the 12th century. Her celestial blue mantle which originated in Constantinople was trailed in full glory through the West, to herald blue's transformation into splendid brightness. By late 13th century transparency was the esteemed value.

'The shadows of plants appear to be blue always' recorded Leonardo da Vinci in his notebooks. With the Renaissance development of perspective, an indigo wash was used to impart distance, or a sense of unreality. Indigo was also used to trace designs. Indigo or azurite replaced the costly ultramarine from lapis lazuli (imported from Afghanistan, thus 'from overseas') to paint sky. The cost of pigments now maintained theological distinctions, 'two florin blue for the Virgin and one florin blue for the rest of the picture.'[4]

Ultramarine remained, for Leonardo da Vinci, the colour 'illustrious, beautiful and most perfect beyond all other colour; one could not say anything about it, or do anything with it, that its quality would not still surpass.'[5]

Janey arrived in England, on a trip with Bill, and visited Tanya in the house in the north. 'God', Janey said to Tanya, 'all these years and not even a peck on the cheek. Let me look at you. Christ, girl, you look just like your mother. In here?'

Janey, who still chain smoked, couldn't believe the cold, white room. Tanya offered her jasmine tea. Janey wanted wine. 'You're out in the sticks here, Tanya. I had a terrible time trying to find a taxi to take me.'

Janey talked the way she wrote letters – without breaks.

'I'm at the Royal. It's the pits. I rang reception this morning and gave them a piece of my mind. You wouldn't believe it, but I can't walk round the bed, not an inch between it and the wall. So, how are you Tanya? Mind if I have a fag? I said to Bill, I bet Tanya's given up the cigs and does yoga. No? Well, given up the cigs. Remember on the ferry, first thing, the Alpine then the peppermint Lifesaver. White wine? I wouldn't mind. Never drink anything else. I only came because of the people. Bill's exhibition? I've done it too many times. To me it's the people that's important, not the place. Jesus, Tanya is this your daughter? Oh, your bloke's daughter? Phoebe, is it? Hello. Do you know who I am? Yeah, that's right, an old friend of Tanya's. I've got a daughter too, though she's a bit older than you. Mine's a big girl. Tanya was my bridesmaid, did you know that? And where do you go to school? You've got a loud laugh for a little girl. Ramsey Street? If your dad wasn't such a meanie, he'd bring you and Tanya out to Australia, you could visit me and see for yourself. No, she and I grew up in Sydney. So, she's told you a little bit about it, has she? Playing out? Oh, I see, outside you mean. See you later alligator. She's a sweet kid. What's that Tanya? Millie's okay. I've instilled it into her, she's gotta look after number one. No one else's going to. It's a tough world. She'll cope but I haven't a clue what she'll do with herself. None of her father's talent. She likes sailing. A photo here somewhere. That's the patio. Just saved those ferns from the fires last year.'

Janey followed Tanya downstairs, where Tanya began preparations for a meal.

'Tanya, I just cannot get over it, you standing there peeling the potatoes leaving the water running, when we've got a water shortage back home. Millie's boarding. Just a single term, I said to her, just while I go on this trip with Bill. I rang her last night, told her about the lost luggage. Didn't I tell you about that? It wasn't transferred in Singapore. Put on a later flight. Bill went and got it the second day in London, thank god. I packed these slacks. I refuse not to be comfortable. But tomorrow night, it'll be the whole works. The jewellery'll come out. Bill hasn't changed. He keeps on coming back with the stuff. I tell him not to but he comes home with it. I've got it with me somewhere, here in my handbag, in this box. Wouldn't leave it. That's the pearls with the diamond clasp. Remember that one? It was the first. Millie was upset when I left. Had a bit of a cry. I told her I wouldn't risk travelling via the Far East again, not with her. Not after last time. Chicken, yes, I like chicken. Vegetables, no. Zucchini? Grate them into the salad then. Well, she had an operation on her back. It was a hair, entered her body and got infected. The surgeon said it's what soldiers got in the war. Because of the sweat, the humidity. Thailand's so humid. Millie complained about this pimple after we'd been there on holiday in January and then she ended up in hospital with it. No, worse than a boil. It was a hundred degrees but I hadn't gone all that way to sit round enjoying the air conditioning. We went sightseeing. A hair enters the skin with the sweat. I think it must have grown down the spine, and you're left with this infection. What? Hair follicle? Well, I wouldn't know about that. She had to have it dug out. I watched. You could see all the little nerve endings waving about. Right on the panty line. More wine? I'll get some ice in a minute. Bill told me I'd been a bad mother, neglected her. It just looked like a pimple to me, and Millie did say it hurt but kids are always complaining about something, and then one morning she couldn't get up. You got another bottle in the fridge, Tanya? Otherwise I'll go and get one. What are the paintings like? The same sort of thing, really. Only paler. Pink and blue. Torsoes, breasts, buttocks. Now it's pegboard and he sticks on bits of driftwood. One thing's extra. He puts on axe handles. Just buys the handles. Wouldn't have blades like that about the house. Not after what you know and I know. Now listen here Tanya, I've felt bad about that all these years. I've never been able to forget it. You can't put the clock back. It wasn't you he was mad at. After twenty years I'd like to forget all about it but I'll never forget. You coming to London for the opening? Glad rags? No, any old thing. Well, Tanya, I think you should. You'll see when you get there. He's done it, that's why. Yes, all of it. There's his mother. I wouldn't call it a portrait exactly. Her face is hers but half of it is this pegboard stuff. And all that went on up to it. Lots of my belly. Lying pregnant, next to an axe handle, above an axe handle. You're the only one who knows it ever happened. You and the doc. That time he bought the axe. It's all nude stuff. One's a car window and through it you see a pale blue axe with the blade melting. *Scream Blue Murder* he's called it. Oh, go on, come. He'd love to see you. God, Tanya, after all these years.'

Tanya did not go to Bill's exhibition. She saw Janey off on

the train the next day. Bill, when he was first with Janey went through a psychotic period for six months, during which he thought he was going to kill Janey, or Tanya, or himself. Then he had a vision of his dead mother. He saw her in the car one day, sitting next to him. After that he was okay. He didn't want to murder anyone. Tanya said to Janey, 'I guess he felt trapped'.

Bill had never loved a woman with blue eyes until he met Janey. 'They're not the same as us', he'd muttered, and Tanya had agreed, leaning into his large, loping Australian body, thinking that she was always coming up against blue eyes in books, eyes of the bluest truth, eyes a sadist blue, that sort of thing, even once of a writer who lived by the Mediterranean so he could be reminded daily of the blue of miners' eyes. The face black with coal dust and the eyes bright as lanterns? No, Bill said, he could never love a woman with blue eyes. He had smiled at Tanya, with his own soft, dark eyes, speaking in his low, soft voice, and she had agreed with him, that people with blue eyes were not the same as themselves. Since Bill, she met a few others of the same type, soft, big Australians, but she'd ended up, twenty years later, with an Englishman who had blue eyes.

The outer, rod-filled margins of the retina are older than the cones at the centre, more primitive in structure, more sensitive, perceptive of movement rather than objects. At the very periphery, they see nothing more than the movements of shadows. When light no longer falls boldly onto the retina, the cones cease to function and the rods start to take over. During this marvellous transition from cone's day to rod's night vision, a shift in perception takes place that brings blue strangely into prominence. Whereas in daylight yellow is the brightest colour, at twilight it is blue. Just before dawn breaks the brightest flower in the garden is blue.

Some time after her accident with the bowl of oranges and Saul's Cézanne print, Tanya started to collect broken pieces of blue and white pottery. She found the first on a beach in Dorset. The sky that day was a forcefield of blue. Sheer, spinning breezes whipped at the shirt she wore over her swimming costume while she followed Saul along the pebble beach. The waves lapped gently, but at deeper levels shifted the stones. Tanya heard the constant little clicks and clatters at each pull of the waves. She found a fragment of blue and white china with edges worn smooth and rounded as the pebbles. It was the largest she would ever find. It showed a chrysanthemum with seventy petals, five leaves on a stem, and a spray of rose leaves behind that.

She worked on her collection at the large table in the bay window of the front downstairs room, where Phoebe sat and ate her meal in the evening. Often she needed to clean the pieces free of mud and grit, because she found them anywhere, in the park, on walks in the country, in friends' gardens. Willow pattern pieces were rare, which surprised her. Her favourite showed an arch of a doorway and a tiled roof overhung by a leafy branch. One evening she was interrupted by a noise. She looked up and saw a man outside. As she left the room and went out into the hall she could hear him rustle past the philadelphus which grew in front of the window. She opened the front door and shouted 'What do you want'. He was already running down the path and through the front gate. By the time she reached the gate herself he had disappeared.

Tanya moved her work upstairs. She began to paint every day, after her meditation. She no longer saw the house or the figure in the kimono but she saw many faces in the water. She bought pigments in order to mix her own paints – antwerp blue, cerulean blue, cobalt blue, indigo synthetic, manganese blue, phthalo (mona) blue, oriental blue, prussian blue, ultramarine blue dark, ultramarine blue light. She painted the faces in the water.

Notes

(1) *Yves Klein 1928–1962, A Retrospective.* The Arts Publisher, Inc, New York, 1982

(2) Violette Leduc: *Mad in Pursuit.* Panther, 1972

(3) W.A. Vetterli: *The History of Indigo.* Ciba Review, Basle, April 1951

(4) Michael Baxandall: *Painting and Experience in Fifteenth Century Italy.* Oxford University Press, 1974

(5) *The Notebooks of Leonardo da Vinci.* ed. with commentaries by Irma A. Richter, Oxford University Press, 1977

The Everglade Kite

Jonathan Lerner

The seat belt sign comes on just as Elliot decides he should learn Spanish. He is reading an article in the in-flight magazine that says new brain cells are generated by learning a foreign language. Elliot fears he is not as sharp as he used to be. Some new brain cells might at least halt the disintegration.

The captain announces an unscheduled stop in Orlando. This irritates the hell out of Elliot. Because he let Jewel book his flight, he didn't know he would have to change planes in Atlanta. (And Bobby had insisted on driving him to the airport. He should have known Bobby would be late.) A flight attendant was reaching to close the door as breathless Elliot trotted up to the plane. Only then did he find he was flying first class, which really pissed him off. Jewel prepaid the ticket on the shop account, but it is Elliot's money now. Well, knowing Jewel, she has him earning triple bonus miles. So he was ready to sip free Scotch and palm the leather upholstery all the way to Miami. But how can you relax when the planes keep tempting fate by landing and taking off, first into that moving-sidewalk marathon at the Atlanta airport, and now again? The real advantage of first class, Elliot sees now, is that he did not have to drag through the narrow aisle of the crowded main cabin both times, banging people's knees with the bag he had no time to check, making a commotion and looking like an asshole.

He lets the magazine flop shut, thinking, Well, I've studied

Spanish once . . . One didn't come up in the schools of Miami without taking Spanish, even back when Elliot was a kid before the Cuban exile community was such a presence in local life. He had accepted heartily the notion of 'Communicating with Neighboring Peoples', always picturing himself in conversations of blooming courtesy with a dark vivacious lady. For a year or two while he was in grade school the Freeds lived in a rented house one up from the seawall at Biscayne Bay. A Venezuelan maid working next door hung out laundry that billowed and sailed in the breeze off the water. Elliot would watch her from his patio, shielded by a hedge of Surinam Cherry, possibly holding his Spanish textbook on his lap, but he never had a conversation with her in any language. Later, when Lena and Sol sent him north to prep school, the fact that he had taken Spanish marked him as slightly odd, and he registered for French. Now he wonders whether the brain has only so many potential cells for each tongue. Maybe his for Spanish are already used up.

Elliot rubs his face in an effort to wipe this thought away. He shaved off his beard only this morning. He isn't used to the way his chin feels, toned up and tight, a sensation he enjoys, or to the sag he perceives in the contour of his cheeks, a sign of decay that alarms him. ('You look great,' Bobby said in the car, turning to lay his gloved fingers against Elliot's cheek for a moment. 'It's a whole new start for you. I'm so thrilled.' They were doing 60, on the Dan Ryan Expressway, in light snow. He pushed Bobby's hand away, motioned out the windshield. 'Just drive,' he told him.)

Elliot fears that this trip is a move that represents his ultimate failure. He is returning home to Miami to take over his parents' business. This is an upholstery and drapery shop that caters to retirees with fantasies of tropical ease. In the years since his father died, the business was maintained by

Lena, his mother, and Jewel Berman, who has worked for his parents as long as Elliot can remember. In the six months since Lena – in the rabbi's unctuous phrase – went on to join her beloved Sol, Jewel has handled the business alone. Elliot has been for sixteen years an art instructor at a community college in a Chicago suburb. Certainly this change means he will come up in the world: he will make a lot more money, will own a business, be in charge. Still, he worries about himself. The teaching had been like anesthesia, a twilight sleep. ('You're turning into a vegetable,' Bobby had said so many times in the long middle period of their friendship – the years after they'd stopped trying to force themselves to be lovers, the years after Bobby quit teaching to open his gallery, their years of burnished intimacy and mutual reliance before Bobby fell in love with Howard. 'Your brain is dissolving into oatmeal,' Bobby once yelled. 'MAKE SOME FUCKING ART OF YOUR OWN.' He might as well have been shaking him by the neck – Elliot's brain did feel like mush afterwards.)

The plane takes off again, and Orlando drops away. Elliot looks down onto an inky emptiness traced with the bobbing lights of a few roads. These roads look insubstantial as shipping lanes, fragile as damp sand causeways diked up out of the ocean of grass that separates Miami from the rest of the country the way the sea sets off an island.

When Elliot was twelve, the Freeds bought a house for the first time. It was a new tract house in an inland suburb called Miramar – a place from which there was never the slightest possibility of seeing the ocean. Lena insisted that they be the first residents of the new subdivision. Miramar then was like a beachhead of civilization, a settlement at the raw frontier of the liveable world. Their lot backed up to a drainage canal, and beyond that, to the west, was only sky, scrub, sawgrass prairies – the waving horizontal distances of the Everglades.

Elliot spent hours on his bike, making lazy circles on the clean new streets where there was no traffic to avoid. Lonely and bored, he began to explore the vast beckoning smoothness to the west. He found that it was neither smooth nor empty. It was thick with broad, ripping leaves that had rasps for edges, with plants that stuck spurs to his legs. It was soggy and chokingly humid and crawling with things that stung and bit. Solitary Elliot often went through it, without ever actually entering. He pedalled his fat-tyred bike along the straight sandy dikes of the canals, and later, when he was old enough, he drove in Lena's coral and gray Oldsmobile sedan: west, north, west, south, west. Every school term, it seemed, the roads and canals pushed further out, marking off newly claimed squares of wilderness. Elliot saw two distinct phases in this process of city claiming wilderness. One was the lag between the penetration of the roads and the filling in of these newly-drained squares with housing developments and shopping centers. This was invariably longer than the second, which was the time it took for all that new concrete-block construction to start looking blighted. Elliot was drawn to know the first interval, from where he lived in the second. Where he lived, the underground lawn sprinklers began almost at once to leave permanent sprays of mildew and rust on the bright new walls of the identical houses.

Sometimes on these rides west, Elliot came across derelict buildings – dank empty huts of concrete block whose origins and purpose were a mystery. Once he found himself pedalling up a stately *allée* of soaring royal palms – dead most of them were, lacking fronds, their cement-textured boles naked in the blank sky. At the head of the drive were the burnt remains of a house, and a greenhouse from which all the panes of glass had been scavenged leaving just a tracery of struts against the blue. Everything seemed to revert so quickly. The enterprise of living in this environment seemed always on the verge of collapse.

This is a short hop, from Orlando, and Elliot does not take his eyes from the window. He means to spy Miami's approach. He means to read its lit highways, the blackout delineations of golf course and canal and shoreline, to be sure it all remains congruent with the map in his head. He had planned this verification. It is an exercise he always performs, flying home, and even though he was here only half a year ago for Lena's funeral, he gives it his full attention. Things can change so quickly in South Florida – whole new towns seeming to emerge from the scrub every time you look.

They would fly in from the northwest, over black Everglade nothingness, and cross the Turnpike, which would separate development from blankness abruptly as a seawall. Suburbs would materialize below, some plotted in squares like graph-paper, and the newer more fashionable ones with streets circling man-made lakes – 'lakes' which are really drainage systems – their curving shorelines faking a topography on the flatness. Four- and six-lane roads would lead east, thickening like old arteries as they neared the coast, where the lights would clot. Then in front would drop out the unlit void of Biscayne Bay. Beyond it, Miami Beach would glitter on its wisp of a barrier island. Elliot expects the city to unfold this way, northwest to southeast, and the plane then to bank briefly out over the Atlantic, pivoting on a wingtip beyond Miami Beach's rim of light, recross the bay, and descend past the towers of downtown Miami to the airport. He is poised to recognize the essential features of urban South Florida.

But he is totally disoriented. Down there is a city, a flat and pulsing electric grid like Miami's – or like Chicago's, for that matter, which he has just abandoned. He twists his head to view as much of the panorama as he can, hunting landmarks and recognizing none. The pilot has brought them in on some other course, to the north perhaps. Then this could be Boynton Beach, or Pompano or Delray down below – places he knows hardly at all. For Elliot, growing up in Miami in the fifties and sixties, these towns were only shallow spots in the sea of grass, patches of exposed marl where the tedious roads north, like bridges, sunk an occasional piling. They were insignificant places, contemptible almost, these blistered seaside communities that in Elliot's lifetime have swelled and burst, run together and congealed into an urban smear a hundred miles long. They were nothing to him, these towns: nothing but the train stations, interchangeable in their dinkiness, in their fake Mediterranean architecture, that punctuated all his journeys between home and prep school; the random junctions where in his college days he might have stood hitching rides from strangers; the sun-blasted filling stations behind which he might have got or given blow jobs. These places north of Miami were nothing to him, and it still shocks him to see them merged into one seamless city. But he must be confused: now the plane is touching down after all at Miami International.

He stands dazed in the airport concourse, first off the plane but already overwhelmed by the cattle surge of passengers from behind. He does not see Jewel anywhere. He has known her all his life, as his parents' chief employee, as his mother's best friend, and possibly – though he does not know how to confirm this intelligence which assembles itself in his consciousness – as his father's lover. Still, he never quite knows what Jewel Berman will look like. She was the first person he ever saw wearing those oversized eyeglasses with squarish lenses and swooping temples. He recalls her in mother-of-pearl glasses studded with rhinestones, about 1956, granny glasses in the Sixties, aviator frames in the Seventies. He doesn't know whether she needs glasses at all, or only uses them as a fashion accessory. Her hair too is always something else. Last time he saw her she had it in a kind of punk arrangement, cut very short but for long, dark-dyed strands coming off the top of her head in a spray. That was a season when Japanese clothing designers were popular and Jewel had worn an outfit of grey sweatsuiting, hugely oversized, with big ersatz characters printed down its front, a jogging suit for a samurai. But she is definitely not here to meet him. Elliot finds a phone.

'Jewel, it's Elliot, were you asleep?'

'Oh, no dear. I'm watching TV.' Her voice is gravelly, the result of a lifetime smoking.

'I thought you were going to meet me.'

'Well I was, but I called the airline. We're used to planes from the north being delayed this time of year, you know. Just take a cab. You have money for a cab, don't you?'

'Of course.' He fishes in his pocket and jangles change, and on an impulse pulls out a quarter. In a rack next to the phone booth is what must be the local entertainment weekly, *Miami Now*. He bends to slip in the coin and draw out a copy. 'OK, I'll call you in the morning.'

'No, not in the morning. I'm at the hairdresser's and then I have lunch with a client. I'll be in the shop by 2 or 3. Call me in the afternoon, when you get up.'

Elliot hasn't slept into the afternoon in probably twenty years. 'OK, then. I'll talk to you tomorrow.'

The taxi driver has his radio tuned to one of the Spanish talk shows and Elliot thinks he may not try to learn the language after all. The moderator and his callers use that ballistic Cuban delivery, the words shooting out in continuous streams, all vowel. Probably the emotional force of the topic helps propel the sound. He thinks he hears 'Nicaragua' and 'El Salvador', but they sound more like 'Niahawa' and 'Eh Sawadoh.' Elliot surprises himself by ordering the driver to turn the radio off. Instead, the man changes stations: salsa music, multiple horns blaring.

The cab idles at the gatehouse to the apartment complex while the guard phones the security office for permission to let them in. Elliot rolls down his window. It is midnight, a night in February, but the air is balmy, a little humid. The ocean smell is strong. He put his head and arms out the window and suddenly feels at home, for just a moment utterly relaxed. Eyes closed, he listens to the sigh and rustle of the areca palms clumped at the edge of the drive. He opens his eyes: the palms and the artfully placed pillows of pampas grass throw soft shadows onto the wall that surrounds the development.

Six years ago, Lena had called to tell him she was looking at condominiums here, and to ask him to come home and help her decide on one. It surprised him. He didn't know she was thinking of a move – but there had never been a time Lena wasn't itching to move. These turned out to be nice apartments. For Elliot, too nice. The marble bathrooms made him nervous, as if the hard glittering surfaces could stun him into losing his grip and would shatter whatever he might drop onto them – a toothpaste tube even, a plastic bottle of shampoo. The arranged perfection of the complex as a whole, with its studied pretense of tropical gardens, its dredged lake and engineered waterfall of cast boulders, made him nervous. The complex was new then, but it still feels empty. Most of the apartments never sold. Three towers went up in a period of real estate boom; the fourth was never begun, and its site is a flat square of sand and parched grass in the midst of all the careful landscaping. But of course, this section wasn't included in the master plan for the underground irrigation system. It's still blank, these years later, like an erasure on the architect's rendering.

The apartments felt damp, when he flew down that next weekend to help his mother choose. They smelled of concrete dust. Their colorlessness had surprised him. Of course, their walls were only painted in chalky white primer, their floors still raw cement – waiting for the decorator, the paperhanger, the carpet and tile men, for Lena and Jewel, the ladies from Freed's fabric shop, perhaps, to discuss draperies and color schemes once an owner was snagged. They even lacked light fixtures; there was only the daylight sifting in through the vertical blinds. Inspecting one, Elliot felt suffocated. He rolled back its sliding glass door and stepped onto the balcony. The sales agent followed him. They were on the twenty-third floor. 'Spectacular, isn't it?' she said, ushering his gaze eastward toward the bay and ocean. The balconies had been designed to jut out so that every apartment could be advertised as offering an ocean view. But that particular apartment actually faced northwest. Elliot ignored her, and stood gazing inland over that glamorless Miami which stretches west away from the waterfront: strewn squares of concrete rooftops stained black by rainborne funguses, singed tufts of palm looking as tiny and brittle as the fake miniature shrubs he used as a kid with model trains. Far to the west, where the Everglades began, he could see a storm or two, charcoal-blue clouds dragging opaque curtains of rain across the edge of the world.

The other apartment Lena was considering was on the ground floor. Well, they called it the third floor – God forbid you should ask somebody buying an apartment in a Miami highrise to tell people they lived on the ground floor – because the numbering started in the underground garage. And instead of a balcony with a view it had a walled patio with a tiny space for a garden. In Lena's car afterwards Elliot paged through the glossy brochure while she drove. 'I think you'd want to be on the high floor, wouldn't you, Mom? It's the floor below the penthouse apparently.'

'I don't know, honey. It might be quieter, and the breeze might be better. But I like the idea of that patio very much. I'd like to be able to plant some things. You can only do that in pots if you just have a balcony. Although some things do just fine in pots. Bromeliads do – but they need shade. A balcony would be too sunny. But hibiscus would be fine, don't you think?'

'Wait a minute,' he said, peering at the page in front of him. 'It has *three* penthouse floors. There's no such thing as having three penthouse floors. That's an oxymoron.'

'Elliot, I did not scrimp to send you to prep school so you could intimidate me with fancy words. It's a very lovely building.'

'I never learned "oxymoron" in prep school. And what is the rest of this terminology? "Master Chamber. Culinary Center". Oh my God, "Salle de Dinner". So fucking pretentious. Lena, how can you even consider it?'

'Darling, please, your language. I'm not taking up house-keeping with the copywriter. It's a very lovely building. I have friends living there already, it's five minutes from the shop, and p.s. this'll be my first new home since your father passed away and I think you should be happy for me instead of making fun.'

Now, waiting for the taxi to be let into the complex, he knows there was no reason to begrudge his mother her arrival here, after so many places that were, to her, too modest or unfashionable – or even to begrudge her the craziness of measuring her own worth by the street address and façade of the buildings in which she lived. He had thought that the apartment on the high floor with the water view was the right choice for her. (He himself moved, a few months later, to an apartment on one of those streets on Chicago's North Side that dead-end at Lake Michigan – an apartment with a tiny balcony from which he could view a slate gray slice of water and sky to his east. No connection between his move and his mother's ever did occur to him.) In the end, Lena chose the ground floor apartment, the one with the private courtyard, and in her few years there, with the help of the climate, turned it into a dense flowered garden that she loved. So Elliot had been wrong about that.

He drops the newspaper he has been clutching all the way from the airport onto the table in Lena's foyer, avoiding his own naked face in the mirror behind it. Time is frozen in his mother's apartment, not by her death but by the decor she created in it, a precise rendition of a particular style of a certain year. Of course Lena's home would reflect that – her ability to capture and package such ephemeral currents of taste has been her great marketable skill. Her mid-Seventies apartment, for instance, had been all shades of green, with occasional lemon and tangerine accents on fields of avocado and lime. In this place, the colors – mauves and grays – are purposely less important than the few oversized objects placed against them: a custom-made twelve-foot sofa in silvery polished silk, and before it a low, purple-black lacquered table the size of a twin bed; in a corner, three huge ceramic floor vases holding sprays of dried branches the thickness of saplings – each object in the room pinlit, to suggest weightlessness despite its bulk. The artifice makes Elliot tired.

There were years in his life when this would have been the moment to roll a joint, smoke, and consider, but he doesn't have any pot now, and he doesn't want to think. He goes to the bar and pours a long Scotch, carries it as he paces through the place. The apartment is sanitized of all the clutter of real life.

Even the insides of the trash cans are shiny clean. The soap on the marble lavatories is new and unmelted. There is not a single dirty dish in the stainless steel kitchen. But the presence of his mother is strong in this cool showroom. Sliding back a section of glass wall, Elliot carries his drink onto the patio, thinking it will be a safe space because it will lack the imprint of Lena's arrangements. But he still can't seem to get it right about this garden. There are her shrubs, looming above the courtyard wall, waving against the sky, gone wild without her care: long attenuated arms of hibiscus with their salmon and pink blossoms wrapped into themselves in the darkness, and masses of night-blooming jasmine releasing perfume so powerful it makes him want to faint.

In the morning, Elliot carries coffee onto the patio and reclines on a chaise longue, shielding his eyes against the screaming light with the copy of *Miami Now*. Although he has a horrendous hangover, he feels compelled to get a little tan. Elliot has the perfect South Florida complexion: smooth olive skin that will darken without burning or drying so that eventually his eyes will be luminous in the shade of his face. His hair is black and thick, and so was the beard which is gone now. This Florida coloring – Semitic coloring, really – always made a big impression up north after his visits to Lena and Sol. ('I'm so jealous of your tan,' was the first thing pale Bobby ever said to him, as they sat next to each other in a faculty meeting one January day; and from this ostensibly superficial remark had been born their long convoluted friendship.)

He opens *Miami Now* and skims an article about a local species of hawk that is endangered. This foolish doomed bird, which exists only in the Everglades, inhabits an evolutionary cul-de-sac. Its beak is curved so that it can eat just one type of snail. As Miami expands, the population of Apple Snails is vanishing, and so, starved out, is the Everglade Kite. Elliot thinks he can remember them from those times, as a kid, when he rode off into the Glades seeking solitude: big dull-brown birds perched high in the cypresses. Everglade Kites, Apple Snails – what else? Dusky Seaside Sparrows, Northern Spotted Owls, gay men with AIDS – he knows he should care about the lengthening list of threatened species, but right this minute it all bores him. He turns the page.

This is the newspaper's design feature, and it takes Elliot's breath away: one photo, centered on a two-page spread, of a house in a garden at twilight. The house is small, traditional, correct. French doors into a living room reveal a wall of books, two facing pairs of chairs, an oriental rug on a cool wood floor. Before the house is a glowing gem of a pool tiled in Greek Key motif. Beyond the restraining edge of its patio, a dense garden erupts. The hard line of paving is lapped and softened by the succulent blades of bromeliads luminous in the fading light, and rising over them he can make out exotic bamboos, lush banana palms, giant philodendrons climbing the bent trunk of a live oak. Though it is a black and white picture on cheap newsprint, Elliot can sense the deep violet of the sky and the deepening greens of the foilage, can catch the ruby patterning in the oriental rug, the Aegean blue in the tiles. It is all serene as the ruin of a temple stumbled upon in the jungle. Now if I wanted someplace else to live, he thinks – because of course he does not see himself remaining in Lena's unbearably contrived apartment – if I wanted something else to do with my life.

There was a period, before he felt totally numbed by teaching, when he toyed with the idea of becoming an architect. ('Go ahead, tell me you're going to sit through five years of school now,' Bobby would say to that, and Elliot always admitted that he lacked the application.) People used to talk about his paintings and sculptures as architectural, back in those days when he still actually made art. 'Elliot Freed's two constructions sit in the middle of the gallery,' a student reviewer had written of his offerings in the seniors' group show at the university, 'like empty houses asking to be entered. They give the illusion of corridors leading in to deep interior spaces. Looking in, you imagine doors you can't see opening into rooms that aren't there.' That was Elliot's first and last notice, positive or otherwise. Its author had gone on to an assistant editorship at *Art in America*, a minor accomplishment which nevertheless depressed Elliot when he heard of it. Anyway, wowing them in college was one thing; knowing what to do, once out in the world, to succeed as an artist, something else. Teaching seemed sensible, strategic at first, a kind of bridge, and surely temporary. By degrees, by the elision of choices, it became instead a compromise, a giving up. It was, finally, as enervating as a hot bath. And now what, he asks himself. Now I am going to be the Freed in Freed's Fabrics, the master draper, the purveyor of pastel, one more fag decorator.

He sees quite clearly, quite alarmingly clearly, that what he intends to do by coming home to take over the business is – well, is nothing. But if I want something else to do with my life – he stares into the photograph, and a tiny spiral bacterium of an idea begins to germinate in his mind. He imagines himself at the center of a lush intimate garden like the one in the picture, at its center not in time and space so much as in conception and actualization, imagines himself close to the hearts of the people whose home it would be. This is a picture of service and beatification: Elliot giving, Elliot treasured. A branch of jasmine brushes his face, sprinkling him with pale tubular blossoms that have exhausted their scent. Irritated, he grabs at it and snaps it off, thinking, I should trim all this back now, Lena must have had a pair of shears. Where would they be?

Instead of getting up to look, he turns another page in *Miami Now*, to a feature about a hospice for AIDS patients. The article consists of profiles of the nurses and volunteers, and their photos – artful portraits showing them appropriately somber, or else smiling as if with some deep knowledge they have gained from their closeness to suffering. He finds this approach infuriating but he is glad to see that his selfish city supports such a hospice – he wouldn't have expected it. He reads with an interest that is sociological, for what it tells him about Miami now, and personal. He knows that while as a gay man he may be theoretically at risk for AIDS, such a likelihood is ridiculously slim. It is many years now since he had carefree sex with anybody – certainly not since the earliest understanding of the disease emerged. Even before, he was never the stereotypically promiscuous gay man. He never had that much self-confidence, could never quite turn himself loose that way, which used to depress him but is a failing for which he now thanks his stars. Still, there are moments when he's certain he has AIDS, the sleepless several days when any purple bloom from an unremembered bump on the shin seems certain to be a Kaposi's Sarcoma lesion, the panic at every swollen gland. And so his curiosity about the AIDS hospice has an element of morbid self-absorption, as if these may be his own future nurses.

One of them, he realizes, he already knows. Todd Weinstein and Elliot went to Hebrew School together, attended each other's Bar Mitzvahs and those of other boys of the same age. The Weinsteins lived in an art moderne mansion on Miami Beach, with Biscayne Bay shimmering past the back yard where an enormous aqua-striped party tent shaded guests at the reception. Well, it probably wasn't a mansion, whatever that may actually be, but that's how Sol and Lena always referred to it. Elliot's own Bar Mitzvah reception was held in an overcrowded hired banquet room at the Eden Roc Hotel. Elliot possesses one snapshot from it: himself pressed between tiny, composed Lena – she wore a tailored apricot silk suit and lipstick a violent shade of plum – and flaccid Sol, under whose eyes, at age 39, were already visible the bruised circles of the hypertensive ill health that killed him. Somewhere in Lena's cupboards would be an expensive album with the rest of the photos from that day, including probably a candid image or two of young Todd Weinstein. Todd Weinstein looks out at him now from the newsprint. He has grown into a handsome man with a long face, hair receding at the temples and a closely trimmed beard – Elliot's hand involuntarily goes to his own face where there's just the slightest stubble. Todd has a web of small creases around his eyes, a mesh of concern. He is a doctor, and has devoted himself entirely to AIDS work – he is the principle founder of this hospice, and he is running clinical trials of several experimental treatments for the disease. The article says nothing about his personal life, but Elliot wonders, imagines, craves to know: is he gay, is he single? They hadn't been very good friends as kids, had certainly lost touch as soon as Elliot went north to school. Had they run into each other once in a while, in line at the movies, or at parties, say, during school vacations? He remembers Todd essentially as a rich kid, an arrogant, bright good-looking boy with lots of nice clothes, with parents who drove matched Cadillac convertibles and played a lot of golf. This is a memory that is tinged at every edge with resentment. Now he is drawn to this person of commitment and evident maturity, and wants right away to call him up, to insert himself right into his life. He craves touch with the usefulness and sureness of that life as he pictures it; he imagines it could somehow complete his own. But he just as rapidly feels deflated by this potential encounter. Dr Todd Weinstein probably wouldn't remember Elliot's name without a mortifying pause, busy as he is with his good works. Todd Weinstein had it all as a kid, and evidently he still does. Elliot resents him all over again, powerfully, and his spirits droop. Depressed, and thinking he should not let himself burn on his first day back in the tropics, he goes inside, to fall asleep on the couch.

Jewel wakes him with a phone call to arrange a dinner date. Elliot decides to leave in time to stop at the mall and have an anonymous look at the shop he has inherited. He finds Lena's car in its spot in the underground garage. It is, as always, a big dark Oldsmobile sedan, a limousine of a car after the little Honda he drove in Chicago. In the dim light he has to steer carefully up the tightly curving ramps to avoid smashing its fenders. It occurs to him that where this car is kept, two levels beneath the apartment building's lobby, is well below sea level, well below the azure waters of Biscayne Bay which lap at concrete buttresses not fifty yards from where he breaks into the light.

He is wondering if he can take a first, at least a fresh, impression of the shop. He spies it from the opposite gallery in the mall, across forty feet of open space. And he winces at the sign. In the old days, before the move to the mall, the business was called 'Freed's Finer Fabrix and Upholstery'. The little flourish of the 'x' had been Sol's idea, circa 1955. It had been executed on the storefront, and on the stationery, in a cursive lettering that swagged away like drapery to become a bolt of cloth unrolling. To Elliot, once he began to think of himself as an artist, this crudely literal image was embarrassing, like a bad cartoon. When they moved the business to the shopping mall a few years ago, after Sol died, the two ladies chose to modernize the image. He suspects this was Jewel's doing, but has never pinned it on her conclusively. Now the word

'Freed's' is very small – retained only for its recognition value to those few shoppers who have been in the area long enough to know it, a small number indeed in this neighborhood where the tangled mangrove shoreline has so recently been dredged and straightened, replaced with blunt seawalls and highrise apartment houses. Below 'Freed's' the sign now reads, in aggressively geometric lower-case type, 'fabrikworx.' Elliot has violently hated this contraption of a word ever since he first saw it. It looks to him like a row of tumbling swastikas, and it makes him gag. To his dismay, he finds his reaction to it has not abated. He heads back to the car, feeling assaulted, by the storefront, by his own future.

Jewel is late, so he sits at the bar and watches. Some people are dressed to kill. He notes a lot of linen and silk, lizard pumps, suede loafers. He himself is wearing a pair of black Levis and a shirt Lena gave him one year for his birthday, a polo shirt made not of cotton but of taupe kid. It is the kind of thing Elliot, an easily intimidated shopper, would never have considered buying for himself. ('Faux cotton jersey,' Bobby had said immediately when he saw it. That's what he's always dug about him: Bobby always *gets* it.) Elliot notes that his outfit is perfect for tonight, in this post-modern shrine to food. He is paying such detached attention to the people who cross his field of vision that he doesn't recognize Jewel until he finishes scanning her attire. Of course, this is again a made-over Jewel Berman. She is wearing blue: a soft-washed, ankle length denim skirt, a man's chambray shirt with the cuffs rolled back easily, canvas espadrilles, all mid-range blues that meld into one another. Her hair is cut very short and lies soft as a cat's fur on her head, in what may just be its natural shade of gray. Her eyeglasses are unfussy, unremarkable. She has the calm, assured WASP look of a rich suburban housewife driving a Volvo station wagon. It's a style he wouldn't have expected to see in Miami, or to make its appearance on Jewel.

She brushes her cheek against his, casually greets people at two or three tables as they are led to their own. 'You look pale, Elliot,' she says when they are seated. 'You need to get some sun.'

'I lay outside for a little while today. I didn't want to burn.' He looks over the menu: bay scallops in mango sauce on angel hair pasta; goat-cheese-and-pancetta pizza baked in a brick hearth.

'You? You don't burn. But then I suppose you're right not to overdo it. Everybody I know has had a skin cancer or two.' She puts down her menu, lifts her glasses, and with a clear-varnished nail touches a scar on the bridge of her nose. 'Myself included. Have the duck sausage ravioli for an appetizer.'

'Sounds good, but I'm not hungry enough for an appetizer. I didn't know you'd had skin cancer.'

'It's nothing, dear. I say, everybody in Florida gets it. You? The way you played outside as a kid in this sun? Forget it. It's just a matter of time, never mind your dark complexion. Do you like cilantro? Lena hated it. But the chicken and black beans with cilantro is just to die. Use a sunblock anyway.'

'Thanks a lot.'

'Elliot! You shaved your beard.'

'You never miss a trick, Jewel.'

'No wonder you look washed out. We'll both have the duck sausage ravioli for starters,' she instructs the waiter. 'Here, Elliot, you choose a wine. I'm sure you know much more about wines than I do. Oh! There's Sid and Marge. You remember the Gersteins. They were friends of your parents. Marge!'

He doesn't know if he remembers them or not. They thread their way toward his and Jewel's table. Elliot shrugs himself up out of his seat. 'You know Lena's boy Elliot,' Jewel prompts. 'Sit down, sit down,' says Sid Gerstein, pushing him down by the shoulder and studying his face. 'Looks just like Solly, doesn't he Marge?' Elliot feels exactly thirteen years old. 'Jewel tells me you've come back to work in the business,' says Marge Gerstein. 'We want to wish you all the luck in the world, Elliot. You know, your mother was a dear friend of mine. What's that you'r eating?'

Jewel holds the plate up under Marge Gerstein's nose. 'Duck sausage ravioli,' she says, rolling her eyes, 'Did you ever? It's out of this world. Listen Marge, give me a ring over the weekend.' The Gersteins resume their progress toward their own table. 'He's a plastic surgeon,' Jewel tells Elliot in a tone meant to convey the information that the Gersteins have plenty of money.

'Well,' Jewel says then, in a businesslike, agenda-setting way. 'So. Are you excited to be back? Are you ready to get to work?'

'I guess so,' Elliot says reluctantly, the hated 'fabrikworx' sign floating in his mind. 'I'm afraid I'll have so much to learn. You're going to have so much to teach me. I'm not familiar with – with the elements you – we – work with. You'll have to teach me. But I'm – I'm not going to run the shop the way it's been.' He surprises himself with his last statement.

'Oh?'

'I want to do design. I want the shop to be an interior design – um – resource. Not a drapes and slipcovers store. A retail design workshop. Like those U-Frame-It places maybe. Where people can come to get any level of help they want.'

Jewel doodles with the tines of her fork on the tablecloth, not looking at him. She does not seem to smoke cigarettes any more, he notices. Elliot falls silent and considers his own words. He did not realize how completely this idea had unfolded in his head. It's all there, but it seems flimsy, unreliable as a construction of paper. He ponders the artful plate of food before him on the table, the pretty arrangement of julienned vegetables. Suddenly he asks, 'Did Lena like it here?'

'Oh, everybody loves this place,' Jewel says non-committally.

They eat for a while in silence. Why not, he thinks. We've got the location, in the mall. It's not intimidating for people to go there. I have the design sense, and I certainly know how to convey it to people, how to help them empower themselves with their own design visions. 'I mean, I don't know the raw materials – the fabrics, the fixtures. Ways of putting things in place. You'd have to teach me about those. I do have the visual sense.' And he thinks, I'd like to give it –

Somebody is waving enthusiastically across the room at Jewel. 'Bunny Stavisky,' Jewel says, waving back and nudging him to do the same. 'You must remember her.' Elliot can't get over the fact that this up-to-the-minute restaurant is filled with people from his square dead parents' scene. He wonders if they come for the food, or what.

'I mean, you know all those things, Jewel. I can learn them from you.'

She runs a hand over the soft fur of her hair, lifts and resettles her glasses. 'I think you might be talking about going after a different clientele. Appealing to different tastes.'

'I haven't really thought it out that much,' he admits. 'But look at all these people in this place. Don't you think they're interested in interior design? Aren't they really our clientele already? Some of them hire decorators to do their homes, but lots of them just want some help in doing them on their own.' He's beginning to confuse himself now. This idea of his is collapsing just as quickly as it opened up. 'Isn't this just what we already do?' Maybe, he thinks, it's just that *I* want to do it, in my own style. Or that I simply want to do it, to have some role in people's lives, any role at all.

Jewel has finished eating and pushed her plate away. 'For a minute I was thinking we would have to change the ad.'

'I guess I need to work my idea out a little more,' Elliot says. 'But I know I have something in mind. What ad?'

'I've put out an ad for a decorator. I don't know if you'll like the way I worded it. But that won't really matter. You'll do the interviewing and you'll hire somebody you think you can work with. Elliot, I'm going to retire.'

She's taken off her glasses, and is facing him with an open, revealed faced he's never quite seen. Now the style she presents, the soft faded blues, the lack of make-up and frill, is like no style at all. It's as if she is finally wearing just her own skin. He can remember Jewel with a beehive hairdo, in purple lipstick and peach lipstick and white lipstick. He likes her better without any. Her new directness makes him want her to stick around, makes him really want to learn from her. But now she's telling him he's being set adrift.

'I'm tired, dear. And I'm sure I'm set in my ways, and they're not your ways, and naturally you want to make the business your own thing. You'll want to bring in your own ideas. You'll make it a younger thing and a more masculine thing, and you'll use your art background, which is something else than what we've been – I'll help you get settled in, but I really think – Do you want some dessert? These people make a chocolate terrine that is just the living end.' She's brightening up.

'No, I'm stuffed.' I also feel like I'm going to puke. 'Look, we need to talk all this out. You're not planning to do this right away, are you?'

'I'll help you get settled. Let's both have the papaya sorbet then. It's light. And espresso.' He's happy now to let her order him around.

Piloting himself home in the big lumbering fuselage of the Olds, with its squashy suspension and damped vibrations, he feels weightless, and alarmingly separated from the pavement, as if the vehicle has taken off. He touches a row of buttons and the windows glide down into the doors, as smoothly as the glass panels roll open to the patio at Lena's. The rush of air puts him back at street level. He's thinking he'd like to call Bobby, as he must have done a hundred other times at 10:30 on a winter's night. But he has grasped finally, the way cows learn to avoid an electrified fence, that it's not the best hour to call (even) a (former best) friend who is engrossed in a new relationship. And anyhow Bobby might not be able to restrain himself. *Empower them*? he can hear him repeat – God, he hopes he didn't say that out loud, although he doubts Jewel would see the ridiculousness of the term. *Empower them* to choose the color schemes for their condos? Bobby would repeat, needling. Oh, Elliot, you asshole . . . No, it's just as well not to call Bobby. Although he misses him, he really does.

He misses the companionship, misses what he once could take for granted. Bobby went with him that first day to inspect the apartment he rented by Lake Michigan. They opened the door that led out to its postage-stamp terrace: an old-fashioned door – creakily hinged, not on slides like the ones at Lena's – with small glass lights between wood mullions. In the coldest part of winter, Elliot came to find out, the frigid winds off Lake Michigan would make thin sheets of ice form on the inside of its glass.

The warm air that blows into the car as he turns into Biscayne Boulevard is heavy with ocean scent, and frangipani scent, and the acrid smell of car exhausts. This is the old shore road north, where Lena's glitzy apartment complex and a dozen like it stand now. Elliot realizes that he has retained from childhood a sentimentally pristine picture of this road. In those days unbuilt ground stretched along it. Thickets of mangrove separated the highway from the bay, so the water, only yards away in places, was not visible. But you could always smell it, and feel its buoyant atmosphere on your forearm where you rested it out the car's window in the breeze. You could always see that unmistakeable light off the bay's surface, yellow tropical light, blue marine light. Now there are all these impressive high-rises between the water and the boulevard. They would seem to embody Miami's promise of holiday glamor, of retirement ease, but he has an idea how many of their apartments are vacant shells, and what portion of the rest are pieds-a-terre for repulsive Latin American oligarchs, the Baby Docs and Somocistas of the hemisphere. And these days between the secure islands of walled apartment compounds the spaces that remain are strewn with the derelict buildings of fast-food franchises abandoned as quickly as their promoters grabbed a speculative profit. The spaces between the high-rises are littered with used car lots, and with dirty book-and-video stores – low, windowless cement-block buildings in the private viewing booths of which Elliot can say for certain men are at this moment jerking their own and each others' penises to climax. The air rushing into the car is warm on his skin. It should feel familiar. But this Miami air feels like the atmosphere of some other planet.

That restaurant threw him. It's as up-to-the-minute as any he ever went to in Chicago – a virtual clone of the one Bobby and Howard took him to on his birthday a few months ago. He remembers the days when to go out to dinner in Miami was to confront mounds of meat and starch in surroundings of rococo excess, experiences that were tasteless in every respect: the point as he apprehended, and rejected it, was to be seen consuming. Maybe nothing has changed but the style and quantities of the food. Still, it seems that the place he grew up in, the world of his parents, has shrunk even as the city has swelled. No doubt some of them increased their fortunes as it happened, but these affluent Jewish couples of retirement age greet each other now in the elegant restaurant with the frayed, forced heartiness of a population under siege. It is as if they have no other place to go. He would bet money that none of them speaks a word of Spanish, that they lose their way in the vast new square miles of the city. They have made a retreat, to their enclave along the bay, with its appliances and illusions of security. And Elliot can see now quite clearly that he is not retreating with them.

He turns the big car west onto Miramar Boulevard. He finds the old house, that house of white concrete on the once-raw street where Lena had insisted they be the first residents. It is smaller than he remembers, and shabby in a way he finds too embarrassingly intimate. An air-conditioning unit protrudes from the window of what had been his bedroom, and where the moisture has dripped from its condenser a yellow streak dirties the wall below it. A child's toys are discarded around the yard like rings of underwear.

And so he drives beyond, toward the Everglades where as a lonely kid he used to go hunting solace. It is twenty-five or thirty years since he has ventured this far in from the coast – the moment he went north to prep school Lena had organized a move to a 'smaller, more manageable' house, in a newer and trendier neighborhood of course, back near the bay shore. Elliot had only imagined how far these suburbs actually sprawled since then. Once he had been able to wade the canal behind his house and find himself on the edge of the wilderness. Now he drives for miles and miles, past shopping malls and golf courses and housing developments all named for other places – Casablanca, Aberdeen, Varadero, Rockport – without even a glimpse of it.

He is looking for the edge again, for that sad shifting solitude where the city meets the sawgrass. He is looking for touch with what was there before the city came, and for touch with something else that might remain. He thought he couldn't get lost out here. He knows so well this pattern of roads at right angles – west, north, west, south, west – roads built on the excavated earth of the drainage canals, the sand roads that kept him out of the muck, protected from the rasping grabbing vegetation even as he glided through above it, roads that are now paved six lanes wide and walled with concrete structures.

He spun a fantasy, as a kid, about that big burnt house he once stumbled on, the one with the glassless conservatory and the *allée* of dying royal palms. In his daydream it was the home of a pioneer farmwoman, a big-boned, large-gestured, straw-haired woman in a man's work clothes whose name was Nicky – a dyke, he realizes now she would have to have been. She led him around to the greenhouse. It was not a hothouse; instead in this sultry climate it was there to keep the temperature down and the atmosphere perpetually misty, to nurture a collection of exotic bromeliads. Nicky invited Elliot in to see them. On his bike, on blazing afternoons with thunderheads piling up to the west, with kites – or were they vultures? – riding thermals in the enormous sky, teen-aged Elliot liked to imagine himself led into this cool rain-forest interior that sheltered bromeliads. He would envision bromeliads, their fleshy blades whorled around pearlescent centers, and the lovely stalks of their bizarre flowers jutting upward, presenting themselves to be kissed.

The Traveller's Husk
Drusilla Modjeska

In the dream I could see Dora. She was standing on a ridge of rock looking out over the valley, and though I was far below her, and her shape no more than a silhouette, I had no doubt that it was her I saw. She stood quite still, not looking at me, nor down into the valley, but straight ahead to the mountains on the other side of the river. In the dream I continued to climb, traversing the ridge and scaling the rock face, hauling myself up by tree roots that had made their way to the surface, or slipping my fingers and toes into tiny crevices worn smooth by the wind. When I reached the top Dora gave me her hand, and I took the last step to stand beside her.

When I looked down into the bush below, and into the cleared space where the zendo was, its buildings as small as dolls' houses, I saw with the eyes of an eagle. I could make out a tray of bread on the verandah table, and beside the shed a geranium in a pot. I could see quite clearly and without strain the paths made through the grass by mice and small marsupial rodents, even by caterpillars. I could see the seeds on the trees and parrots waiting. I could make out the spines of leaves, the sleeping places of echidnas, snakes warming themselves beside the tank. All these things I saw, and seeing them pleased me, for nothing that I saw, nothing human, nothing non-human, claimed importance over any other thing. Houses, caterpillars, all were equal. My eyes saw not with perspective, nor without it exactly. It was more like a pointillist painting, though even this is not right for there were clear lines of connection. My eye moved easily from detail to detail, and it was by accretion that everything was named and the dream's balance achieved.

In the dream I stood on the ridge with Dora, who for that moment was no longer old and no longer sick; it was not that she was young exactly, rather without age or self-consciousness she stood there. I took the cardigan which she indicated was heavy on her shoulder. I folded it neatly and held it over my arm. She took off her apron and without turning to me indicated that it too was weighing on her. I took the apron and folded it over my arm. Then I took her dress, her petticoat. My arms were filling up with her clothes. I tried to keep them in order, so as not to crush them, but the silky stuff of the petticoat slipped to the ground, and as I bent to pick it up, I dropped the cardigan. Dora stood beside me, quite bare. Not naked, I wouldn't say that, but shiny somehow, and lightened. On the ground where her clothes had been, a spiny carapace.

2. The valley where the zendo is isn't at all the valley in the dream, though there is a ridge of rock above the trees not unlike the escarpment Dora stood on. But without the eagle's eyes, one could not have made her out from where we were, and nor could I standing beside her have glimpsed more than a flicker of roof, a chimney perhaps, a plume of smoke. In any case when I awoke it was dark.

The bells rang at five. A light bell, rung with the sweetness of song, enters dreams without damaging them. Outside, figures move, clad in black, dark against dark. Under creamy hurricane lamps, the black cushions wait. A sharper bell rings, and before night has finished, or day begun, the bows are made, incense lit, and the dark figures settle. I have seen dawn come often enough when I've been woken early by the church across the street. Never before have I sat into the dawn and watched the precise changes of light, not coming stealthily as one dozes, nor with the surprise of interrupted concentration, daybreak taken in stages around the kettle. On that cushion, facing a wall with windows to one side and the other, but none ahead, I saw the day come neither by stealth nor by surprise, neither smoothly, nor in jerky spasms. A textured, highly detailed coming of day marked at the moment of change by the raucous bellowing of kookaburras. And yet, though I say change, there was no moment when one could say that the border had been reached, or a line crossed. It remained the same, yet also different, day clearly no longer night, nor night day, while on our cushions each of us sat, the same and changing, both. In front of me on the wall, a small scuff mark that took shape out of the dawn; a skier on a slope, a chrysalis, a pig rooting in straw: or a man stooped in prayer, a monk, or an angel perhaps.

When the next bell rings and the dark figures bow and rise, moving outside onto the verandah, the cliff at the other end of the valley is already lit with sun. I lift my eyes, which have been lowered as is required on retreat, and look into a valley that was deep in darkness when we arrived the night before. "Like a bowl," Louise had said, describing it, "small and round with steep sides." The zendo is at its deepest end so that the hills curl in from the left and from the right, while straight ahead, behind a dipping saddle, is the ridge of sandstone that is graced each morning by the first glimpse of sun, illuminating one focus for attention, while I take my place in the line and return to the wall where the monk prays, the skier skis, and the angel broods. And when the bells ring again, and breakfast is carried in, and the dark figures call their praise with folded hands, *porridge serves the zen student in ten ways*, the servers wait, facing out into the valley with their backs turned on the clattering teeth and the breath sucked in. They can see, as eating we cannot, that the hill to the left which at the ringing of the earlier bells seemed host only to the scraggy fullness of the gums, had revealed, hanging above us, a sheer cliff of rock, mauve and pink, unmoved by the valley flat below, but offering its blessing nonetheless to the wide verandahs where we walked, and to the cows who had moved up to inspect us, their stringy saliva dripping onto the boards.

3. It was the first retreat arranged only for women. There had been some opposition within the sangha. There had been women with doubts, as well as men with anxieties. The women had come; the men were left to consider their qualms. With the back trouble and jitteriness that comes with city living, my doubts were different. I had not been reassured by the meeting for those making their first retreat, though my links with the sangha are various and I've sat with them often enough. We waited in a not yet practised silence for the fifth woman to arrive who'd make up the complement of beginners. When she came, I realized that had I considered who I'd known as habitually late, I might have anticipated her arrival; but as it was I didn't. So it was with some dismay that I recognized in her the one who'd led the move to expel Joss and me from our writing group. That was fifteen years ago, we had a rugged aesthetic then, as if writing could be policy, like law reform, or child support. To demand the integrity of language and gesture, or to admit to uncertainty was at best self-indulgent, at worst counter-revolutionary. Vacillation, hesitation, inwardness: these were the cards we played. No wonder we were expelled.

'Should I go,' I asked G.

'Why not?' he said.

'The war,' I said, rather than confess the triviality of other battles. The war in the Gulf had started; the war we'd waited for all summer, rounding the kids up off the beach in order to be back in time for the news. Like everyone else, I'd spent two days in front of the television, staying up at night as if it were the Olympic Games or Wimbledon, watching the tally go up on the board. Later, one by one, the women said they'd doubted whether they should come, as if war demanded their presence as spectators in a city lit up and expectant. I doubt if I was the only one in the valley who broke the rules and listened to a surreptitious radio.

4. As the sun reached the roof of the dojo, and pressed against the furled blinds, the little monk praying before me became a fighter plane in a pall of smoke. The cows retreated to the other end of the paddock, backed in towards the dry creek bed as if the smooth pebbles and parched trees would cool them. By turning my head very slightly, I could see that Louise, her spine usually so straight, was bowing into the heat. As if in response, I straightened my back, lifting into the sulphury air as though by making the gesture I would alleviate the pressure of a different death that sat flush up against the wall with me.

In another city, two hundred miles inland, Dora lay dying. Dora, who'd once taught me, and who'd continued to teach, offering succour, or perhaps only understanding, a full sort of attention, when I turned from student to whatever it is that follows, not friendship exactly, more the regard of those who know that an inheritance passes between them. The last time I'd seen her well enough to be out of bed, her shoes, as polished as ever, were laced with string. Beware of strong emotion, Louise had warned as we'd driven along the river flat, watching for the road that would take us over the saddle that gives the first impression of sandstone and mountains. Like a sudden gust of wind, or a blush, anger lifted through me. With it came fear, and the necessity of movement. My arms flew up as if they belonged to someone else, and I rose with them. Standing, I made my bows and walked out into a stinging heat.

In the creek bed there were bones picked clean by the crows, a broken piece of mirror. I walked from one stagnant waterhole to the next until I could see the dusting of blue plumbago where a house had once been. I climbed up through the casuarinas and eucalypt saplings to the apple trees, the olive, the stone wall that had once marked a chimney, the outline of flattened soil. Did they, the settlers, find serenity in those gnarled apple trees, or see the elegance of the olive, building as they were a bulwark against threat and unfamiliarity, up under the scarp for protection. It seemed to me that day that the traces they'd left were not so much an embellishment, which I would once have thought, or a chance juxtaposition, as a condensed and rectangular rendition of an impossible hope.

When Annie brought Mildred back to the valley, she insisted on clambering up to the house where she'd been born.

'Look at it,' she said. 'How did any of us live here.'

She kicked the dry earth.

'It can't always have been like this,' Annie said. 'There are still good farms round here.'

'That's what they say,' Mildred said. 'That the valley flowered. Not in my life time it didn't.'

'So what happened?'

'Who knows,' she said. 'Too many people. We were six kids, not that that was many then. And the other one, buried up the back. It was the floods, the doctor couldn't get through. Though they got out easy enough when they took Amy away. It was raining then, the river as high as I saw it.'

'What did they take her away for?' Annie asked.

'It was a long time ago,' Mildred said, 'and best forgotten.'

5. As I came down the hill I watched the women, one by one, bow and leave the dojo. I watched them take their hats and do up their sandals. A women's retreat: deviation from the samurai order; innovation. The women took their positions on the grass for the dance exercises that had accounted for my second worst qualms.

I circled behind the buildings, staying in the trees but keeping the small figures of the women in view. Galahs with pink breasts watched their surreal choreography from the dojo roof. One of the women, the one who was training to be a doctor, younger than most, moved towards me up the hill. I watched her passing into and out of bright pools of sunlight. Thinking herself unobserved, she bent and moved to a rhythm entirely her own. With one hand on a tree, she balanced, letting her body fall forward, her eyes lifting with her arm towards the sky, and one leg raised behind her in a graceful curve. She moved to a flat rock and tried to repeat the gesture without support. Moving swiftly, as if after prey, I was beside her before she saw me. Her eyes faltered momentarily, there was a pause, and then she took the hand I offered, and with it my admiration and service, given at that moment in perpetuity. Like a diva she lifted her other arm to the great arc of sky, and turned a perfect circle, tracing the valley with the dipping movement of her foot.

6. There is a koan that goes like this. I first heard it in a class of Dora's, a riddle to demonstrate to us our dualistic thinking. In China, during the T'ang dynasty, there lived a man called Chokan. He had two daughters. When the elder girl died, he devoted himself to the younger, his Sen-jo. As she grew up he

turned his attention to the question of a suitable husband for her, and eventually selected a good and strong young man. But Sen-jo had already taken her cousin Ochu as her lover. She had grown up with him in a union blessed since childhood, and she considered herself betrothed to him.

When Chokan announced that his choice of a suitor was to arrive in the village, Sen-jo became cast down and sad. Ochu, unable to bear the prospect of witnessing the betrayal, left the village without saying farewell. He took his boat and rowed into the night. As he rowed he noticed the outline of a figure running along the bank. He put into the shore to see who it was; and there was Sen-jo, tear stained and adamant.

Together they travelled to a distant land where they lived as man and wife. Five years went by. Sen-jo gave birth to two girls. But though she loved Ochu and the children, she was weighed down by the dishonour she'd done her father. All this she told to Ochu. And he admitted that he too longed for his homeland. 'Let us go back,' he said, 'and beg forgiveness.'

And so they returned. At the port, Ochu left Sen-jo and the girls while he walked to the village. He went directly to Chokan's house, confessed the whole story and bowed his head at their ungrateful behaviour. Chokan received him kindly.

'Which girl do you mean,' he asked.

'Your daughter Sen-jo,' Ochu replied.

'That is not possible,' Chokan said. 'Sen-jo is here in the house with me. Since you left the village without bidding her farewell she has lain here; she lies here now.'

Mystified, Chokan refused Ochu's invitation to go with him to the port. Instead he sent a servant to check the boat. When the servant returned, reporting that it was indeed Sen-jo who waited there, Chokan took Ochu into the house. 'She has not spoken since you left,' he said. 'It is as if she has been absent in mind, or drugged. Now I see that her soul left to follow you.'

So saying, he showed Ochu into Sen-jo's room. Hearing the story, Sen-jo rose from her bed, still without speaking, and walked out into the village just as Sen-jo and her children stepped from the cart that had brought them from the port. The silent Sen-jo moved forward to greet her, and as she did, the two were united and became one.

If Sen-jo's soul was separated, the koan asks, which was the true Sen-jo?

Zen students still study this koan today.

7. If you follow the creek into the next valley and travel away from the river for an hour or two, you reach the base of an escarpment that curls round to join the cliff above our valley. If you climb part of the way up and follow the line of the cliff back towards us for the better part of another hour, you will come upon a long ridge of overhanging rock, and shallow caves. There, painted in ochre and charcoal are the drawings that once mapped the universe of the Dharginung people: lizards, turtles, wallabies, spirit men, a human hand. Mildred said the Dharginung still lived up there when she was a child, she saw them sometimes.

'They'd walk along the edge of the valley, in a line,' she said. 'We'd see them in the evening, or the early morning. I don't know where they were going. They'd come back along the edge of the crops, or where the boys had ploughed, and then up the track behind the house, and into the bush.'

She looked up to the scarp. In the afternoon sun it turns a tender, mottled pink.

'Did you speak to them?' Annie asked.

'Sometimes Amy gave them cakes,' Mildred said. 'I think she knew how to speak to them. I was just a kid. And, well, later, by the time I'd grown up, they'd gone.'

8. In the dojo, rivulets ran along the curve of spines, pores opened, the air smelled of armpit and sweat. Nothing moved. Behind me the girl as vital as a dream, her gown spread around her. Beside me the one who was pregnant leaned back on her arms. Louise's back was straight, her hair tightened and pinned on her head. In front of me the figure on the wall lay down in obeisance. The roof shifted with the weight of the sun. Even the cicadas were quiet. There were no stories that could accompany us through the heat. No anecdotes. No desires. Only koans and the free fall of meditation stripping us of boundaries, and even memory. Time slipped a cog. And then, as the sun reached an angle that would let it through the window on the other side of the dojo, a sudden streak of sunlight lit my wall through a crack under the furled blind. The monk lifted his head in praise. On the other side of the room a hand snapped down the blind.

9. The gate read: *Private. Keep Out. No Through Road.*

'I don't remember this,' Louise said. The light was growing dim.

'There are gates marked on the map,' I said, turning on the torch.

'But not this sort of gate,' she said.

'I don't see where else we could be,' I said, tracing my finger along the line I was certain we had travelled. 'This has to be right.'

Louise opened the gate. A light came on outside the house. A dog barked. We drove on.

'This looks better,' she said, as the headlights picked up the milky trunks of the gums. A steep corner. A steep descent. A field planted with potatoes. No, with melons. It was hard to tell in the dark. The track became two ruts divided by long grass. We were going down steeply.

'I don't remember this,' Louise said.

There was no sign that other cars had passed. There was nowhere to turn around; on one side the melons, on the other a ditch, dense scrub. Ahead of us a gate, and on the other side, cows.

'I remember cows,' Louise said.

'They're bulls,' I said. She opened the gate. I wound up the windows. We were in a paddock. There was a faint outline of tracks. We drove on. The tracks divided. We stopped, got out, shone our torch along one, then the other. We could hear the bulls breathing in the dark behind us.

'They're small bulls,' Louise said. 'More like bullocks.'

'Even so,' I said.

For the rest the paddock was silent. The bush came in to meet us. Ahead, steep hills. Above us a black sky out of which no bombs fell. 'It was beautiful down there,' the pilot had said. 'Like fireworks exploding in the dark.'

We turned and drove back along the ruts, the car's base sliding over the silvery grass, and up the steep ascent, the steep curve, close to the side, we had to take it fast, just as well it wasn't wet; no damage done, back into the bush that was all that had ever looked familiar, back towards the house.

The farmer and his son were waiting in the middle of the track, shining a powerful torch into our headlights. We stopped. They were angry. We could hear in the farmer's words phrases rehearsed for a lawyer's letter. I sprang to a guilty defence. Louise got out of the car.

'But in the country,' I said, 'gates often say private and you have to go through them.'

'How awful for you,' Louise said, 'People blundering through your property at night, never knowing what damage they've done.'

'Did you close all the gates?' he asked.

'Oh yes,' she said. 'Certainly.'

'Did you disturb the cows?'

'They came towards us,' she said, 'but they didn't seem disturbed.'

'Where did you turn round?' he asked.

'In the paddock,' she said. 'We didn't harm the crops. The melons.'

'Potatoes,' he said.

He smiled. The moment passed.

'We're lost,' I said.

'I can see that,' he said. 'You're Zen Buddhists I suppose. The second lot tonight.'

He gave us directions. We'd missed a sharp turn half a mile before his gate. We looked at the map and saw our mistake. We apologized and set off as he seemed to indicate. The dogs tore around us, barking, jumping at the door. The farmer shouted. We stopped. The dogs jumped at the window. The shouting continued. 'He must be shouting at the dogs,' I said. The dogs retreated. We were half way across the dam before we knew the shouting had been for us.

'You've driven over our irrigation system,' the farmer said. I'd noticed black piping running across the dam's embankment.

'If it's bent,' he said, 'it's ruined. You went over it twice.'

'We thought you were shouting at the dogs,' I said.

'Turn the car round,' he said.

I did as he directed us. 'That,' he said, pointing to the track that branched decisively to the left, 'is the road. Do you see it? Or must I lead you? And there,' he said, flashing his torch into the unseeing night, 'is the gate. Be sure you close it when you leave.'

I put the car in gear. Louise got out again. She offered names and addresses. 'If there's damage,' she said, 'we'd want to repair it.'

He demurred. 'No,' he said.

'Well let us wait while you look,' she said.

He walked the hundred yards to the dam. His son leaned against the car. 'What d'you want to come out here for anyway,' he said. 'Why can't you be Zen Buddhists in town?'

His father came back. We watched him walk into our headlights.

'You've done two hundred thousand worth of damage,' he said.

Even the dogs were silent; the bush, everything. He laughed. There was a pause, like a breath being let out. We laughed.

'No,' he said. 'It seems to be all right.' He shone his light along the track we should have taken.

'Is there anything else we can do wrong you should warn us about?' I asked.

'There's plenty you can do,' he said, 'without me helping. But not between here and the gate.' He tapped the roof of the car.

'I'm going back to my osso buco,' he said.

'It's a fine place you've got here,' I said.

'We love it,' he said.

10. Mumon's commentary on the koan is this: 'If you are enlightened in the truth of this koan, you will then know that coming out of one husk and getting into another is like a traveller's putting up in hotels. In case you are not yet enlightened, do not rush about blindly. When suddenly earth, water, fire and air are decomposed, you will be like a crab fallen into boiling water, struggling with its seven arms and its eight legs. Do not say then I have not warned you.'

11. At dusk I follow a dark figure towards the tank. I watch the hem of her gown as it catches on the flattened tussocks. Parrots scavenging for drips scatter at our approach. She moves to one side of the tap; I move to the other.

We wait, eyes lowered, each for the other, then reach towards the water at the same time. Our eyes meet. Hers are the colour of fresh almonds: the one from the writing group. Mine travel up past the trees, and the cliff, to a trail of vapour in a still-light sky. I fill my basin. She grins. I bow, all the way to the waist.

12. There are no mirrors at the zendo. Only a black rectangle of glass that at night is lit by hurricane lamps. In it the reflections of the women are indistinct. I move my arms and look for the responding gesture. On the other side a woman puts a fresh sprig of leaves on the altar. In the glass I catch a movement, but without a guiding reflection, I cannot get a sense of who it is I see.

As darkness gathers, the angel on my wall is plump and calm, and in the dry creek bed frogs begin to call, an accompaniment to the angry scuffles of bandicoots mating. In silence we eat. The yellow soup is thick but insubstantial, the apples tasteless from too long in store. Afterwards, a woman sings. Another joins her. The girl lifts her arms above her head. Above us only stars move. Sometimes a bat. Hungry I fall asleep and dream under the pop of a contracting roof.

13. Six weeks later, when I sat with Dora before she died, the war in the Gulf had moved from air to ground. Her last book had just appeared; too late for her to see its reception. And just as well, perhaps; the ponderous respect that is accorded the dead and dying would have rankled, as if the rough edges that made them themselves were shed with their passing. When

suddenly earth, water, fire and air decompose, the ancients warned, meaning death, do not be caught like the crab with its seven legs flailing.

When I put my hand on Dora's head in a gesture of tenderness she never allowed in life, I could feel her skull press into my palm. Her hair was as silky as fresh grass. I felt it for hints of a perm, for I had never seen her without her row of curls. I remembered her at a Palm Sunday rally, dressed for a day in town, holding the microphone in her gloved hand, her words clarified, somehow, by her odd fastidiousness. It was she who first showed me that the fleetingness of life requires of us many disguises, though it wasn't the disguise of gloves that she meant; and as I came to know her, at first disconcerted to see in her a woman who wasn't teacher, as if before my eyes she'd shed a skin, I began to understand, for others if not for myself, that we are true in many forms. Buffeted by changes that seemed to come too fast, I'd complain to her that faith eluded me, and that at those moments, rare enough, when it was glimpsed, I was incapable even of naming.

She'd smile at me then, and warning against resisting the river, she'd send me back to my desk, as if to a cushion and a blank wall. *Art approaches as a healing and redeeming enchantress*, she liked to say, quoting Nietzsche. *She alone may transform.* 'Transform what?' I asked.

When Dora visited me in the city, she'd cross the street for the early service. I'd hear the click of the gate as she came back in for breakfast. Scrambled eggs was what she liked. 'Dear girl,' she'd say, looking into the pan, singing as she turned the toast.

What did I want of her? Wisdom? Illumination? Or just forgiveness? There is no reason why she should accept the role I cast her in. Her struggles were no less.

At her request, her coffin was carried bare from the church: no flowers, no disguise.

14. It was during the second night in the valley that I dreamed of her. When the bells rang the next morning, I was hauled from a heavy enchantment, back into a world where perspective ruled, hierarchical and exaggerated, where death waited, and eyes dimmed. In the dojo my knees and hips locked into furious resentment. The monk sat bolt upright. The angel made preparations for flight. Wind passed through the room lifting hair, a thong, a blind. Outside the trees began to moan at its presence.

After breakfast, porridge to serve the zen student, watery and thin, I left the vegetables to be chopped by others.

I lugged my sleeping bag and pack to the car. The boot slammed closed, as sudden as a retort. Women turned their heads. I opened the boot again, found my camera and closed it carefully. At the far end of the paddock I snapped the dojo with its roof that perfectly combines the pitch of Japan with the spread of an Australian verandah. Above the cliff, clouds were gathering, coming in from the south.

In the photo there seems to be movement at the point where the trees thin out and the cliff lifts above them. For a moment it seems as if there are shapes making their way down from the rocks, but it is nothing but a shadow. Or the angel from the wall; it's hard to tell.

15. To Goso, the monk replied: 'Coming and going leaves no traces at all. You travellers, please do not ask which path I once took.'

16. At the river I waited for the ferry upstream from the township where Amy had been taken, for what I don't know,

and where Mildred had gone as a domestic, fourteen years old, to do out the rooms at the pub, and where the Dharginung were hanged for stealing, and left as a warning, the cob of corn he'd taken jammed in the mouth of a boy. There is nothing more sinister there now than an advertisement for corsets flapping on a post.

'Easy does it,' the ferry master shouted as the gates opened to unload the city cars it had brought from the other side. She was wearing heavy boots and an Akubra with her summer dress. 'There's nothing over here to hurry for,' she said, banging her hand on the bonnet of an impatient car. On this side of the river, which I was waiting to leave, was dirt road: corrugations, pot holes, blind corners.

17. At home, I lay upstairs on the bed, as if dreams could be revisited and sleep regain an eagle's vision. Instead I remembered the first night I'd slept in that room and how in the morning the light came through the blinds in bright slats, filling the room while we slept, catching the motes of dust that stirred with our movements. 'Oh yes,' I said when I woke and saw the spire, 'oh yes'. Even then, as I turned by instinct to the one beside me, something quite different moved in me, and though I noticed it, there was no name I could bring to it. Now while I lie still, G opens the door and walks into the faint smell of rosewater and the Sunday feel of bells from the church. Sometimes I go across for communion, but after the solitude of zazen, I don't like the handshaking, the head nodding, the guitar playing. The vicar wears running shoes under his cassock as if that will bridge the gap between the church and the street. Dora would discuss in endless detail plans and possibilities with the vicar's wife. But from the vantage point of my window on the other side of the street, there is no gap. Church and street are one. At night teenagers fuck in the

porch, and in summer lovers have picnics beside the graves; pickpockets exchange their loot under the trees, children show each other their things, and animals and insects are left to their own imaginings. Their mingled sounds and the voices of people praying, and the thud of shoes along the pavement, one barely distinguishable from another, float up through the window of the room where I wake each morning to the spire, lifting out of a sea of leaves and slate, that planes use to guide them safely in.

This is not something I ever managed to describe to Dora, that moment when the arrangement of things becomes horizontal and, just for that moment, everything is held in balance, and the day begins.

This story is written in memory of Dorothy Green, 1915–1991, and with thanks to Gilly and Tony Coote.

Mumon's commentary is taken from Zenkai Shibayama, *Zen Comments on the Mumonkan*, Harper and Row, 1974

The Stone Poles of the World
David Craig

All over the world, in Mongolia and the Arctic, in North Africa and Palestine and Scotland, stories were told about clashing rocks or pairs of rocks like the jambs of a gateway. Often they flanked the door to the Otherworld; they were the Jaws of Death, or a miraculous gate beyond which lay Oceanus, the Isle of the Blessed, the Realm of the Dead. According to the Karens of Burma, 'in the west there are two massive strata of rock which are continually opening and shutting, and between these strata the sun descends at sunset.' The space between the rocks could house the water or the bread of life. Any being, whether animal or human, who passed through in a quest for these most valuable things was unlikely to get out again unscathed. As the gates clashed shut, they crushed or cut off the ship's stern ornament or the hindlegs of the hero's horse, the hare's scut or the stork's tail-feathers.[1]

Al this means that nowadays, in our search for the sites or surviving tangible symbols of these myths, we are looking for pairs of rocks which will probably be remarkable in their own right, great salient monuments to elemental forces, with a gap between them which is frightening to jump, a seaway which is stirring to sail across. Their strength challenges ours and sets bounds to our life.

The prime site of that kind in Europe must be Gibraltar and its straits. Hercules, god of strength, for his tenth labour had to steal the red oxen of Geryon, grandson of Medusa the Gorgon, who lived a hundred miles west of Gibraltar at Gades (now Cadiz). On his journey west he came to a rock barrier and tore it apart, leaving two pillars between which he passed. That is to say, five and a half million years ago the ocean broke through the limestone reef between the places the Phoenicians were to call Calpe (later Gibraltar) and Abyla (later Ceuta, due south of Gibraltar across the Mediterranean). Mediterranean was then a desert basin, deeper and hotter than Death Valley in California today. The shifting of the plates in the earth's crust had cut it off from the primeval ocean which has now been named Tethys (after one of the Titans). Over two million years it had dried out, leaving a few brackish lakes like the Dead Sea. Then the melting of polar ice and glaciers after an Ice Age raised the oceanic levels and salt water poured in from the west in a waterfall five kilometres high. It poured for at least a hundred years. The waters came brimming up crags the colour of old bones, all round the rims of what are now Spain, Sardinia, Italy, Yugoslavia, Ithaca, mainland Greece . . . Our own species had not yet evolved but tribes of erect hunters, australopithecines, lived in what is now Morocco. The roar of the falls, the teeming mists, the rainbows making their arcs will have formed a pillar of cloud by day, marking a place the peoples could no longer pass on any sally northward as they followed the bison and the musk-ox.

That waterfall and the sea-way, whose current still flows at over four knots and roughens the surface between Algeciras and Tangier into a welter of whirlpools and overfalls, must have been unsurpassed as a display, intimidating and inspiring, of the world's primal strength. Presently, as the brains of our forebears grew large and complex enough to store legends and think in symbols, that strength was embodied in Herakles/Hercules, in the Aegean cultures, and further east and south in

Melkarth, Sesostris, Baal, Sandon the lion-god of Tarsus, Attis, Tammuz, and Vishnu. Hercules, like the giant cut into the chalk downland at Cerne Abbas in Dorset, wielded a club and leaned on it when he was tired. A Freudian interpretation would see that club as phallic. The Graeco-Roman (also the Babylonian, Egyptian, Indian, and Scottish) myths emphasize more the whole gamut of powers, in the earth, the waters, and the skies, which set the conditions for our lives.

The Rock of Gibraltar is not much like a pillar and its opposite number, Monte Hacho in Ceuta, is still less so, but the upright symbol was crucial and sucked into itself many different natural shapes. In ancient Babylonia pillars embodied the idea of the 'world spine' or 'world tree' and pillars for worship carried stone heads in the shape of a lion, a ram, a lance. At Calpe/Abyla, or Gibraltar/Hacho, the notion of pillars as twin jambs of a great gateway is especially potent because what lay beyond was the impassable and unknown. When the Spaniards followed in the wakes of Columbus and Magellan and set out across the Atlantic for El Dorado, the land of gold (and silver), they dropped the negative from the old motto *Ne plus ultra* and moulded onto their coins the words *Plus ultra*, asserting that there *was* more beyond. Modern empire-building had begun. The symbol they chose for their pieces-of-eight and doubloons was the twin Herculean pillars with a garland twined round them.[2]

So the almighty dollar-sign was born. No doubt it's far-fetched to see anything in fact that recently the dollar sign has lost half its substance – one of the two uprights – and retained the mere ornament, that sinuous ribbon–$. The pillars and the ribbon with the motto still flank the Spanish coat-of-arms.

The winning of Geryon's cattle by Hercules is especially rich in meaning because it is an occidental myth. For people in the Graeco-Roman and North African worlds, the sun set in the strait between the Pillars. Geryon's red cattle symbolized the light and heat of the sun as it went down in the west. Hercules reached Geryon's hide-out at Gades by commandeering the golden bowl of Helios and sailing westward in it along the river of Oceanus. His defeating of Geryon and his ally Cacus (a fire god and son of Vulcan) was a victory for light and water over darkness and drought.

As we flew in to Gibraltar down the Spanish coast after the sun had set, a black island seemed to float amongst the swarm of yellow and orange lights. The plane dipped. The black island grew – was it an island or a mountain? The plane banked, north and east again, and we were skimming past a scarp of haggard rock which tapered six hundred – eight hundred – a thousand feet into the sky. A few days after we arrived, the air roared and out of it came the yellow-camouflaged Tornadoes of the RAF. They had just completed their Herculean mission to destroy all the bridges, all the power stations and waterworks, and all the conscript soldiers in modern Babylonia, that is to say Iraq. The modern airstrip is tarmac laid over the sand-bar which joins the Rock to Spain. A few hundred yards down the eastern shore from that highest cliff, you can touch the last remnant of the dunes left over from the Mediterranean's Dead Sea phase – a bluff of hard sand striated in layers of yellow and brown. Above it slopes the biggest 'roof' in the world – the thirty-four hectares of corrugated iron sheeting which were laid over the Great Sand Slope to make a water catchment.

The whole island (for that is what it feels like) is a prodigy of rock-work and fire-work. You walk down Bomb House Lane and pass beneath jutting strongpoints called Tank Ramp and ramps named after Kavanagh, Hargreaves, Cratchett – NCOs, or so one imagines, with smoke-stained faces, scorched moustachioes, and several fingers missing. Lord Airey's Battery and King's Bastion stare over the modern harbour and naval base from redoubts faced with colossal limestone blocks blasted and chiselled out of the body of the Rock. The major hole in it now bears an angelic Christian name, St Michael's Cave. For those who lived here between the Phoenicians and the Moors this was the entry to Hades, in keeping with the popular ancient belief in a doorway to the Otherworld formed by clashing mountain-walls. Concerts are held in it now – rows of plastic chairs stand on the rock floor, wetted by drips from the naked roof.

The cave twists and burrows off into the dark, its sides horned and frilled with stalactites, stalagmites, and unnameable formations like growths in a diseased gut. The more pillared of the forms are intelligibly shaped, with rippled collars like craft-shop candles. Most of the calcite secreted by the fissures in the walls has coagulated in long drools and stretched skins like organisms dreamed up by Dali.

Cavers used to explore the labyrinthine Lower Cave below St Michael's. Rockfall has put a stop to that quite recently. We can still penetrate the Rock in the steps of the pioneers. In the summer of 1782 the Company of Soldier Artificers tunnelled towards The Notch, a col between the main face and a spur, hoping to mount a gun there to blast the Spaniards. The Great Siege had beset the Rock for three years. The mine, or gallery, was the idea of Warrant Officer Ince. When the smoke in the tunnel became unbearable, he thought of blasting holes sideways to let in fresh air from the north side. How many of his men were deafened, blinded, or mutilated by then? Nowadays you walk down a slowly descending tunnel – light breaks in from the left – you step into a bay perhaps twelve feet high, with a vaulted roof hewn out of rock, and twenty feet wide. Its mouth is barred with iron rods. Mediterranean light dazzles. At your feet there is a sheer drop of six hundred feet to the airstrip. Swifts skim past, and the occasional Boeing 737. The drill-holes grooving the walls are often barely a foot apart and you realize with dismay the effort it cost the Artificers, dinting with sledgehammer and iron bit, to plant all those charges, working on minimal water rations, shielding their eyes and ears from explosion after explosion. Here was a whole sub-culture of kindling and shattering, of man-made earthquake. The two look-out boys with the sharpest sight were nicknamed Shot and Shell. When Ince realized that the vents would make good fire-posts, Lieutenant Koehler designed a carriage from which 24-pounder guns could be angled more steeply downward than had ever been achieved before. The Spaniards threw a quarter of a million rounds at the Rock during the Siege. Now they could be answered with red-hot shot poured from the heights. Just fifty years ago the Upper Galleries were blasted still deeper to make air raid shelters in case Franco joined the Axis and tried to recapture the Rock for Spain. Down in the town it shook me to see 'ARP Shelter' on the lintels of various old bunkers – my first meeting with 'Air Raid Precautions' since I was a boy in Aberdeen during the Second World War.

Because Gibraltar stands up hugely out of land and sea, it exemplifies supreme elemental force, intense hardness, intense heat, and because it therefore made a strongpoint, it *attracted* fire and the terrible Vulcan-like hammering of the Spanish smiths and gunners. Now that the British infantry have gone from Gibraltar and it is losing importance as a fuelling base for warships and fighter planes, its hellish aspect can be effaced a little and its paradisal population of birds and apes and flowers is softening the ugly war-mask. To explore the wild garden of the east side, I took a path signposted 'Mediterranean Steps'. It twisted off into the *maquis* past an Army mesh fence and a blockhouse. Flowering bushes rooted in limestone scree closed behind me in aromatic coverts. Giant candytuft held up their broad pink rosettes, butcher's broom sparked yellow, the leaves of succulents with purple flowers shone darkly green as though varnished, tall yellow umbellifers were putting out fat new shoots, and dwarf palmyra cut spiked green discs out of the blue expanse between Europa Point and the Moroccan coast. The path, a thread of rubble and dust, led under the white faces of the Levant Cliff, past the twin mouths of Goat-hair Cave. Now and again I couldn't avoid re-entering the social world, by cement steps, under the walls of a bricked-up blockhouse festooned with old barbed wire, coming out on emplacements still armed with obsolete guns. When I climbed the 200-foot cliffs of Buffadero Bluff with an Army instructor who was about to leave the Rock for good, we had to regain the foot of the cliff after each route by climbing down the *inside* of an iron ladder festooned with wire, struggling to save our thighs and elbows from the rusty barbs. The cliffs themselves were a hanging garden, every ledge brimming with mauve and orange blossom, with yellow daisies whose coronas of petals printed circles of pollen like little suns on the legs of my climbing trousers. As we pulled over onto the level at the top of Sawtooth Slab, our fingers grazed gulls' eggs of pale turquoise-blue with brown blots, lying on dusty ledges among wisps of fluff. Below us freighters and small tankers plied to and fro, and the small fast 'Winston boats' that smuggle cigarettes into Spain. The fuming blue reef across the water was the shoreline between Ceuta and Tangier, piling up into the mountains of the Rif. It was there we would have to go to find the other Pillar.

This turned out to be ambiguous, tantalizing. As the hydrofoil from Algeciras buckets across the snaking and whirling currents of the Straits, limestone ribs and massifs begin to rear and show their vertical grain. The mountain range on the eastern-Moroccan border near Ceuta rises more than seven hundred metres above sea-level – should the southern 'pillar of Hercules' not be there? In the centre of Ceuta the pier of rock called Monte Hacho forms the foundation of the 4000-year-old castle but it is a much lesser thing than Edinburgh Castle rock and hardly a fit jamb for the gates of the Sea of the Middle of the World. We want a counterpart for Calpe/Gibraltar. But where to look? Outside the shipping office on the quay, a small dignified leathery man, bald and aquiline, dressed in a meerschaum linen *jelaba* with a hood, a silver medallion on a chain, and white slippers with no heels, appoints himself our guide and instantly decides what we want to see.

'You want to go to Tetuan – is market – only 25 kilometres. All very typical things – these Berber people, Bedouin, they bring all-kind things. Dancing you will see, playing for the snake. This man, he drive you. Is all correct. I am Morocco Tourist Board. 6000 pesetas – whole thing.'

But I am utterly intent upon Hercules. I name him, adding several other words with no pretence at sentences or phrases even. 'Hercules,' I say many times. 'The Pillar. Abyla? The Pillar of Hercules?'

Our man twirls his hand helplessly. 'For that you must go Tangier. 100 kilometres.'

I repeat my simple demand: 'The Pillar of Hercules.' If I

knew more Spanish, or *any* Arabic, I might have been less singleminded. I hold my ground, saying 'The Pillar' from time to time and pointing eastward at the pale masses of mountain rearing and scooping among steamy cloud. A compromise emerges: the driver will take us all to the mountains, *then* to the market.

We drive through dusty suburbs, between stands of umbrella pine and eucalyptus, past barracks of the Army and the Spanish Legion. 'All they do,' says the driver over his shoulder, 'is eat and sleep.' The mountains have disappeared behind their foothills. They reappear near and high, the skyline hanging between shapely peaks, half a mile from the coast. Opposite a gap in the eucalyptus forest the driver pulls off the road, stops, and points. 'The woman – is like a woman. You see?'

On a col between summits, features jut. A brow, tilted back almost to the horizontal. An orbital ridge, the bridge of a nose, the lower jaw. They compose the face of a head lying back, turned upward. White hair of fine-weather cloud skeins over the features, slowly unravelling. Set in between brow and nose a dark socket hollows; yellowish scree weeps from it down the mountainside. The grain of the limestone, drawn from the profile, gives each area of the face, forehead, cheek, and jowl, the look of very old skin sagging, of muscle whose tone has gone forever, a face in a hospital bed, sleeping its last sleep.

'Is called Dead Woman,' says the driver. 'Monte Muliere Muerta. Hercules marry this woman. In the mythologia. The wife of Hercules. Mythologia.' Can I climb the mountain? No – it is in another country. Can we at least drive along the coast road below the rocky slopes? It is prohibited – military zone. Up there on the skyline, dapples of sun on the cheeks and forehead suggest bygone smiles. The shreds of cloud sink and thicken: the face is grave, expressionless. The cloud lifts, evaporates: in full sun she is calmly asleep.

That mountain, which I hope to return and climb this year, looked a much more worthy counterpart to Gibraltar than Monte Hacho. It lacked the singleness of a pillar but the massif as a whole was a fit gatepost for the Straits. It is pointless, however, to pose the question: Which *was* the Pillar of Hercules? The matter is not on the plane of verifiable truth, any more than we can 'decide' which was the place on the shore of Ithaca where Odysseus landed to surprise the suitors or in which cave Eumaeus hid his herd of pigs. Historically speaking, the Phoenician sailors must have pointed to one or another rock formation as they sailed past and credited it with the legend. That is beyond our knowing. The naming of mythic or sacred places happened on the tongues of the people (at least until the stories sung by the bards were written down) and was bound to change, die away, and reappear, as do the lyrics of folksongs. Later that same day we could not be quite sure whether or not the Dead Woman was the *wife* of Hercules – had the driver not once called her the 'mother'? As wife she 'might have been' either Megara, whom in his madness he killed along with their children, or Deianira, who unknowingly gave him the shirt steeped in the Centaur's poisonous blood to win him back from Iole. But if the mountain was 'really' his mother, then this would agree very well with Ovid's story of his birth and the infant crag a few miles east in Ceuta could have been seen as issuing from between the great stone hips of the Moroccan mountain.

A few days later we crossed the Mediterranean again to explore *les Grottes d'Hercules*, which we had found on a French Michelin map. They are just south of Cap Spartel where the Straits expand to become the Atlantic. The shore of coarse sandstone is fretted grotesquely by surging salt waters. A guide in a hooded brown *jelaba* led us into a maze of caves. He repeatedly lit a petrol-soaked cloth in a bottle to show us the walls. On every side they were hollowed as though stacks of coins, each one two feet in diameter and eight inches thick, had been pressed into malleable rock and left their shape in it. Each 'coin' was a millstone chiselled out when the place was a mine, 2,500 years before the Romans according to our guide. The querns were used to grind maize and olives. In places a stone had been cut on the vertical; in others the initial circle had been made with a compass, then cut in deeply but the stone left *in situ*, perhaps when demand fell away.

Even the natural walls at the cave mouth were scooped and groined, as though the god, or his Eastern Counterpart Melkarth, had leant against them when they were still plastic and left the impress of his muscles – as though they were the mould that had produced him. The rock had a very coarse open texture, which would have let air permeate and keep the grist cool. Outside, from the 75-foot level down to the water's edge, hundreds of circular scoops marked the sites of cut-out stones, some of them worn by the sea into natural-looking potholes. Bosses showed where a stone had been cut round, then left, and the salt water had worn away the surrounding rock. Men with long bamboo poles were fishing, or dozing in hollows above the reach of the waves. It would have been pleasing if Hercules' labours had included some mention of mining or grinding. It is pleasing in another way to find that *any* well-shaped site along that shore, any evidence of the superhuman and human forces that threw up and shifted, reft and sculpted the world's hardest stuff, could be symbolized in a vivid story.

The passage between stone sides, the circuit between stone poles, not only fitted terrain all over the world, it also worked as a metaphor for a crucial test or a deed that mattered and was achieved with difficulty. In the Scottish Highlands a couple could make a 'handfast' marriage by clasping hands through a hole in a monolith. On the shore west of Sligo in the Republic of Ireland, near the village of Iaskaigh or Easkey, there is a split rock called the Finger-stone of Finn MacCool – a granite erratic ten feet high, thirty feet long, and twenty feet across. A glacier must have dropped it here after rafting it from the mountains of Connemara fifty miles to the south. The rock has parted just enough to let a person squeeze through. You must pass through it three times: if it does not snap shut on you, then you are a just person – an amiable myth, since it enables absolutely everybody to pass the test (unless, of course, unjust persons back away from damnation and show themselves up).

In the Highlands, of Scotland, at the head of Glen Einich on the slopes of the Cairngorms above Strathspey, a pair of rock landmarks called A'Cailleach and Am Bodach, the Old Woman and the Old Man, face each other across the head of the loch. The head of the glen is Coire Odhar, the dun cirque. Grassland a quarter-mile square spreads out in a shallow basin. This was a shieling, where the people lived with their herds and flocks in summer. At the back of it looms a mountainside split by a chain of white waterfalls. The Cailleach and the Bodach stick out of the slopes on either side. When they came into sight for the shieling people moving up from Coylumbridge and Inverdruie, they would have known that their ten-mile trek with children, animals and dairying tools was nearly done for another year.

Such natural 'totems' are all over the Highlands but a pair in relation to each other is uncommon. A *bodach* was an old man; the word also contains *bod*, penis. One blunt, dark spur across the mountains on the Aberdeenshire side is Bod an Deamhain – cautiously translated by the Victorians as Devil's Point. A *cailleach* means 'old woman'. The *Cailleach Bheur* was the earth-mother, who trampled to and fro across the northern lands with a creel full of rocks and earth on her back. When the creel tipped, mountains were made. In the Cromarty Firth she was the south-westerly gale which came 'yelling round the Heel of Ness with a white feather in her hat'.[3] She was the flood that drowned travellers in fords. When she forgot to close her well on Ben Cruachan with her stone slab one night, the water brimmed over and formed Loch Awe. When she washed her plaid in the strait north of Jura, she stirred up the contrary tide-races, the most turbulent round Britain, with their fierce flow and spinning overfalls. Her day is March 25, virtually the equinox, when winter's last cold gales arrive. At that time her son, who has fallen in love with a beautiful young woman kept prisoner by his mother, runs away with her on a white horse and the Cailleach drums up a storm to forestall them then thrashes the grass with her rod or hammer to stop it growing.

The land was full of rocks that broke the plough. The wind filled the fishermen's sails and could sink their boats. The water could flood and drown as well as quench. So the people faced the difficulties of the land by embodying the whole mixed nature of it in the one giantess or god, her face blue-black, her hair 'white as an aspen covered in hoar frost'. A Gaelic quatrain from Argyll, 'Bha aon suìl ghlumach 'na ceann', creates this definitive image:

> In her head was one deep pool-like eye
> Swifter than a star in a winter sky;
> Upon her head gnarled brushwood
> Like the clawed old wood of an aspen root.

We first approached Einich from Glen Feshie, the next glen to the west, skirting the northern slope of Carn Bàn Mòr, the big white hill, and making for Sgor Gaoith, the rocky peak of the wind. We worked steeply down a narrow headland jutting towards Loch Einich. It narrowed and fell away on either side – one slip would send us bouncing down gullies ending in chockstones, then nothing, then the rasped-metal surface of the loch fifteen hundred feet below. Now a chasm faced us, eighty feet deep, cleft north/south through the rib. On its far side there she was, A'Cailleach herself, her stone profile louring against the shieling pasture, hoary grey against briefly sunlit green. Her cranium is low, her aquiline nose a yard long from bridge to nostril, her grey eye the size of a melon under a brow cut in a perfect shallow arc. (Another of the Cailleach's names was Mala Liath, grey eyebrow.) Under her nose the upper lip purses deeply in to a mouth that has been empty of teeth since she was young. Her chin recedes into her squat neck and shapeless trunk. She's a colossal squaw who grimly supervises the pastoral work of the little people below, tacitly challenging them to smirk at her deformity.

As for the Bodach, he's hard to identify, in spite of the seemingly exact instructions in chapter 16 of Seton Gordon's *The Cairngorm Hills of Scotland*, which had put us onto the pair in the first place. Several broken pinnacles totter along the ridge to the east. We skirted the headwall and struggled through a torment of hummock and bog and lochan and amphitheatres floored with boulders like charnel-pits full of old men's heads. We contoured northward along collapsing slopes strewn with clumps washed down by incessant rains, peering upward at each crag, willing it to shape itself in a rough human likeness. Could it be that one where two lateral rocks make a mouth, or an eye? That stack which merges back into the broken cliff and never quite makes a body or a head? In the next few days, approaching southward down the whole length of the glen to follow in the track of the shieling people, we never quite saw a male totem among the rocks but the Cailleach was not in doubt, a superbly salient earth-mother who needed some kind of counterpart for the completeness of the myth. She even had her handmaiden or daughter, a slender blade standing her ground amongst the barely stable scree halfway down to the lochside.

The Cailleach's relationship with the Bodach was teasing. Both 'resented a mortal entering their domain after certain hours. They were also rivals: if one was angry at an intruder, 'the other would at once encourage the offender with friendly cries.' When no humans were about, they threw boulders at each other.[4] This is fairly whimsical, so much so that it almost smacks of a fancy made up on the spur of the moment to divert a scholarly visitor in a kilt, like Seton Gordon . . . But not all myths are fundamental, they are also a seedbed of story available to people at play, pleasing themselves, letting their imaginations loose. Certainly those stories of the Cailleach and the Bodach quarrelling would have been told at the evening ceilidhs down in the shieling houses, three of which still show in the grass as oblong earthworks twenty feet long and twelve feet broad. The people traditionally came up here at Beltane, May-day, the great summer festival of the Celts. 'Women knit, sing, talk, and walk as free and erect as if there were no burdens on their backs, nor in their hearts . . . All who meet them on the way bless the trial, as it is called, and wish it a good flitting day.'[5] The men would see their families on their way and then turn back to resume their work at the fishing or at harvesting in the Lowlands. In Glen Einich the animals were sent up a few days before and a herdsman went with them as far as Craobh Tillidh, the tree of the return, then left them to walk the six miles by themselves to Coire Odhar. The tree, or its scion, can still be seen between the track and the river of Am Beanaidh, a pine with dense bunches of needles and a hefty trunk and limbs which glow bronze at sunset: the last tree on the trail, an outpost from nearby Rothiemurchus, the Plain of the Great Trees.

In the mellow days of May, June, and July, hunger and the weather ground the people less harshly. During the time of the Big Sun, from Beltane to Halloween, the Cailleach was transformed into a grey boulder and stayed that way, always moist, until the time of the Little Sun came round again. While she was in abeyance, the young folk in the shieling could play and flirt and twine stories round the baleful godheads waiting up there in the crags. A Gaelic quatrain, 'Ann am bothan an t-sùgraidh', evokes this time which was the nearest the Highlanders got to an idyll:

> In the bothy of courting,
> With birchwood stopping the door,
> The cuckoo and the ring-dove
> Sang for us on the trees . . .[6]

These myths were not moral – concerned with right and wrong. Like the religion of the Phoenicians, they were inspired by the powers and processes of nature, which by and large must be accepted or worked along with. This applies along the gamut from the Near and Middle East to the Scottish Highlands. In Tyre, Melkarth was Baal, chief of the 'primitive groups of nameless deities' – the oldest gods, most deeply rooted in nature. Baal was a storm god, nourisher and destroyer, lord of wind, earthquake and fire, personification of sun-heat. The Egyptian Baal was Shu; his consort Tefnut, like the Cailleach, was a rain-spitter, plague-spreader, and blower-up of gales.[7] There were no temples to the Cailleach; she is found *in* the earth itself, she emerges from it in certain places. These were 'sacred' in that people saw there an epitome of the powers that were beyond them – that preceded and outlasted them. To form them into a myth, to embody it in a human likeness as in the Moroccan or the Scottish mountains, or to suppose that a being with a human likeness shaped those pieces of the world, was to gain a hold on reality through your imagination to see it as that much less random or amorphous, that much more definable and predictable.

These powers continue to play upon our world, quaking, eroding, fertilizing, although the cultures that imagined them as godheads have passed away. The sites themselves are not everlasting. The Cailleach is slowly, slowly splitting off from the Peak of the Wind, when she goes she may take her scion with her to drown in the loch, and the Bodach may have gone already. In the Mediterranean basin the tectonic plate that carries Africa is inching northward again and may presently close the gates which Hercules opened five and a half million years ago.

Notes

(1) Ananda K. Coomaraswamy, *Selected Papers* I (Princeton, 1977), pp 522–43; Arthur Bernard Cook, *Zeus*, III (Cambridge, 1940), pp 976–86.

(2) *A Literary and Historical Atlas of America* (Everyman, 1930 ed.), pp 108–9 and Plates I, VI; *The Times Atlas of Archaeology* (1988), p 274, fig. A.

(3) Donald A. MacKenzie, *Scottish Folk-Lore and Folk Life* (1935), pp 136–67; Raghnall Mac Ille Duibh, 'The earth mother and the cailleach', in *West Highland Free Press*, July 12 1991.

(4) Gordon, *Cairngorm Hills*, pp 132–3; Peter Drummond, *Scottish Hill and Mountain Names*, Scottish Mountaineering Trust, 1991, p 182.

(5) W.H. Murray, *The Isles of Western Scotland* (1973), p 232; I.F. Grant, *Highland Folkways* (1961), pp 73–4, 128–9; Raghnall Mac Ille Duibh, 'What were shielings made of?', in *West Highland Free Press*, July 24 1990.

(6) MacKenzie, *Scottish Folk-Lore*, pp 137–8; Mac Ille Duibh, 'What were shielings made of?'.

(7) Donald A. MacKenzie, *Egyptian Myth and Legend* (n.d.), pp 307–9; *Scottish Folk-Lore*, p 146.

The Story of the Jar
Lucy Goodison

11.30 am

The archaeologist ducked into a room off the courtyard clutching a bundle wrapped in Greek newspaper. The sun glared down on the garishly restored ruins of the palace of Knossos. It bristled with tourists travelling from the 'House of the Sacrificed Oxen' to 'The Queen's Megaron', and on to 'The King's Megaron or Hall of the Double Axes'. The small antechamber to the 'Throne Room' was already full. On the imitation wooden throne a blond man posed for a photograph, sweat standing out in droplets on his pink shoulders. Beside him a woman in flowered shorts fanned herself with a

guidebook. The archaeologist squeezed past the rest of the group and sank onto a stone bench with a wince of pain. She set down her package carefully and took out a compass and a notepad. With the compass she began to measure the angle of the sunlight striking the steps. She started to make notes.

The tour guide's English was irregular: 'This is the Throne Room where King Minos received the visitors. The ancient ambassadors wash their feet in this bowl and stand here to listen his wise judgements. Or if any of his people have a problem they come here for the King to help them.'

The sun rose slowly on the last few degrees to noon. The visitors jostled each other for a better view, fumbled with their cameras, checked their bum-bags, mopped the flesh that bulged around their sunwear. They peered listlessly at Sir Arthur Evans' reconstructions, at the bowl found several metres away but now securely concreted to the floor of the room, the walls rebuilt and the frescoes repainted like a set for a historical drama. A curtain of light hung airlessly outside the small room while inside the visitors, impatient with the tour guide's bored patter, hovered uneasily as if seeking something – some romance? some hope? – lacking in their own lives. When he finished, they poured out after him onto the bleached courtyard.

12.25 pm

At the archaeologists' hostel lunch started at noon sharp as usual. The house, once owned by Sir Arthur Evans, stood across the road from the Knossos palace. It was a low, white building, shrouded by trees. Its paintwork was slightly peeling and on one side a faded decoration of replica Minoan murals in crimson, blue and gold, celebrating the bull's head and the double axe, hinted at a grander past. In front of the murals a verandah with wooden rails looked out into a yard where, under a faded awning strung between pine trees, the archaeologists sat at a long wooden table. A frisbee and children's sandals littered the dusty earth around them. The professor's brood of five had already swept from the table brandishing their chess game, disputing in high-pitched voices whose turn it was to play in their 'Brain of Britain' tournament. Their mother trailed after them, clutching a beach towel and a half-eaten peach. She was a short heavily-built woman, once red-headed, but now looking altogether faded as if the colour had been drained from her and left an empty vessel.

The sun beat down on the pine trees and beneath the awning the gathering at the table was silent – there was only the cicadas' relentless barrage. The professor resumed his inter-rupted discourse. 'There is no continuous tradition of female vessel figurines in this area. One wonders whether the village potter had actually visited the museum and pinched the idea from ancient Minoan models.'

A clay figure on the centre of the table rose regally out of her newspaper wrapping. Her glaze was shiny, the paint of her blue and pink edging patterns sharp, her face bright with a mischievous smile. Her thin springy arms were also handles: one curled down onto her hip, the other balanced a pot effortlessly on her shoulder. The professor adjusted his trousers over his capacious belly and gazed at her like a child eyeing a new toy. 'She's a fine specimen. Do they have a traditional kiln there?'

'No, an electric one,' the archaeologist replied. 'The door was open, you could still feel the heat coming off it. They said it was hard working at midday in this weather.' With the eyes of the company suddenly upon her, she struggled to look dignified while tackling the final, sticky stages of eating a peach.

'Whom did you speak to?' the professor asked.

'A large woman with clay on her apron. She said her husband was out.'

'Interesting, interesting. Pity no traditional kiln. Not many around these days. Female potter, you think perhaps?' His nose twitched. He took off his glasses and dangled them from his fingers. His smile was approving, his attitude of authority benign. He smoothed down the few remaining grey strands that lay across his head. The scalp gleamed as if his brain shone through.

The archaeologist was hesitant. 'I'm not sure if she was the potter. Some people would be delighted if she were – those who suggest that women were the first potters.'

'Piffle . . . Eyewash . . .' snorted the professor.

'There's very little evidence either way. But you do get women closely linked with the jar in the Pandora story. The gods made Pandora – the first woman – as if they were making a pot. They shaped her from earth and water.'

'Ah,' the professor replaced his spectacles forcefully as if to banish any shadow of doubt or disagreement, 'But then she is the one who takes the lid off the jar and thus unleashes every evil and misfortune onto the world. Except for Hope which remains inside.' He chose his words precisely and pointedly. 'Pandora's Jar stands for the release of what would much better be kept in its place, a veritable can of worms. Hardly a positive prototype for a female connection with pottery.'

The archaeologist took a deep breath and spoke formally: 'But the earliest version we have of the myth is from Hesiod,' she said, 'Eighth century BC. The older material from the second millenium BC tells a different story. I'm thinking of the pictures engraved on the Bronze Age rings and sealstones, and the "vessel-goddesses" made like a pot and often carrying one. To me that material suggests that hundreds of years before Hesoid there was a more positive, reverential attitude to both the female and the vessel.' She swiftly disposed of the peach.

'Hmm. Hardly consistent with the Pandora myth.' The professor's eyes surveyed his audience for signs of assent. His smile was less expansive.

She continued speaking, slowly and clearly. 'Perhaps women were always associated with vessels. And the attitude to the jar or vessel changed over time, as attitudes to women changed and deteriorated. The little writing we have from the Bronze Age doesn't include any stories. But perhaps there was an earlier, oral version of the myth where the female vessel appeared in a different light.'

'Sounds as if you're treading dangerously thin ice here.' The professor's boyish expression became petulant. 'Let's not get carried away. If you were planning to publish something along these lines you'd have to make your case very carefully with clear, hard evidence.'

'That's exactly what I'm talking about – the material evidence from the Bronze Age.' She bit her lip as if afraid she had said too much.

The professor narrowed his eyes and mouth. 'It's very easy to push the evidence in one direction if one has an emotional involvement, an axe to grind so to speak.'

In the uncomfortable silence the cicadas blared and heat settled on the gathering like a heavy blanket. Finally the archaeologist ventured: 'But the makers of received opinion are no more "objective" than anyone else. Don't you think everyone has an axe to grind?'

'As long as it's not a double axe, dear.' The professor raised his eyebrows and peered coyly over his spectacles, signalling the end of the conversation. On cue the gathering responded with a round of obedient, mirthless laughter. The fresh-glazed clay figure with her pink and blue patterned dress continued to smile as if at her own private joke.

4 pm

'Not lean on the glass case please,' barked the museum guard. In the air-conditioned room, the neon lights flickered. A thin shaft of sunlight came through an upper dormer window, a reminder of the still-burning afternoon heat outside on the busy streets of Heraklion. The archaeologist leant as close as she could without touching the glass. The case contained an Early Minoan vessel shaped like a woman, but not any woman one has ever met. She read the label: 'Funerary offerings from *tholos* tombs of the Mesara plain: Ritual vessels and anthropomorphic vase from Koumasa, approx. 2,000 BC.'

The vase had two brown dots for eyes and a slightly sloping protuberance for a nose. Two severe eyebrows almost met in the middle, in what could be a frown. Or was she just looking hard? Perhaps she was commanding the passer-by to look at her? A double painted band circled her neck. Her head leant back and there was a slight stiffness to her neck; if she had a chin it would be up, but she had no chin. Two small lumps of clay had been stuck on to indicate breasts. They looked purely informative, passionless. Extravagantly painted stripes and crosses in red and black decorated her front, where the pottery was cracked. She didn't so much carry the miniature vessel as let it grow out of her. She needed no hands to hold it, or at least no hands that the archaeologist could make out. The mouth of the tiny vessel was open, irregular, and a snake spread around her shoulders with spots along its length shading from red to black. She had no arms, no waist, no legs and no genitals. But she was clearly a woman. She bore the snake without any emotion, letting it rest around her shoulders, hanging over the front and curling gently inwards to where her waist would be. At the back her head was flattened and a handle – set slightly on the skew – suggested a hand that must have once lifted and poured her. Over her body a hint of paint here and there was a reminder of how much had been lost of her original appearance, let alone of her significance to the people who made and used her. In the museum, dwarfed by the larger pots around her, she looked concentrated and self-sufficient. She showed no dismay at her new surroundings, no shock at her 4,000 year journey, as if she had simply slipped through a fold in time. The grainy, unsmooth clay had a soft creamy texture like flesh.

Behind the vessel a face framed by a mass of long dark hair suddenly appeared. 'I've done my three sketches. That's enough of museums. How's your leg?'

'You gave me a shock.' The archaeologist laughed as she put away her notepad, 'I thought for a moment you were part of the display.'

'One of those skulls the Minoans kept in their kitchens?'

'Not with all that hair.'

'They had long hair when they were alive. I've seen the pictures.'

'I do need to sit down.'

As the archaeologist's companion knelt with a dramatic courtly gesture to offer her a knee there was a loud shout from the doorway, 'Please do not lean your baggages against the case!'

He lept up again and rapidly assembled his sketch-pads. 'The guard's snarling. Get me away from the dead and their keeper.'

She led him through to the next room, picking a way round displays of tiny seals, miniature stone jars and terracotta animals, vessels shaped like ungainly birds, jokes in pottery. She stopped at a cabinet containing a pair of clay feet. 'Hardly any weapons, you notice. Except this knife – it's meant to have been used for human sacrifice at Anemospilia.'

'Do I have to get the guided tour?'

'Before we go I want to show you the stuff they found at the Fourni cemetery at Arkhanes. We'll be there later this afternoon, we'll see the sun set behind Mount Juktas. I'm sure you'll get an idea for a painting, especially if you've seen the finds.'

'More bones.'

'Some bones. A chopped-up horse skeleton. But also an intricate gold ring, and jewellery. Late Minoan, a bit later than this stuff. And some of those little marble figurines like the ones from the Cyclades.'

He pulled a face. 'Cyladic figurines are dick-heads. I need a cup of tea.'

6.30 pm

The gnarled branches of the olive tree twisted away from the trunk like the tentacles of an octopus, or like arms holding offerings. Its tiny green fruits were hard and unripe, and its silver-backed leaves shivered and shimmered, catching the evening sun which rolled solemnly down the slope of Mount Juktas towards the sea.

She sat on a small stool beneath the tree, leaning back against the trunk, her flounced skirt tucked between her legs. Her braid of hair rested on her shoulders, and her creamy brown skin was wrinkled in places from the sun. Her breasts rose and fell with her breath, and the light from the sinking sun danced on the small blue stones in her necklace.

At her feet the girl crackled the dry leaves as she made herself comfortable. 'I'm waiting,' she said, 'Tell me the story.' She put her hand into the larger hand, sinewy and tanned, with its oval gold ring. The ring was barely the size of a ripe olive, and yet the scene it showed was complex, a miniature world crisp with detail and so exuberant that its figures seemed to move with a life of their own. On one side of the scene a tiny tree – like the one above them – grew out of some sort of structure. A dancing man with a narrow waist reached up to touch the branches in a gesture of honour. A broad-shouldered woman wearing a flounced dress stood in the centre. One of her arms bent up from the elbow, the other rested at her side, and a gentle curve which snaked through her body suggested that she was dancing. Beside her on the ground was a large jar over which a man in a loincloth had flung his naked body. His pelvis curved sinuously towards the jar, his hair flowed in a long braid down his back. His arms were thrown forward as he embraced the vessel. The girl ran her forefinger over the ring's minutely clear design.

'Will I ever have a ring like this?'

'Perhaps.'

'This very one?'

'It may be buried with me when I die.'

'I'm waiting.' She buried her head in the woman's lap. 'Tell me the story about the jar.'

'Again?'

'Again. The sun has nearly set. It's a good time.'

'At the beginning of everything there was a jar.'

'Was it light or dark?'

'Neither. Both. No one used those words. You always disturb my rhythm if you ask questions.

THE STORY OF THE JAR

'The jar was large and round, baked red like the last moments of sky on a summer day. Its outside was smooth and creamy, warm to the touch like skin. Inside the jar was the sun, like a womb bursting with life. The jar was too large to carry and too small to see. Tinier than the white on your finger nail, but if you travelled to the middle of the jar you would be journeying forever.

'The sun, the *ka*, floated in the waters of the jar. As it shone it made a golden path across the waters like the train of the long dress of a woman returning home at evening from the fields or from a dance. The golden *ka* danced on the wave edges as on a gemstone skilfully cut with a careful hand. And then suddenly the water rippled and broke the sunshine into a thousand fragments like a vessel dropped from high onto a stone floor.

And each sliver became a new life – a pair of horns, a branch,
An olive, an orange and a stone. A wind, a shadow,
And all the sounds and savours – a bleat, a bark,
A tiny flower of thyme, all in the jar.
All sprang into being from care and chance
Effortless, fully formed . . .'

As the story became a song, the young girl's eyelids slowly drooped and closed, nestling on the older woman's lap.

'But it was hot and wet, no room to breathe,
They kicked and quarrelled, screeched and squashed and squealed
Until the *ka* soared out of the jar
Like a seed from a pod that bursts,
Or like a ball thrown by a girl
And caught by her friend who jumps and curls and bends
Her body like a soft green twig,
And then the water followed. Chattering, singing,

Spreading itself like a silver girdle round the waist.
And then out tumbled everything,
Big and small, arguing and dancing,
And stretched out in the sun . . .'

As her chant continued, the young girl stirred: 'I fell asleep.'

The woman edged the heavy head from her lap, 'Please move a bit, dear one. You are squashing my *ka*. It hurts.'

'How much did I miss?'

'They came out. No longer all mixed up like a cooking pot. They sorted themselves from this and that into the way that things are now.'

'Except on best days . . .'

'When we go back to what we had before
Inside the jar. We take the wings, the horns
We find again those happy mixtures
When things now separate once joined hands,
When everything was many and was one.
Inside the jars they wait, those secret shapes
Like the seed that waits from year to year to feed us.
That's why we bend and dance
Around jars on the best days. We carry wings and move.
That's why we go into the circles of the dead
Their seed homes where they lay still
Their sun circles, to retrace the path that goes around
And comes back like the day . . .
But you're distracting me, that is a different story . . .'

'Now the *ka* jumps . . .' prompted the girl.

'So high . . .'

'So hot, everything ran for cover,
Held its breath, hated and hid.
The flowers wilted . . .' the girl took up the refrain. 'I don't like this bit. She goes too high. I like it when she falls, like now.' She looked west as the last fingers of the setting sun

reached through the trees, drawing a luminous half-light over
the circular buildings around them on the slope.

'And that is why we dance each twilight,' resumed the woman,
'Refreshed like drinking water after sweat.
But the *ka* kept falling, she sank into the sea
And dancers shivered and grew sad.'
'Don't forget the bird they sent to search. And the boat the
moon lent her to sail in . . .'
'Of course. And so she travelled shining through the darkness
Till morning came. Just as when someone dies
We put them in a jar or tomb,
We cry but they come back to us
The jar breathes hope. Loss and return,
Mourn and rejoice, evening and dawn.
And that is why we dance in circles like the *ka* and
Celebrate the changes. Those shifting moments
Between the still glare of noon and the dark silence,
Those moments of motion we celebrate.'
'You sang some of it differently this time.'

The last slice of gold had sunk behind the mountain and a
breeze stirred the leaves on the olive tree.

'To keep you awake. That cool wind is unfolding mists on to
us, hungry ghosts asking questions. They don't belong here.
But what's a little wind. I'll finish quickly.'
'And that is why . . .
'And that is why we dance
Evening and morning to welcome sun and dead and plants and
        trees
And that is why we go back to the jar.
We touch it when we need our strength. We hide there
When we need to rest encircled and embraced. We go there
When the way is lost and needs refinding. We go to know
Yesterday, tomorrow and today. We go back in to find

The half-remembered pictures from our sleep,
The bonds between things that we have forgotten.
And out of it each time things are created new,
The same and changed.'
She took a breath and with a closing cadence added:
'We tell this story because it helps us live. And
Different people tell a different story.'
'Why are you stopping there?'
   'My legs are stiff. A draught is creeping round my neck.
We're out of time. The story is over.'

8 pm

'I still don't understand why we got the smallest room. There's
two of us and all my canvases.'
   'Hierarchy. Know your place.'
   They dropped their bags, kicked off their shoes and fell onto
the two iron beds which they had earlier wedged side by side
against the whitewashed wall. On the shelf by the bed the
fresh-glazed clay figure with her pink and blue patterns smiled
knowingly.
   'I'm glad to be back from that creepy cemetery.'
   'I thought you were busy with your sketches.'
   'Until it started getting dark and that mist came in.'
   'Paranoia?'
   'You can talk. All you did was go on about your bad leg and
osteopaths' bills and how you are still limping months later.
Once you'd finished with your compass you couldn't get out
fast enough.' He started to leaf through his sketches and she
snuggled against him.
   'That circular *tholos* tomb in the sunset had a little side room
where they found an important woman buried. A priestess

they think. Rich finds, including that gold ring in the museum – the one with the dancers and the jar.' She paused.

'Hope I didn't catch anything sitting there.'

'In the ossuary next door they found 200 skulls.'

'Now she tells me. Ghoulish lot, the Minoans. Any of the stiffs-in-pots – what d'you call them – *pithos* burials?'

'Not sure.'

'No wonder they were spooked about jars – like that Pandora story the prof was going on about at lunch.' He took an empty teacup from the shelf and peered into it: ' "What's in this lovely pot – aaahhh! it's dead great-granny!" '

'They might have liked the dead. They moved them around enough.' He held his nose and peered into the cup again, "Hello, Mrs, fancy a stretch?" So what do you reckon was originally in Pandora's Jar?'

'Dunno. But I bet it wasn't all bad.'

'Perhaps it was like those bran tubs at the fair . . . Every loser gets a prize.'

'Even if it's only a plastic keyring.'

'I'll do a painting.' He sat up excitedly and struck a pose: ' "Pandora's Lucky Dip." '

'Please don't. Some of us have a reputation to consider.'

'Not even as a fantasy?'

'Fantasies are officially banned in the academic world.' She reached for the after-sun lying on the floor. 'Can you rub this on my back?'

He lifted her t-shirt and began to smoothe the lotion over her brown shoulders.

'Their fantasies are mostly disguised as archaeological theory, like the Knossos "Priest-King", "King Minos" and the "Mother-Goddess" with her "son and consort".' She sighed. 'Your hands on my back are magic.'

'Your spine's preparing to strike. Relax. You're only with an archaeological ignoramus here.'

'Sorry. Can you rub further down? What gets me is the way people reconstruct ancient Greece into their own private Disneyworld, and then claim it's historical truth. Hey presto – a vision of just male rule . . . a benign aristocracy . . . a perfect big cosmic Mummy at the beginning of history . . .'

'Thank you, doctor. I need a tissue to get this oil off my hands.'

'I stuck some tissues inside the pot-lady. The Minoans' life must have been so different. People should just keep an open mind about it.'

He planted a kiss between her shoulder blades. 'What about human sacrifice? Another fantasy?'

'Hard to say. The evidence isn't clear.'

'Was it at that cemetery we went today?'

'Not there. But perhaps nearby at Anemospilia. A Greek archaeologist has excavated what he thinks is proof of the sacrifice of a young man. And here at Knossos they've found other evidence, two children perhaps . . .'

'Stop. My turn for a kiss.'

'There must be remains underneath us here, under this very building. It's only a stone's throw from the palace.'

'I'd rather not think about it,' he said. She smiled and kissed his eyelids.

Outside the professor's children played frisbee in the dusk. Inside the room sketch pads slid onto the floor as the archaeologist and her companion fumbled with each other's clothing.

'I wish we had a double sheet.'

'I'll wrap my wings around you.'

'I'll sting you.'

Under the bare light bulb they locked limbs. The silence

was broken only by their breathing, the hum of a single mosquito and the occasional rattle of a lorry passing on the main road from Heraklion.

'The curtains aren't drawn properly. The professor's kids were just outside.'

'Relax, doctor. The window's too high.'

'They've gone quiet.'

'Turn the light off.'

In the dark the iron beds shuddered as their bodies moved in a private uncourtly minuet before collapsing slowly and wordlessly into a deep sleep.

12 pm

A woman outside on the verandah was playing the grand piano. Dead bodies lay all around her, men in faded trousers and brown jackets or jumpers. They lay still. Then as she played one of the bodies stirred. Suddenly, with a cracking sound, one man's legs shot up into the air at right angles. The woman at the piano turned round in terror.

'Nnnn-No, it's not my turn . . .'

'What's the matter?' They both sat upright in bed.

'A nightmare.'

'What's the time?'

The headlights of a passing lorry flashed in through the window, picking out two startled faces.

'I dreamed I was kidnapped . . .' He leaned forward and his long hair fell tangled over his chest. 'Something to do with black magic . . . they were going to kill me – people were watching – I killed him first. In the stomach. With a big kitchen knife like the ones we have at home.'

'I was having a strange dream about a woman playing the piano.'

'What's the time?'

'We forgot to set the alarm.'

'Have you packed your compass and stuff for the morning?'

'It's a long drive to Koumasa for dawn. I need a crap.'

She picked a path across the pitch-black room, stumbling over a sketch-pad. She felt her way along the steps around the side of the hostel past the verandah. In the shadows the wooden table, scene of the midday conversation, was deserted, a photograph thrown into negative. She found the door. The light didn't work. She stumbled over another object, a jar of 'Azax' the Homeric Greek hero reborn as British scouring powder and sold back to Greece misspelt. She recalled the polite classical conversation of lunch as she found her way to the toilet seat, felt for the paper and the plastic wastepaper basket.

6 am

Brightness already spilling onto the black dome of the sky silhouetted the peak of the mountain which rose like a wall directly above the graveyard. The stone circle of the *tholos* tomb, nestling on the high slopes, gleamed dully and felt cold to her touch. The walls of the two other tombs loomed faintly out of the gloom.

Dawn would be a long time coming. She breathed deeply. The air was full and fresh and she could smell the mountain herbs. Around her second by second everything was changing from absence to presence, from one colour to another, as the light slowly spread. She heard the muffled sounds of people stirring in the distant village. A solitary dog barked. The darkness embraced hollows and bushes, and slipped gently away from higher places. Far, far across the Mesara plain a point of light settled onto a grey mountaintop. She had had no food yet. She sat down and drifted slowly towards sleep. A woman's face leaned in towards her, changing from young to old and back to young again.

Waking with a start, she saw that the sun had gathered to a faint halo at a point on the skyline. All around her plants and grasses were springing fully formed out of the darkness. A small procession of ants passed in front of her foot. The sky was now like a dome of milk. Tucking her skirt under her, she shut her eyes and tried to remember the steps of the dance. She seemed to be travelling down a long passage. Images brushed past like goats, too fast to catch. In the darkness she could feel others beside her. We are moving together, don't leave me behind. Each day is a new life.

Now the golden light around the mountain peak above her was vivid, the sky almost blue. The landscape was alight. Shadows leapt across the checkerboard Mesara plain. But still the *tholos* tomb was in shadow. The heavy arched doorway facing the mountain waited stolidly for the crowning birth of light. She stood up and stretched her limbs. She took out the fig she had brought with her. It was soft to her touch as she pressed her thumbs into the purple flesh. Inside, it was blood red with a feast of soft golden seeds resting at the centre. The fruit was sweet and fibrous, and stuck in her teeth.

The sun finally rose. A sliver at first, gentle as a flute solo, then like a deafening chord. Boldly it threw an arm of light directly in at the tomb doorway, warming the deathplace of years. She began to dance as if from memory, circling her pelvis and raising her arms so that the first touch of the sun could warm her hands and burn into the centre of her palms, so that she could carry the sun's warmth down to fill her belly, so that she could bring the sun down to earth. As she danced, her body rippled like the sun's reflection in a bowl of water, returning the warmth from her outstretched hands.

'What are you doing?' I thought you had a bad leg.'

'Not now.' She stopped dancing. 'How are your sketches?'

'The sun took ages, but still everything changed too fast.'

'Time slithering back on itself.'

'Speaking of which, if you've finished your studies, I've been waiting 4,000 years for you and I'm dying for a cup of tea.'

Contributors

Rosalind Belben's most recent novel, *Is Beauty Good*, was published by Serpent's Tail in 1989, together with the reprinted *Dreaming of Dead People*, which had first appeared in 1979. She is the author of three other works of fiction and of radio plays. In 1987 she had a grant from the DAAD Berliner Künstlerprogramm and continued to live for a while in what was then West Berlin. She was born and grew up in Dorset.

Jean Binta Breeze is a poet, storyteller and director. Her writing includes poetry – *Ryddim Ravings* – and the plays *Moon Dance Night*, *The Healing Touch* and *In and Out the Window*. Her first film, *Halleluja Anyhow*, was screened at the 1990 British Film Festival and on Channel Four television. She has two children and divides her time between Jamaica and Britain.

David Craig was born in Aberdeen in 1932. He has a daughter and three sons. He is married to the writer Anne Spillar, lives in Cumbria and teaches Creative Writing at Lancaster University. He loves to hill walk and rock climb and has written *Native Stones: A Book About Climbing* (1987) and the rock-climbing guide to Buttermere (with Rick Graham). He has written literary criticism (*Scottish Literature and the Scottish People*, 1961; *Extreme Situations*, with Mike Egan, 1979). Now he writes poetry (most recently *Against Looting*, 1987; *The Grasshopper's Burden*, 1992), fiction (*King Cameron*, 1991) and prose (*On the Crofter's Trail*, 1990).

Jenny Diski was born in 1947 in London where she still lives. She has written five novels: *Nothing Natural* (1986), *Rainforest* (1987), *Like Mother* (1988), *Then Again* (1990) and *Happily Ever After* (1991). She has also written two plays for television.

Lucy Goodison has spent many years of her life absorbed in studying ancient Cretan symbols. She has written about them for her PhD thesis *Death, Women and the Sun* (1989) and in her book on the mind/body split, *Moving Heaven and Earth: Sexuality, Spirituality and Social Change* (1990). She has also written about self-help therapy and issues in mental health and learning difficulties. She runs groups on dance and dreams at the Women's Therapy Centre in London, and practises massage. She has a teenage daughter.

Juan Goytisolo's *Whirling Dervishes* is one of a series by Spain's major living novelist on the diversity of Islamic culture. The exploration was prompted in the early 1960s by physical attraction for North African workers in Paris. Juan Goytisolo rediscovered the fertile coexistence of Christians, Jews and Muslims in medieval Spain and then placed the burning modernity of mystics like Rumi and John of the Cross at the centre of his own writing about the *mestizo* richness of contemporary life.

Peter Bush works as a freelance translator and television consultant. He has translated Juan Goytisolo's autobiography, a selection of his essays, novels by Juan Carlos Onetti and poetry by Jaime Gil de Biedma. He was consultant to the

Channel Four Rear Window documentaries on Juan Goytisolo, and *Islam in Spain*.

Thomas Keneally has served on a number of Australian Government Councils and Commissions, including the Constitutional Commission, which was looking at a review of the Australian Constitution. He was President of the National Book Council of Australia, a member of the Literary Arts Board of Australia Council and Chairman and then President of the Australian Society of Authors. He received the Order of Autralia in 1983 for his services to literature. He is Chairman of the Australian Republican Movement. He has held various visting Professorships for Creative Writing on both the East and West Coasts of America. In 1991 he was appointed Distinguished Professor at the University of California at Irvine, where he teaches in the Graduate Writing Program. Thomas Keneally is married with two daughters. He divides his time between Australia and the US.

Jonathan Lerner was born in Washington, DC, in 1948. He was active in the New Left and underground press of the 1960s and 1970s, and co-authored the book *Voices from Wounded Knee*, an oral history of the 1973 confrontation on the Pine Ridge Indian Reservation. His novel *Caught in a Still Place*, the story of a bi-sexual love triangle in a post-apocalyptic future on the Florida coast, was published in 1989 by Serpent's Tail.

Drusilla Modjeska was born in 1946 and grew up in England. She moved to Australia in 1971 and now lives in Sydney. Her most recent book, *Poppy*, which is published in the UK by Serpent's Tail, won the Australian National Book Council's Banjo Award for Non-Fiction, and the New South Wales Premier's Award.

Marsha Rowe first came to Britain in 1969 from Sydney. She worked on *OZ* magazine and *INK* before co-founding the feminist magazine, *Spare Rib*. She edited the *Spare Rib Reader*, the anthology of the first ten years. Her previous anthologies for Serpent's Tail are *Sex and the City* and *So Very English*. She has contributed essays and stories to various anthologies, including *Serious Hysterics*, and is currently preparing a further anthology and *Breath*, a book about asthma. She lives in London and is married with one daughter.

Founded in 1986, Serpent's Tail publishes the innovative and the challenging.

If you would like to receive a catalogue of our current publications please write to:

FREEPOST
Serpent's Tail
4 Blackstock Mews
LONDON N4 2BR

(No stamp necessary if your letter is posted in the United Kingdom.)

CHARGE

(Electric Series #1)

E. L. TODD

Fallen Publishing

Charge

Editing Services provided by Final-Edits.com

Prologue

Volt

My story has been told a million times.

I was a wild stallion that couldn't be saddled. Freedom rang in my heart like a loud bell. The future had no hold over me because I could never look past the forthcoming day. I lived in the moment, tasting it and feeling it in my very blood.

Until I met her.

She grounded me with the force of gravity. As if she had the ability to move mountains and station them, she put me in place.

And I never moved.

Which is why I'm asking her to marry me.

"What do you think?" The saleswoman held out the ring. It was a princess cut diamond with flawless quality. With every shake of her hand, the prisms within the jewel showered the walls with rainbows.

It was perfect. "Great. I need a size five."

Instead of smiling because she made a sale, and probably a commission, she grinned in a genuine way, the kind that reached her eyes. "She'll love it. Trust me."

She would love anything I got her. But she would definitely love this.

My jacket felt much heavier than it did when I first entered the store. An invisible weight pressed down on my shoulders, giving me the kind of pressure that felt welcoming rather than daunting. I pulled out my phone and called the first person who came to mind.

"Hey, wanna go out?" Derek's voice came over the phone, and judging by the conversation in the background, he wasn't alone. It sounded like Jared was with him, along with the other guys.

Which was perfect. "I have some big news."

"Your insurance company approved the dick implant?"

Nothing could hurt my ego tonight. It was practically made of steel. "No. They said your brain transplant was more important."

"Burn…" His face wasn't visible, but his tone made it clear he was rolling his eyes. "Are you going to tell me, or am I going to guess for the next hour?"

The ring was hidden deep in my pocket, the black box keeping it safe from unwanted scratches. The velvet lining and protective film would keep it sparkling and clean, ready to be revealed at the right time. "I'm proposing."

"Shut the front door, man."

"I'm serious."

"What? Volt Rosenthal is going to take a wife?" I could tell he turned away from the phone, his voice becoming muffled. "Guys, check this out. Volt just told me he's going to propose."

They immediately erupted in yells, screams, and straight-up gibberish.

Derek returned to the phone. "Where did this come from? I didn't even realize marriage was on your mind."

"Well...sometimes you just know." We hadn't been together very long, only a year. But I knew couples who'd been together for five years and it was clear they still weren't ready to get married. The measurement of time was subjective to whoever was experiencing it. "Just got the ring."

"Damn, you're serious then."

Now it was my turn to roll my eyes. "Yes."

"Then we definitely have to hit the town. Where do you want to meet?"

I stepped to the end of the sidewalk, letting people pass me. Manhattan was one of the biggest cities on earth, but the seven million inhabitants made it feel cramped. My eyes wandered to the bar just a block over. "How about Tito's?"

"Tito's? Where the fuck is that?"

"Corner of 23rd and Broadway."

"I've never been there, but it's your night. See you in ten minutes."

"Ten-four."

He finished the phrase. "Over and out."

I shoved the phone into the front pocket of my jeans and felt the nerves get to me. Now that I'd told my best friend, everything just became real. I had an expensive engagement ring in my pocket and a question to ask. When I pictured myself getting down on one knee, I felt excited. Her bright blue eyes would somehow become brighter, and the same joy that burned in my heart would burst like fireworks in her smile. Instead of feeling scared, I felt driven.

I crossed the street once the light turned green then made it to the entrance of the bar. I'd never been there before, but that was the beautiful thing about Manhattan. You could live in the city your entire life and still not experience every thing about it.

I walked inside and felt the warmth from everyone's body heat press tightly against me. My jacket was suffocating, but I kept it on because of the diamond ring in the pocket. I'd rather sweat to death than risk losing it. When I looked into the diamond, I saw her face. I couldn't just buy another one to replace it.

The NHL playoffs were on every screen, and everyone crammed together to see every play as it unfolded. I headed to the bar to get a drink but stopped when I recognized someone.

With long blonde hair and a petite frame, a woman I knew better than anyone else in the world stood. Her blue eyes were soft, but not dull. They contained innocence more pure than the snowcaps in the Swiss Alps. Like ice crystals that hung from igloos, they reflected the deep blue color of the sky.

Her skin was fair like the surface of a ripe peach. It was soft to the touch and warm against the mouth. I'd tasted her a million times—and she tasted just as sweet as she looked.

But those lips were kissing someone else.

She wore dark skinny jeans that led to brown heeled boots. The only reason why I noticed was because I bought them for her birthday. The saleswoman at the store spent nearly the whole day helping me pick them out because I didn't know shit about shoes.

Her arms were wrapped around the waist of some guy, and she looked up into his face with a wide smile. Her perfectly straight and white teeth were intricately designed to fit a flawless face. When he said something, she chuckled, and then she leaned in to kiss him again.

And again.

The bartender asked what I wanted to order, but his words sounded like a distant echo. My ears could pick up on what he was saying, but my brain couldn't process the sounds into information.

The guy ran his hands up her arms then gripped her shoulders, giving them a gentle squeeze. He had a thin layer of facial hair from not shaving that morning, and his eyes glowed for hers just the way hers did for him.

And then it hit me.

It was Leo—her ex.

Despite the pain it caused me to stare, I couldn't look away. Instead of feeling my heart pick up its pace to a terrifying speed, it slowed down. My body slowly shut down, cutting off circulation to every organ.

Because that was the only way it could protect me.

I never fantasized about a moment like this because it wasn't something I ever thought possible. But I assumed if I were in this situation, I would march over there and give the guy a beating he would never recover from. Then I would turn my gaze on her and say something so hateful she cried.

But I didn't do either of those things.

I kept staring, unable to believe what I was seeing with my very own two eyes. I tried to be logical and give her the benefit of the doubt. Maybe they were just friends who were affectionate. But with every kiss, that possibility was erased. He wasn't even some guy she just hooked up with.

They had a relationship.

The box suddenly felt lighter in my pocket, losing all of its meaning and significance. The image I had for my proposal was cracked like a dried twig. The dream shattered into a million pieces, becoming forever broken. The pain that burned inside me was agonizing. I'd never experienced anything like it. I'd take a broken leg or cracked ribs over this.

But even then, I wasn't angry.

I felt stupid.

Foolish.

And hopeless.

I had every right to march over there and give her a piece of my mind. I had the right to make a scene and storm off. I had every right to say exactly what was in my heart.

But I didn't want to do any of those things.

Because in that moment, I realized my feelings didn't matter. If she did this to me to begin with, then I meant

7

nothing to her. Every kiss and every touch was just a show. It was all an act.

So why would she start to care now?

She wasn't worth my time or my heartbreak. Call me proud or call me stubborn, but I wasn't going to let this woman even know what she'd done to me. In fact, I was going to hurt her far more than she ever hurt me.

She'll see.

Chapter One

Taylor

Cardboard boxes were scattered around my small apartment. The hardwood floor was the same color as the boxes, so it was difficult to differentiate between the two. I didn't have a lot of stuff to begin with, but that didn't make moving any easier.

The guys carried my furniture into the living room—the new couch I bought from Macy's as well as the other pieces of my living room set. Their strong arms bulged as they carried the weight, and I broke a sweat just watching them.

Sara walked inside carrying two boxes. "Shit, why is this so heavy?"

Right on the side in black permanent marker was the label BOOKS. "Read the label next time."

Sara dropped the box on the ground, making a loud thud that nearly shook the apartment. She put her hands on her hips and tried to catch her breath.

"Dude, don't drop my stuff. You'll break everything."

"You can't break books."

"So you *did* read the label."

She dodged the question by changing the subject. "What do you need these for? You're done with school, aren't you?"

"It's always good to have them for a reference."

"That's what Google and Wikipedia are for."

"As an academic, I don't use Wikipedia."

Sara narrowed her eyes on me, calling bullshit with just a look.

"Okay, I use Wikipedia for everything. But don't tell anyone that."

"There you go."

The guys finished unloading the truck, and after I gave them a big fat tip and lunch, they left. Sara and I sat on the floor in the living room, and slowly, we went through my things.

Sara opened the box of living room accents, a few sculptures and picture frames. Whenever we stopped talking and her mind began to wander, she always had a sad look on her face. The past lingered behind her eyes, haunting her.

"Thanks for helping me unpack."

She snapped back to reality. "Of course. Like I'd ever let my best friend handle this on her own."

"I wish you would show that same compassion for my things..."

She rolled her eyes. "If the box said china, I wouldn't have dropped it."

"Actually, china is stronger than regular plates. You could throw them at the wall, and they still wouldn't break."

"How do you know stuff like that? Random crap?"

I shrugged. "I don't know. I guess I'm a sponge."

"A sponge?"

"You know, I absorb everything."

She made a face when she didn't understand the reference, and then she returned to sorting through my things. "When do you start your new job?"

"Monday." I was nervous as hell, but so damn excited at the same time.

"Teaching little pretentious brats at a private school..." She turned up her nose in disgust. "Count me out."

"They aren't pretentious brats. They're kids."

"Whatever," she said. "They'll still wipe boogers on you."

"I'm teaching high school, not preschool." Sara wasn't exactly the most maternal type and never had been. But when she had her own kids, the instinct would kick in. It happened to all women.

"I wonder if there will be any hot teachers there..." She waggled her eyebrows at me in a playful way, but it looked a little ridiculous since her eyebrows were so blonde they were white. It was difficult to see them move.

11

"It doesn't matter if there are. I don't sleep with my coworkers."

"Why not?" she asked. "Wouldn't it be perfect if you married a teacher? You would both have summers off."

"I admit it would be nice, but it's not a part of my criteria." Not that there was a list of prerequisites in my pocket. I was open to any type of guy—funny, outgoing, anything really. But dating someone I worked with had catastrophe written all over it. "I'm more excited to be in the classroom. I feel like I've been going to school forever, and now I finally get to do what I love."

"And they must be paying you pretty well since you're at a private school."

The pay wasn't amazing, but it was enough to get me a decent apartment, a savings account, and some spending money. I couldn't ask for more than that. Besides, as a teacher, I was given a pension, something that was so rare these days it was almost nonexistent. "I'm not complaining."

Sara sorted through the picture frames, looking at the image of my parents, brother, and me at the top of Mt. Rainier in Washington. Her eyes lingered on the photo longer than necessary before she moved on.

"Everything alright?" I picked up on her moods easily because I was intuitive. Part of my job was understanding human emotion without asking questions. In order for my students to succeed, I had to understand what they needed without them ever telling me.

"Yeah, I'm fine." Her voice belied her true sorrow. It was suddenly soft and raspy at the same time, as if she were living in a distant memory that strained her voice without speaking.

I knew what troubled her, even if she didn't speak a word of it to me. She and her boyfriend broke up a year ago, and the anniversary of that date was just around the corner. I wasn't sure the specific date, but it was near. "You want to talk about it?"

"Not really."

I completed my Teach For America training in Nashville, Tennessee so I'd been separated from Sara for over two years. We'd been best friends since childhood, but I went away to college then moved to the South. We kept in touch by texting and occasionally Skypeing, but we missed out on significant life events.

"It's still hard, you know?"

I busied myself with the plates, organizing my dishware and glasses. Each was secured in bubble wrap and had to be carefully removed before being placed on the ground.

"As time goes on, it gets easier, but I'll never really get over it."

"You'll be alright, Sara. Healing takes time."

"But I guess not knowing what happened is what haunts me." Her bottom lip trembled slightly, but tears didn't form in her eyes. "We were fine. We were happy together, and everything was perfect...and then he just left."

"Maybe there was someone else?" No one wanted to entertain the idea of their lover cheating, but that didn't mean it wasn't a possibility.

"No. He wouldn't do that." There wasn't an ounce of hesitation in her voice.

Since I'd never met the guy, I didn't have an opinion about him. And when they started seeing each other, I talked to Sara even less than I usually did. In fact, I didn't even know what he looked like. She'd taken all of his photos and shoved them into a box under the bed. "Then maybe he started to feel differently."

"But the last time I saw him, everything was normal. He told me he loved me and kissed me..." She shook her head, like that would get rid of the pain. "But then the next time

14

he saw me, he just dumped me. I'm not even going to sugarcoat it. He *dumped* me."

"Did you ask him why?"

"Of course." She stopped organizing the books and just stared at the ground. "But he said he just wanted to take a step back. Then he walked out—no further explanation."

"Could he have been mad about something?"

"No..." Her eyes were still hazy.

Lingering on the past and analyzing every word of a prior conversation wasn't healthy. Soon, people began to see things that weren't there to begin with. They felt emotions that hadn't existed at all. Memory was subjective—and dangerous. "Let it go. You're going to find someone really fantastic, and this guy will seem insignificant in comparison."

"Yeah...I suppose." Her voice trailed off as she continued to ponder it. "It's just, I think he was going to propose."

"Why do you think that?" I doubted it. Why would he flip that suddenly if that were the case?

"He'd just been different lately...wanting to go on a trip. We'd never been on a trip before."

Continuing to live in the past was just making it worse. "Sara, want my advice?"

"I guess." She turned her gaze back to me, finally coming back to reality.

"Whatever happened a year ago doesn't matter. He let you go—and that's his loss. You'll find a much better man someday, and he won't hesitate to ask you to be his wife."

Finally, Sara smiled. "You always know the right thing to say."

"Because I'm your best friend."

Invigorated, the life came back into her eyes. "And you'll always be my best friend."

***

My first day of class was uneventful.

I read off the syllabus and explained my expectations for the school year. A sea of blank faces stared back at me, every student still in summer mode. Their eyes glanced to the windows, dreaming about their vacation by the pool. They looked like a group of lifeless slugs.

It wasn't exactly what I fantasized about.

Getting them to focus was the most challenging part. So I had to do the thing I hated most—I had to be a hardass. I gave them a pop quiz about the elements just to light a fire under them. Each and every one of them disliked me, but at least they would take me seriously.

By the end of the day, I was already dreading the following one. It would take at least two weeks for these kids to get into the full swing of things, and the parents were already shoving themselves down my throat asking about field trips and the academic decathlon.

I walked into the break room and ate the lunch I skipped earlier that day. I could go home, but I was too exhausted to do anything besides sit and eat my tuna salad sandwich and my sliced apples.

Ms. Lane poured herself a cup of coffee before adding a packet of sugar. "Long day?"

I wasn't even sure if she was talking to me because her back was to me. But there was no one else in the room, so I had to be the person she was talking to. "You could say that."

She turned around and sat in the seat across from me, her coffee steaming toward her chin. She was my age, possibly a year older. "Principal Rosenthal tells me you're from Teach For America."

"I am."

"Cool. Me too."

"Where was your program?"

"In California."

"That's great." I stopped eating my sandwich because I didn't want to have fish breath. "I'm glad I have a fellow alumni here. How long have you been at Bristol Academy?"

"This is my third year." She stirred her coffee before she blew the steam away. "I love it here. Great kids and great funding. We're taking a trip to the museum next week."

"That's great." I hadn't decided on the type of field trips we would be doing. First, I wanted to build a relationship with my students and figure out what they could handle.

"I'm Natalie, by the way." She shook my hand.

"I'm Taylor."

"Let me know if you need anything. I'm always here to help."

"Thanks." I'd probably have to take her up on that offer.

"Are you new to New York?"

"Yeah. I lived in Washington for college. Then I went to Tennessee for my master's."

"You get around."

"So to speak."

"Maybe I can show you around sometime. I was born and raised here."

"Sure. That would be great."

She blew on her coffee again before she left the table. "Well, I should get going. I've got papers to grade."

"Already?"

She held her head high as she walked out. "What can I say? I'm a hardass."

***

By the end of the week, I got into the swing of things.

It was all about accountability. I had to make good on my threats so the kids knew bad behavior wouldn't slide, and I had to give them fun activities so they wouldn't become restless with boredom. The combination of those two things brought stability to the classroom and facilitated learning.

After the bell rang, Natalie walked into my classroom. She took one look around at the desks perfectly aligned with their rows and the absence of paper and gum. "Wow...your kids are actually clean."

"They aren't allowed to leave unless everything is picked up."

"Good call. I didn't learn that until my second year."

I packed all the assignments into a folder and shoved it into my bag. I'd probably be grading papers tonight while the TV played in the background. Maybe Sara would come over and paint her nails while she droned on about work.

Misery loves company, right?

"You have plans tonight?" Natalie asked.

19

"Just a hot date with my assignments."

She chuckled. "I'm going out with some friends. You should come along."

Now that I was in a new city, I needed to make some new friends. I planned on being there a long time, and I couldn't hang out with Sara all the time. I loved her to death—but sometimes, she drove me crazy. "I'd love that."

"Great. I have some hot guy friends, so I hope you're single."

I grinned from ear to ear. "Single and ready to mingle."

"Perfect. Do you know where The Lion and The Snake is?"

Was that a zoo?

She answered the question I never asked. "It's a bar near Fifth and Broadway."

"Oh, okay. I'll find it."

"Alright. See you at eight." She walked out and swayed her hips in her loose skirt.

"I look forward to it."

***

Despite the fact it was September, it was still warm in the city. I wore a long dress that nearly touched my feet. It was loose around the legs and the waist, and I wore a pink cardigan just in case it was chilly inside the bar.

I found the place easily, thanks to Google, and walked inside. The second I entered, I realized I was underdressed. Actually, I was overdressed. Women wore dresses that were so short their asses nearly hung out. Heels that were five inches tall or more were on their feet, and I couldn't look at them without wanting to topple over.

I felt like a stick in the mud.

Just when I decided to go back and change, Natalie spotted me. "Hey. You found it."

"Yeah, I did. Thanks to Google."

She held a glass of wine in her hand, and she wore a tight black dress that highlighted every curve of her toned body. It left nothing to the imagination because it was so skintight. She looked amazing in it. When she looked me up and down, she tried to keep the smile on her face. "You look cute."

I knew she didn't mean that and was just trying to be nice. "I thought it would be casual."

"In New York, nothing is casual. You can't even run to the store at two in the morning to grab a carton of milk without wearing makeup. And don't even think about going to the gym in a t-shirt and shorts. You better have a bangin' outfit."

"Thanks for the tip."

21

She linked her arm through mine. "You look beautiful in anything, so you're good. Let's get you a drink, and I'll introduce you to everyone."

"Okay."

She got me a glass of whatever she was drinking then pulled me into the rear. There was a small table with a comfy sofa, and beside it was a dartboard. Two guys were playing a game while another sat on the couch with his beer in his hand.

When I took a look around the bar, I realized why it had such an interesting name. Mounted lion heads were everywhere, and the walls had long cobras engraved into the marble. It was artistic chaos, but still really cool.

Natalie pulled me onto the sofa. "Jared, this is my friend Taylor."

Jared finished drinking his beer before he turned to me. He had blond hair and green eyes, looking like someone that just returned from Ireland. He shook my hand with a firm grip. "Nice to meet you, Taylor."

"You too." He was a good-looking guy, and I wondered if this was the man Natalie wanted to introduce me to.

"Taylor is a teacher too." Natalie tried to pull down her dress so the top of her thighs wouldn't be revealed, but it was no use. "We work at the same school."

"Cool," he said. "You've been there long?"

"Actually, I just started. Natalie was nice enough to be my friend since I'm kind of a loner right now."

"A loner?" he asked.

"I just moved to the city." I should have explained that earlier so he wouldn't assume I was a total loser.

"A newbie?" He clanked his beer against mine. "Well, I'll be your friend. Trust me, I have great references."

"He's the biggest piece of shit I've ever met." One of the guys playing darts came around the couch and rolled up his long sleeves. "He'll borrow five dollars from you and never give it back."

Jared rolled his eyes. "I didn't realize you were so hungry for five bucks."

"It's the principle, man." His blue eyes turned to me, and he shook my hand. "You're the teacher, right?"

"Yes."

"I'm Derek—Natalie's brother."

"Oh..." I searched his face and didn't see any similarities. "That's cool."

"Yeah, she's lucky to be related to a stud like me." He flexed his arms.

"A penny-pinching stud," Jared teased.

"I'm a penny pincher?" he asked incredulously. "You're the one who won't pay me back. If it's only five dollars, why haven't you opened that thick wallet of yours?"

The third guy returned the darts to the board then introduced himself. "I'm Cam. And I'm sorry you have to listen to this bullshit. I want to say it's rare, but it's not."

I shook his hand then chuckled. "I teach high school. Believe me, this is nothing."

Natalie looked at Jared and Derek then turned to me, rolling her eyes so dramatically they might get stuck in the back of her skull. "Losers, right?"

"You're the one who hangs out with your brother," Jared jabbed.

Derek slapped his knee and laughed. "Good one, bro." As soon as his laughter died down, he switched gears. "Now give me my money."

Cam leaned toward me and whispered in my ear. "This argument has been going on for two weeks…"

"Wow. It looks like they need to find something else to fight about," I said.

"You're telling me," Cam said with a chuckle.

I sipped my wine and listened to the argument continue. Natalie and her friends were nice, welcoming me into their group without asking too many questions. And it was nice to hang out with them rather than be interrogated.

My eyes glanced around the bar and looked at the strange architecture. They didn't have anything like this in Washington or Tennessee. The fact it was so odd made it beautiful. It seemed like I was in a different place, a different time.

A man rounded the corner and came directly into my line of sight. Suddenly, the mounted lions and threatening cobras no longer seemed interesting. The black wallpaper became an obscure background, and the person who just walked into my life took the stage.

I knew I was staring, but my body and mind had separated into two different entities. They no longer cross-referenced or worked together. My heart was beating painfully slow while my mind worked a million miles an hour.

The deep blue eyes were startling. Speaking of distant lands and different times, they showed a past only told by the greatest storytellers. They were deeper than a gushing volcano full of lava, but they were softer than a rose petal. Blue eyes were common. I'd seen them a million times.

But I'd never seen these.

He wore an ordinary gray t-shirt, something he could have bought at any retail store. But his extraordinary body filled it out well, providing definition and depth from his powerful physique. The sleeves were tight from his bulging muscles, and his waist was thin with even thinner hips.

His dark jeans hung low around the waist, enough to give him a noticeable V formation. Even without seeing his bare skin, it was clear he owned that chiseled form, the type of image only carved out of solid granite.

My observations happened in a nanosecond, and once I processed the heat in my cheeks and felt my suddenly parched mouth, I understood the immediate effect this stranger had on me.

His eyes turned my way once he entered the room, and instead of seeing the same look of desire on his face, I saw absolutely nothing. There was no change in feeling or mood. I was just another face in a sea of others.

And I felt disappointed.

Instead of walking past the group, he joined it, listening to his two friends bicker about the unpaid debt.

"Stop being a pussy and just pay me," Derek demanded. "Are you the kind of man who doesn't pay his debts?"

"Are you the kind of pussy who begs for money?" Jared countered.

26

The man watched them argue back and forth.

"Dude, just pay me," Derek argued. "Then this stupid conversation will stop."

"Or you could just stop talking," Jared countered. "And then the conversation will stop."

I was barely listening to a word they said because I was still occupied with the stranger just a few feet away from me. Now, I could smell his cologne. It was masculine and musty. But was it cologne at all? Or just his natural scent? If so, I liked it.

He opened his wallet and pulled out two twenty-dollar bills. "Here. The debt has been settled, and the feud is over." He shoved a twenty into each of their chests before he grabbed his beer from the table. "Let's move on."

Derek grabbed the twenty then shoved it into his pocket. "Works for me."

"I'm going to buy a pretty girl a drink tonight." Jared shoved the bill into the front pocket of his shirt.

"You still won't get laid." Abruptly, the man turned to me and extended his large hand.

I'd never done this before in my life, but I examined his hand. I eyed his dry knuckles, his thick fingers, and measured the size of his palm in comparison to mine. It was the first time I was attracted to something so mundane.

27

He waited for me to take his hand, still hanging in midair.

I placed my hand in his but didn't shake it. I just let our hands touch. My middle finger touched the top of his wrist, and I could feel his distant pulse. It was beating slowly, calm and confident—just like the man himself.

His eyes were on mine the entire time, absorbing every feature and reaction. He still hadn't spoken a word to me, his face doing all the talking.

I finally shook his hand and felt mortified. I was clumsy and awestruck. He didn't need to know me to understand what my reaction meant. Everything about him affected me, and I was embarrassed how obvious that was. "I'm Taylor."

"Volt."

It was the strangest name I'd ever heard, but somehow, it suited him. "Natalie brought me."

"Good. Her only job is to bring cute girls." He pulled his hand away but still didn't give me anything other than his stoic expression. He was ice-cold but still warm to the touch.

I didn't react to his words because I wouldn't allow myself to.

"It's a pleasure to meet you. Can I get you a drink?"

I was still holding my glass of wine, which was nearly full. "I'm okay. But thank you."

Without saying another word, he walked away and left his friends behind. He didn't explain where he was going, and the rest of the group didn't think his behavior was odd.

Natalie came back to my side. "You want an easy and hot lay? He's your man."

"What?" Did everyone know how hard up I was?

"Volt. I told you I would introduce you to a hot guy. Well, there he is."

"He wants to be set up?" I tried to keep the hope out of my voice. He was dark and dangerous, clearly someone I should steer clear of. I doubted a man like that would need help finding a date, but sometimes miracles happened.

"No," she said with a laugh. "He just sleeps with everyone."

Chapter Two

Volt

The soft sheets were tangled around my waist, hugging me with smoothness. Diana's leg was wrapped around my thigh, her warm skin matching the same temperature as mine. Laura lay on the other side, her sculpted back against my bicep. I wasn't sure what time it was, but it was time to get up.

Sunlight filtered through my open window and penetrated my bedroom. I didn't draw the curtains shut the night before so the apartment was several degrees warmer than I would prefer.

Diana stirred when I did then cuddled into my side. "Morning..."

"Morning, baby."

She pressed her face against mine, rubbing her lips against my scruff before she placed a soft kiss against my mouth. Her hand rubbed my chest gently, feeling every line and groove.

Laura woke up next and turned my way, her tits pressed against my arm. She kissed my shoulder then licked it in a playful way. Her long hair brushed against me as she moved, and the strands were just as soft as her skin. Her hand slowly traveled down my chest until she reached my waist under the sheets. She wrapped her small fingers around my thick shaft and pumped up and down.

I wasn't sure what time we went to sleep last night, but it was probably early in the morning. My body was wiped out, and I wasn't eager to thrust and pump like I did last night.

But my dick disagreed.

Laura moved down to my waist and started licking my balls, pumping my cock as she sucked my delicate skin into her mouth and massaged it with her inner cheek. Then Diana placed my long shaft into her mouth and gave me slow strokes, pushing me to the back of her throat just before her gag reflex was initiated.

I shoved another pillow under my head so I could watch everything they were doing with a perfect view. I dug each hand into their hair and gripped it tightly, moaning from deep in the back of my throat.

***

Diana and Laura left, and I walked to a nearby coffee shop to get a hot cup of joe. The girls used all my coffee beans, so I was out of fuel. It was nearly three in the afternoon so it was late for coffee, but I couldn't start my day without it.

After I walked a few blocks and navigated around people like they were cattle, I came to the entrance of the shop. But I stopped when I saw something peculiar right in front of me.

The woman I met last night was standing in the center of the sidewalk holding out an enormous map of New York. Her brown hair was flying with the breeze, and she kept turning the map upside down as she tried to decipher it.

What was she doing?

She wore denim shorts, sandals, and a white t-shirt with a giraffe on it. Like last night, she wore clothes I didn't see women wear. I was used to short dresses and miniskirts. This woman was dressed like a schoolteacher, classy and casual at the same time. A man bumped into her as he passed, and she was nearly put off-balance because of it.

Instead of talking to her, I continued to study her, unable to take my eyes off her. I thought she was pretty, like I thought of most women, but I also thought she was strange—awkward. When we met last night, she didn't say much, and she did a lot of staring. If she was anything like Natalie's other friends, she was obsessive and clingy.

I learned to steer clear of those a long time ago.

It would be easy for me to turn around and walk the other way like I hadn't spotted her, but my feet remained in

33

place. After examining her for a few more seconds, I walked up to her. "Hey, sweetheart. You look lost."

She kept her eyes glued to the map and didn't look up. "What gave you that idea?" She laughed in a natural way, beautiful and soft. She held herself with a strict posture, shoulders back and her head held high. It was a completely different stance than the one she had last night.

"First of all, no one uses maps anymore."

"My phone died, and now I can't find it." She turned the map right-side up again. "And I can't remember where my apartment is…"

"Talk about a bad day." She still hadn't looked at me, and I began to wonder if she ever would.

"I'll figure it out. It might just take me a while."

I placed my hand on the map and pushed it down so she was forced to meet my gaze. "Or you could rely on a gentleman to steer you in the right direction."

A smile was still on her lips when she looked up. It was only there for a brief second, but it was long enough for me to see her perfectly straight teeth, plump and beautiful lips, and the same laughter in her eyes. She didn't have any makeup on, but somehow her features were more distinct that way. Once she realized it was me she came face-to-face with, that smile disappeared quicker than lightning could strike the earth. "Oh, hey… What are you doing here?"

"I was just about to get some coffee when I saw a lost puppy." I gave her a smile so she knew I was only teasing her. "Can I help you? I have a phone that already has Google Maps installed."

She folded up the ridiculously big map and shoved it into her purse. "Maybe that's a good idea. I couldn't see anything on that thing. And there was no key. Who makes a map without a key?"

"And who reads maps in this day and age?"

She rolled her eyes. "I lost my phone, alright?"

"Have you tried calling it?"

"It's dead so that didn't work."

"Hmm…"

"It's probably somewhere in the mess of my apartment."

"That's a good place to start."

"I thought I had it on me when I left, but by the time I got here, I realized I was wrong."

"And where exactly were you trying to go?" This girl must be ditsy to lose her phone and get lost in the same day.

"I was trying to get to the Museum of Natural History but realized I was going to the MET instead. Now, I'm just trying to get home so I can find my phone."

How did anyone get those two mixed up? "We definitely need to find you that phone. What's your address?"

"Ugh..." She bit her bottom lip as she tried to remember.

Seriously, she didn't know that?

"I know it's on East."

That didn't help at all. "That's a pretty big street." I kept my agitation to myself because being a dick wouldn't help anything. "What's the cross street?"

"I can't remember that either."

Geez, woman.

"I know how to get there from work. So, if you can direct me to Bristol Academy, I should be able to figure it out."

She worked at a school? I hoped she was a janitor for the kids' sakes. "I know where that is."

"Great. Which way?" She looked at the cross street then looked the opposite way.

She would only get more lost if I gave her directions. "I'll walk you there."

"You don't need to do that—"

"I don't mind. Let's go." I started off without waiting for her to follow me.

When she realized this was really happening, she walked beside me. "It's pretty late for a cup of coffee. Do you drink a lot?"

"I just got a late start this morning." *Really late.*

"Oh…" She looked away like she figured out exactly what I'd been doing the night before.

"So, do you get lost like this on a daily basis?"

"Lately, I have." She pulled her sunglasses out of her purse and placed them on the bridge of her nose. They were aviator sunglasses, and they looked cute on her small face. "I've only been here for a week. I'm still not used to everything."

Now it all made sense. She wasn't some stupid girl. "You just moved to New York?"

"Yeah. It's been a really big change."

"Where did you move from?"

"Nashville."

She didn't have even a hint of an accent so I suspected she wasn't born and raised there. "Cool. Did you move for work? For a guy?"

"Not a guy. For work."

I realized I'd been asking her a lot of questions, and I needed to back off. I hated it when people interrogated me, so I shouldn't do the same to her.

"Thanks for walking me. That map wasn't helpful."

"No problem. New York is a big place—especially without a phone."

"I'll never make that mistake again. I'm usually organized and prepared for anything, but I still haven't unpacked all my things so my apartment is a bit of a mess."

"Understandable."

"It's pretty ironic that I ran into you."

"Why?"

"Natalie just told me last night that I shouldn't go anywhere without makeup because you always see someone you know…and she was right. And I don't even know that many people right now."

"You look good without makeup, so you're fine."

"Thanks…" She adjusted her glasses again and kept walking. "So, Volt is an interesting name…"

"It's my middle name." I had the lamest first name ever, and I didn't like it when people called me by it. It didn't fit my personality or my identity, and I rarely told people what it was.

"Oh, I see."

We passed a few blocks before we finally reached the area where the school was located. It took up the entire block because it was a big school. There were quite a few prestigious private schools in the city, and Bristol Academy was one of the top three. "You work here?"

"Yeah, I teach math and science."

"Really?" After my first impression of her, I couldn't hide my surprise. She didn't strike me as the academic type, but apparently, she was the nerdy, awkward type. "Do you like it?"

"This is my first year teaching, so I'm not sure yet."

If Bristol Academy hired her as a starting teacher, then she must have had an impressive resume. Prestigious academies never did that sort of thing—and I would know. "You'll love it. It's a good school."

"I can tell. The staff is friendly and the kids are great."

"Because they're all geniuses."

She chuckled. "Some of my students are smarter than me—but I'll never admit it to them."

I stopped when we reached the entrance to the school. The gates were closed, and the campus was shut down for the weekend. No one could get in there if they tried. "Well, do you know your way from here?"

She shielded her eyes from the piercing rays and looked across the street. "Yes. I can see my building."

Then she should be fine. "Alright. I'll see you around."

"Thanks so much for helping me. I know I must have looked like a weirdo standing there with a map in my hands."

"I didn't mind. And yes, you looked like a weirdo." I gave her a teasing smile so she knew I wasn't really being an ass.

"People warned me that New Yorkers are coldhearted and brutal. But in my experience, they've been nothing but nice and friendly." She shrugged and gave me that pretty smile I spotted when I first saw her. It was the kind that formed in her cheeks as well as her eyes. Her green eyes naturally glowed under the sun, and even in the darkness of that bar, they emitted their light like a star in the sky.

She wasn't the typical type of woman I was attracted to. I liked women in short dresses, with thick hair and heels that made them almost as tall as me. I liked the flirty and sexy kind, the ones who stuck their tongues down my throat the moment they laid eyes on me.

Taylor was nothing like that.

But now I really looked at her, seeing the young smile on her lips and the gentleness in her eyes. She was her own breed of beauty, a rare kind that many people never got to see. "That's because you're a pretty girl. And everyone is nice to pretty girls."

Chapter Three

Taylor

The students were gone, but I stayed behind my desk and finished grading lab reports. We just did a lab that measured the water displacement of pennies. The kids seemed too advanced for it, so I'd have to think of more challenging things for them to do. If they were too bored, they would become reckless and loud.

And that would give me a headache.

Natalie stepped inside with a folder of papers under her arm. An empty coffee mug was in her hand, and it said *#1 Teacher*. She wore a necklace with her keys hooked at the end, and every step she took was accompanied by a gentle rattle. "How was your day?"

"My kids are bored," I said with a sigh.

"Oh, no. You'll have to step it up."

"You're telling me." I placed the cap on my red pen and set it on the desk. "What's up with you?"

"The guys really liked you the other night."

"They did?" I asked in surprise.

"Yeah. Thought you were charming."

I thought I stuck out like a sore thumb. "Well, that was nice of them to say. It seems like you have a fun group."

"It's okay," she said. "It is what it is."

I wondered why Natalie hung out with her brother. It wouldn't be the first time I'd heard of siblings being close, but it was usually because one of them was dating a mutual friend. That didn't seem to be the case with them. "I liked them too. Made me feel welcome."

"You never hooked up with Volt?"

My body immediately stiffened, and I felt my cheeks redden. At the end of the night, I saw him leave with two pretty girls, so I knew whom he went home with that night. "Uh, no." My initial attraction to him was physical, and now that I knew more about him, I realized he wasn't my type. He was the kind of man who had no intention of settling down, wasn't looking for a girlfriend, and broke hearts like they meant nothing. "He was nice but...not my type."

"How is he not your type?" She sat on one of the desks and crossed her legs.

"He seems like a player."

"Well, he is."

"And that's not what I'm looking for."

"Really?" she asked. "I thought you'd want a welcome lay, to see what this amazing city has to offer."

I wasn't against one-night stands, and I wasn't one to turn down good sex, but a meaningless fling wasn't on my list at the moment. Now that I'd started my career and settled down, I was looking for a husband to start a family with. I was twenty-seven years old, and I'd already had my fun. "I'm sure I'll find a good lay soon. But it's hard to enjoy it when I know it'll never go any further."

"Please don't tell me you're one of those girls who needs to get married right away."

Her words ruffled my feathers and set me in a sour mood. Like she hadn't understood a word I said, she immediately labeled me. "I spent my youth partying and having a great time. I enjoyed that lifestyle, but now, I don't miss it. I'm ready to move on and settle down. I'm looking for Mr. Right, and I don't think there's anything wrong with that. Just like I don't think there's anything wrong with you for enjoying your freedom and sleeping with whomever you want." I was a nice person who kept my judgments to myself, but once people started pushing me around, I bared my fangs and my claws.

"Taylor, I didn't mean it that way. I just want you to loosen up."

I wasn't going to loosen up with Volt. He was ridiculously sexy, at a dangerous level, but he wasn't the man for me. Maybe one day he'd be the right man for someone else, but I knew I wasn't the woman who would make him realize that. "Have plans tonight?"

"Derek, Jared, and I are going bowling. You want to come?"

Did she always hang out with her brother? "Sure." I didn't have anything else to do.

"Great. We have even numbers for a team."

"Perfect."

***

Pizza and beer were on the table, and we took our turns bowling.

"You're up, Tayz." Jared winked.

"What did you just call me?" I grabbed the pink bowling ball from the machine because, you know, pink is my favorite color.

"Tayz," Derek said with a nod. "I like it."

"It suits you," Jared said. "Taylor is too long of a name."

"It has the same number of syllables as yours," I countered.

Jared started counting on his fingers. "Oh shit, she's right."

I tried not to smile before I turned to the alley and bowled. I hit nearly all the pins, but two remained.

"You got this, Tayz," Derek said. "Focus."

"Why are you cheering her on?" Natalie asked. "She's not even on your team."

44

"Well, she has a nice ass," Derek said with a shrug.

I rolled my eyes then bowled again. My aim was true, and I knocked down the two remaining pins. "I got a spare."

"She's a pretty good bowler," Derek said.

"No kidding," Jared said. "Maybe you two should switch." He moved out of the way just before Derek could punch him in the shoulder, and then he headed to the machine that spit out the balls.

I sat down, and Derek took the seat beside me.

"You know what?" He grabbed his beer but didn't take a drink. "I don't know too many girls who can pull off bowling shoes. But, girl, you make them look hot."

My lungs immediately tightened in preparation for a laugh and my chest heaved. Unable to keep it in, I let a loud laugh escape my lips. "Oh my god...that's the cheesiest line I've ever heard."

"But it's true. You make them look awesome."

"Well, thank you. What a nice compliment."

"So, you don't think Jared is a looker, right?"

The question gave me whiplash because I had no idea where it came from. "Uh, he's okay."

"But you aren't into him?"

"He's a nice guy, but no." The only person who gave me that queasy feeling in my stomach was Volt. The second I

45

laid eyes on him, the butterflies exploded from their chrysalises and soared. I wasn't sure what my problem was, but I was always attracted to the dangerous ones. We'd have our fun, and I'd get my heart broken—again and again. But I wasn't doing that this time. I wasn't looking for just any man—but the right man.

"Perfect. Because I'm totally single and looking for a lady." Whenever Derek said cheesy things, they didn't come off sleazy. He had an innate charm that made him harmless and actually cute.

"Thanks for the heads-up."

"And Jared is Natalie's man."

He is? "She told me she wasn't seeing anyone."

"Well, she's been in love with Jared forever, but he's not into her."

Every puzzle piece came together, and the full picture was revealed. "That's why she always hangs out with you…"

"It's sad, really," he said. "She makes it so obvious."

"Why isn't he into her?" Natalie was smart, beautiful, and fun to be around. What more could Jared want?

"I don't know. We grew up together, so I guess he sees her as a little sister."

"Does she know this?"

"No. She's totally naïve and thinks no one suspects her feelings for Jared. I've tried telling her a few times, but she just denies it. I feel bad for her because she just looks desperate."

I eyed Jared and Natalie in the seats across from us. He said something funny, and she leaned in and grabbed him by the bicep as she released a laugh that was real but also fake.

"See what I mean?" Derek followed my gaze. "She makes it obvious."

I'd have to help her. Friends didn't let friends look clingy and obsessive. "Thanks for letting me know."

"I just don't want you to waste your time with Jared." He leaned in and winked at me. "When you have Grade A, top choice meat right here."

His lines just got worse and worse. "I think you're cute and very sweet, but I'm not interested." There was no reason to be rude to him when all he'd ever been was nice, but I didn't want to lead him on either. He was a good-looking guy, but there was zero chemistry between us. I'd had more chemistry with cute dogs than this guy.

"That's fair," he said. "But maybe one day you'll change your mind."

I highly doubted that, but I wasn't going to shoot him down again. "Yeah. Maybe."

***

After Sara and I went shopping all day, I walked into my apartment and dropped all the bags of useless stuff on the ground. I got new shoes, a few sundresses that were on clearance, and a new pair of shades. Since I got my first paycheck, I decided to do something reckless with it.

My apartment was finally clean and organized, so I didn't have anxiety the second I walked in the door. My office was ready to go, and my Internet and cable were set up as well.

I got a text message from Natalie.

Hey, we're watching the Yankees game. Come over.

Come over where?

To Jared's place.

I really needed to tell her she was making a fool of herself—and I needed to do it soon. *I'll be there in twenty minutes.*

Perfect. See you then.

After I grabbed a six-pack of beer, I headed to his apartment. I had my phone this time, fully charged, and I used that to navigate to his place a few blocks away. I walked inside and greeted everyone.

48

"Just in time," Derek said. "It's the second inning." He grabbed the beer from my hands. "And you brought presents."

"I don't know if beer is considered presents."

"It is to me." He carried it into the kitchen.

"Hey." Natalie wore a Yankees jersey, and she welcomed me with a hug. "We've got pizza."

"I'm not hungry right now, but thanks. Just ate at Buffalo Wild Wings."

"Man, I love that place." Jared wore a Yankees jersey as well, and that's when I noticed Natalie was wearing the same exact one. "The teriyaki is the best—hands down. Who'd you go with?"

"My friend Sara."

"Who's Sara?" Natalie asked.

"She's my best friend. We've known each other since…" I couldn't even recall when we met. "Forever."

"I didn't know you knew anyone else in the city," Natalie said. "That's good you have someone to show you around."

"Yeah, she's great. She went through a breakup a while back, and she's still not over it quite yet." She was so devastated when he left her that I wasn't sure if she would ever recover. It'd been a year, and she still wasn't the same.

"I've been there, done that." Natalie grabbed a beer and handed it to me.

The guys were together on the couch, and I found myself disappointed when I didn't see Volt there. I refused to ask about him because that would just feed my interest. I already decided he was off the table and not worth the heartache, so I needed to stick to that decision. "Hey, I have an idea."

"What's up?" Natalie asked.

"How about the two of us go out tomorrow night? Just us." Not Jared and the rest of the guys.

"And do what?" she asked.

"Let's hit the bars and pick up some cute guys." Or at least she could pick up a cute guy. If she kept hanging around Jared, she would never find anyone else.

To my sadness, she glanced at Jared. "Uh—"

"It'll be fun. You're the one who said I needed to loosen up a little. You do too." I knew I should tell her what Derek said to me, but I couldn't bring myself to do it. Any woman would be humiliated if the guy she loved knew exactly how she felt and why she hung around all the time. I didn't want to say the words, so getting her to meet someone else was a better way of accomplishing my goal.

"Well, I—"

"Then it's settled."

"What's settled?" Volt walked into the apartment with a bottle of whiskey.

Right on cue, I squirmed. I felt the butterflies grow to the size of flying watermelons. My eyes immediately went to his, falling into the deep chasm of solid blue. I was trying to stop my friend from embarrassing herself, but I realized I was doing the same exact thing. I needed to get it together and not let him affect me like this—no matter how hot he was. "Natalie and I are going out tomorrow night. You know, picking up some tail."

"Yeah?" he asked with a playful grin. "Why don't the two of you just pick me up instead?" He walked past us and greeted the rest of the guys. "I've got whiskey to make manhattans."

"Sweet." Jared walked with him into the kitchen.

And there it is. The reminder I needed that he's just a player. Ready to sleep with anyone—no strings attached. No heart involved. No chance of a future.

No, thank you.

Why was I attracted to a man like that? Instantly, my lust died away, and I finally stopped thinking about him that way.

Which was a relief.

51

Jared and Natalie sat on one couch while I sat alone on the other. Derek just left to get more beers, and Volt hovered behind the back of the couch, sipping his manhattan slowly. I noticed he never had a beer—always hard liquor.

Volt eventually took the seat beside me and rested his glass on the end table. "Is this seat taken?"

"Nope." I didn't take my eyes off the TV, even though only a commercial was on. My fingers were wrapped around the Heineken I was drinking. The glass was cool and wet from the condensation, but the crisp temperature was welcome in the heat.

His gaze turned my way and was directed onto the side of my face. I could feel his stare, slowly burning with every passing second. "How was work this week?"

I wanted to push him away so my attraction would die for good, but when he was being a nice guy, it was difficult to keep my walls up. The second he came knocking, they were down. "Good. I'm not challenging my students enough, and I'm trying to figure out a way to change the curriculum without deviating from the quarterly lesson plans."

"Bristol Academy is a private school. You should be able to do pretty much whatever you want."

"Not really," I said. "Common Core is still being shoved down our throats."

His eyebrows rose, and somehow, even that was sexy.

"Bristol Academy accepts some federal funding for students who need scholarships to attend. Therefore, we're at the government's mercy."

"I didn't realize that."

"It's something they introduced this year. So, I have to stick with the lesson plans but keep them engaged at the same time."

"Have you tried Teach and Go?"

"What's that?"

"Have the students do literature-based activities in science, such as presentations, plays, interactive games, etcetera."

"But that's a problem because—" I halted in midsentence when I realized something I never noticed before. "How do you know so much about this stuff?" Did he have a kid in the school system? Were his parents teachers? He didn't strike me as an instructor himself, so that wasn't possible.

"I used to be a teacher." He said it nonchalantly, like this information wasn't a revelation. The whole time I'd been talking about my teaching experience, and he never mentioned his once. But then again, I never asked what he did for a living.

"Really?"

He nodded. "English and history at Northgate Assembly. It's a private school across town."

I couldn't hide the shock on my face. "Seriously?"

Instead of being offended, he had the grace to smile. "It's shocking, I know. But yes, it's true."

After I realized just how rude I sounded, I tried to backpedal. "I'm sorry...you just don't strike me as the teaching type."

"I was. I really liked it."

"You don't teach anymore?" The fact he took two women home and had a threesome like it was no big deal didn't make him a great role model. But then again, his personal life had nothing to do with the classroom, so it shouldn't matter.

"I stopped a few years ago."

"May I ask why?" Volt was suddenly fascinating to me—in a way he never was before.

"I opened an academic preparatory program in Manhattan. Its purpose is to prepare all students for their SATs. It's a glorified tutoring program, but in this case, the students actually see results. Our pass rate is the highest in the country. We have students from private schools and public schools."

"What's it called?"

"First Chance Education."

I'd heard of it before, but I couldn't recall where. "Wow. That's really cool." Sometimes tutors were geniuses, but they couldn't teach the material in a way the students could understand. Having a large tutoring program that truly prepared students at any academic level was amazing.

"Thanks. We have a lot of clients who can attest to its effectiveness. I've had students jump from a seven hundred to a twenty-one hundred. I'm not kidding."

With scores like that, he seemed to be talking about two different kids. "That's amazing." I'd always heard students fall behind because they didn't have the resources they needed. It was a story told too many times, and the ending was always the same. "How did that come about?"

He leaned back into the chair, his shirt fitting snugly against his powerful chest, and then took a drink. "It was an idea I had a long time ago. Students continued to stay behind after class because they needed extra help—usually with English. After a few weeks, I had more students than desks. It was becoming too much work on me and too stressful for the students because they weren't getting the attention they needed. That's how the concept was formed. And frankly, there are a lot of teachers out there who don't have their students' best interests at heart. They get tenured and stop caring. How is that fair to the students?"

When I told people I wanted to go into education with my chemistry degree, they told me it was a waste of potential. I could make a lot more money working in a lab or doing research. But none of those things ever interested me. I was always passionate about educating—and even more passionate about kids. To listen to someone share those same views at such a deep level was comforting.

"Over the course of a year, I put everything together, and once it was open, it immediately boomed with clients. I have a lot of tutors and specialists working one-on-one with students who needed the attention. After a few years, the business became a corporation, and we have new locations in major cities."

I couldn't wrap my mind around everything he said. "That's truly an incredible story."

"It's still hard to believe everything happened the way it did. It got off the ground pretty quickly, and it's a resource that's getting used thoroughly."

"Will you implement this service to low-income schools?"

"Eventually. My goal is to receive government funding so all students can afford to attend if they want to go."

Volt seemed like two different people. He was a cocky womanizer by night, and by day, he was an academic leader. I never would have guessed he was capable of this kind of contribution to society. But then again, I really didn't know him. "You don't teach anymore because you're tutoring?"

"No. I have employees who do that. I'm the CEO of the company."

What did that mean?

He must have seen the question in my eyes because he answered on his own. "I run the business side of things, but sometimes, I take students who aren't getting what they need. There can be conflicts between certain students and the tutors, and I have to step in. But that doesn't happen very often."

He dropped a lot of information on me in five minutes, and I needed more time to process it all. I would definitely Google the company the second I could—when he couldn't see me.

"I just realized how long I've rambled on for." A slight grin stretched his lips. The kind that didn't really affect his mouth but reached his eyes. "Sorry about that. When it comes to work, I have a lot to say."

"It's okay. I found it interesting."

He turned back to the TV and rested one ankle on the opposite knee. His hand rested on his thigh, his large fingers reaching out. His hands intrigued me in ways I couldn't describe. I couldn't stop picturing them on me, gripping my hips or spanning across my back. Those hands could do so much to me, and I wanted to borrow them for the evening.

***

I said my good-byes then walked out the door.

Volt came behind me then caught up to me, his footsteps in stride with mine. "Can I walk you home?"

"I'm okay. But thanks."

"Are you sure?" he teased. "You won't get lost?"

I shot him a glare, but I never meant anything less in my life. "I can manage. My phone is fully charged."

"Let me walk you home anyway."

"Really, it's fine—"

"I love walking in the city at night, so it's perfect." He placed his hands in his pockets and looked away like the conversation was finished. He was pushy in an antagonizing way. The kind that wasn't worth fighting over.

Now I was back to being annoyed with him.

We reached the sidewalk then walked together down the street. When the sun was gone, it wasn't nearly as warm. The humidity was still prevalent, moisture sticking to our skin in heavy drops. But the unrelenting heat had passed.

"Do you like the city so far?"

I kept my arms across my chest as we walked. "There's no other place like it."

"That didn't answer my question."

"I guess I'm still homesick."

"For Nashville?"

"Actually, Washington."

"Really?" he asked. "You made it sound like you haven't been there in years."

"But you never forget your first home." I missed the lush greenery, the endless trees that stood everywhere you looked, and the fact Mt. Rainier was in the background no matter where you were. "I'm sure I'll get used to this new place. And one day, I'll love it."

He kept a foot between us, but sometimes his elbow would brush across my shoulder.

"Have you lived here your whole life?"

"Born and raised."

"Could you imagine living anywhere else?"

"I don't know. Maybe."

"You know what I've noticed about New York?"

"Hmm?" He was nearly a foot taller than me, so when he turned my way, he always had to look down.

"People always seem to be in a hurry here, but they don't have anywhere to go." The statement was contradictory, but that didn't make it untrue. People were always rushing to get to the next place, even if they didn't need to be there. It was nonstop—always.

"I know what you mean."

"In Washington, it's slow. People take their time to get places because there's so much to see. I miss that sometimes."

"It sounds like your heart belongs in a small town."

"I won't make that decision until I give New York a chance." It was beautiful in its own way, with majestic skyscrapers and brilliant lights that burned as far as the eye could see. The people were just as much a part of the city as colors to a painting. Neither one could exist without the other. Despite the maze of roadways and underground tunnels, it was an efficient city, getting people where they needed to go in a timely manner. There was always something to treasure if you looked hard enough.

"It's good to keep an open mind."

We passed a few food and newspaper vendors before we finally made it to my block. "I can take it from here."

"Come on. Let me walk you to your door."

"I appreciate the sentiment, but I can get there on my own."

"I don't know... I'll never get the image of you trying to read that map out of my head."

I wanted to roll my eyes but couldn't manage it. "You'll never let that go, will you?"

"You looked pretty ridiculous."

Since he was going to get his way no matter what, I let it go. "You know what? I'd rather be weird than boring."

"That's very true. But I never said you were weird."

"Actually, I think you did."

He grinned at the memory. "Oh wait, you're right. But I meant it in a good way."

We entered my building then took the stairs to the fifth floor. He didn't need to accompany me all the way there, but at least the evening was almost over. "Where do you live?"

"On Park Avenue."

I wasn't familiar with the city to know exactly where everything was, but I knew where Park Avenue was—and I knew what kind of real estate it contained.

"It's close to the office, so that's a perk."

I was certain there were a lot more perks that came along with it.

He stopped when I reached my door and pulled out my keys. "Now I know exactly where to bring you when you get lost again."

I wanted to throw down my keys and stomp my foot. "Give me a break."

He chuckled but stopped when he realized it was really starting to bother me. "For what it's worth, I thought you were cute standing there in your giraffe shirt looking like another lost tourist."

"Cute?" *That word was in his vocabulary?*

"Yeah. Why do you think I stopped?"

I touched the metal in my fingertips and felt the strain from his gaze. His blue eyes were inviting and piercing at the same time. Sometimes, I thought he could swallow me whole, and other times, I thought he could spit me out after chewing me into tiny pieces.

He stared at me for nearly a minute, his eyes unreadable but his intention clear. I could feel the sting in the air, the rush just before a lover's kiss in a doorway. There was no explanation for my prediction. It was just a feeling deep in my gut, an instinct that told me something was about to happen.

I wanted it to happen.

But I also dreaded it.

I wanted my attraction to die like a wet fire and never rekindle. But every time I thought I turned cold, he brought me to life once more. He said sleazy things, but then he said something unbelievably sweet.

He took a step forward, closing the distance between us. At lightning speed, he dug his hand into my hair and pulled me in for a kiss. He took exactly what he wanted without thinking about it, like he had every right to. He didn't think twice about what I wanted or how it would make me feel. He just saw—and he conquered.

But I didn't want that.

I pulled away just before his lips could land on mine.

Stunned, he dropped his hand. The confusion on his face told me this never happened to him before—that a woman had never rejected him.

In that moment, I realized exactly what I wanted. I wanted a man's lust, but I also wanted his love. I wanted to be kissed like there was no one else he'd rather be kissing. I'd never been in love, and now that was all I wanted.

And I would never have that kind of future with Volt.

I was just some girl in that moment. I was a pair of lips he could kiss, and my bed was a mattress he could screw on. I was one of the many women he would forget the second the fun was over. He would see me again and pretend nothing happened at all, and then he would completely lose interest in me because he got exactly what he wanted.

"I'm not the kind of woman you're looking for." My eyes bored into his, showing him every ounce of sincerity I possessed. "And you aren't the kind of man I want."

Chapter Four

Volt

I hadn't stopped thinking about the final conversation we had in front of her door. The urge to give her a hot kiss came over me because of how pretty her eyes looked. And my body craved something sexy and fast.

But she turned me down.

She pulled away before my lips could even touch hers, and the repulsion in her eyes was painful. She stared at me like she wanted me, but she wanted nothing to do with me.

I didn't understand it.

I didn't put too much thought into my actions before I did them—at least, physically. If I wanted to kiss a woman, I kissed her. If I wanted something more, I took it. In that moment, I wanted her. I wanted that soft mouth on my body. I wanted to hear her moan as I moved inside her all night long. She was shy and gentle, but I wanted to bring out a new side in her.

But she didn't want me.

She said I wasn't the kind of man she was looking for.

And she wasn't the woman I wanted either.

What exactly did that mean?

I should just forget about it and move on with my life. I didn't know her, at least, not very well. We met two weeks ago, and she was still a stranger in my eyes. She would come and go like everyone I encountered.

But I couldn't stop thinking about her.

Was it guilt I felt? Something else?

I spent my week working at the office. Emails from concerned parents never died down, and I was holding interviews for new tutors. The interview process was daunting and suffocating. I couldn't take anyone who wasn't the best of the best, and I couldn't hire someone who didn't care about the success of the students. My livelihood depended on their compassion.

I started this business with the best intentions, but it inadvertently made me rich. Money wasn't important to me years ago, but once my heart was broken and my world was shattered, I relied on it to make me happy—just as I relied on all the women. That didn't make me a bad person. It was two birds with one stone.

I met a few beautiful women and brought them back to my apartment, but the sex was mediocre—and that was being nice. Something was holding me back—a dark conscience about the last conversation I had with a woman I hardly knew. When it didn't go away, I knew I needed to clear my head.

So I had to talk to her.

I knew where she worked because I was familiar with the campus. I'd interviewed there once before, and I was on good terms with the presiding principal.

Because he was my father.

I walked down the halls and eyed the clock in the corner. The bell was about to ring any moment, and the students of Bristol Academy would take off down the halls.

I reached her classroom and peered through the small window in the door. She wore a teal blue dress that was loose around her entire body, and nude pumps were on her feet. She dressed like a typical schoolteacher, nice but never intentionally looking sexy. Taylor wasn't the kind of woman I was used to, but I still found her attractive.

She just finished writing something on the board when the bell rang, and the kids dashed for the door. I stepped out of the way just in time before I was crushed by the throng of eager students.

The students filed into the hall, and soon it was a moving sea of kids in their school uniforms, dark blue vests with matching slacks. The girls wore the same thing, but I remember the skirts they used to wear in my youth. My hand had slipped underneath them too many times.

When the classroom was vacated, I walked inside.

Taylor sat behind her desk, her brown hair pulled over one shoulder. A coffee sat in the corner, probably cold and stale since it was brewed that morning. Packets of lab reports were stacked beside her, and the lack of red ink suggested she hadn't graded them yet.

When she didn't notice me, I walked farther into the room and approached her desk. That's when I noticed the scent of vanilla and oranges in the air. It was a strange combination, but the mixed scent was soothing. I recalled the scent when I leaned in to kiss her, but I didn't really get to enjoy it.

I still wore my suit because I just left the office, and the clothing was stifling. I'd wear a t-shirt and jeans every single day if I could get away with it. It was more comfortable than this blanket.

Taylor finally looked up when she realized she wasn't alone. "Sorry, didn't see you there—" She halted when she understood exactly whom she was talking to. Once the surprise melted away, disappointment replaced it.

And that made me feel worse.

Was she that upset because I tried to kiss her? She behaved as though I tried to steal her wallet or something.

She recovered from the shock and collected herself. "Hi. What brings you here?"

I scanned the walls of her classroom, seeing the different projects the students had made. Illustrations of black holes and their gravitational pull were plastered on every wall, and I couldn't help but be impressed by each student's interpretation. They even had calculations of the force projected along the orbit of a satellite. "I wanted to stop by and see your classroom. I like it." In the back was the lab equipment, and on the back shelf were small motors in the process of being constructed. Everything they were doing was far more advanced than I ever did as a student.

"Thank you. But I can't take the credit since the students made everything."

"You should take some credit. After all, it was your idea."

A red pen was held tightly in her fingertips. The tip pressed against the paper, and it started to bleed on the lab report.

I glanced at it. "You should put the cap on."

She saw what she did and quickly pulled the tip away. She capped it then tried to figure out what to do about the large pool of ink. "I should be able to make that into an A…"

I pulled up a chair and grabbed the pen. "Let me see." I carefully sculpted an A with the ink, making it look like a cheeky design Taylor was giving to her student.

69

Taylor studied it with approval. "You saved the day. You know how these parents can be...overanalyzing everything."

"All too well." In my experience, all of the single moms wanted to get too friendly with their child's teacher...and some of the single dads as well. I blew on the ink until it was dry then capped the pen.

Once that was done, it became awkward again.

Taylor placed the paper aside and cleared her throat, addressing the tension. "How can I help you, Volt?" Her gaze turned elsewhere, avoiding any kind of eye contact with me.

When I studied her from afar, she had the strongest sense of confidence, but once I was next to her, that strength evaporated. I couldn't tell if I intimidated her or made her hot. "I wanted to talk about what happened last week."

She finally turned her gaze on me, her hands moving to her lap. "There's nothing to talk about. Let's just forget about it and move on. I know I have."

Ouch. "I never meant to offend you."

"You didn't."

Hostility was emanating from her in high-voltage waves. I could feel it pierce my skin like tiny particles of radioactivity. "Look, I know I screwed up somehow, and I'm trying to make it right. Please meet me halfway."

"Trying to make what right?"

"Whatever this awkwardness is. What exactly did I do to bother you?" In that moment, I realized how strange my behavior was. I never let anyone get to me, bother me like this. But Taylor had me rethinking my actions and thoughts.

Taylor finally dropped her front, letting her walls come down enough to allow her vulnerability to shine through. "I just don't want to be treated the way you treat all the women in your life."

Her comment made me stagger. "What's that supposed to mean?"

"I'm not a woman you pick up in a bar, have a threesome with, and then never call again. And I don't want to be treated that way. I don't know what I did to give you the impression that I'm looking for an easy lay, but that's not on my roster."

"Whoa... What?" How did she know all of that? "Taylor, you don't even know me."

"I don't?" she asked. "So you're saying my assumption is inaccurate?" She challenged me with her look.

"Well…" Actually, it wasn't inaccurate at all. All I wanted was meaningless sex, cheap booze, and then to wake up the next day and do it all over again. When I kissed her on the doorstep, it was exactly what I wanted. I wasn't going to lie about it. "No, I guess you're right."

"And there's nothing wrong with that, Volt. I don't judge you for it. But I don't want to be on your target list."

Over the past year, I'd never made a pass at a woman and been turned down. Most of the time, they came on to me. I had regulars that stopped by at three in the morning, and I always had a full booty call list. I stopped keeping track of how many women I slept with because I didn't have enough fingers and toes. And my brain couldn't remember every name. I thought Taylor was pretty that night, and like with all the others before her, I went for it.

"I just don't want to be treated that way, that's all. Like you can kiss me whenever you want because you're entitled to my lips. I'm not a woman you can just grab and take. I'm a person."

I didn't truly feel guilty until that point—when she rammed the truth into me. "I'm sorry." I never apologized, even when I knew I was in the wrong, but the apology escaped my lips automatically. "I wasn't thinking."

When she saw the sincerity in my eyes, her gaze softened. "It's okay. I didn't mean to be so harsh. I don't mind being kissed when I'm on a date or when the guy walks me to my door...but I knew that wasn't the kind of kiss I wanted. I didn't feel like a person—more like an object."

That was exactly how I viewed her, so I couldn't blame her for drawing that conclusion. "You had every right to feel that way." I hadn't misread her that night. In fact, I hadn't bothered reading her at all. I just took the shot because I assumed she would want me—like an asshole. "I hope you'll accept my apology."

"Of course I do." Her gentle spirit had finally returned, and she actually gave me a smile. It wasn't a forced grin, the kind you knew was fake. This one was genuine—and it was beautiful.

"Good." The weight finally left my shoulders, and I could breathe again. "I hope we can move on from this and forget about it."

"Maybe we can be friends."

"Friends?" I asked, unsure what that word even meant. Friendships were rare for me, and the only ones I had were with men. And even then, I wasn't close to them. I didn't share every aspect of my life with anyone. In fact, I never told anyone anything. Derek and I used to be closer, and he'd still claim I'm his best friend, but I didn't feel the same way anymore. Solitude was my only friend now.

"Yeah," she said with a chuckle. "Do you need to brush up on your vocabulary?"

"I don't have many friends."

"You seem to be pretty close to the guys." She grabbed the pen and slowly spun it in her fingertips. That's when I noticed different planets of the solar system were painted on each of her nails, and her thumb displayed a comet. It was childish—but cute.

"We hang out." But that was the extent of it.

"That's pretty sad… I wish I had more friends, and you don't want any friends. Ironic."

That did make me sound like a sad person—pathetic. "You're actively looking for new friends?"

"And that's pretty hard in a big city like this. People are always coming and going all the time. No one has the chance to stop for a cup of coffee."

"Well, I can be your friend. And I'll take you out for a cup of coffee."

"Really?" she asked. "You expect me to take a pity invite?"

Now that the suggestion was out in the open, I didn't dread it. In fact, it might be nice. "You want to be friends or what? This offer expires."

She chewed her bottom lip as she tried to come to a decision.

I glanced at my watch. "Time is ticking."

"Okay. But only if you buy me a scone."

"That's what you want?" I asked with a laugh. "A scone?"

"Orange and cranberry. They're my favorite."

She reminded me of a child excited to visit Disneyland for the first time. An innocent smile was on her face, and her eyes were lit up like Christmas Tree Lane. "I'll buy you whatever you want."

***

We walked into The Muffin Girl and stood in the line that wrapped around the store. Taylor stood beside me and peered into the glass windows that displayed all the baked goods inside. There were pies, cookies, and assorted pastries.

"Is this place always so busy?" She pulled her hair over one shoulder and showed off her earrings. They were small globes hanging from silver hoops. Her look was geeky, but she somehow made it look cool.

"Yeah. But it's the best bakery in town. If I'm going to show you around the city, we have to make a stop here."

"Wow. I'm excited." She pressed her face to the glass and eyed a chocolate and strawberry scone. "That looks good."

I didn't have much of a sweet tooth. I drank my coffee black and skipped cake at birthday parties. I was boring and predictable. "Then get it."

"But that blueberry muffin looks good..." She pointed to the basket of muffins on the lower shelf.

"Good thing this line is long so you'll have time to make a decision."

She chewed on her nails, still indecisive.

The corner of my mouth upturned in a grin. "You have the perfect personality for a teacher."

"Yeah?" she asked. "I would say thank you, but I'm not entirely sure what that means."

"You're playful—not stiff. Kids respond to that." I only taught for five years before I opened First Chance Education. But in that amount of time, I was able to understand what students really needed from their instructors—and the type of people they responded to. I knew Taylor would leave a lasting impression on them even though I'd never set foot in her classroom during the school day.

"I don't know about that. I'm having a difficult time getting them to listen."

"Really?" We moved farther up the line, talking loudly over the chatter of the bakery. Blenders were going off, and the cash register kept beeping with new orders. The kitchens were operating at full speed, toasting bread for sandwiches and making new pastries.

"Yeah. I'm not sure what the problem is. At first, I thought they were unchallenged. I gave them some complicated projects, but that didn't fix the problem. I'm not sure if it's the Common Core standards that's throwing them off..."

"Interesting." Private schools tended to have obedient students, especially those at Bristol Academy. Taylor's experience was rare—and strange. "Do they know you're a new teacher?"

"I never said I was."

Students had a way of finding the truth—no matter how hard you tried to hide it. "Kids talk."

"Even then, I don't know what difference it makes."

"When students know you're new, they like to test you—see how far you'll go."

"Ha. I'd like to see them try." We moved up the line some more, and she examined the pecan cookies in the window. "Dude, those look bomb."

What did she just say? "Did you just call me dude? Wait, back up. Did you just use bomb as an adjective?"

She pointed inside the window. "Do those not look like the most delicious cookies you've ever seen?"

I shrugged. "I'm not much of a sweet tooth."

She cringed. "Just when I thought we could be friends."

I stared at the back of her head and felt that old smile tug at my lips.

We reached the register and ordered our coffees. After the man took our order, he said, "Anything else?"

"Yeah," Taylor answered. "Can I have...?" She fidgeted with her hair as she tried to make a decision. "Can I have the chocolate strawberry scone?"

"Sure—"

"No, I want the blueberry muffin instead."

He typed it into the register. "Okay."

"Actually, I want a scone. That's what I came here for anyway."

The cashier hid his irritation poorly and fixed the previous entry before making the new one. "Anything else?"

Taylor had her hair wrapped around her hand at this point. "Actually, I want a pecan cookie."

Now the guy looked like he wanted to kill her. "Are you sure?"

Taylor flinched at the threat in his voice. "Uh…"

As entertaining as this was, I had to intervene. "Give her two of everything and a dozen of those pecan cookies."

"What?" Taylor asked. "I don't need all of that."

"You can take it home with you."

"But—"

"Ring us up, please." I handed over my card to speed things along. There were thirty people in line behind us.

The guy didn't hesitate as he grabbed my card and slid it through the machine. "Here's your receipt and have a good day." He grabbed a white paper bag and shoved all of the pastries inside before he handed it to Taylor.

She had to carry it with two hands because it was so heavy.

I carried our coffees to a table outside and took a seat in the small patio enclosure near the alleyway. Picnic tables were lined on the small grassy area, and umbrellas were erected to keep the sun out of our eyes.

Taylor sat across from me and set the heavy bag on the table. It made a noticeable thump. "That guy must think I have no self-control."

I sipped my coffee and watched the people pass. "And he would be right."

"I didn't need all of these."

"Take them home and eat them later."

"You didn't have to buy them all. I could have paid for them."

"I didn't mind." I sipped my coffee again. "So, which one are you going to have? Or is that a dangerous question to ask?"

She opened the bag and peered inside. "I don't know... I'm leaning toward the muffin."

"It's what the bakery is known for."

"Then I'm sold." She pulled out the blueberry muffin and picked small crumbles from the top before popping them into her mouth. The second the first bite was in her mouth, her eyes rolled into the back of her head. "This is off the hook."

Off the hook? "Is that how you talk when you're in the classroom?"

"I would if I were eating this muffin."

I chuckled then snatched a piece and popped it into my mouth.

"Hey. I thought you didn't have a sweet tooth."

"Well, you wore me down." I quickly chewed it and swallowed.

"What do you think?"

I slowly nodded. "You know what? This really is off the hook and da bomb."

She covered her mouth and laughed, almost dropping her muffin. "I didn't say *da*. You added that word all on your own."

"And it's fitting." I took another piece of the muffin and ate it.

She pushed the enormous bag toward me. "Have whatever you want. There's plenty to go around."

"I'd rather split this one with you. I can't eat a whole one by myself."

She pressed her lips together like she was trying not to laugh. "Sorry, you sound like a girl."

"A masculine one."

"You have to keep your body under six percent body fat?" she teased.

I immediately smiled because I liked the fact she guessed so accurately. "Actually, yeah."

She rolled her eyes. "Not my style. I love food too much."

"Your body doesn't imply it."

"Why do you think I always wear loose dresses?" She gave me a knowing look, like she defeated me in an imaginary battle. "I've got a tummy and some serious thighs."

I didn't believe that. I could admit she wasn't a supermodel, but she still had a great rig. "Women are always hard on themselves. Not sure why."

"Now that I've seen the type of women you go home with, I know exactly why. Men want a perfect woman who eats like a pig but doesn't gain a pound anywhere. They have to hold their liquor just like a man, but they have to be a classy drunk as they do it. I can't do either of those things so I'll never be the perfect woman. But you know what? I'm fine with that. I still get that D from time to time." She waggled her eyebrows before she sipped her coffee.

I forgot about the conversation we were having momentarily because I was absorbed with the playful look on her face. Now that she cooled her jets, she was actually fun—and funny. "What's your type?"

"Type of what? Ice cream?"

"Sure. But that's not what I was asking."

"Mint chip," she answered. "And what were you really asking?" She picked at her muffin until nothing but the wrapper was left.

"Your type of man." Because I clearly wasn't it.

"I don't really have a type." She covered her lips with her fingertips as she continued talking. "I'm not picky."

"Come on, you must have an idea."

She wiped her hands together to dissolve all the crumbs from her fingertips. "Well, I like guys who don't take themselves too seriously. You know, they can make fun of themselves. I like someone who's honest and genuine. And they have to make me laugh. If he's not my best friend, then it'll never work."

Whenever I asked that question to women, I never got that response. "But what about their features?"

"I don't care about that. Cute is cute."

"There must be some physical attraction to a relationship. Otherwise, it'll never last. One partner will cheat. It's a guarantee."

"Well, I do value physical attraction. But it's definitely not the most important factor in a relationship. I want a nice guy. You know, someone trustworthy."

There was no such thing. "Guys aren't trustworthy. They're all dogs."

"Not all of them." She grabbed a cookie from the bag.

"Yes. All of them."

She broke off a piece and looked at me. "Does that include you?"

I'm the biggest dog of all. "Absolutely." I should've felt ashamed for saying that, but I wasn't. I'd been hurt so irrevocably that I was never the same. My heart disappeared that night, and I never found it again. My friendships were never the same because I couldn't even trust my buddies. All I wanted was to screw because feeling meaningless pleasure mixed with nothing was better than feeling heartbroken all the time.

Taylor didn't take a bite of her cookie because all of her attention was directed at me. "I don't believe that."

"I kissed you, didn't I?" Just an hour ago, she was pissed at me for it.

"You aren't a dog for kissing me. When I pulled away, you stopped. A real asshole would have pressed me against the door and forced the kiss to happen against my will. So, no, you don't fall into that category."

She didn't know the truth. She suspected I spent my nights screwing anything that moved, but she didn't understand just how bad it was. I'd broken hearts and beds. I'd broken promises and plans. I was entirely selfish and only cared about myself. There was no way to misinterpret what I really was.

"When I was lost in the city, you helped me. You could have turned around and walked away, but you didn't."

"That doesn't make me a good person." Not by a long shot.

"It doesn't make you a bad person either."

The conversation was beginning to make me fidget. I took a long drink of my coffee just so I would have something to do.

"Is there a reason why you are the way you are?"

Like I would ever tell her. "No."

"You don't do relationships at all?"

"No." I'd had this conversation with a lot of women, and my same answers were making me feel numb.

"Is it because you haven't found the right woman yet?"

I laughed because her question was just stupid. "I'm a permanent bachelor because I like it that way. I like sleeping around and making the rounds in different beds with different women. Sometimes, I like two girls at once, even three. I have a specific palate, and that's just how I am. I don't apologize for it, and I never will."

She studied my face like she still didn't believe me. "It's interesting."

"What?" *My sex life was interesting?*

"You're so compassionate when it comes to young minds and education. You started an entire company with the intention of helping people. When you talk about your years as a schoolteacher, it's with fondness. But then you have this side of you...which is dark and twisted. It's so contradictory that I don't believe what you're saying. There is a reason why you're this way—I just don't have a clue what it is."

Instead of being impressed by her observation, I was ticked. I didn't want people to read me, to analyze my behavior and try to understand me. Once, I was an open book with no secrets. But now I was closed off from everyone because I was ashamed of my stupidity. I let someone trick me, mislead me, and I allowed her to make a complete fool out of me. My walls reached the sky, and I didn't like it when people tried to tear them down.

Taylor must have known she crossed a line. She felt it in the air and shifted her weight slightly, as if she was trying to get away from it. "I offended you. I'm sorry."

I stared at her without blinking, unable to control my rage and irritation. "Don't try to figure me out. Don't analyze me. I hate that."

"Okay."

"Otherwise, our friendship is done."

Instead of looking away, she met my gaze. There wasn't a trace of fear or intimidation. "You got it."

I wanted to storm off, but something was keeping me there. I liked the way my life was, how sheltered and shadowed it was. When someone risked that and peeked through the clouds, it bothered me. But yet, I remained.

She opened the bag and pulled out the other blueberry muffin. She handed it to me, giving me a smile that would cheer anyone up. "My peace offering." She grabbed my hand and placed it within my fingers.

It was hard to stay mad when she did something so innocent and cute. I felt the soft muffin in my grasp before I took a bite. "Better not be poisoned."

"Oh, no. I would never poison my *friend*."

Chapter Five

Taylor

Sara shoved her hand inside the paper bag and pulled out a pecan cookie. "I've eaten ten of these. I can't stop."

"They're good, huh? I went to this bakery downtown, and it was amazing."

"Which one?"

"It's called The Muffin Girl."

"Oh, I've heard of that place. There's another location next to my work."

"I didn't know it was a chain." It seemed too cozy to be corporate.

"I don't think it is. It's just expanded."

That part didn't surprise me. The place had a warm atmosphere, and it smelled so good that they should have an air freshener in that scent.

"Go there with anyone?" she asked.

"Yeah, a friend."

Sara had become a couch potato over the past year. She didn't want to go out or do anything. When we did hang out, it was at my place or hers. "A guy friend?" she asked hopefully.

"Yeah, actually. But he really is just a friend."

"Is he hot?"

So hot it should be illegal. "He's definitely a looker. But I don't see him like that."

"How can you not?"

"He's not my type. You know, he's the manwhore type."

"Oh…gotcha." She nodded like she understood that all too well. "Steer clear of him. You'll think he'll change for you, but he never will. When a man has too many options, he never sticks with one thing."

I suspected Volt's behavior arose from a deeper level than indecision, but I didn't dwell on it. He was fiercely private, and I wasn't going to stick my nose where it didn't belong. "I really like being his friend anyway. I get a lot more enjoyment out of it than if I were to sleep with him."

"He's gay?"

I laughed. "No, definitely not. But he shows a more humane side of himself when I'm off-limits."

"Why do guys act so strange once pussy is involved?"

I shrugged. "I think that's a question women will ask until the end of time."

"Yeah, probably," she said with a chuckle.

The Bachelorette was playing on the TV, and I just finished a game of Candy Crush on my phone. "You wanna go out this weekend? Hit up a bar and find some cute guys?"

Like always, she sidestepped the question. "Nah. I have a long week."

I tried not to roll my eyes. I wanted to be there for my friend while she went through a hard time, but it'd been a year. She should be over it by now. And I needed to go out and mingle. Maybe the perfect guy was out there—waiting for me just as I was waiting for him.

***

"Back left pocket." Jared hit the ball, and it rolled right into the hole. "Boom."

"Shut up, asshole," Derek said. "Get on with your turn."

Jared moved around the table until he found his next shot.

Natalie stared at his ass, practically drooling.

I hoped no one else noticed. "Hey, Nat."

She snapped out of her trance. "What's up?"

"Let's go barhopping tomorrow," I said. "Meet some sexy dudes."

"Tomorrow?" she asked. "Well, I—"

"Perfect," I said. "We'll meet at The Lion and The Spider—"

"The Lion and The Snake." Like always, Volt appeared out of the shadows and graced us with his unexpected presence.

91

"Whatever." I rolled my eyes and nudged him in the side. "She knew what I meant." When my elbow connected with his stomach, I felt a solid slab of concrete. It actually hurt my arm a little.

"I doubt it," he said. "And what will you two be doing there?"

"We're going to meet our future husbands." I held my beer in my hand and watched Natalie's expression. She definitely wasn't into the idea.

"Your future husband?" Volt asked. "In a bar?"

"What's wrong with that?" I asked.

"You aren't going to meet a good guy in a bar."

"Okay, cupid," I said. "Where will I meet a good guy, then?"

He adopted a stumped expression. "I don't know... The library?"

I turned back to Natalie. "Ignore him. Let's go."

"What about dating apps?" he asked. "Tons of chicks use those."

"I don't want to do that," I said. "I'm sure it's fine, but I want to meet someone organically."

"Or there's Tinder." He grinned from ear to ear. "I speak very highly of that app."

I nudged him in the stomach again.

This time, he grabbed my arm and dragged me into him. "You wanna play a round?"

When I was this close to him, I smelled his familiar scent, the masculine tone mixed with body soap. "A round of what?"

"Pool." Without waiting for my answer, he pulled me to our own table and grabbed two pool cues. "Do you know how to play?"

I glared at him—venomously.

"I'll take that as a yes." He racked the balls and set them up on one side of the table. "Break, sweetheart."

"Her name is Tayz," Derek called from the other table. "Get it right, bro."

"Tayz?" He turned to me, a permanent grin on his face.

I approached the table and positioned my stick. "Yes. I'm cool like that."

"Your students call you that?"

I lined up the shot then slammed the stick hard into the cue ball. It slammed into the triangular formation and sent the balls flying everywhere, sinking a solid into the corner pocket. "No. But that would be fun if they did."

He eyed the balls on the table with a look of approval. "Where did you learn to play like that?"

I shrugged. "I'm a natural." I prepared for the next shot but missed.

"But not humble." He leaned over the table, his back perfectly straight and etched with muscle. His thick arms stabilized the shot before he struck. Two stripes went into the same pocket. "Now, I'm a natural, but I'm not going to say it."

"You just did."

"No. I *showed* I'm a natural. Big difference." He moved to a different spot on the table and prepared for the shot. He was right beside me, so when he was about to hit the ball, I tickled him in the side.

His stick veered off to the right, and he knocked the cue ball forward, missing all the other balls. He laughed then jumped away. "Someone's a sore loser…"

"I'm just making it more challenging for you. You know, since you're *so* good."

"Well, maybe I'll make it challenging for you." He gripped his pool stick by his side with a threatening look in his eyes.

"You wouldn't dare."

"I guess we'll find out."

I walked around the table and tried to figure out what shot I was taking next.

Volt remained on the other side, trouble written all over his face. His dark eyes hinted at his mischievous nature, and the slight smile on his lips was even more threatening.

"You better not come over here."

He held the pool stick in one hand and shoved his other hand into his pocket, but his fake hostility didn't diminish.

I finally found a shot I wanted to take, and the second I set up, he made his move. "Touch me and you die."

His fingers moved into my ribs, and he tickled me fiercely.

I laughed and got the attention of everyone else in the bar. I dropped my pool stick because I was frantically trying to get away. "Let me go."

"Tell me I'm the pool king."

"What?" I said as he continued to tickle me.

"I'm the pool king—say it."

"That doesn't even sound cool."

He tickled me harder. "Say it."

"Fine. You're the pool king." And I lost all self-respect for myself for saying it.

"Good girl." He patted my rear then stepped up to the table to take a shot.

"Hey, it's my turn."

"Damn, I was hoping you wouldn't notice."

"I always notice when someone's trying to take me for a ride." I lined up the shot and felt my shooting star earrings swing from my lobes. I kept the shot stabilized as I jabbed the stick into the cue ball. But I didn't sink any of the others.

"Tsk...tsk. Don't be too hard on yourself. You're playing with a master, after all."

I wanted to chuck the cue ball right at his face.

"So, what are you and Natalie doing at The Lion and The Spider?" He gave me a teasing grin, taking another jab right after the previous one.

"We're going to find some hot dates."

He lined up his shot then sank another ball. "What did I tell you? You aren't going to find a good guy in a bar."

"Says who?"

"Anyone with a brain. Men only go to bars because they know they can pick up women for a fun night. Trust me, I know about this stuff."

"You can't make that assumption for all men."

"Yes, I can." He took another turn but missed.

When it was my turn, I stepped up to the plate. "You can't make a generalization like that. I'm sure there are tons of men who go out every night hoping to find a woman they can have a meaningful relationship with."

His only reaction was a laugh. "Maybe in a Disney movie."

"It's true."

"Every guy is looking for an easy lay. And if you aren't an easy lay, they'll pass you by."

I didn't believe that. I refused to believe that.

"I'll take you out and give you some help."

"What?" I blurted.

"I'll go out with you to the bars, and I'll find you a good guy. But I'll also prove my point that there aren't any."

"I can get my own dates. But thanks."

"Come on," he said. "You can pick out a girl for me."

"Eww," I said. "I'm not picking your sex buddy."

"You can watch us too, if you want." He waggled his eyebrows.

"I'm about to barf on this pool table. And I suspect it'll be really hard to clean."

"Not our problem." He landed another shot then moved to a different spot on the table. "So, what do you say?"

"I'm supposed to go with Natalie."

"Can't you go with her some other time?"

I glanced behind me and saw Natalie and the guys absorbed in their game. They weren't paying any attention to us.

Volt watched my actions, growing more interested.

I came around the table and stood by his side. "I'm trying to get Natalie to go out and meet someone."

"Why?"

"Because..." I nodded toward Jared.

He followed my gaze and turned back to me. "Because?"

"She's into Jared, but he's not into her. She looks desperate, you know? I can't let her make an idiot out of herself."

He shrugged. "I don't see how that's your problem."

"She's my friend."

"But you haven't known her long."

"So? That doesn't matter."

"I guess I could sleep with her." He shrugged like he was trying to be humble when doing something heroic.

I glared at him.

"What?" he asked innocently.

"You will not sleep with her."

"Why not?" he countered.

"Because she's your friend. You don't sleep with your friends."

"I know, but you want to help her out, right?"

"I want her to move on and have a relationship with someone else. A night of hot sex won't change anything."

He grinned like he was remembering a fond memory. "You obviously haven't had any hot sex, then."

"Yes, I have." I sounded far more defensive than I meant to, and I knew that was because all I'd ever had was mediocre sex. Sometimes I would get off, but most of the time, I wouldn't. I wasn't sure if it was the size of the ship or the motion of the ocean. But whatever it was, it wasn't working. Maybe it was me. *Geez, I hoped not.*

Volt smiled like he saw right through my words. "I'm always at your disposal if you need to let off some steam."

"Don't be gross."

"Sex isn't gross."

"It is with you."

"What's that supposed to mean?" he countered.

"You probably have chlamydia or something."

"I always use condoms, and I get tested regularly—I'm good."

"Even so, I'm not interested."

"Whatever," he said. "When you change your mind, just let me know."

I'd never change my mind. I liked him much more as a friend than a fuck buddy. I'd never sink that low. "Don't hold your breath."

"So, when are we doing this?"

"Doing what?" I hadn't agreed to anything.

"Finding your Prince Charming."

"I never said I was looking for Prince Charming. I just want a nice guy."

"In New York City, there's no such thing. Maybe you should go back to Washington."

I would if I could.

"You can come so I can prove how wrong you are."

"And how will you prove that?"

"I'll find a nice guy."

He chuckled. "Good luck with that."

"I'm serious."

"I'm sure you are." He walked around the table like he owned the place and everyone in it. His arrogance was charming at times, but now it was just annoying.

"My priority is getting Natalie out of her funk."

"She's not your problem, Tayz. If she wants to follow a guy around, that's her right."

"But I think she'd feel differently if she knew everything."

"Then tell her."

I couldn't do that. She would be so humiliated she would never recover. "I think it's easier if I just find someone else for her. She's smart, beautiful, and really sweet. She deserves a man who notices her as much as she notices him."

He shook his head then lined up his next shot. "Why can you go out with her but not with me?"

"Why do you want to go out with me so bad?" I countered.

"If I walk in with a woman, all the others will fight for me more."

"That doesn't make any sense." He should be off-limits.

"Women like a man they can't have."

That's disgusting. "I would never go after a man in a relationship."

"The rest of the world doesn't share your morality."

Volt had a strange outlook on life. He thought everyone was innately evil and there were no good people in the world, which was strange since he molded the minds of young people and prepared them for the world. He told me not to analyze him, but I couldn't help it. I wanted his secrets, answers to unspoken questions. "I think most people do."

He shook his head in response.

"Friday night, then?"

"I'm down." He hit another ball and sank it into the corner. All that remained were the eight ball and some of my own solids. "After that, we're going to teach you how to play pool—because you suck."

Chapter Six

Volt

Somehow, without even realizing it, Taylor became my friend.

When I first met her, I thought she was some awkward woman, and then I got to know her better and I wanted to have a one-night stand. But then she told me off and demanded the respect I didn't give her.

And boom! We were friends.

I'd never had a friend that was a girl. There was always sex involved, and if sex couldn't be had, there were some decent hand jobs. Natalie and I were friends, in a way. But I viewed her as Derek's sister most of the time.

After I got off work, I was walking to my apartment when Taylor texted me.

The Muffin Girl.

She usually sent me these cryptic text messages, and it was my job to figure out what she was trying to say. *Now?*

She sent an emoji of a blueberry muffin.

That wasn't too complicated to decipher. *On the way.*

She sent me a picture she took of herself. She was shoving the entire muffin into her mouth like a snake that was swallowing a mouse whole.

I chuckled and typed a reply. *Damn, that's sexy.*

Then she sent me an emoji of a hand flipping me off.

I laughed then shoved my phone into my pocket. I walked to the bakery and spotted her sitting outside at one of the picnic tables. She wore a long pink dress with a purple cardigan over it, her usual classroom attire. She looked like a stereotypical schoolteacher, classy but also a little nerdy. Her long brown hair was in curls, and she wore a large sun hat to keep the sun out of her eyes. She looked like she belonged at the beach—minus the cardigan. "When you start a dating profile, you should make that picture as your profile picture."

"So no one will be interested in me?"

"No one is going to be interested in you anyway."

She gave me a playful kick under the table.

"What's this?" I spotted the coffee and muffin on my side of the table.

"I figured you didn't want to wait in line."

"But how did you know I would come?"

She shrugged. "You don't have any friends besides me, so what else would you be doing?"

She made me smile bigger when I didn't think it was possible. "Touché."

"So, how was your day?"

"Pretty boring. I was in my office the entire time."

"Looking at porn? Or working?"

I chuckled. "I don't watch porn."

She stopped in midbite and gave me an incredulous expression.

"I really don't." I had no reason to lie—especially to her.

She looked at me like she didn't believe a word I said.

"Why would I watch porn when I'm getting laid all the time? Believe me, I don't need my hand for anything besides writing with a pen."

"I guess that's true," she said. "For a second, I thought you were lying because all guys watch porn. Shit, I even watch porn."

I was about to grab my muffin but stopped when I heard what she said. I immediately pictured her lying in bed with her hand between her legs. Her bedroom was dark, and the light from her computer displayed her flushed cheeks and parted lips. She breathed deeply, moaning as she watched some man pound into his partner. Her fingers worked her pussy aggressively, bringing her to the edge of a powerful climax.

"Volt?"

I zoned out for a moment there, and I wasn't sure how much time had passed. "Huh?"

"You just got a weird look on your face."

Because I was picturing her masturbating—and I got a hard-on from it. "I realized I forgot something at the office."

Thankfully, she bought my excuse. "Work has been a struggle lately."

"What's up?"

"I'm having a hard time getting the kids to pay attention. The other day, I was lecturing and spotted them exchanging notes in the reflection of the whiteboard."

"Did you say anything?"

"No. I didn't see the point." She picked at her muffin. "I know kids aren't going to be soldiers, but I expected more from them."

"Do you hold them accountable for bad behavior?"

"Yes. When I'm not pretending I don't see it..."

"Are the assignments too much or too little?"

"I thought I wasn't challenging them enough, so I increased the workload and increased the difficulty of the content, but it doesn't seem to have made a difference. They just aren't interested—for whatever reason. These kids are future diplomats, physicians, and rocket scientists. I just assumed they would be eager to learn."

When it came to the culture of a classroom, there wasn't any specific factor that determined how it would flow. "In my first year, the kids gave me a hard time. They knew I was a brand-new teacher who was learning the ropes as I went. But when I became the wrestling coach, it really smoothed things over."

"What does that have to do with anything?"

"I became a member of their community. I was a face they saw outside the classroom, and I had a respectable position within the school community. The more involved you are with the school, the more respect they'll give you."

"Never thought about it that way."

"It really makes a difference."

"But what could I get involved in?" she asked. "I'm already teaching all day and preparing lesson plans at night when I go home. How would I squeeze in another activity?"

"Maybe you could do a club or something."

"Eh." She shrugged with disinterest.

"Academic decathlon?"

"God, no. That will take up all of my time."

"Did you play sports in high school?"

"Does sunbathing count?"

I laughed when I pictured her laying out on the school lawn. "I don't think so."

"I guess I could find something… I just don't want to take extra time out of my day. I have a million things to do as it is."

"It'll help you get tenured quicker."

"It will?" she asked.

"Yeah. The more courses you teach and the more involved you are in the school, the more likely it is they'll want to keep you indefinitely."

She stared at me with impressed eyes. "Good thing I have a friend who can share all of his secrets with me."

"I don't know if they're secrets, but I'm a fountain of knowledge."

"Well, I'll look into it tomorrow and see if there's something I can get involved with. So these brats will start listening to me."

"I can sit in if you'd like."

"Sit in?" she asked.

"You know, observe your class for a week and analyze it. It might be helpful."

"You would do that?" she asked incredulously.

"Why not?" We were friends, right?

"That would help me out so much. I need an expert to point out what I'm doing wrong and what I'm doing right." She clutched her chest in gratitude. "Thank you so much."

"It's really not a big deal. And I'll definitely point out every little thing you do wrong." I took a bite of my muffin and winked.

She was so grateful for my offer that she didn't seem to care. "I'll get it cleared with administration."

"Don't worry about it. I'll take care of it." It'd be a lot quicker if I did it on my end. I knew all the right people in all the right places, including my father.

"Well, thanks for helping me out. I'm sure you have more important things to do."

"I really don't mind. Besides, you bought me a coffee and a muffin. I have to repay you."

"I'm repaying you for buying that enormous bag of pastries that I didn't need."

"Did you eat them all?"

She looked away and avoided the question.

"Seriously? You ate all of that?"

"Not in one day," she snapped. "And my friend ate some too."

"Your friend? I thought I was your only friend."

She threw a crumb at my face. "No, you aren't. She and I have been friends forever."

"Is she cute?" I was always looking for new tail.

"She's not your type."

"Is she a man?"

"She got out of a relationship recently, and she hasn't mended yet."

"Even better. I can help her get over her ex."

She rolled her eyes. "I'm keeping her away from you."

"Now that she's forbidden, I want her more…"

"Are you five?" she asked incredulously.

I shrugged. "I'd say I'm sixteen—immature and just hit puberty."

"You hit the nail right on the head." She finished her muffin then downed her coffee. "Well, I have to get going. I have shit to grade."

"Their work is literally shit?"

"Unfortunately." She patted me on the shoulder and walked off.

I craned my neck uncomfortably and watched her walk away. She swayed her hips as she walked, and her brown hair bounced as she moved. Her ass was decipherable in the dress, and I stared at it until she was out of sight.

***

When I picked her up on Friday night, she was wearing one of her schoolteacher dresses. It was loose around her body and had bees all over it. She wore a necklace with a dangling beehive and sandals were on her feet.

"You're going to change, right?"

"What's wrong with this?" She looked down at herself, having no idea what I was talking about.

"We're going to a bar. That's not how chicks dress."

"But I don't want to wear a miniskirt and a tube top. I can't pull it off."

"What the hell are you talking about?" I checked out her ass the other day, and it was perfect.

"I'm twenty-seven years old. I'm ancient."

"And I'm thirty-two. What does that matter?"

"I can't dress like a twenty-one-year-old anymore. I don't have the body for it."

It took all my strength not to roll my eyes. "That's the biggest tub of horseshit I've ever heard of."

"It's true. Plus, I'm a schoolteacher."

"That means you can't have a life outside the classroom? You think you're going to run into one of your students?"

She crossed her arms over her chest, giving me a pissy look.

"Let me prove it to you." I walked into her apartment without being invited and immediately headed for the bedroom I assumed belonged to her.

"Please, come in…" She shut the door and followed me.

I opened her closet door and peered at my options. Honestly, there weren't many.

"Please, go through my things…"

Her clothes were carefully coordinated by color and season. The back of the door held a jewelry hook, where her necklaces of the universe and animals hung. On the top shelf were her shoes, most of them sandals.

I was looking into an old woman's closet.

"I don't even own anything sexy, so you're wasting your time."

I moved her clothes over the rack and quickly browsed through them, searching for something somewhat sexy.

"You're wasting your time." She sat on the edge of the bed behind her, her arms crossed.

Tucked away in the back corner was a slender black dress. It was a tube top with a sweetheart shape in the front. When I held it before my eyes, it looked like a flimsy piece of material that would barely cover anything.

It was perfect.

"This." I tossed it on her lap.

She squinted as she examined the dress, like she didn't know what it was. "I forgot about this. My friend got it for me."

"Because she knew you'd look hot in it."

"Like, three years ago."

"Shut up and put it on." I rummaged through her closet until I found black heels that matched.

She held the dress up in front of her face. "I doubt it even fits anymore."

She was slender, so I was sure it was fine. "Just give it a try."

"I'm going to look ridiculous if I wear this. I'm going to stick out like a sore thumb."

"You already stick out like a sore thumb." I set the shoes on the bed beside her. "Now get to it."

She sighed as she held the dress in her fingertips. Then she looked up at me, an expectant expression in her eyes.

I didn't know what the holdup was. "What?"

"Do you really think I'm going to let you watch me change?"

Wasn't thinking. "I was hoping you would just go for it."

"Nope."

I left her bedroom then stood on the other side of the door. "I want to see it on you. Don't you dare take it off before I get a peek."

"What if it doesn't fit and it's halfway up my thighs?"

"I still want to see it."

"Believe me, you don't."

"Stop talking and start changing."

She fumbled on the other side of the door, hopping around as she tried to get the skintight dress on. A few humphs and heaves reached my ears, and I expected the worst. It would be on upside down, or worse, backward.

"You done yet?" I leaned against the door with my arms crossed over my chest. I looked directly into her living room and kitchen, examining the way she decorated her home. Beige couches contrasted against the hardwood floor, and colored pillows were arranged on the cushions. Her kitchen table was made of black wood, and it stuck out in comparison to everything else. It was elegant and sleek, but it also had personality—her personality.

"Yeah, I think so. But I look terrible."

I rolled my eyes.

"I really do."

"I'll be the judge of that. Can I come in?"

"Wait..."

My hand was on the doorknob, but I didn't turn it. "What?"

Her humor disappeared, and all that was left was a grand sense of vulnerability. "Volt, don't laugh at me."

My hand gripped the doorknob, and I felt sympathy wash through me. "I would never do that."

"Because I don't look anything like those girls you see in bars and clubs."

"Maybe that's not a bad thing." I kept talking to her through the door.

"No, it definitely is."

My hand hadn't left the doorknob. "Can I come in now?"

"I guess…"

Now I pictured the dress so tight on her body it showed every flaw rather than every highlight. It was stupid of me to suggest this idea and make her feel insecure. I tried to help, but instead, I made it worse.

I walked inside and tried to keep my face expressionless, so she wouldn't see my true reaction. Telling a girl she didn't look good in something automatically sent you to douchebag hell. And since I put her in this position to begin with, I deserved to go there.

But when I looked at her, all my fears disappeared.

The dress molded to her body like it was made for her. It hugged her slender waistline, giving her an hourglass shape that was so prominent my mouth went dry. Her tits fit into the sweetheart cups, pushing them together and forming a subtle line of cleavage. She had petite shoulders, well rounded with glowing skin. Her collarbone was defined just below her neck, and the hollow of her throat formed when she moved slightly. The dress stopped just

115

above her knee, and even though her feet were flat on the floor, her legs still looked toned and her ass perky.

She stared at her image in the full-body mirror, and instead of being impressed by what she saw, she seemed mortified. "I look stupid as hell."

"What are you talking about?" I couldn't take my eyes off her. "You look hot."

"Shut up." She pulled her hair over one shoulder, trying to use it as a shield to hide herself from view.

"You do. Are you looking in a broken mirror?"

She fidgeted in place and didn't meet my gaze.

"What exactly's wrong with it?"

"It's just really tight, and I don't have a hard body."

"Okay... I haven't heard that term since the eighties."

"Well, it's a perfect description for the situation."

Was this woman totally blind? "Tayz, you look like a damn fine woman."

She rolled her eyes.

"I'd totally be all over you if I spotted you across the room."

"When you first saw me, you ignored me," she countered.

"Well, yeah. But I'd already decided to hook up with those two other chicks."

She shook her head like she didn't believe me.

"I'm telling you, every guy will be looking at you tonight. You can have your pick of the crop."

"I don't want to give them the wrong impression."

"Then don't. Be yourself."

Her fingers moved through her soft hair.

"You want to find Prince Charming? Well, you don't have to. Now he'll come to you."

She finally stopped touching her hair and turned to me. "You swear I don't look stupid in this?"

"Cross my heart, hope to die, never stick a needle in my eye."

"Wait... What?"

That was my own version of the vow. "I'd rather die than stick a needle in my eye, so that's how I say it. But the meaning is the same. I'm not yanking your chain."

"Really?" Up until this point, I'd never seen a needy side to her. She was usually confident, sometimes awkward, but never desperate. It was as if she needed my absolute approval before she'd leave the house.

I grabbed both of her shoulders, noticing how soft they were, and positioned her to face me. "Absolutely." I held up one hand to her, my pinkie extended. "Pinkie promise."

When she glanced at my hand, she smiled. All her teeth were on display, and it was one of those smiles that reached all the way to her eyes. She didn't always do this, just on rare occasions. "Pinkie promise." She interlocked our pinkies together, and we shook.

I felt my own mouth stretch into a wide grin. I loved seeing that confidence in her eyes, knowing I wouldn't lie to her—not with a pinkie promise. "Now let's go out and get laid."

***

We sat together on a couch, our drinks in hand. Her legs were crossed, and I found myself glancing at her toned thighs more than looking around the lounge for my next catch.

Heads turned her way the second they noticed her, and their eyes hardly left her face. Heads were turning my way too, followed by the sounds of high-pitched giggles.

Taylor eyed a guy in the corner. He wore jeans with a dark blue t-shirt. He was on the thinner side, without the same kind of muscle tone I possessed. It surprised me she was checking him out considering he wasn't the most handsome man in the room.

Well, besides myself.

"I think he's cute." She nodded in his direction then sipped her drink.

"Really?" I couldn't hide my disdain. "You're way out of his league."

"Why do you say that?"

"Because he's, like, a hundred and twenty pounds. His clothes look like they're from a thrift store, and his watch looks like a toy. What do you see in him?"

"I've been watching him, and he smiles a lot. When he talks to his friends, he's usually laughing. He seems like a good guy. You know, the kind that's a loyal friend and a good man."

She gauged all of that just from watching him? "But are you attracted to him?"

"He's cute. I mean, he's no Brad Pitt, but I'm not looking for Brad Pitt."

"Every woman is looking for Brad Pitt."

"Looks are the least important trait to me. I told you that."

"They mean the most to me."

"Yeah, I know," she said with a laugh. "You've made that clear." She sipped her drink and continued to watch Skinny Boy. "How do I talk to him?"

"You're going to hit on him?" I asked incredulously.

"Yeah. Why not?"

"Because you're way out of his league. I'll put it into terms that you can understand. He's Pluto, and you're the sun."

"You don't even know him. How can I be out of his league?"

"I can just tell."

"Well, who do you like?"

I hadn't been paying much attention, actually. "Uh, not sure." I scanned the bar and found a group of pretty girls in the corner. They were staring at me, probably hoping I'd make a move on one of them—or all of them.

"I think I'm going to talk to him." She set her drink down on the table. "What should I say?"

I couldn't believe this was happening. She was going to walk up to the guy, looking like a bombshell, and he was going to pass out. Guys like that never got hit on by girls like her. "Honestly, you don't need to say much."

"Should I make a joke?"

"Just say hi." Trust me. That was all she needed to say.

"Alright. Wish me luck."

I would, but she didn't need it.

She rose from the couch and adjusted her dress. Then she slowly walked over to where he stood in his circle of friends. Her hips swayed as she moved, and she had the grace of a queen. I'd never noticed the way she walked before, but then again, I'd never seen her in heels. Her long brown hair trailed behind her back and looked delicious against her fair skin. She had a few freckles on the back of her shoulders. They looked like kisses from the sun.

Skinny Boy turned his gaze on her, and the moment he took her in, he couldn't hide his surprise—and his pleasure. He held his beer in his hand and didn't take a drink. All of his focus was pinpointed on the perfect woman right before him.

I watched them talk to each other, and within a few moments, he laughed at something she said. They were both smiling, hitting it off right from the beginning.

I sat on the couch alone and suddenly felt out of place. I spent most of my time in solitude because that was how I preferred to live. Just being with my own thoughts was enough entertainment. But once Taylor walked away, I felt a new sensation of loneliness. It was different than it ever was before. Somehow, I felt colder.

The cushion beside me dipped when someone took the vacated spot. It was a young blonde with green eyes and fair skin. She wore a short dress that revealed things that should be hidden. "Hi. You look like you need another drink."

I turned to her and realized I'd seen her before—only I hadn't. I'd seen a million of her. Just like everyone else in the crowd, she blended into the background. She wasn't unique. She wasn't special.

She wasn't memorable.

***

"How's work?" Mom passed me the bowl of potatoes.

"Good. About the same." I scooped the potatoes onto my plate and passed the bowl to Connor, my younger brother.

Connor served himself before he set the bowl on the table.

"What about you?" I dug into my roast and marveled at the flavor. Mom had always been a good cook, and I hardly ever had home-cooked meals. I lived off protein bars and protein shakes because I never took the time to figure out how to work a stove.

"Things are great," she said. "The shop is slowing down for the holidays, but that just means I have more time off." My mom owned a wedding dress boutique. She sold dresses to future brides and loved every aspect of her job.

"Maybe you guys should take a trip," I suggested. "Enjoy the downtime."

"I wish," she said. "Your father is way too busy at school."

"I'm putting out fires all over the place," Dad said after he took a few bites. "I love Bristol Academy, but the parents run the show more than I do."

I immediately thought of Taylor but decided not to mention her. If I mentioned any woman, my mom would jump down my throat. Ever since my last relationship fell apart, my mom had been anxiously waiting for me to find someone new. She knew I was going to propose, and she was so disappointed when it didn't work out. "The beginning of the school year is difficult."

"Not only difficult," Dad said. "I have this new teacher who seemed promising in the beginning, but the parents keep complaining about her. The students say she's all over the place, and it's hard to follow what she's teaching. And she gives out too many projects that take time away from the schoolwork for their other classes."

I stopped eating. Taylor immediately came into my mind again, and I hoped he wasn't referring to her. She was working her ass off. "What does she teach?"

"Science."

Damn.

"She came through Teach For America, and since her resume was so impressive, I decided to give her a chance and forget her lack of experience...but that was a mistake. I may have to replace her after winter break."

This couldn't be happening. "Dad, maybe she's trying something new with the kids. You know, challenging them."

"Well, they aren't learning."

"How would you know that unless you tested them?"

"I am, actually. Unannounced, I'm going to give out an exam that covers everything they should have learned up to this point. If those scores don't compete with the students of the previous year, she's gone."

My appetite disappeared completely.

"She's a very nice woman and seems passionate about her subject, but I can't keep taking these complaints from the parents. Since it's a private school, they hold all the power." He wiped his plate clean then sipped his wine. His hairline was starting to recede, and his sweater vest was the same one he usually wore to school. We had some similar features, but we looked nothing alike. Connor, on the other hand, was the spitting image of him.

Now I wanted to get the hell out of there and go to Taylor. I had to do something to stop this. Even though I'd never seen her in action, I knew she was a good teacher.

She didn't work for the paychecks. She worked to enrich lives. "Thanks for dinner, Mom. It's delicious."

"Thank you, dear," she said.

Connor was quiet, eating in silence.

"Anything else new besides work?" Mom asked. She didn't bluntly say what she meant, but when her tone changed, I knew exactly what she was getting at.

"No. My life is pretty boring." I drank my wine to mask my unease.

"So…no one special in your life?" Mom stared at her plate and tried to act casual.

I loved my mom and respected her, but I wished she would get off my ass. "No one serious."

"Dear." Dad gave her a gentle look. "Volt will settle down when he's ready."

Thank you, Dad.

Mom stopped eating and placed her fork on the plate.

That wasn't a good sign.

"It just seems like you haven't bounced back." Now Mom looked me in the eye, turning into the protective and intrusive mother that she was. "You're different, and I'm just concerned. Your father and I are always here to talk."

It was difficult to stay annoyed when she seemed so sincere. "Mom, I'm fine."

"But you aren't," she whispered. "I hate her for what she's done to you. That hopeful look in your eyes isn't there anymore. You're just…darker. I miss the man you used to be. You were carefree, easygoing, and happy…"

I hadn't been happy in a long time. And I wondered if I ever was happy. Stupidity had blinded me, and I was in a relationship that never truly existed. I was simply in love with a woman—who didn't love me back. "Mom, I appreciate your concern. I really do. But I'm fine. I'm not rushing into another relationship until I find the right woman." I was a terminal bachelor, and I was happy with that fate. I'd have fun flings that would last throughout weekends and trips, but nothing beyond that. But how could I ever say something like that to my mom? That I'd given up on love forever.

My parents got married young, but they've been happy ever since. They hardly ever fought, and when they did, it didn't last long. After being together for over thirty years, they still made eyes at each other over the table. Their youth and beauty had faded away years ago, but love and respect had grown in equal measure. They had a partnership based on honesty and loyalty.

And sometimes that gave me hope.

"Well, I'm happy to hear you're still actively searching for Ms. Right," Mom said. "I thought you were just...passing time." She took a bite of her broccoli before she pushed her food around, avoiding the awkward subject of my sex life.

I wasn't a total dick. I felt bad for lying to my mom, but I couldn't lay out the truth like I did to other people. And the one excuse I made was Connor. He had a good head on his shoulders, actively dated, and brought different women around. One day, he would get married and pop out a few kids.

So, my parents would have grandchildren.

And I was off the hook.

***

"Hey." Derek walked inside my office without knocking. He usually announced his presence with the quick pace of his feet against the hardwood floor as he approached my door. My secretary's pointless attempts to stop him were also an indication.

"What's up?" Instead of working like I should have been, I was trying to crack a Rubik's cube. Whenever I had a daunting amount of stuff to do, I became overwhelmed and didn't know where to start. That's when I busted this little toy out. It distracted me enough to clear my thoughts and start over.

"Dude, you haven't cracked that yet?"

"It's not exactly easy."

"I could do that in five minutes."

I stopped twisting the different sides around. "Yeah? I'd pay serious money to see that."

"Then you're on."

I tossed the cube to him.

With a cocky grin on his face, he started randomly twisting the sides to align the correct color sections. His grin slowly started to fade away as the puzzle grew more complicated. When he reversed his progress and put himself in an even more difficult situation, that smile dropped altogether.

His irritated silence became my victory song.

"Whatever." He tossed it back. "It's a stupid toy anyway."

"You're lucky I'm not going to make you pay me."

"Better not. You know I'm broke."

"What's up?" I tossed the cube in my desk and stood. "Want to get lunch?"

"Starving. I'm craving sushi."

"I'm down." He and I left the building together and settled into the restaurant after a short wait. We ordered our food and made small talk about work before our plates finally arrived.

I used my chopsticks to pick up balls of rice and place them in my mouth.

"You've been hanging out with Tayz a lot."

I grabbed a roll and dipped it into the spicy sauce before I plopped it in my mouth. "Yeah, I see her around."

"But you hang out with her a lot," he pressed. "Are you sleeping with her?"

"No." I glanced at my watch to see how much longer I had on my lunch break. "If I had slept with her, I doubt I'd still be talking to her."

"Then what do you guys do together all the time? Any time we're together, the two of you are huddled in a corner."

"We're friends." It didn't feel weird saying that, not like it used to. She really was just a platonic friend, someone I hung out with. "We have a lot in common, and we have the same sense of humor."

Instead of stuffing his face, he hung on to every word. "But you sleep with everybody. Why haven't you slept with this one?"

I hadn't slept with *everybody*. Natalie was another woman who'd never graced my bed—because that would be weird. There were a few rules I never broke. And one of them was screwing your friend's sister unless you were in love with her. "Actually, I did try to go for it a while ago, but she turned me down."

"Really?" he asked in surprise. His face slowly started to light up like the sun was rising in the distant background of his eyes. He didn't hide the fact he had a thing for Taylor. I just wish he knew she didn't have a thing for him.

"Yeah. She said she wasn't that type of girl."

"I know. She has some class."

"Yeah," I said in agreement. "She's not a prude either. She doesn't want to sleep with someone unless it might be going somewhere. And she knew I just wanted a one-night stand."

"Then you become friends?" he asked with both of his eyebrows raised.

"Yeah. I'm not sure how that happened. I apologized to her, and then overnight, we were friends. Weird, huh?"

"I guess. You don't have a thing for her?"

"No." I was never going down that road again. I opened my heart to someone, and she made a complete fool out of me. I was humiliated, heartbroken, and ashamed all in one night. "She's a great girl. Really. But she's not for me."

"Then maybe she's for me." He waggled his eyebrows.

Taylor already told me about her experience with Derek. I didn't want him to waste his time on a woman he could never have, and I also didn't want him to keep pestering Taylor. "She's not interested, man."

"What?" he said defensively. "How would you know?"

"Well, we went out the other night, and she left with some guy." Who wasn't anywhere near her level. She could have walked out with any guy of her choosing, but she chose some skinny nerd guy. I knew she didn't care about looks, but come on, she could do better.

"She did?" he asked in disappointment.

"Yeah."

"What happened?"

"Not sure. Haven't talked to her yet." I went home with the blonde woman who made a pass at me. She was an easy lay and didn't talk much, so I couldn't think of a reason not to go through with it. Besides, I didn't want to go home alone—even if I didn't remember the girl's name the next morning.

"Damn." He released a long and irritated sigh. "Maybe that guy was just in the right place at the right time."

"It's not random, dude. She liked him, so she made it happen."

"But if she met me under different circumstances, things could have been different. Maybe it's because I'm Natalie's brother. She sees me as off-limits."

Derek had been my friend for a long time, so I wasn't going to laugh in his face. "Maybe. I think it's safe to say she's off-limits to both of us. But being friends isn't the worst thing in the world." Truthfully, I actually liked it. I hadn't had that kind of relationship with someone in a long time. Derek and I used to be close, but I pulled away after my heart was broken. It was impossible for me to trust anyone. I didn't exactly trust Taylor, but she pierced my inner circle pretty quickly—abnormally quickly.

"I was wondering when you were going to tell me about Taylor." Now Derek stopped eating. The atmosphere was different, and I felt out of place. I was about to sip my iced tea but changed my mind.

Derek didn't ask a question, but it felt like he did. The hostility was undeniable, but I didn't have a clue where it came from. One moment, we were having a normal conversation. Then, out of nowhere, he attacked. I held my silence because I didn't know how to cooperate.

"It just seems like you don't tell me anything anymore."

Again, it wasn't a question. But now I knew for certain he was ticked about something. I didn't have a clue what it could be, but something was obviously pinching at his side.

Derek tilted his head as he examined me, like I chose not to answer his direct question.

When the silence was no longer tolerable, I spoke up. "Dude, what's up?"

"I'm telling you what's up, but you haven't answered any of my questions."

I gave him the same stoic look, wishing he could remember exactly what he said and how he said it. "You didn't ask me any questions."

"I just feel like you don't talk to me anymore. I admit we aren't girlfriends or sisters, but we've never kept each other in the dark before. You don't tell me anything, and I have to get my news secondhand. To this day, you still won't tell me what happened with—"

"Don't say her name." I hated hearing it. If I were about to hook up with a girl with the same name, I'd send her packing. That's how much I hated it.

"Whatever." He continued on like he hadn't been interrupted. "You called me and told me you were going to propose, and then a second later, you guys are broken up. What happened, man? Did she say no?"

133

I never got the chance to ask her—thankfully. "It's nothing personal, Derek."

"But it is personal. I thought I was your best friend."

"You are." Actually, I hadn't had a best friend in a while. And if anyone came close to that title, it was Taylor. But he didn't need to know that. "I'm just not that talkative anymore."

"But you've completely shut me out. And for the past year, you've been a completely different person. It's like night and day. I'm worried about you."

"I'm fine, I assure you."

Derek's eyes narrowed in frustration. "But you aren't fine. If you can't tell me what happened with—"

"What did I just say?"

"If you can't even hear her name, then you aren't fine."

He had a point there—a big one.

His hostility disappeared instantly. Heartbeats passed before his voice came out gentle. "Did I do something? Did I push you away? Offend you?"

The sincerity in his voice made me feel like a dick. "Of course not, man."

"Then what's with the distance? What's with the coldness?"

I couldn't explain these feelings to someone else, not when I didn't fully understand them myself. My life completely changed that night when I saw her in the bar with her ex. It was clear she didn't just bump into him and the flames rekindled. They'd had a relationship—and for a long time. All those nights I made love to her and told her I loved her, she was lying and sneaking around behind my back. I questioned my intelligence and perception. This was going on right underneath my nose, and like a stupid idiot, I didn't even realize it. I wasn't just hurt, but mortified. I allowed someone to do this to me, to play me. How could I ever tell my friends what happened? It was embarrassing. "She and I had irreconcilable differences and—"

"Cut the shit."

I stumbled in my speech. "I don't want to talk about it, Derek. Plain and simple."

Hurt slowly crept across his face.

"Like I said, it's nothing personal." The only people who knew what really happened were my parents. That was because I couldn't lie to them. My mom would yank it out of me eventually, and since she won every battle we were in, I surrendered.

"How can it not be personal when I'm your best friend? Dude, what could have possibly happened that made you this way? Did she kill someone?"

Yes. Me. "I don't want to be constantly reminded of it. If I told anyone, that truth would echo eternally. I could never shake it. It would always be there."

"You think I'm going to think less of you?" he asked incredulously.

If he didn't, he should. "Just drop it, man. You have your secrets too."

"Not big secrets. Just the kind where I wipe the history on my phone when I'm done jerking off."

He wouldn't let this go, and I wondered if he ever would.

"Volt, come on."

"Just drop it, okay?" I wasn't going to budge, not on this. "I don't want to talk about it anymore."

Derek stared at me coldly, like he had a lot more he wanted to say.

I stared back, standing up to him in my silence.

"Whatever the reason is, I guess it doesn't really matter." He leaned over the table and lowered his voice. "But this is different." He pointed between us, his chest to mine. "And I don't like that."

I didn't like it either. "You're right."

"Can we at least move forward? And let it be different this time?"

I could try, but I definitely couldn't make a promise. "Yeah."

"Alright." He leaned back in the booth and stared across the restaurant. His eyes lingered there for a while before he turned back to me. Heavy silence filled the air, and the tension was still there. "So, you really don't think I have a shot with Tayz?"

Chapter Seven

Taylor

The graded essays were sitting on my desk in alphabetical order. Like every day, the students grabbed their work before they sat at their desks and silently waited for class to start. I stayed up late the night before getting through these essays about the pasteurization process of milk and how that technique was discovered by Louis Pasteur.

I had a long week, and I wasn't ashamed to admit I was tired. I loved my job and my students. Pushing them to be better learners and human beings was something I innately loved.

But damn, it was exhausting.

My classroom door was opened, but no footsteps sounded in the hallway. It was too early for the students to arrive. It was even too early for most teachers. Someone knocked on my open door and caught me by surprise.

Volt walked into my office, a visitor badge pressed onto his black suit. He wore a gray collared shirt with a black tie, looking like a powerful man who had complete dominance over the city. I didn't see him in a suit very often, and when I did, I was always impressed. He had the perfect body to fill it out, all hard muscle. Even though I just saw him as a friend at this point, I couldn't deny he was still hot.

Like, really hot.

"Can I come in?" He was already inside my classroom so that was a moot point.

"Sure. But what are you doing here?"

"I came to help with your class. Or do you not remember my offer?" He leaned against one of the desks, his arms across his chest. He just shaved that morning, so his chin was free of hair. He looked good that way, but I actually preferred the slight scruff that usually covered his chin.

"I remember. But a heads-up would have been nice."

The corner of his lips rose in a smile, and that same smile reached his eyes. "Do friends really need to give each other a heads-up?"

"When they stop by your job, I think so."

"Do you want me to leave, then?" he asked like a smartass.

"No." I hated to admit it, but I needed him. "I could use your expertise."

"Still having a hard time, huh?"

"I'm not sure what the problem is. Do they not respect me? Do they think I'm incompetent with the subject? Am I too stern? I have to say, classroom management is a lot different in real life than it is in theory."

"I know what you mean. I had a hard time my first year too. Honestly, every teacher does."

"But I'm doing everything right..." At least I thought I was.

"We'll get to the bottom of it. Just relax."

"I am relaxed," I argued.

"You sound defensive to me." That same smile was there, rugged and mixed with boyish charm.

I shot him a glare.

"How'd it go with Skinny Boy?"

"Skinny Boy?" Was I supposed to know who that was?

"That guy from the bar."

"He has a name." And it definitely wasn't Skinny Boy.

"Well, that's how I know him," he said. "And that's how I'll keep referring to him."

"Don't be an ass—" I spotted the first student of the day file into the classroom, and judging the smirk on his lips, he knew exactly what I said. He approached the desk and took his essay before he sat in his seat at the back of the classroom.

Volt grinned, enjoying every second of the tension.

I tried to keep the embarrassment out of my face, knowing if I gave into it that would make it worse. "Well, Mr...." I faltered when I realized I didn't know Volt's last name.

"Rosenthal," he answered. "I'll be in the back of the class." He walked to the rear and took a seat at the large wooden table. He rested one ankle on the opposite knee and continued to give me that irritating smile.

***

Once the last student walked out, I was relieved the school day was over. Having Volt watch my every move was unnerving, to say the least. During my student teaching, my advisor evaluated me, but that was different.

Volt left the table he was occupying and joined me at the front of the room. He hadn't taken any notes. All he did was stare.

I met his gaze and waited for him to speak, but his mouth was shut.

His thin lips led to his stern jaw, making his stoic face impossible to decipher.

"So...what do you think?"

"I think a lot of things. But how about we get something to eat while we talk it over? I'm starving."

I was hungry too. I didn't have a prep period, and I didn't get a lunch because some of my students stuck around to discuss the grades on their essays. "And I'm thirsty."

"For a shot?" he teased.

"A lot of shots, actually."

We left the school grounds then headed to a pub just a few blocks over. Their food was decent, but their beer was awesome. I got a huge glass of ale and didn't feel guilty for drinking at three in the afternoon.

Volt didn't care either. In fact, he'd probably drink at ten in the morning and still wouldn't give a damn.

I got a burger with onion rings and cheese and the greasiest French fries known to man.

Volt got a salad.

I rolled my eyes when I looked at his food, shaming him for eating healthy all the time. The only time he didn't was when he ordered alcohol. I didn't give a damn and inhaled everything placed in front of me. "So, what did you think?"

"How sensitive are you?" He drank his beer while his eyes watched the baseball game in the corner.

"I have a backbone of steel."

"Are you sure?"

How bad of a teacher was I? "Yes."

"Alright." He set his beer down and turned his head my way. We were sitting right at the bar, side by side on the stools. "You're all over the place, Tayz."

All over the place?

"You jump around so much that the kids are having a hard time keeping up. One moment it's micro, and the next, it's evolution."

I admit it was unorthodox, but a lot of the subjects were intertwined. "But that makes it interesting. If the curriculum was predictable, they would get bored."

"But they should be bored, Tayz. It's school. They aren't supposed to like it."

"But I don't want them to feel that way. Learning can be fun."

"Then make it fun. But don't throw them off balance all the time. Students learn better when pathways are predictable."

"But that's not how it is in real life." How would these students ever succeed if they were so pampered?

"Look, you're wasting time by throwing them off. Their concentration can only last so long. And maybe you think you're making it complicated, but the kids just think you're confused."

"But—"

"You asked for my advice, and I'm giving it to you." His blue eyes were calculating, almost threatening. "You have a hard backbone or not?"

"Of course I do. But—"

"The kids were passing notes in the back of the class, and you didn't even notice."

Now I tried not to be hurt. "I was busy—"

"You're paying more attention to what you're doing at the front of the classroom rather than what your students are doing in the back. Your focus should always be on how they're responding to what you're doing. You're in your own little world up there."

Maybe my backbone wasn't as hard as I thought. I felt like an idiot.

"You need to move around the classroom, stand in places they don't expect. That will force them to behave because they never know what's going to happen. Also, I suggest making a seating chart."

"I did make a seating chart."

"Based on where they sat on the first day. Of course they're going to sit next to their friends. And when they sit next to their friends, they're going to fool around. Make a new seating chart and put them next to people they don't know. That will limit classroom disruption."

Why hadn't I thought of that?

"We're going to go through your lesson plans and change things around. Also, what field trips have you gone on?"

"None."

"Really?" He seemed to be most surprised by that.

"Yeah. They aren't succeeding enough and don't deserve it."

He was about to take a drink of his beer but stopped. "Tayz, parents of this school expect at least four field trips a year. That's what they're paying big bucks for. They want their kids to be cultured and broad."

"I know, but—"

"Also, all the other teachers at this school are masters of their craft. You're sticking out like a sore thumb in comparison. The kids notice stuff like that. And that's why they don't respect you."

This whole time, I thought I was a good teacher. But in reality, I was a joke. I was doing my best to give them a great experience and make learning fun, but I was just making an idiot out of myself. I stopped eating because my appetite evaporated quicker than a drop of water in the hot sun. All my motivation to do better ceased because I felt incompetent. How did I get this job in the first place?

Volt studied my expression, and when he realized how much I was aching, his sternness waned. "You aren't a bad teacher. That's not what I'm saying."

"Really? Sounds like it." I drank half my glass and still wanted more.

"I know you care about these kids. It's obvious just from watching you. I just think you're channeling your knowledge and passion in the wrong way. We'll get it right. Don't worry about it."

I rested my chin on my propped hand and stared down into my beer.

"Hey." He nudged me playfully in the side.

I ignored him, depressed.

He wrapped his arm around my shoulders and leaned his face close to mine. That masculine scent washed over me, making my heart throb a little less. He gave me a gentle squeeze. "Taylor, you got this. I know you do."

"No, I don't."

"Yes, you do. Every teacher struggles in their first year. There's nothing wrong with you."

"But the year has already started. I'm not sure if I can change the atmosphere of the classroom. After the first few weeks, it's pretty much set."

"We can change it," he said firmly. "I'm here to help."

I still lacked the motivation.

"You're going to be the best teacher ever. I promise."

"That's a big promise to make."

"Well, I was the best teacher ever at one point, and I can teach you my ways."

I didn't tease him for the comment because I was desperate. "Well, thanks for helping me. I appreciate it."

"Of course." He dropped his arm to the middle of my back and rubbed it gently. It was the most affection he'd ever given me, the sincere kind that actually meant something. In fact, it was the most affection I'd seen him give anyone. The lustful kiss he tried to give me once before was such a random blur. I felt like another nameless woman about to share his bed. But that condolence, that touch, actually meant something.

When he finally pulled away altogether, I suddenly felt cold, like a rainstorm just emerged over my head and released endless drops of water. It took several seconds for my body to heat up again.

"So, how'd it go with Skinny Boy?"

Time had slowed down for just a moment, and it took my brain a few seconds to speed up and catch the present. "His name isn't Skinny Boy."

"Then what's his name?"

"Drew."

"Eh." He shrugged. "I'm still calling him Skinny Boy."

"He's a nice guy. I like him."

"You do?" He seemed both surprised and disappointed. "That guy? Who wore a *South Park* shirt to a bar?"

"Hey, I like *South Park*."

"Well, so do I, but I'm not blasting it with my attire."

I liked Drew. He made me laugh, he was polite, and he wasn't full of himself. He was the kind of man who opened every door, didn't try to kiss me after we just met, and actually called when he said he would call. "We're going out again on Friday."

Volt drank his beer. "Did you sleep with him?"

"No." I was surprised he would even ask that. "You of all people know I'm not a one-night stand kind of chick."

"If you really like someone, things can change. Did you kiss him?"

"Why are you asking me all these personal questions? You asked me to not ask you anything."

"No. I said don't *analyze* me. You can ask me whatever you want. We're friends."

I decided to put him to the test. "Did you go home with anyone?"

"Some blonde."

"This blonde doesn't have a name?"

"I'm sure she does, but I never asked what it was."

He was such a dick. Geez.

"So, did you kiss him?"

"No." We had a few drinks, and he walked me home. He got my number and asked if we could go out again.

"Because he's too skinny?" he teased.

I nudged him in the side. "Stop picking on him. He's a very sweet guy."

"You don't know him well enough to say something like that."

"Well, I'll find out more on Friday."

He drank his beer again, taking an extra large drink. "Tell me about him."

"Why do you care?"

"Because." He gripped his beer as he stared me down.

"Sorry, was that a complete sentence?"

"Because you deserve someone who's good enough for you. You're my friend, and I have to keep an eye out for you. No one knows the dogs better than I do, so you should trust my judgment."

"I don't need a protector. I'm doing just fine on my own."

"But it doesn't hurt, right? You're trying to find Mr. Right, and I can save you some time."

Despite the harsh way he was speaking, his concern was actually kind of sweet. It didn't seem like Volt cared about anyone but himself and his students. Somehow, I made the cut. "In Drew's defense, you haven't met him. So you shouldn't judge him."

"Then tell me about him."

"Alright." I gathered up all my information before I spit it out. "He's a lab scientist for NYU. He lives in a one-bedroom apartment in Manhattan. His dad passed away from a heart attack, and his mom is a chef for a steakhouse. He has one sister."

Volt processed all of this without looking impressed. "What's a lab scientist?"

"He takes samples and identifies diseases and microorganisms."

"Sounds lame."

I kicked him under the table. "It's actually a really interesting job. You need a master's to do it."

"But it probably doesn't pay anything."

I scoffed because it was ridiculous. "He makes way more than I do. And I don't care how much he makes. That's irrelevant to me."

"Well, if he's going to take care of you, it should be relevant."

"Are you like this with Natalie too?"

"Nah. She has Derek for that."

"Well, I'm going to keep seeing him because I like him. What you think doesn't matter."

"You do care what I think."

"I don't remember saying that."

"No. But I can tell."

I grabbed a fry and shoved it into my mouth, wanting to talk about something else. "How was that girl you went home with?" I wondered if he would really answer such a question.

"Sex-wise?"

I nodded.

"She was okay. I did all the work, but that's usually how it goes." He talked about his sex life like it was a routine procedure he did at work. He even sounded a little bored.

"If you don't like the sex that much, why do you hook up with strangers?"

"I've met a lot of really good lays doing it that way. They're regular booty calls, when they aren't in relationships and whatnot."

So, he really would answer anything I asked. Our friendship had reached a new level. He must trust me. Or at least be comfortable with me. "Why don't you do relationships?"

"Because I don't do love." He answered the question like he'd done it a hundred times. The indifference that emanated from him was heartbreaking. To feel loss was terrible, but to feel nothing was worse.

"Is there a reason why?"

"I don't think people truly love each other. I think relationships are just about security. People don't want to be alone, or they aren't financially independent to be alone. They use each other until something better comes along. And there's no such thing as monogamy. No one is ever faithful, and we're all prey to our hormones."

Damn, that was a dreary outlook. "I don't agree with any of that."

"Good for you."

"That means you don't think your parents love each other."

He looked away and felt the top of his beer with his finger.

"And you don't love them."

"I do love them," he argued. "There are different kinds of love that do exist. I just don't believe in the romantic kind."

"So, why are your parents together?"

When he didn't meet my gaze, I knew I had him. "There are some people who truly love each other, but it's so rare that it's not worth depending on."

"I think it happens more often than you think."

"And I think we have a difference of opinion."

Something did happen to him. Something made him this way. I didn't know what it was, but I suspected a woman left him or cheated on him. It scarred his heart, and he never really recovered from it.

And that broke my heart. "When was the last time you were in a relationship?"

"So long ago I can't even remember." Finality was in his voice, telling me this subject had come to an end.

"I think you're going to find a woman you can't live without, and she's going to make you so damn happy that you'll forget what it was ever like to be sad. Every single day for the rest of your life, you'll wonder how you got so lucky to find someone who completes you so utterly. You'll have a long and happy life, and every woman of your past will become a ghost."

His face turned to mine, and a new expression was there. It wasn't stoic, but it wasn't emotional either. His eyes turned an unusually bright blue, reminding me of the shallow waters of an exotic island. Time and space stretched endlessly through his eyes, showing a multitude of memories that seemed to go on forever. His entire soul was open and bare, but I couldn't read a single thought or idea. Was it doubt I saw? Or was it hope?

***

"How's teaching?" Drew asked from across the table. Our meals had been demolished, and all that remained was the endless basket of bread in front of us. We kept eating it, and the waitress kept bringing us more.

"It's okay," I said. "I'm struggling a bit right now."

"You'll get the hang of it. It's a noble profession." He wore a collared shirt with the sleeves rolled up. His forearms were slender, just as slender as mine. He was on the thinner side, and it must come from a fast metabolism because he ate just as much as I did.

"I hope so. I have a friend giving me some pointers. Maybe that will do the trick."

"There's no shame in asking for help." He ripped the bread apart before he slathered it with butter.

I wish I could eat like that and stay thin. "How's the lab?"

"The same," he answered. "I sit at the microscope all day."

"That's still interesting."

"Maybe I can come to your class and do a demonstration sometime."

"The kids would love that. I'm always looking for ways for the students to learn about new careers. It might point them in the right direction."

"When I was in college, I saw a presentation from a lab scientist. And that's when I chose it for a profession."

"There you go."

We made small talk about TV shows and music. The conversation flowed well enough, and he was always polite. He didn't talk about himself too much, and he always listened to anything I had to say. I think Volt would like him if he actually gave him a chance.

After dinner, Drew walked me to my door. "Thanks for going out with me again."

"Thanks for taking me to dinner."

"I didn't mind in the least. Looking at a pretty girl over a good dinner is the perfect way to spend an evening."

He was a smooth talker. And since he seemed sincere, it made me like him even more.

He eyed my door before he leaned in and gave me a PG kiss on the mouth. It was soft and sweet, and it lit me up in the right places. He may not be a body builder, but I cared more about what was on the inside than the outside. And Drew had the kind of qualities I liked.

"Can I take you out again?"

"You've already taken me out twice. How about I take you out?"

"Whoa, a beautiful woman wants to take me out on the town? Lucky me."

"You deserve it."

"I'm glad you asked me out in that bar. I thought you were pretty, but I also thought you were out of my league."

My eyes softened at the comment. "That's a sweet thing to say. But no, I'm not out of your league. No one is."

**

Sara was getting on my nerves.

"Dude, you never want to do anything." We were hanging out at her apartment, like we did every time I saw her. She never wanted to leave the shelter of her home, and she was practically living under a rock.

"I just don't feel like going out."

She needed to get over this breakup. It'd been a year, for crying out loud. I texted Drew. *What are you doing?*

Playing COD.

Am I supposed to know what that means?

Sorry, Call of Duty. It's a video game.

Oh, cool.

Why?

Well, my best friend is a turd who needs to get out of the house. Do you have a friend I can set her up with? We can go on a double date.

Actually, I have a few friends.

Great. Can we go out tonight?

I'll have to check with them, but I'm sure that works.

Thank you. You're a lifesaver.

Maybe you can give me a kiss as a thank you.

Score.

I turned to Sara. "Get dressed. We're going out to dinner."

"I'm not hungry."

"Well, get hungry. 'Cause we're going."

***

Sara wasn't pleased about the double date, but since there was nothing she could do about it, she got over it and was tolerable. The guy Drew picked out for her was Rick, and he seemed nice enough.

Drew and I talked quietly to each other on our side of the table.

"I think Rick likes her."

"How can you tell?" I asked.

"He likes blondes."

"Hope he likes the heartbroken ones, specifically."

He shrugged. "We'll find out."

Sara and Rick talked quietly among themselves, and it was mostly Rick asking all the questions and participating in their conversation. It took Sara nearly an hour to break out of her shell. By the end of dinner, she was actually laughing and having a good time.

Thank god.

"Sometimes you need someone to push you to get back on the horse," Drew said. "I've been there."

"Yeah?"

"I got out of a relationship a few years ago, and it was hard for me to get back in the game."

"Why did you break up?" I asked.

"We just fell out of love," he said with a shrug. "Sometimes that happens."

I'd seen it happen, but I'd never experienced it myself.

After the guys split the bill, we went our separate ways. When Rick said he was going to walk Sara home, I almost did a backflip right on the sidewalk. She was finally living her life, letting the sun shine through. Maybe Rick wasn't her future husband, but at least he was a start.

Drew walked me to my door like he had several times. He gave me a kiss goodnight, but when he pulled away, it seemed like he didn't want to leave. He stared at my lips like he wanted to kiss me again—and not in a PG way. I hadn't had a good lay in a long time, and I liked Drew. I could see it going somewhere. Maybe we wouldn't make it to the altar, but we would make it somewhere. "Want to come inside?"

He grinned from ear to ear. "Definitely."

***

"This week has definitely been an improvement compared to last week." Volt met me at the front of the classroom once the students were gone. "I think you're getting the hang of it."

The students still weren't responding as well as I wanted, but it would take them a while to adjust to my new teaching methods. "I have a lot of emails from parents. Really don't want to answer them."

"Don't ignore them. That's the worst possible thing you can do. The parents have all the power, especially in private schools since they're paying top dollar for their child's education."

"That shouldn't matter."

"But it does. If they don't like a teacher, they can get them fired with a snap of a finger."

That was ridiculous.

"That's why it's so important to be tenured."

"So you don't have to worry about getting fired all the time?" I asked incredulously.

"Pretty much." He straightened his tie then grabbed my folder. "Let's work on your lesson plan. Want to come to my place?"

I'd never been there before. "Sure. Do you have food?"

"I have food and beer."

"Excellent."

We left the campus then walked to his apartment a few blocks away. He lived in a nice building overlooking Central Park. We took the elevator to the top floor then walked into his apartment.

The second I walked inside, I knew it was his place. Leather sofas were arranged in the living room with dark, cherry wood furniture. A large flat screen was on the wall, and the balcony connected to the kitchen overlooked the park. A round table sat there, the place where he probably had breakfast every morning. It was the size of a palace compared to mine.

"This is where all the magic happens." He tossed his jacket on the couch then loosened his tie as he walked to the table. He threw the fabric over the chair then walked into his kitchen. "What are you in the mood for?"

"Depends. What do you have?"

He poked his head into the fridge. "Bud Light."

"Yuck. That's piss."

"I know."

"If you know, why do you have it?"

"Someone must have left it here. How about Corona?"

"Eh. Do you have any wine?"

"Cabernet?"

"Yes." Finally, something that didn't taste like a Fourth of July party.

He pulled out the bottle and poured two glasses. "All I have left is some leftover pizza."

"Any kind of pizza is good with me."

He pulled out the box, and we sat at the kitchen table. We didn't bother using plates. We ate the cold pizza right out of the box and with our elbows on the table. We looked over my lesson plan for the following week and made the appropriate changes.

"So, how's Skinny Boy?"

I knew Volt would bring it up at some point. "I don't know whom you're referring to."

"Yes, you do." He had a gleam in his eyes, telling me he enjoyed teasing me.

"I'm dating a guy called Drew. Is that whom you're referring to?"

"AKA Skinny Boy."

I rolled my eyes.

"What's new with him?"

I remembered our night together with fondness. He stayed over, and we had breakfast the next morning at a little diner around the corner. "Things are really good. We're getting serious."

"Really?" The teasing note left his voice.

"Yeah. He slept over the other night." I flipped through my lesson plan and decided I should just throw the whole thing out. "Do you think the cheek swab lab will still work?" I remembered doing it when I was in high school, and I liked it.

"Whoa, what? He slept over?"

"Yeah." I looked at him, unsure what the big deal was.

"So you slept with him?"

"Yeah."

His expression was unreadable...and ice-cold. "How was he?"

"Oh my god, I'm not talking about that with you."

"Why not? I tell you about all my conquests. It's not like I asked how small his dick was."

I smacked him in the shoulder.

"What?" he asked innocently.

"Stop picking on him."

"That's never gonna happen, so you may as well not bother. And how was he?"

I shrugged. "It was good."

"Just good?" he asked. "A man is supposed to rock your world until your vocal chords go out. Not just be satisfactory."

"He's not Christian Grey."

"Then dump him."

"You're ridiculous, you know that?"

"Did he make you come?"

My jaw almost dropped. "Volt—"

"Did he?" he pressed.

I shut my mouth and turned away.

"So, he didn't."

"The first time you sleep with someone is always awkward."

"Uh, no. I'm a gentleman. And gentlemen make their ladies come."

"How heroic…"

"I'm serious," he said. "If he can't complete that simple task, then he's no good. Kick him to the curb."

"Relationships aren't all about sex."

"But the good ones are."

I turned back to my lesson plan. "Should I do the cheek swab thing?"

"No. One of my students had a sperm swimming around in her mouth. You don't want to go there."

"Seriously?"

"You're the perfect woman, Taylor. This guy should be busting his ass to be with you, not half-assed pussy shit."

My neck almost snapped at the sudden change in subject. "I'm the perfect woman?" Did Volt just give me an amazing compliment?

"Yeah. You're classy, smart, funny, whatever. And those kind of girls don't go out with losers like him."

"Again, you don't know him."

"He should have cared enough to finish you off. There are tons of ways to do that."

Now I regretted telling him the truth. "Just drop it, alright?"

"You told me you were looking for Mr. Right. I'm trying to save you some time here."

"I care more about having a good relationship with a good man. I want someone I can trust, who makes me laugh, and is a good guy all-around. I'm looking for a partnership, not just a night."

"Why can't you have both? Why can't you have the perfect relationship and have amazing sex?"

"I'm not saying I can't. I'm just saying I don't value it as much."

"Well, you should. And it's clear you've never had good sex."

"That's not true," I said defensively.

"Yes, it is. You've never had that kind of orgasm that curls your toes. You've never had the kind of pleasure that makes you scream so loud people think you're dying. You've never had a man give it to you so hard that you actually enjoy being sore the next day. I can tell, Taylor. And that's just a shame."

Goose bumps emerged on my arm. When my hair stood on end, I knew he was right. When he described it in that way, I knew I'd never experienced it. I'd been with men who made me come, but not like that. But I refused to admit it.

"Are you going to keep seeing him?"

All these questions were giving me a headache. "Maybe I liked it better when we weren't friends. Fewer questions."

"Well, too late. You're stuck."

"Stuck?"

"Yeah. Friends forever. So, are you going to go out with him again?"

I tried to dodge the question by looking away.

Now I could feel Volt roll his eyes. "You're wasting your time. And I'll be there to say I told you so."

***

Sara and I were shopping at the mall. All my clothes were ancient and starting to lose their color and elasticity. Maybe a change of wardrobe would make the kids listen to me.

"So...you like Rick?" We hadn't talked about it since that night. The last thing I heard was he walked her home. But what happened after that was a mystery.

"Yeah," she said quietly. "He's cute."

"So...did anything happen?" I was so eager for her to move on that I couldn't care less who she chose to mess around with. She needed to get back on the horse—any horse.

"No. We just said good night, and he left."

167

Damn. "And that's it?"

"Well, he got my number, and we're going out on Saturday."

Seriously? That was the best news I'd heard in a long time. "That's so great. You guys will have so much fun."

"I hope so. It just feels weird dating again."

"It shouldn't. You've waited long enough." *Too long, actually.*

"I'll see where it goes."

I hoped it would go to the bedroom. She just needed to get under a man so she could move on and scope out the other fish in the sea. "Good for you. Maybe we can do another double date."

"Yeah, that would be fun."

***

Drew came over, and we watched TV in my living room. I had a platter of cheese and cured meats sitting on the coffee table, and we sipped our cabernet as we sat close to each other.

I kept thinking about what Volt said. Sex with Drew wasn't amazing, but did that really mean anything? I'd been with a decent number of partners, and I'd never had that mind-blowing kind of sex that people talked about. Maybe I was the problem. Maybe Drew thought it was amazing, and I just didn't.

"Rick told me he likes Sara. Thinks she's charming."

"That's great."

"He says she's a little rusty, though. He can tell she hasn't dated in a while."

"Yeah...her relationship ended a while ago. But I think she's getting over it. I've tried getting her to date for months, but nothing worked. But I guess she likes Rick."

"A perfect match." He clinked his glass against mine before he took a drink.

I looked into his eyes as I drank my wine, thinking about his full lips and how they would feel against my mouth.

When he set down his glass, I suspected a kiss was coming. That worked out in my favor because if he didn't kiss me, I was going to kiss him. His hand moved to my arm before it slowly slid up to my shoulder. He let it rest there for a few heartbeats before his fingers moved to my neck then my hair. A deep breath escaped him, smelling like wine, before he leaned in and pressed a kiss to my lips.

I felt the heat like I always did. But I had to admit, the foreplay before the sex was better than the sex itself. Maybe if we fooled around longer before we got to the finale, the explosion would be better.

An intrusive doorbell rang, and not just once, but three times in a row.

Drew ended the kiss abruptly, immediately flinching at the unwelcome sound. "Expecting anyone?"

"No." Who the hell was that? I was about to get laid before I was rudely interrupted.

"Well, it sounds important...since they rang so many times."

"It's probably a kid or something." I walked to the front door and tried not to look too vicious. I'd scare the kid away for good if he saw how pissed I was. When I opened the door, I didn't come face-to-face with a kid. I was looking at a six foot two grown man who was so beautiful it was painful. His rugged jaw led to soft and thin lips. His blue eyes were brighter than usual, hypnotizing. "Volt?"

"Hey, Tayz." He wore dark jeans and a gray t-shirt, not his usual attire if he wanted to go out and do something. Then he held up a bottle of wine. "I say we drink and watch *South Park*."

He'd never come over unannounced before. I didn't mind him stopping by, but it was a little weird since I was seeing someone. It didn't exactly make me look good. "Uh..."

Volt walked inside like he lived there. "I was on the subway this morning, and you'll never guess who I saw." He stopped when he spotted Drew sitting on the couch. The bottle was still in his hand, and he almost dropped it.

I needed to defuse the situation as quickly as possible. "I suppose it's time the two of you met each other. Volt, this is Drew." *Not Skinny Boy. Drew.*

Volt stared at him coldly, and it didn't seem like he was going to say anything.

"Drew, this is my friend, Volt. We've been working together on my lesson plans and class-management projects."

"Didn't know you had company." Volt spun the bottle in his hand.

"Well, you certainly didn't ask as you barged in here," I snapped.

"You barge into my place all the time," Volt argued.

"What are you talking about?" I asked. "Not once."

Volt sat on the couch where I'd been sitting and extended his hand to Drew. "Nice to meet you. Heard all about you." A malicious gleam was in his eye, the slight kind that Drew didn't pick up on.

"Likewise." Drew shook his hand and quickly dropped it. "I hate to say I don't know much about you."

"Taylor and I are besties."

What the hell did he just say?

"You know, as the women call it," Volt explained.

Drew examined him closely, his eyes narrowing. "I think I recognize you now. You were in the bar when Taylor and I met."

Volt tapped his fingers against his temple. "You're a smart guy."

Now that Volt knew Drew and I were on a date, why was he still here?

"Whatcha guys doing?" Volt asked as he rested his arm over the back of the couch.

"What does it look like we're doing?" I snapped. "We're on a date."

"Oh." Volt looked at the display of fine cheeses and meats but still didn't get up. "They are having a *South Park* marathon. We should watch it."

"Maybe tomorrow." I sat down on the couch and was forced to the opposite end, Volt in between Drew and me.

"So, you work in a lab?" Volt asked.

"Yeah," Drew answered. "I work in the medical office at NYU."

"Then you mainly examine specimens for STDs," Volt teased.

I rolled my eyes even though neither of the men was looking at me.

"I guess," Drew said with a chuckle. "It seems to be the number one thing people come in for."

"Been there, done that," Volt said. "So, Tayz tells me you two are getting pretty serious."

I'm going to murder him. I mean it. "Volt, why don't you just go?"

Volt held up his hand to my face without looking at me. "Let the men talk."

Now my eyes burned with lava.

"I guess," Drew answered. "We're having fun too."

"Good," Volt said. "Always have to have some fun." He poured himself a glass of wine. "Sports fan?"

"Not really," Drew answered.

Volt stared at him like he didn't know what to think. He was shocked. "You don't watch sports?"

"If they're on, I guess. But in general, no."

Volt still had the same blank look on his face. "Then what the hell do you do all the time?"

"I play games."

"Like board games?" Volt asked incredulously.

"No. Video games," Drew answered. "Like Call of Duty. Stuff like that."

Volt turned my way, and without saying anything, he gave me a look that said, "Seriously? This guy?"

I gave him the same look of loathing in return.

Volt sighed before turning back to Drew. "What are your plans for the future?"

Drew gave him a blank look. How was he supposed to respond to that?

"Stop interrogating him," I hissed.

"I'm just curious," Volt said without looking at me. "Where do you see yourself in five years?"

"Uh, is this a job interview?" Drew asked. "Because last time I checked, I wasn't applying for anything."

Volt narrowed his eyes in obvious threat.

"He's just joking." I tried to defuse the tension as much as possible, but I suspected nothing I did would make a difference. I clapped Volt on the thigh and smiled through the ordeal. "Now, I think it's time for you to go."

"What about the *South Park* marathon?" Volt asked.

"Maybe some other time." He was really cramping my style and ruining any chance I had of getting laid. I wouldn't be surprised if Drew just walked out since he was being interrogated like a prisoner of war.

Volt sipped his wine, and it didn't seem like he was moving anywhere. "At least let me finish this exquisite wine."

I glared at him. "It was five bucks at Target."

He sipped it again. "Well, it's delicious."

I sighed and leaned back into the chair, irritated that Volt ruined my evening.

Chapter Eight

Volt

I just finished a game of Candy Crush on my phone when Scott walked into my office. I immediately shoved my phone into my pocket so I wouldn't look like the laziest boss in the world. "What's up?"

His glasses were sliding off his nose, and sweat was sprinkled on his forehead. "My mom just called. She's been in a car accident."

Oh, shit.

"She's at the hospital. Can I go?"

What kind of question is that? "Of course. Don't worry about anything."

"All my clients left for the day, so I just need someone to man the front desk." His voice was raspy like he hadn't drunk enough water. His vocal chords had shriveled like leaves in a hot desert.

"Don't even worry about that." I left the chair and came to his side, wrapping my arm around his shoulder to console him. "Take care of your mom. Work will always be here when you get back."

"Thanks, Mr. Rosenthal." He gave me some form of a smile before he walked out.

I watched him walk down the hallway and disappear before I went to the front desk. My fingers moved through my hair, and I released the breath I was holding. Scott was a great guy, and I pitied him for going through this. If something happened to my mom, I wouldn't know what to do with myself. I'd always been close to my parents. The last thing Scott needed to worry about was work. I could handle it for the rest of the day until I found another worker to cover for him.

I sat at the front desk and pulled out my phone again. The office was dead quiet because everyone had left for the day. First Chance Education was on the tenth floor of one of the many skyscrapers in Manhattan. Large windows covered the rear wall, and a perfect picture of the city was captured. I remodeled the floor and transformed it into a glorified coffee house, giving it a comfortable aura so the kids would feel at ease when they were being tutored. People could laugh all they wanted, but I believed having an environment like this really made a difference in the learning process. I learned about it in a case study when I was doing the research.

But now that I sat at the front desk, I was bored out of my mind. The silence was deafening, and this crisp suit was becoming more uncomfortable by the minute. I hadn't had a private tutoring session in over a year because I did all the management and paperwork, so I wasn't even sure what to do with myself. All I had to do was wait a few hours before we were officially closed. Then I could be on my way to the gym and home.

I turned my attention to my phone when I heard the elevator beep. The monitor near the ceiling said it was approaching my floor. I was about to have a guest, which surprised me since it was seven o' clock in the evening. Most kids were home by now.

The doors opened, and instead of a concerned mother or father walking out, it was a high school student. His jeans were whitewashed and faded, having enormous patches in both knees. Strings of fabric hung from the area, the beginning of another rip. He wore a red t-shirt that looked too small for him, as if he grew out of it a few years ago. The end barely reached the top of his jeans. The backpack over his shoulder was packed to the max, looking heavier than a car. He pulled out his map and looked around the lobby.

I whistled quietly and raised a hand. "You're in the right place, kid."

He quickly shoved the map into his pocket and approached the desk, timid and uneasy. He didn't make direct eye contact with me, keeping his head low and trying to avoid as much attention as possible.

Which was pretty difficult considering he was the only person in there.

"What can I do for you, kiddo?" I put my phone away and gave him all my attention. When he was this close to me, I noticed his haircut. It was peculiar, to say the least. The brown locks trailed down his forehead, but it was uneven all the way around. There was no way a professional would have done that, so I could only assume he did it himself.

Small freckles sprinkled his face, and a tiny nose blended in with the rest of his features. He looked too small to be in high school—and definitely too skinny. He opened his backpack and pulled out an application form. His messy handwriting filled the blanks, barely legible.

I took the paper and didn't tease him like I normally would. He didn't exactly seem like the joking type. "Carmichael High?" That was the poorest school in the city, hands down. Nearly every student was in the food program, and they were using the same textbooks from the eighties.

"Yeah." He adjusted the single strap on one shoulder.

His application said he was a sophomore and quickly approaching sixteen. I'd never had a student from

Carmichael walk into this office before, but there was a first time for everything. "How can I help you?"

He pulled his hair off to the side even though it wasn't in his eyes. He looked at me head-on but seemed uncomfortable doing so. "I want a tutor."

"Sure thing. What subject?"

He shrugged. "Whatever."

Whatever? "There's not a specific class you need help with?"

He fidgeted with his strap again. "I guess math and English."

That was a better answer. "We have a few different programs you can enroll in. Annual programs, monthly, etc. Is there something you specifically want?"

"Well, I want to prepare for the SAT."

"Then you probably want the annual one."

He shrugged then dug into his pockets.

I watched his movements, wondering what he was doing.

He pulled out a few bills and a collection of change. "Do you have a payment plan? I have some for a down payment." He placed everything on the counter between us. It amounted to $28.75. It was chump change to me, but probably a fortune to him. "Is this enough?"

Not by a long shot. That was barely enough to pay the tutor for just one hour. "Not quite." I pulled out a financial aid form, assuming this kid was from a low-income household just by looking at him, and handed it over. "Just fill this out, and you won't have to pay a dime."

He took the form and read through it, looking stressed rather than relieved. His hand automatically moved through his hair, pulling it back and revealing more of the side of his face.

And that's when I saw it.

A distinct purple bruise high on his upper cheekbone. It faded underneath his hair, difficult to see with the naked eye.

My laid-back manner disappeared, the concern coming through. "What's your name?"

He kept looking at the form. "Why does it ask for my parents' income?"

"We just need to verify that so you'll qualify for after-school aid."

He set the form on the counter. "Never mind. Thanks anyway." Then without saying good-bye, he walked away.

"Whoa, hold on." I rose out of my chair and kept him in my line of sight.

He was already at the elevator and hitting the button.

"Kid, hold on." I came around the desk and headed to the elevator, not wanting to run because that might freak him out more than he already was.

He walked into the elevator and hit the button, the doors closing and hiding him from view. Then it began to move, sinking to the bottom of the building.

I put my hands on my hips and stared at my distorted reflection in the closed doors. Something didn't feel right with this kid. He looked like a mess, he refused to provide his parents' information, and then he ran from me like I was going to make his life more difficult.

But now he was gone.

***

I sat at our usual table with two muffins set in front of me. The sun was shining, but the few trees around the area sprinkled shade to keep it cool. My aviator sunglasses were on my nose, keeping my eyes comfortable.

Taylor emerged from the crowd and headed for the table. She wore a sundress with a pink cardigan, alligator earrings in her ears, and she had a tote bag with the globe on it. Even if I didn't know her, I could tell she was a teacher just by looking at her.

And she looked pissed.

She dropped into the seat across from me and tore the sunglasses off her face, letting me get the full scope of her anger. "What. The. Hell."

I pushed the plate toward her. "I got your favorite—a chocolate muffin."

She shoved it back across the table. "I don't want your sorry food."

I didn't believe that for a second. "Alright. I'll just eat it then." I reached for the muffin, watching her expression the entire time. As I suspected, her anger diminished as her appetite took over. If she let me have this muffin, then she would have to stand in line for twenty minutes to get another. And chances were, they'd probably be sold out by then.

She grabbed the plate and dragged it back toward her, keeping it out of my reach.

I grinned from ear to ear.

"Why did you crash my date last weekend?"

We hadn't spoken in a week because I knew she was mad at me. I gave her some space so she could cool off. Obviously, that didn't work. "Look, I didn't know you guys were on a date. I just came by like I would any other time. It's not like a schedule was posted on your door."

"But when you found out I was on a date, you stuck around."

"So?" I asked. "I wanted to see what he was like. And by the way, I'm not a fan."

She reached across the table and snatched my muffin. Now she had two.

"Ooh...big punishment."

"How would you feel if I crashed one of your dates? I just hopped in and got right between you?"

I couldn't stop smiling at the arousing image in my head. "I'd love that, actually."

Her cheeks tinted immediately. "Don't be gross."

"What?" I asked innocently. "I'm just being honest. I love threesomes. Sometimes pleasing one woman is just too easy."

"Ugh, I hate you."

"No, you don't." If she did, she wouldn't have met me for lunch. "Speaking of pleasing, does he still suck in bed?"

"I never said he sucked."

"Because he clearly isn't doing any sucking." I waggled my eyebrows.

She grabbed a piece of muffin and threw it hard at my face.

I let it bounce onto the floor, where a group of pigeons ripped it apart. "Has he made you come yet?"

"Yes," she said defensively.

"How many times?"

"What does it matter?"

"It does matter. Is he bringing you to that special place every time?"

She turned her attention to the muffin and started to eat it. "I'm not having this conversation with you."

"Why? Because you know I'm right?"

"Right about what?"

"That the sex isn't working and you need to find someone else."

"Volt, sex isn't everything."

"But it's a lot."

I grabbed my muffin and dragged it back to my side of the table. "So, he only makes you come once in a while?"

"I don't know," she said as she picked her muffin apart. "I'd say once every four times."

I almost spit out my food because I was disgusted. "And he calls himself a man?"

"Shut up, Volt."

"No, that's bullshit."

"Why do you care so much about my sex life?" she argued.

"Because you're my friend. And friends don't let friends have terrible sex. If you were Derek, I'd say the same thing. He was with this one chick who hated blow jobs, so I told him to kick her to the curb. And guess what? He did."

She rolled her eyes. "Stuff like that isn't as important to women."

I laughed because it was absurd. "Women are just as sexual as men. They like sex, and they shouldn't feel ashamed to say it. You clearly haven't had a great experience in the bedroom. If you had, you wouldn't be settling."

"Not settling."

"You so are."

"Look, enough of this conversation. Just stop crashing my dates."

"He wasn't even that interesting," I said. "And he plays video games? What is he? Five?"

"Hey, I like video games," she said defensively.

"This guy is a total nerd. What do you see in him?"

"For your information, he's very sweet."

"If you care about sweetness, eat a peach."

Taylor made a deep sigh, expressing her obvious irritation with me. "I'm done talking about this."

If she wanted to settle for some skinny guy who didn't know how to tap her headboard against the wall, then fine. She was the one missing out. "Whatever."

She kept her head down and ate her muffin quietly. When the tension became too much, she broke off a piece of her food and tossed it to the birds. Her nails were bright green, reminding me of a neon light show. I noticed she did her nails in different colors, always bold and striking. "How was your week?"

"Fine." I thought of the kid who came into the office. I never got his name, and I kept wondering what happened to him. I watched the birds walk past our feet, searching for any crumb they could have possibly missed.

"It doesn't sound fine." She pulled the wrapper off the muffin and ate the remaining pieces.

"I just had a weird interaction with a kid."

"What does that mean?" She set her muffin down, more interested in me than eating—which was a first.

"He came by the office and tried to sign up for tutoring. When I told him he had to fill out a financial aid form, he took off."

"That's not too strange."

"He had a bruise on the side of his face. And he's the first kid I've ever had from Carmichael High."

Taylor became very still, her breathing shallow. "A bruise?"

"It was past his cheekbone." I used my hand to mark the area on my own face. "He has uneven hair that covered most of it, but I spotted it. He wanted to pay for the service on his own, but he only had a few bucks. When I asked him to list information about his parents, that's when he took off."

"That doesn't sound good..."

"I never got his name. And I haven't stopped thinking about him."

"Maybe you can trace him down by going to the high school."

"If I don't have a reason to be there, it's going to look really bad."

"Don't go on campus. Just watch from across the street."

"I guess I could do that." The short interaction I had with him was enough to stick with me for a lifetime.

"I think you should."

My parents were upstanding citizens, and Connor and I always had what we needed. Not just financially, but academically. My dad was always a role model to me, and he gave me the resources to succeed. When I noticed the other students on the lunch program or getting sent to the principal's office every other day, it made me realize how much I had. I was the valedictorian of a school with two thousand students, and that never would have happened without my parents' encouragement. I always pitied students who didn't have that kind of support at home. "Me too."

***

The bell rang, and kids filed out like ants leaving the anthill. They grabbed their bikes and skateboards and took off, heading to the skate park or to get a drink from Starbucks.

My eyes scanned the crowd, searching for the small boy who stopped by my office. Carmichael High was oversaturated with students, and it was a sea of nameless faces.

But luck was on my side, and I spotted him.

After most of the students left, he approached the bike rack and unlocked his mountain bike. It looked too old to be usable, and the chain was barely hanging on. He pulled it from the bars and was about to hop on when he noticed the problem himself. He kneeled down and fixed it like he'd done it a hundred times.

That's when I made my move.

I crossed the street and headed down the sidewalk until I was near enough to speak to him. I stood over him, my hands in the pockets of my suit. My shadow covered his face.

He looked up when he noticed me. "What?" At first, he didn't recognize me, but after he took in my features, he made the connection. "What the hell do you want?" He stood up straight and pulled his bike close to him, ready to take off again.

"Whoa, calm down. I just want to talk."

"I don't want to talk to you."

"Why is that?" I kept my hands in my pockets and seemed as unthreatening as possible.

"Because you're a creep who follows kids around, maybe?" he said like a smartass.

To defuse the situation, I smiled. "Following kids around isn't my thing. I only came here because I had a meeting with the principal. And that's when I recognized you. So, chill."

"Really?" he snapped. "What's the principal's name?"

This kid was brighter than I gave him credit for. "Principal Littleton." I happened to know everything about the New York school system, both public and private.

His suspicion died down but didn't disappear altogether. The bruise that was on his face last week was gone, but there was a new one on his arm. I tried not to stare.

"You got a minute to talk?"

"No." He secured his chain and hopped on the bike.

I wanted to stop him, but there wasn't much I could do. "If you're still interested in the program, there's room for you."

"I don't have any money." He started to pedal away.

"There's no fee."

"I'm not filling out that stupid paper." He gave me one final look before he started to pick up speed.

I was going to lose this kid if I didn't do something. "You don't have to. You don't even need to tell me your last name if you don't want to."

To my luck, he hit the brakes. He turned the bike around and faced me, his hands gripping the handlebars. "Are you lying?"

"No. I wouldn't lie to you." I kept my cool even though I was panicking inside. Something told me I couldn't let this kid go. I had to intervene in his life, make him come to my tutoring program. If I lost him, I'd regret it forever.

He studied me with suspicion before he pedaled back to me. "So, I don't have to fill out any paperwork?"

"No."

"My dad won't find out I'm there?"

Why would he want to hide tutoring from his own family? That just made me more uneasy. "Not unless you tell him yourself."

"Why is it free all of a sudden?"

Because I was paying for it. "We have special programs for all students with different needs."

Finally, he dropped his uneasiness. "When can I start?"

"Whenever you want. We have a lot of different tutors you can choose from, based on your needs."

He twisted the handlebars slightly, his eyes looking off into the distance like he was thinking.

I noticed he was careful with his words. He thought about every action before he made it, like every little thing mattered. He had the thought process of a diplomat, wise beyond his years.

"I want to take the SATs." He looked down like he was embarrassed.

"Sounds like a good plan."

"But I'm terrible at math and English. Actually, I'm terrible at everything. I was hoping I could score high enough to get into a junior college or something…"

I noticed his jeans were the same ones he wore when I first met him. And now I wondered if that was the only pair of jeans he owned. "We can make that happen."

"Yeah?" he asked in surprise.

"Absolutely." I was definitely the best tutor in the building since I was the only one who had been a teacher at one point. My knowledge wasn't necessarily better, but I understood how to work with special-needs students—like this one. "What should I call you?"

"Clay. What's your name?"

"Volt."

He raised both eyebrows. "Mr. Volt?"

"No." I gave him a smile. "Just Volt."

***

I walked into the bar and spotted the gang mingling near the couches in the rear. My eyes immediately went to Taylor, seeing her in a charcoal gray dress that hugged her hips perfectly. Purple heels were on her feet, and despite the clash, they looked great on her. Her calf muscles bulged out impressively, and her ass was even perkier than usual.

I grabbed two drinks then made my way over there. "This is for you."

Taylor already had a drink, but she took mine anyway. "What's this for?"

"I always buy hot women drinks. And you look damn fine tonight."

The corner of her lip automatically rose in a semi-grin. Half embarrassed, half flattered, she turned away and set her previous drink down. "Well, thanks…" She took a sip then savored the taste on her tongue. "Just hope it's not spiked."

"Nah. I don't need drugs to get a woman into bed." I drank my beer while my eyes remained glued to hers the entire time. "So, who picked this out for you?"

"What?"

I looked her up and down. "This ensemble."

"That was all me, thank you very much."

"You've got great taste. And you know exactly where you got it from."

"Cosmo?" she asked playfully.

"We both know it was me."

Natalie came over wearing a skintight dress and heels that were so high they might break her ankles. I knew she dressed to impress, but there was only one person she was trying to attract—and he didn't notice her. "I was wondering if you were going to say hi to the rest of us."

I gave her a short wave. "Hey."

She eyed us back and forth suspiciously, a few drinks already swirling in her belly. "Okay, seriously. What's going on between you two?"

"Between us?" Taylor asked incredulously.

"Yeah," Natalie said. "The two of you are always tucked away in your own little world, and you always hang out. There has to be something you aren't telling us." She backed us into a corner and wouldn't let up.

"We're just friends," Taylor said. "I already told you that."

"Friends with benefits?" Natalie leaned forward like she was in on our little secret.

"I wish," I said. "But no."

"You guys are two peas in a pod," Natalie said. "And I've never seen Volt be just friends with anybody."

"I'm just friends with you," I pointed out.

"But that's different," Natalie said. "You and I don't just hang out."

"What are we doing right now?" I countered.

"But not alone," Natalie said.

"What's the big deal?" I asked. "Tayz and I are close friends. There's nothing weird about it."

Natalie still seemed suspicious after the entire conversation we just had. "In my experience, a guy and a girl can never just be friends."

"Well, believe me," Taylor said. "That's all we are, and that's all we'll *ever* be."

My head snapped in Taylor's direction, and my mind replayed the way she emphasized *ever*. My stomach squirmed with discomfort, and I suddenly felt hot around the collar. I took a drink to mask whatever it was I felt.

"Fine," Natalie said. "Whatever."

"Besides, I'm seeing Drew," Taylor reminded her. "And I really like him."

I couldn't help it. I had to roll my eyes—and I had to roll them hard. "Nat, please tell me you think this guy is a joke."

She shrugged. "He was nice to me."

"He weighs, like, a hundred pounds." No man should ever be that skinny.

Natalie shrugged again. "We all come in different shapes and sizes. Who cares?"

"I don't care," I argued. "But Taylor deserves the best, and I think we can all agree he's not it."

Taylor was about to sip her drink but stopped when she heard what I said. Her eyes softened in a beautiful way, and it made me want to keep saying those sorts of things.

"Aww," Natalie whispered. "I wish someone would say something like that to me." She trailed away and returned to the guys, taking her place right beside Jared.

I cleared my throat and tried to change the subject. "Did you ever tell her about Jared?"

"No," Taylor said with a sigh. "I just can't bring myself to do it. If it were me, I'd be mortified."

"Don't you think it's worse for her to keep this up?"

"We're going out tomorrow night to pick up a guy for her. I think if I can get her to move on with someone else, it'll be a lot more convenient."

"I guess you're right." I scouted the room and searched for a pretty woman to take home, but no one caught my eye. It was a sea of short skirts and heels.

"Did you ever find that kid?"

I pivoted back to her. "Yeah. Found him at the bike rack."

"What happened?"

"I got him to come to tutoring. He starts Monday."

"How did you get him to fill out all the paperwork?"

"I didn't." There was no way Clay would come if I asked him to do that. "I'm tutoring him for free."

"Aww…"

"He doesn't know that, though. He thinks he received a qualifying scholarship...some bogus shit I made up."

"That's so sweet, Volt."

I shrugged because I didn't know what else to do. I liked this kind of attention from her, when she looked at me like I was some kind of hero, but I hated getting it from other people. "No student should ever be turned away because of lack of funds."

"You're absolutely right." She shifted her drink to the other hand, and unexpectedly, she wrapped her arm around my waist and hugged me. Her head rested against my arm.

I stood absolutely still because I couldn't process what was happening. "What are you doing?"

"Hugging you."

"But why?"

"Because I love this side of you...the sweet and compassionate one."

I looked down at her and waited for her to pull away, but she never did. My arm automatically wrapped around her waist and pulled her into me, and that's when I realized it was the first time I'd ever hugged her. The scent of her shampoo entered my nose, and it made me think of a summer meadow. The affection was strange, but welcome at the same time.

And I liked it.

When I looked up, I spotted Natalie staring at us. She shook her head and rolled her eyes. Then she mouthed, "Just friends, my ass."

Chapter Nine

Taylor

We walked into the bar and immediately grabbed our drinks before we headed to a standing table. Natalie was wearing a sexy dress, showing off her perfect legs and slender waist. But she looked uncomfortable—like this was the last place she wanted to be.

"See anyone you like?" I scanned the crowd and saw a few cute men scattered around.

"Eh." She shrugged then stirred her drink.

She wasn't even trying. "How about that guy in the black shirt?"

She glanced at him. "He's okay."

She was giving me nothing to work with. "Natalie, what's your deal?"

"What do you mean?" She set her drink on the table.

"You never date. And when we're out, you aren't interested in anyone. I'm starting to think you're a lesbian." Coming out and saying I knew she was in love with Jared would just embarrass her. She had to tell me on her own terms.

She nudged me in the side playfully. "Maybe I am."

"Oh, whatever. I'm not your type."

"Why not?"

"I'm short and brunette...you seem like someone who would be with a tall blonde woman."

"I guess," she said. "Maybe like Charlize Theron?"

I realized we were getting way off topic. "I just don't see you very active in the dating world, which is strange since you're young and in your prime." If I kept nudging her, maybe she would spill her secret. "I've only been in town for a few months, and I've already snagged a boyfriend."

"That's because you're cute."

"Whatever." I smacked her arm. "You're cute too. Now tell me what's up."

She kept her fingers wrapped around her glass like it would keep her steady. "Alright. The truth is..."

I leaned forward and waited for the official announcement.

"I have a thing for Jared."

That was the biggest understatement—of the year. "Really? I had no idea."

"I've had feelings for him forever. Every time I try to shake them, I just can't. I keep hoping that he'll finally notice me and stop thinking of me as his friend's little sister."

If this had been going on for years, I doubted that would ever happen. "Then maybe it's time you move on and find another great guy. Natalie, this is New York. There are a ton of amazing men."

"I know, I know. But everywhere I look, I see Jared."

This was worse than I thought. "If it's not going to happen with Jared, you need to take a step back. Staying hung up on him will only waste your time and ruin your chances of meeting a great guy."

"You're right." She breathed a heavy sigh like she wished I weren't.

"So, how about we start now?" I turned back to the guy in the black shirt. "Go over there and talk to him."

"Just like that?" she asked incredulously.

"Introduce yourself and offer to buy him a drink."

"I've never hit on a guy before."

"It's not hard. Just have some confidence. Guys like that."

"And what if he says no?"

I shrugged. "So what? Then move on to the next guy."

She pulled down her dress and fixed her hair. "I don't take rejection as well as you do."

"It's really not that bad."

She turned to me. "How do I look?"

"Hot as hell. Now go get some." I turned her around and gave her a playful push.

She walked to the corner where he stood with his friends. She walked with grace, her shoulders back and a sway in her hips.

This night was going far better than I imagined. I stayed at the table and drank my beer, delighted to sit back and enjoy the show. I sipped my drink and realized I already drank the entire thing.

And I needed another.

Just when I turned to the bar, I stopped in my tracks. Drew was standing at the end of the bar wearing his typical jeans and t-shirt.

He told me he was going out with the guys tonight, so this must have been the spot they chose.

Excitement welled up in my heart when I spotted him, but just as quickly, it disappeared.

Because he wasn't with the guys.

He was talking to a cute blonde against the wall. She had a drink in her hand and a pretty smile on her lips. His arms were across his chest, but he was standing dangerously close to her.

My mind immediately wanted to make a bad assumption, but I convinced myself I was just jumping to conclusions. The bar was dark and the limited light distorted people sometimes. She was probably just a friend he ran into. No reason to be upset.

I decided to walk over there and say hello. I hadn't seen him in a few days, and I missed him. The bar was crowded and the music was loud, so I had to navigate through the sea of bodies to reach him.

Just when I was a few feet away, I stopped.

Because he kissed her.

He had her pressed into the wall as he kissed her passionately. One hand dug into her hair while the other gripped the small of her back. He practically ripped her clothes off in excitement.

All I could do was stand there and watch.

My hearing became muffled, and the music changed to the distant echo of a throbbing bass. The conversations around me died down, and only a high-pitched ringing burned deep in my ears. My heart was racing like I was about to compete in the Boston Marathon. My body died in that moment, but it also came to life at the same time. I stared at Drew as he kissed her, and despite the horrible scene I was looking at, I couldn't stop. It pained me, wounded me, but it was so awful it was hypnotizing.

Finally, I pulled myself together and turned around. I needed to find the nearest exit and get the hell out of there.

Anyone else would have confronted him and slapped him hard across the face. Or at least thrown a drink at him. But I didn't do any of those things.

I chose to run instead.

When I finally reached the sidewalk and pushed past the people trying to get inside, I inhaled the cool air. It smelled like smoke and rat piss, but it was still a haven to me. Without realizing it, my eyes bubbled with tears until they slid down my cheeks. I didn't realize just how much Drew hurt me until I felt the hot liquid reach my chin then drop to the concrete below.

I shouldn't cry because no man was worth my tears.

He didn't deserve anything from me.

I wiped the tears away with my forearm, smearing my makeup in the process. I sniffed loudly to stop the liquid from seeping from my nose. Once I was in some kind of control of my emotions, I went to the first person who came to mind. I went to my closest friend in the world. I went to the one person who could actually make me feel better.

I went to Volt.

Chapter Ten

Volt

Ring. Ring. Ring.

I was reading in bed when the irritating sound snapped me out of the story. I set aside *The Count of Monte Cristo* and kicked the covers back.

Ring. Ring. Ring.

I glanced at my nightstand and realized it was 10:30 p.m. The only person who would come to my door at this time of night was a booty call, but they wouldn't announce their presence in such an obnoxious way. Plus, they usually texted first just in case I was already booked for the night.

Ring. Ring. Ring.

"Shit, I'm coming." I walked past the living room in just my sweatpants then reached the door. I flung it open, ready to tell off this clingy woman for pissing me the hell off. "What the hell—" I stopped in midsentence when I came face-to-face with Taylor.

Her eyeliner was smeared.

Her mascara was running.

Her eyes were red.

Her cheeks were tinted.

Dumbfounded, I stared at her. My brain couldn't comprehend what I was looking at. There wasn't enough time to process everything. I couldn't tell if this was real or just a dream. I wanted to say something, but my brain had turned off for the moment. How could someone look so beautiful when they looked their worst?

She pressed her body into mine and wrapped her arms around my neck. Her mouth crushed against mine, and she gave me the hardest kiss I've ever received in my life. Her hands gripped me everywhere, needing every part of me. She threw herself into me completely and utterly. Her lips moved against mine at record speed, heating me up in a nanosecond. Her fingers dug into my hair and gripped me tightly. She came closer to me, trying to be absorbed so we were a single person.

I breathed against her mouth then gripped her hips tightly. I felt every inch of her, the feminine curve of her hips and the steep plunge of her back. The skin of her arms was so smooth, and when I reached her hair, I actually moaned into her mouth. Explosions were erupting inside me, and we hadn't even begun.

It didn't matter why she was there. She wanted me, and never in my life had I wanted someone more. We were feeding off each other, needing each other to keep this feeling alive.

This wonderful feeling.

I picked her up and slid her legs around my waist before I backed her against the wall. My throbbing dick was pressed against her through my sweats, and I grinded with her against the wall as I showered her mouth with kisses. My tongue danced with hers in the most erotic way, and I thought I would come then and there.

One hand gripped the back of her neck as I felt her, loving the sensation of her body against mine. She was pinned under me, entirely mine to enjoy. I'd wanted her in the past, and a part of me always wanted her, but now I couldn't think of a time when I ever wanted someone else besides her. "I love your kiss." I loved everything about her. The softness of her lips turned me on, the way she gripped me in desperation made me feel like the man she needed, and the way she squeezed my hips made me feel like a goddamn king. "I've never wanted a woman more in my life."

Her hand went to my sweatpants, and she yanked them off, getting them down to my thighs. Then her hand went to my boxers, yanking them down. "Fuck me, Volt. Fuck me hard."

The dirty talk would normally make my dick twitch because of how sexy it was. But those words had the opposite effect.

I felt used.

I felt like a warm body.

I didn't feel like anything.

The connection I had with her was severed. The hot and blinding heat between us halted in midstep when I understood what this was.

She was just using me.

I pulled my lips away and looked into her face, seeing the desperate arousal coursing in her eyes as well as her lips. But I also saw the overwhelming sadness, the depression—and the heartbreak. "You're crying."

"No, I'm not." She yanked my boxers down farther.

I pulled them back up, knowing I couldn't sleep with her—not like this. "Baby, what's wrong?" My hand cupped her cheek, and I suddenly recognized the salt on my tongue. The salt of her tears.

"I'm fine." She kissed me, trying to pick things up again.

"Why are you crying?" I pulled away again even though I didn't want to. I wanted to keep kissing her.

She reached her hand into my boxers and grabbed my rock-hard dick. She stroked it like a pro, her thumb gliding along my tip and catching the pre-cum before she gave me a good pull, spreading my own liquid down to my balls.

Fuck.

Her mouth pressed to mine, and she kissed me as she rubbed me hard, giving me the kind of hand job I'd give myself.

I couldn't kiss her back because her hand felt so good. My mouth was idle, breathing into hers as she made my dick ache to be inside her. Everything about her touch was euphoric. She set my nerve endings on fire and made me yearn for the greatest release of my life.

I wanted to say no, but I couldn't. Fuck, it felt too good.

I carried her to my bedroom, still breathing into her mouth as she jerked me off in the sexiest and most sensual way possible. I set her on the bed and moved on top of her, ready to have some amazing sex with a gorgeous woman.

She pulled my boxers down to my thighs and allowed my cock to emerge. She took one look at it and licked her lips.

Oh, damn.

I lifted her dress up and revealed her slender waist then grabbed the top of her thong and prepared to yank it off. It was the first time I saw her bare skin. I noticed how flawless she was. She had beautiful legs, curvy hips, and firm abs just underneath the skin.

She was perfect.

She kept stroking me, making more liquid ooze from my tip.

My hand shook as it grabbed her thong. I wanted to pull it off and shove myself inside her—all night long. But then I looked at her beautiful face, still marked from the tears she had shed. No matter what she did, whether she wore makeup or not, she was beautiful.

And that's why I couldn't do this.

Somehow, I found the strength to overpower my dick and take a step back. I released her panties then pulled her dress down. Then I pulled the covers back and got beside her, tucking my dick back into my sweatpants.

He throbbed in protest.

Taylor went for it again, reaching right for my waist.

I grabbed her hand and steadied it. "No."

"Volt, come on. I want some amazing sex, and I was told this was the place to go. Isn't that what you're known for?"

"Yes."

"Then get inside me."

My spine actually shivered, but I kept my focus. "I'm known for screwing women who mean nothing to me. But you don't mean nothing. You mean everything."

She pressed her lips to mine and tried to seduce me. My words went through one ear and out the other. I doubt she even heard them. "Please…"

God, she was killing me. "No."

"I want meaningless sex. I'm telling you that's what I want."

And I wanted to give it to her. I wanted to be inside her all night long and ignore the sun when it came up the following morning. I wanted her to scream my name over and over until her voice broke. I wanted every fantasy to happen—with her. "But it's not what you deserve."

She finally stopped trying to grab and kiss me. All she did was stare, a whirlwind of emotions in her eyes. I didn't know what she was thinking, but she was obviously thinking a million things at once.

"I won't give you a night of sex that you'll regret in the morning. I won't use you when you're at your lowest point." I pulled her against my chest, cuddling with her. My arm wrapped around her small waist, and our faces were close together. "But I'll give you this." My hand moved to her cheek and gently pulled her hair from her face. Her eyes were still red and glossy, the aftermath of unstoppable tears. "Now tell me what happened."

She stared at me for nearly a minute, her thoughts unknown. Then she spoke. "I went out with Natalie tonight. Everything was fine until I saw Drew..."

I didn't understand what she was upset about, but instead of asking questions, I let her keep talking, knowing she would get to the point when she was ready.

"And he was making out with some woman." Her tears bubbled all over again, turning into globs of misery. They were the size of hail, and they carried the same weight. They billowed over and streaked down both cheeks, shining like diamonds.

Pain erupted everywhere in my body, and not just in my heart. A physical affliction had wounded me, but I didn't carry the scar. More than anyone, I knew exactly how she felt. I knew what it was like to walk into your worst nightmare and never walk out of it.

She sniffed then wiped her tears away, shame written all over her face. "I know I shouldn't cry. Crying is stupid and for weak people."

"Crying is a sign of emotion. Those who don't cry are the weak ones because they're too cowardly to actually feel anything." I stroked her cheek and wished I could make all this pain go away. Now I was even more grateful I didn't give in to my physical demands and do something I could never take back.

"I thought you would be annoyed by it..."

"Do I look annoyed?" Without looking at my face, I knew she could see the sadness in my eyes. Whatever was in my heart reached the surface, thudding with misery. "Did you love him?" She was so worked up over it I could only make the assumption.

"No. So I know my tears are even more stupid."

I wiped a tear away with the pad of my thumb. "Not stupid."

"I just feel stupid, you know? I trusted him and thought he was someone worth trusting. But then he goes and...it makes me question my judgment."

I knew exactly what she meant. "Did you slap him?"

"No. I just walked out."

"So, he doesn't even know he's been caught?"

She shook her head.

"You'll tell him off later?"

"I guess. Whenever I'm up to it. It's not about pride, but I don't want him to see me this way. I don't want him to realize how much he hurt me. I just don't want him to know how well he played me."

I knew that feeling better than anyone. "Yeah."

"I guess you were right," she whispered. "You can say it."

"Say what?"

"I told you so." She didn't look at my face, her eyes directed at my chest.

"Taylor, I didn't want to be right. I hate that I am."

"Yeah, me too."

I ran my fingers through her hair, a failed attempt to comfort her.

"I came here because I wanted to do something to forget about the pain. I want to fall into something stronger than misery. You're a sex machine, so I thought this was where I should go." She didn't need to explain herself, but she continued to do so. "Maybe you're the one who has everything figured out. You have these meaningless flings that never go anywhere. And you never get hurt. You never feel pain. Maybe you have everything figured out, and I'm the one who doesn't have a clue." She released a sarcastic laugh that lacked any type of humor.

"You don't want to be like me."

"The grass is always greener on the other side, and your side looks like a green lawn right after a storm."

"The truth is...I'm pretty lonely." I'd never said that to anyone before, including myself. I kept up a charade, not for everyone in my life, but for myself. It was the only way I could convince myself that I was okay. "I think that's why you and I have become such good friends. You keep the loneliness away. You give me everything I'm lacking."

Her eyes drifted to my face, and they looked like glossy orbs. "You give me a lot too, Volt. The second I saw him kissing that woman, this is where I wanted to be. I didn't go to my best friend's place. I didn't call my mom. I came here...to be with you."

"And I'm glad you did." Even without the opportunity for sex.

She pulled the sheet farther over her shoulder and got comfortable on the pillow. "Do you mind if I sleep here?"

"I wasn't going to let you go, Tayz." I pulled her into my chest and ran my hand down her back. She felt nice against my body. I could feel the echo of my beating heart when I pressed against her.

And I could feel hers.

"Volt?"

"Hmm?" My lips ached to kiss her again. It was the most natural thing I wanted to do, to feel our mouths move together.

"Thanks for not sleeping with me."

When she kissed me the second she walked through the door, I wanted her badly. My entire body zoned in on the prize. But when she told me to fuck her, I knew I didn't want it anymore. She didn't want me to kiss her when she felt used, and now I knew exactly how that felt. I didn't want her to be meaningless—because she could never be meaningless. "Yeah."

***

The strobe lights shone across the walls and changed patterns with the tempo of the song. The bass was loud, making it feel more like a rave than a club. Everyone danced on the floor, either high or drunk out of their minds.

I lingered near the entryway to the bathrooms, my arms across my chest and my eyes locked on the prize. I never lost my target, always carefully waiting for my opportunity. Women came and went, but I never took their offers.

Then he made his move.

He set his beer on the counter and left the girl he was with, some blonde with a boob job. He moved around the dancing crowd in the center, hugging the wall as he maneuvered to the entryway where I stood.

Discreetly, I turned my face away and blended with the shadows.

He passed me, heading for the men's restroom.

I followed his trail, lingering behind him with enough space between us so he wouldn't grow suspicious and glance over his shoulder. The line for the women's restroom was endless, but there were no guys in line for the men's bathroom.

I entered the bathroom after him and immediately turned the lock behind me. It closed with an audible click, sealing us inside and preventing new visitors from entering the restroom.

Drew turned at the sound, his brown hair messy from the woman digging her fingers into it. He wore jeans and a t-shirt that made his body look even smaller than it already was. His eyes widened in recognition when he saw me.

I stepped closer to him, the threat unmistakable in my eyes. Now that I was this close to him, I couldn't stop my hands from shaking. The image of Taylor crying in my bed was permanently scarred in my brain. It made me so angry I felt like an erupting volcano.

He stepped away, his hand slowly rising to keep me back.

And that's when I snapped.

I pushed him against the wall and slammed my fist into his face, making blood squirt from his nose at the first strike. The sight of blood didn't stop me, and I hit him again, blackening his eyes then cutting his lip. Rage fueled me forward, and I bloodied him so much he was unrecognizable.

"Stop!"

"Fucking cunt." I threw him on the ground then kicked him hard in the ribs, flipping him onto his back. The blood from his face drained onto the tile and made it slippery.

"What the fuck was that for?"

That pissed me off again, so I kicked him right in the face. "You know exactly what that was for, asshole. Come near Taylor again and I'll kill you." I'd make good on my word, and I didn't need to shed any more blood to prove it.

I made my point.

***

Taylor sat across from me, looking sad like she did every day. She was taking the breakup hard, which surprised me. She seemed like a woman who would bounce back from everything.

She picked at her muffin with her gaze downward. That's when she noticed my hands. "Why are your knuckles so bruised?" She grabbed both of my hands and examined the purple swelling.

I quickly pulled them away and hid them under the table so she couldn't inspect them any further. "Boxing."

"I didn't know you boxed."

"Sometimes. I like to mix up my exercise routine."

"You don't wear gloves?"

I made up a quick excuse. "I put them on wrong."

"There's not too many ways to do that…"

If she kept digging, she'd find something I didn't want her to find. "Has he called?"

"No…and it's been a week." She returned her focus to her muffin even though she wasn't eating it. She just picked at it, making one piece into several smaller pieces.

"Forget about him, Tayz. You're too good for him."

"I don't want him to call because I miss him. I don't want him to call so I can hear him apologize. I guess I just want to act like he didn't affect me. Get the last word in kind of thing."

"But you don't need that. Just put it in the past and forget about it."

"I feel stupid too. I thought he was a good guy, but he just turned out to be a player."

"It's his loss." I wanted to make her feel better, but nothing I did or said seemed to make a difference. "What are you doing on Saturday?"

She shrugged. "Probably grading papers."

"As fun as that sounds, how about we go to a Yankees game instead?"

"I do love baseball."

"Attagirl." I gave her a playful tap under the table.

She tapped me back. "And I'm a sucker for chili dogs."

"Aren't we all?"

"Should we invite anyone else?"

I didn't want to bring the gang along. I preferred spending my time with just her. I could be myself in every way imaginable. Somehow, she put me at ease. "I only have two tickets."

"Bummer."

"Derek talks too much anyway. Did Natalie ever hook up with anyone?"

"She started talking to this guy, but I'm not sure what happened. She didn't say much more about it because she was too busy asking me if I was okay. She said she wants to kick Drew in the nuts then slap him across the face."

Already beat her to the punch. "He definitely deserves a bitch slap."

"She told me about her feelings for Jared. I tried to steer her away from him as much as possible."

"Do you think you made an impression?"

"I think it planted a seed. Hopefully, that seed will grow with some water and sunshine."

I liked the metaphors she made.

"Any new girls in your life?" She asked the question with a sigh, like she didn't really want to know my answer.

"Not really." Actually, I hadn't hooked up with anyone all week—which was a first for me. Despite the fact Taylor gave me a short hand job, it didn't seem awkward between us. But I wasn't going to lie, I'd been thinking about that hand job a lot—in addition to her kisses.

"No honies around?"

I hadn't been looking. "Guess not."

She eyed the time on her phone. "Well, I should get going. If we're going to that game tomorrow, I better grade those papers tonight."

"I can come with you if you like."

"And watch me grade papers?" she asked incredulously.

"I can watch TV or something. Keep you company." I didn't want to leave her alone right now. One of my biggest fears was Drew would call and beg her to take him back, and she wouldn't have the strength to say no.

I had to make sure she said no.

"Sure," she said. "If you're up for it."

"I am." I threw our trash away and walked with her down the sidewalk.

She held her purse over one shoulder, and her eyes were on the ground. "Thanks for being my friend during all of this. I know there are better ways for you to spend your Friday night."

Actually, there was no better way I could spend my Friday night. "You're my best friend, Tayz."

She smiled as she looked at me, her eyes glowing. "You're my best friend too."

Chapter Eleven

Taylor

Sara took me shopping and out for ice cream to cheer me up. Sometimes a frozen treat was the only thing that could lift your mood. At least, that was the case for me.

Sara kept discreetly glancing at me as if she thought I would burst into tears at any moment.

"I'm fine, Sara."

"I know you are," she lied.

"Then why do you keep staring at me?"

"Just want to make sure there's nothing on your face… That's all."

Yeah, whatever. "Drew really hurt me, but I assure you, I'll get over it." I didn't want to be one of those girls who moped around after a guy wounded them. There were better things to do with my time than let some guy drag me down. But I needed some time to finally get there.

In the meantime, I'd eat ice cream.

"I know you will. You're the strongest chick I know."

"Thanks." It was a compliment I didn't deserve, but I'd take it right now. "Everyone has been smothering me with love. It's been nice." Volt was in the lead, taking me to ball games and just hanging out at my apartment so I wouldn't be alone with my thoughts. I never asked him to do anything, and he made all those gestures by himself. "Volt has been the sweetest. Not sure what I would do without him."

"Your other boyfriend?"

Everyone teased me about my relationship with Volt, and I knew it was easier just to let it go. "My other best friend."

"You can't have more than one best friend."

"You can if the other one is a dude." And frankly, I spent more time with him than her. Now she spent most of her free time with Rick, and before that, she was Debbie Downer. "On the night I caught Drew, I went to his place and did something really stupid…"

She dropped her spoon into her cup, abandoning it in light of my gossip. "Did you guys get it on?"

"A little bit." Without even realizing it, the corner of my mouth lifted.

"Say what?" She slammed her hand on the table. "Girl, what happened?"

"Keep in mind that I was a little crazy at the time. I just saw Drew grinding against some blonde in a nightclub."

"Shut up and get to the good stuff."

"When Volt answered the door, we started making out. He picked me up and pinned me to the wall as we continued to devour each other like we had fasted for the past week."

Sara hung on every word. "And he's hot, right?"

"Oh god, yes." *One of the hottest guys I'd ever seen.* "And such a good kisser."

"Go on."

"We were getting hot and heavy against the wall, and I just wanted some meaningless sex that would make me feel better. He's the king of manwhores, so I thought he was the best place for that kind of service. But then he pulled away and stopped."

"No!" Sara was even more disappointed than I was.

"I gave him some strokes in his pants to change his mind, and it almost worked...but then it didn't." When I stuck my hand down his pants and gripped his rock-hard cock, I was expecting a specific size. Average, maybe a little bigger. But when my fingers grasped his base, I released a quiet sigh into his mouth, shocked by what I was grabbing.

"How is he down there?"

I shouldn't share Volt's personal information, but Sara wouldn't quit until she heard the truth. "Let's just say I thought it was his leg at first."

She gasped and covered her mouth. "What a hunk."

"I know. It's the biggest one I've ever touched. I couldn't believe it."

She looked away like she was reliving an old dream. "Muriel was big in that department...miss that."

"I'm sure Rick is more than perfect too..."

"Like I'm ever seeing him again."

"What? Why?" I thought things were going well. Sara was out of the house and off the couch. The cushion was stained with old popcorn butter and Ben and Jerry's ice cream.

"I can't keep seeing him after what Drew did to you."

I stared at her blankly because I didn't understand the correlation. "What does that have to do with anything?"

"Because he's Drew's friend. I'm not going anywhere near that asshole ever again."

"But that's not fair. Rick didn't do anything."

"But I don't want to ever be in the same room with that guy. If I keep seeing Rick, it's bound to happen."

"That's still not right. I really don't care if you keep seeing him." In fact, I would encourage it.

"No. You're my best friend."

"But—"

"Rick is his best friend, which would mean I'd have to have a relationship with him. And hell no, I'm not having a relationship with a man who hurt my best friend. I want nothing to do with him, and I better not see him again because I may go to jail for the shit I'm about to pull."

Her loyalty made me smile, giving me the first feeling of happiness in a while. "Well...thanks."

"No problem. I'll find someone else."

"Yeah. There are a lot of great guys in the city."

"What about Volt?" She waggled her eyebrows.

"He's off-limits," I blurted. I didn't think about what I said before I said it. The idea of him screwing my best friend immediately made me feel vomit in my throat.

Sara raised an eyebrow. "Is he now?"

I knew what the look meant. I'd seen it a hundred times. "Not because I have feelings for him, but because it would make things awkward for me if you broke up." Not if they broke up. *When* they broke up.

"Even if it was a one-night stand?"

"Definitely a one-night stand. Sara, he's my closest friend besides you. I can't afford to lose him." When I first met Volt, I was attracted to him, but I didn't like him very much. It took me a while to look past his callous shell before I saw the beauty underneath. Or maybe it just took him a while to show the beauty underneath. Either way, he was now an integral part of my life. He helped me out at work and was the person I went out with on the weekends.

"Oh, really?" Her left eyebrow was arched so high it was about to fly off her face.

"Yes. Really."

"So, you're saying there's not a single chance that you have feelings for this guy?"

"None."

Now her right eyebrow rose. "Oh, really?"

I hated it when she tried to act like some genius detective. "Yes."

"Not even a tiny bit of a chance?" She held her forefinger and thumb together and waved it in front of my face.

"No."

"You made out with him and jerked him off, but you don't feel a thing?"

"Sara—"

"You have to feel something for this guy. I'm sorry, but I don't believe your bullshit."

"I admit I'm attracted to him. But who wouldn't be?"

"And you call him your best friend, which means you're attracted to him and you like him as a person. If you ask me, he sounds like the perfect guy."

I laughed because it was absurd. "He's not the perfect guy."

"Why not?"

"He's the biggest manwhore I know. He doesn't do relationships, just sexcapades."

"What does that have to do with anything?"

"Because when we first met, he said that was all he could give to anybody. When I realized he was hollow and superficial, I stopped thinking about him that way."

"Obviously not if he was the first place you went for some action."

I narrowed my eyes because I was growing irritated. "Look, I was just depressed and didn't really know what I was doing."

"Were you drunk?"

"No..."

"Then you knew what you were doing."

"Sara, I don't have feelings for the guy. I'm not sure why we're even arguing about it because I would have told you the truth if I did."

"Maybe you're in denial."

"Nope." My desire to be with him died once he tried to kiss me on my doorstep. That feeling of indifference, of looking like another warm body, turned me off so completely that I wanted nothing to do with him. In order for real passion to emerge, there had to be some feelings there. But with Volt, he didn't feel a single thing for me. After that, I really saw him as a friend—and nothing more.

"You said he was an amazing kisser."

"I'd be surprised if he wasn't since he's kissed all of New York."

"Or maybe you had some serious chemistry." She gave me a knowing look.

This was getting old—and fast. "Sara, let it go. Now you're just getting on my nerves."

"Fine. I'll drop it." She picked up her spoon and began eating again. "But that doesn't mean I'm not thinking it."

***

Volt walked me home after the movies.

"I liked it." He walked beside me with one hand in the pocket of his jeans.

"You only liked it because there were titties."

"So?" he asked with a laugh. "I think titties stop a movie from being ordinary and make it extraordinary."

"Does that mean every porno is a cinematic masterpiece?"

"Absolutely."

I rolled my eyes and kept walking. "I thought you didn't watch porn?"

"Not regularly, but I have. Every guy does it."

"But if you're getting laid all the time, why would you need to watch it?"

"Well, it's very rare when I do watch it. And it happens when I can't get laid. But since I have quite a sexual appetite, I need to do something."

"You haven't had any conquests this week?" It seemed like Volt picked up four to five women a week. It happened everywhere he went, the grocery store, the dry cleaners, anywhere that women went.

"Nothing lately…"

That was a first. "How is that possible?"

"I haven't been feeling well, so I've taken a break." He put his other hand in his pocket.

In the time I'd known him, I'd never heard him take a break from the bedroom. "Are you sick?"

"Kind of under the weather."

"You don't seem sick." I hadn't heard a sniff or a cough.

"It's been mostly the stomach flu. Ate some bad tacos or something."

"Gotcha." Now that made sense. We kept walking until we were just a block from my place. There was a bar nearby, but I hadn't had a chance to stop by. There was so much to see in the city but never enough time.

Just as we passed it, Drew stepped outside with a discolored face. Old bruises covered his cheekbones and his eyes. And there were a few old cuts along his bottom lip. It happened so quickly, I wasn't sure what I was looking at. It took a moment to focus.

Drew noticed me in that instant, and instead of looking confused about why I hadn't called or even apologetic for not calling me, he halted in midstep with a look of horror on his face. He took one look at Volt then took off at a dead run. He pushed past people on the sidewalk and hauled ass.

Did that really happen?

Volt kept walking like he hadn't noticed anything.

"What was that?"

"What?"

"Drew just took off like a madman was chasing him."

He shrugged. "Beats me."

None of it was making sense. Drew didn't even know I caught him in the act at that nightclub. And now he was covered in bruises like he took a serious beating. The second he looked at me, he ran off in terror. What was I missing?

The fact Volt didn't find it suspicious was even more suspicious.

"Did you do something?" I stopped walking and faced him head on so I could look into his face.

"Do what?" He had the same bored expression on his face like he couldn't care less about this conversation.

"Something with Drew. Because he looked pretty terrified."

"Well, I'm a pretty terrifying guy." He started walking again.

"Volt." I grabbed his arm and pulled him toward me. Now I knew something was up, and I couldn't ignore it. "You did something, didn't you?"

"Like what?"

What else could explain the bruises and the way Drew took off? "You hunted him down, didn't you?"

Volt shook his head. "Like I don't have better things to do."

"And you kicked his ass."

He rolled his eyes. "Again, I don't care enough to do something like that. Now let's get to your apartment because I need a beer."

"Volt." My voice became threatening, telling him I wouldn't drop this until I got the truth out of him. I silently pressed him, eye-mugging him until he caved. He would tell me the truth if I asked him for it. "Tell me what happened."

Volt slowly began to cave, a resigned look on his face. "If you want me to apologize, you're wasting your time. I don't feel bad for what I did, and I never will feel bad for what I did."

My heart slammed hard into my chest, making me ache. "What did you do?"

"I hunted him down in a club, where he was making a pass at some other bimbo, and when he went into the bathroom, I followed him inside. And that's when I made him wish he were dead." Volt held my gaze without blinking, a hint of his former rage shining in his eyes. There was no regret in the look—and definitely no remorse. "He hurt you, so I hurt him more."

Speechless, I just stared.

Volt stared back, prepared for whatever I might say.

"You didn't have to do that."

"I know."

"And you shouldn't have. You could have gotten hurt—"

He released a sarcastic laugh.

"Or he could sue you."

"Don't care."

"You didn't need to defend my honor like that. I appreciate it, but...you didn't need to do that."

"I have your back until the end of time, Tayz." The angry look in his eyes slowly started to fade away. The man I knew was slowly coming back to me, the rage and hostility becoming something of the past.

"Even so, I—"

"What's done is done." He started to walk again. "No one hurts my best friend and gets away with it."

Chapter Twelve

Volt

Clay walked inside right at 3:30 p.m.

He wore the same ripped jeans and flimsy t-shirt. One of the zippers on his backpack was broken, so the bag hung open when it was on his back. He sat in the chair across from me and set his stuff on the ground. There were no bruises on his face today, but his hair was still a mess.

He looked homeless.

"Hey, Clay." I had the stack of books beside me because I suspected he didn't have the things he needed.

"Hey, Volt." He faced me across the small table and immediately looked out of place. He examined the room, studying the gray walls and mahogany furniture. It was a type of luxury he probably never experienced in his life.

"How's it going?"

"Fine." He didn't ask me the same question in return. Up until that point, he still hadn't looked at me.

"Are you ready to study?"

"I guess."

I opened the SAT book and turned it upside down so he could read the words. "We're going to start with vocabulary. You'll read each sentence and determine the meaning of the underlined word." It was the shortest section of the SAT but arguably the most difficult one.

"Uh, okay."

I pointed to the sentence and waited for him to begin.

He stared at it blankly before he glanced at me. When he saw my stare, he turned back to the paper. Instead of his eye following along with the words, he just stared at it.

What was the holdup? "How about you read it out loud?"

"It's okay," he said quickly.

My eyes narrowed. "Then what does antagonist mean in the sentence?"

He kept his eyes glued to the paper, and minutes went by without him saying a word.

I gave him all the time he needed so he wouldn't feel pressured, but when three minutes passed, I assumed he didn't have a clue. "The best way to approach this type of question is to read it completely and understand what the sentence is about. Then you can backtrack and make an appropriate guess."

"Okay."

"So, how about you read the sentence out loud." I was curious to know what his reading level was at the moment. It was probably lower than the sophomore level, but how low?

He shifted his position several times before he began reading. "The...he...here..."

"Hero."

"The hero," he repeated. "de...de...fe..."

"Defeats."

"The dra...drag..."

"Dragon in the...cas...cas—"

"Castle. He is the...ant...ant..."

"Antagonist."

"Antagonist." He continued sounding out the rest of the sentence like a five-year-old, and it took nearly ten minutes for him to arrive at the end of the sentence. By the time he got there, he forgot what he just read.

He was even more behind than I feared.

I'd never had a student with such poor reading skills, and I feared how bad his math would be. If I wanted him to get a decent score on the SAT, I'd have to teach him everything—from the beginning.

Clay rested his temple against his palm and stared at the surface of the table. The spunk he showed before was nonexistent. The shame wafted from him in waves.

And I pitied him. He didn't have any of the resources to succeed, and without my help, he would walk away from high school without even graduating and probably get caught up in some bad shit.

I was his only hope.

"That was a good start, Clay."

The disbelief on his face was unmistakable. "It was?"

"Yeah. We've got a long way to go, but I've had students start at lower levels." That was a lie, but he didn't need to know that.

"Really?" He straightened in his chair and put his hand down.

"Yeah. But it's going to take a lot of hard work. I hope you're up to it."

"I am."

"Great." I gave him a smile before I turned back to the notebook. "Let's move on."

***

I glanced at my phone for the fifteenth time and hoped there was a message from Taylor.

There wasn't.

I got home late that night but didn't want to hang out in my apartment. I wanted to go out and do something, but I didn't want to go out alone. I wanted to be with Taylor. She made me laugh in ways I hadn't felt since I was a child. She made me feel good about myself even on my worst day. And she just made me happy in general.

But I saw her last night and the night before…and the night before that. If I kept this up, it was bound to annoy her. She wasn't my only friend, and I certainly wasn't hers.

Now I was overthinking everything, wondering what she thought when I asked to see her. What did she think when I just stopped by her apartment?

Why did I care?

After sitting around for long enough, I just went ahead and texted her. *Dinner plans?*

Nope. Forgot about it since I'm buried under lab reports.

Sounds like you need a break. Pita Paradise?

Uh, duh.

That was her favorite place to eat, so I knew she wouldn't say no. *I'll see you there in fifteen minutes.*

K.

I went to my closet and pulled on a dark pair of jeans and a gray t-shirt. It fit my chest perfectly, and the jeans hung low on my hips. Whenever I was trying to attract attention, this was the type of thing I wore. I examined my arms in the mirror and felt the muscle. When they didn't look big enough, I got on the floor and did twenty push-ups. Blood moved to the muscles and made them bulge.

I left my apartment and headed to the restaurant. I got there first because I was closer, and I got a table in the garden located on the side of the restaurant. Plants and flowers were scattered around the enclosure, and birds still chirped despite the sun's absence.

My heart was beating fast.

Why was it pounding so hard? Why did I feel the rush of blood to my head? Why did I feel the distant tingle in my fingertips?

Taylor entered the restaurant then approached the door to the patio. This was where we ate last time, so she probably just assumed that's where I would be. She wore a champagne pink dress that fit snugly around her waist and flared out around her hips. Nude pumps were on her feet, and her legs looked long and toned. Her brown hair was in loose curls, pulled over one shoulder, and looked soft as hell. She hardly wore makeup like usual, but her eyes seemed to stand out that evening.

I swallowed the lump in my throat.

When she spotted me, she smiled then headed my way.

I didn't know what to do. I froze on the spot. That dull ache in my chest returned in full force, and my mouth was painfully dry. I tried to think of what to do and wasn't sure why I was thinking at all.

She reached the table and placed her clutch on the surface.

That's when I darted out of my chair and wrapped my arms around her. The impulse came out of thin air, and when my arms were wrapped around her small figure, I felt at peace. It was the same sensation I felt when we were lying in my bed together. I could feel the distinct curves of her hips as they led to her waist. I detected the indentation of her ribs through the fabric. Her smell washed over me at the same time, and a vivid image of us kissing came to mind.

Taylor froze when she felt my embrace, clearly not expecting it. Her arms rested on mine, and she held her breath. "Uh, everything alright?"

Realizing how stupid I looked, I pulled away. "Yeah. Of course." I shoved my hands in my pockets so fast I actually missed and threw them down my thighs. I tried to cover it up by acting like I was brushing something off my jeans.

Her eyebrow rose.

"It seemed like you needed a hug...after all those lab reports."

When her eyebrow fell, I knew she took the bait. "True. They are daunting." She reached for her chair.

Like the idiot that I was, I moved behind her and pulled the chair out for her. I hadn't pulled a stunt like this in so long, I couldn't remember. It surprised me most of all that I had any manners.

Taylor fell into the chair and looked at me over her shoulder.

I pretended everything was perfectly normal and sat across from her. Her gaze was drilling into my face, the disbelief more paramount than the awkwardness. I grabbed the menu and pretended to browse it even though I already knew what I was having.

Taylor kept up her stare for another minute before she grabbed her menu.

I knew I was acting like a weirdo. But I had no idea why. The last thing I wanted was for her to question me about it because I didn't have any of the answers. "Hummus?" We usually ordered a plate to share.

"Like we would ever come here and not order it. I'd never forgive myself."

I chuckled. "You're right."

The waiter took our drink and food order, and once he was gone, so were our menus. Now I had nothing to hide behind. I had to stare at her and keep my aura of confidence even though I felt anything but collected.

Taylor stared at me with her usual expression. A ghost of a smile was on her lips, and her eyes had a distant twinkle. They were unusually glossy, slightly wet at all times, and they reflected the light better than any other pair of eyes I'd gazed into. Right now, they reflected the white lights hanging in the garden just behind me. It looked like a constellation of stars in her eyes. As if she held the answers to the mystery of our very universe.

I could look into them all day.

"Volt?"

The sound of conversation became louder when I was brought back to reality. My eyes took in her entire face, and I saw her lips moving. "Sorry?"

"I asked you to pass the dessert menu three times. Are you okay?"

"Yeah, I'm fine." I grabbed the plastic stand and accidentally knocked over the bottle of oil. It tipped on its side but didn't break, thankfully. I quickly righted it then handed over the menu.

She took it, but her suspicion was directed right at me.

Before she could ask the question she had every right to ask, I changed the subject. "Already thinking about dessert before we've even had the appetizer? That sounds about right."

A smile formed on her lips, and she looked down at the menu. "That's how I roll."

I felt sweat form on my forehead, and I quickly wiped it away. My heart was beating so fast it actually hurt. My dick was hard in my jeans, and my breathing was haywire. I wasn't sure if I was having a panic attack or just a heart attack.

All I could think about was the softness of her lips. They felt perfect against mine. When they brushed past one another, they took hold before they broke apart again. The distinct taste of cherry was on her lips, concentrated from her ChapStick. I'd never been so turned on from a kiss in all my life. I was even fantasizing about it.

I hadn't seen her naked, but now I kept picturing how she would look. Her tits were average, but I bet they were firm and round. Her nipples would probably feel amazing in my mouth.

I shifted my weight in the chair because my dick was pressing hard against the zipper.

Her words kept echoing in my mind. *Fuck me, Volt. Fuck me hard.*

God, I couldn't stop thinking about it.

I'd been aroused before, but this anxiety had never accompanied it. My feet had been pulled from the earth, and I floated far above the ground. I couldn't catch my footing, and I spun out of control. Chills ran up my spine, but I was painfully hot at the same time.

I didn't even know who I was at the moment.

The waiter set the hummus and pita bread in front of us, and Taylor immediately grabbed a piece. She scooped the bread into the creamy hummus and popped it into her mouth. She closed her eyes and released a quiet moan from her lips. "Oh god..."

My dick twitched, and my heart raced even faster. I knew she was talking about the hummus, but I pictured her talking about something else. A vivid picture of her lying on her back underneath me, her tits shaking with every thrust I made, exploded into my mind.

And I pictured the face she made when she came.

***

"Taylor seems to be doing better." Derek sat across from me at the table in the bar.

I glanced over to see Taylor and Natalie standing near the TV. They both had a drink in their hands, and they were watching the game. "Yeah. She's bounced back." I stared at her curves in the black dress she wore, and I knew I wasn't the only man turning her way.

"That guy was an idiot," Derek said. "Taylor is so fucking hot. Why would you—"

"Say that again and you won't have any teeth." My hand formed a fist on the table, and I stared him down like an executioner.

Derek was just about to take a drink of his beer but decided against it. "I'm just saying—"

"Don't say anything about her, alright?" I forced my hand to relax, and I turned my gaze back to Taylor on the other side of the room. "She's not a piece of meat. How would you feel if I said that about Natalie?"

"Wouldn't give a damn. And I'm surprised you would give a damn."

"She's my friend." I didn't need to explain it further than that.

"Just your friend?" Suspicion was heavy in his voice.

"Yes. *Just my friend.*" I watched Taylor laugh at something Natalie said. I couldn't hear the sound, but I imagined it in my head because I'd heard it so many times.

"Dude, you spend every waking hour with this woman. She's not your friend, and we both know it."

"Don't act like you know what I'm thinking or feeling. Trust me, I don't have a thing for her."

Derek rolled his eyes then drank his beer. "This has something to do with *her*. I know it does."

I knew who he was referring to, and I was grateful he didn't say her name. It was the ugliest name I'd ever heard. When I hit on a girl with that same name, I ditch her in a heartbeat. "It doesn't."

"She did something to you, didn't she? That's the only explanation. Because you changed overnight."

"Drop it, man."

"I don't know what happened between you two, but whatever you have with Taylor is different. I can tell."

He could? "You don't know anything about our relationship."

"I know she's replaced me as your best friend." He sounded a little bitter, like he was trying to mask it but failed to do so.

"No, she hasn't."

"Cut the shit. Yes, she has. A guy and a girl can't be best friends unless one of them is gay. And I know you aren't gay, so that must mean Taylor is a lesbian."

"Shut up, man."

"Whatever." He fell silent and took a long drink of his beer.

I didn't have feelings for Taylor. I refused to go down that road—with anyone. I'd already had my heart ripped out of my chest and it'd never healed. The scars were still there—along with all the memories. I'd never been afraid of pain in all my life, but heartbreak was something that affected everyone.

And it affected me.

To put myself out there again and get trampled was something I'd never consider. I liked my life the way it was, going from woman to woman and never having anything significant with them. I forgot their names and faces the moment we were finished.

It was so easy.

But I hadn't done that in a while. I stayed home every night waiting for Taylor to text me. I convinced myself I was just trying to look after her after Drew hurt her, but now I wasn't so sure.

I wasn't sure of anything.

My eyes wandered around the room until I found a pretty girl. Blonde or brunette, I didn't care. Tall or short, what difference did it make? I had to prove to myself that my heart was still my own. Taylor was just my friend, and the only feelings I felt for her were lust.

And lust alone.

I pounded into Trish and listened to my headboard smack against the wall. I was giving it to her hard and rough, trying to fuck the feelings out of my heart. Her legs were wrapped around my waist, and she was moaning loudly, wanting even more than I was already giving her.

Her nails dragged down my back, cutting into me slightly. I liked the pain. It made me feel alive.

She already climaxed just a minute ago, and now it was my turn to take the plunge. My body was covered in sweat, and every sensation felt so good. I wasn't thinking about Taylor. I was just thinking about sex.

I made my final thrusts into her, feeling the delectable sensation start deep in my groin and spread out everywhere. I stared at her blonde hair and watched it change to brown. The strands got longer, reaching her shoulders and her tits. Her green eyes immediately turned blue, crystal clear like the water of a tropical island. Her lips changed from thin to plump, and her moans even changed in tune.

And then I came.

"Taylor…" I filled the tip of the condom with the most seed I'd ever released. My body became blinding hot, and all the sensation increased by tenfold. It was the best orgasm I'd ever had. My head swirled in a rush of emotions, all of them physical and undying.

The orgasm seemed to go on forever, and when it finally dwindled, reality came back into play. Her hair became blonde and her eyes green. She didn't stare at me with a look of satisfaction, but a look of horror. "Fucking asshole." She pushed me off violently, causing me to roll over onto the sheets.

She grabbed her dress and hastily pulled it on before she stepped into her heels and stormed out of my apartment. I knew she was gone when my front door slammed shut.

I lay back and stared at the ceiling, still breathing hard. The undeniable truth hit me like a slab of bricks. Now I couldn't deny everything I felt. Taylor was on my mind, and she infected every inch of me. I couldn't shake her because she was a part of me.

And that terrified me.

me, he darted to the refrigerator and popped off the lids of two beers. Then he returned and handed me one.

I took a drink before I set it on the coffee table. My lesson plan for the next week was spread out, right beside the first midterm I would be distributing in a few days. It was worth a lot of points, and I wanted Volt's opinion before I handed them out. If the parents didn't like it, my life would be more difficult.

Volt sat at the far end of the couch and hugged the armrest. He was so far away he couldn't see the lesson plans unless he leaned over and craned his neck down in a painful way.

Something didn't feel right. He hadn't said a word to me, and he treated me like I had a deadly virus that was contagious. "What's wrong?"

"Nothing." He drank his beer again.

"Then why are you sitting way over there?"

"It's more comfortable."

"But you can't see any of the papers." Seriously, what was his deal? He got weirder and weirder.

He eyed the space between us with uncertainty. Then he finally made the move and slid over, purposely keeping extra space between us. And he gripped his beer like he needed it to keep living.

I'd come to know Volt pretty well over the past few months, and I'd never seen him act this way. He was a completely different person, someone I didn't even know. "Are you sure you're alright? You've been different lately."

"I'm not different," he snapped. "I've just been tired at work and stuff. You didn't do anything."

I didn't do anything? "I never asked if you were mad at me."

"Well, I'm not. I don't feel anything toward you."

Even weirder. "Okay…"

"I picked up this girl the other night. Trish something…"

Even his tone of voice wasn't the same. His features were slack, and the usual playfulness he displayed was absent. "Good…do you like her?"

"I don't like anybody. Single forever. I already said that."

Now his hostility annoyed me. "If you're going to be a dick all night, just go. I have a lot of stuff I have to do."

"How am I being a dick? All I said was I don't do relationships, and I won't change my mind."

And it was random as hell. "I know…you said that already. I'm not even sure why we're talking about this. I assumed you were here to help me with work. But it seems like you have something else on your mind."

"I have nothing else on my mind."

262

I just wanted to get out of this conversation—pronto. "What do you think of this midterm?" I handed it over.

He set down his beer and flipped through the test, taking his time and reading every single question. He leaned back into the couch and finally sat normally. He rested his ankle on the opposite knee, and his features began to soften and fade from the scowl he walked in wearing.

"How's it going with Clay?"

He pulled his eyes away from the exam and looked at me. The look was normal again, and the man I knew was looking back at me. "He's even further behind than I imagined."

"That's too bad."

"His reading level is elementary."

I cringed.

"I have some time to prepare him for the exam, but...that's so much content to cover."

"And a lot of hours."

"But this kid seems motivated. He said he wants to score high enough to at least get into a junior college."

"At least his expectations are realistic."

"I just feel bad for him. My parents gave Connor and me everything, and I'm not talking about financial stuff. Dad always helped me study, and Mom always helped me build all my projects and stuff. They pushed me to succeed and knew exactly how to do it. Kids like this...don't stand a chance."

"It's heartbreaking."

"It really is." He shook his head and turned back to the exam. Instantly, he changed back into the soft and compassionate man I loved. This side of him was so gentle it was unreal. I loved it when he came out. I just wish he stuck around longer.

"So, what do you think?"

"I think it's a little challenging..."

"Isn't that the point?"

"I mean the questions themselves—the way they are written." He grabbed a pen and marked it up. "You're trying to trick them with every question."

"Not in a mean way," I argued. "This is how every test will be when they get to college."

"But these kids are juniors. They aren't quite there yet."

"Well, they need to be prepared." I wasn't going to give them a simple and straightforward test. Every exam I ever had required meticulous concentration just to decipher what the question was even asking. If I didn't prepare them now, they would be thrown off course when these kinds of exams happened.

"Maybe put a few like that, as bonus questions."

Oh, hell no. "I'm not giving extra credit. I'm not that kind of teacher."

"Then throw out the questions altogether."

My ears were about to blow out smoke. "I'm tired of having to attenuate my teaching style to please everyone. That's not what education is about. I want these kids to dislike me but thank me later. How can I accomplish that when I'm trying to make the parents happy? And they aren't even teachers, so they don't understand what needs to be done."

Volt shut the packet and tossed it on the coffee table. "Baby, listen to me."

I was so pissed off, my nose was about to ooze with lava, but when he said those words, I was suddenly jerked in a different direction. "Whoa, what?"

Volt's face blanched when he realized what he said. "I mean, you're acting like a baby."

"No, I'm not," I snapped. "You just—"

"Just do what I say until you get tenured. When you get to that level, you have a lot more freedom to do whatever you want. But you're a brand-new teacher, and you are

265

being scrutinized at a microscopic level." He grabbed my wrist and gave it a firm squeeze. "I hate to say it, but you're their bitch—for now."

"I'm nobody's bitch."

He shrugged. "Everyone is somebody's bitch—at one point in time."

***

"What do you think of this guy?" I turned my computer toward Natalie, who was sitting beside me at my desk.

"Eh. He's okay."

"Yeah...he's the best I found." Once my profile went live, I got a lot of takers. But most of them were weird, divorced, had no profile picture, or just plain creepy. This guy was the first one who seemed decent. He lived in the city, worked as an accountant, and he wasn't bad to look at. "But I have a bad feeling about this. I think I'm just going to waste my time."

"You won't know until you give it a try."

"But I may end up dead by giving it a try."

She rolled her eyes. "You'll be fine. I can come with you if you really want."

"Maybe we can just do that GPS sync on our phones so you'll know where I am just in case I go missing..."

She smacked me in the arm. "That's not gonna happen. Don't even think like that."

I responded to his message and agreed to a date on Saturday night. After I hit send, I knew it was final. There was no going back now. I was taking a risk to find Mr. Right. But I had a strong feeling this guy wasn't him.

***

Volt and I didn't talk for the rest of the week.

Which was very odd.

We usually talked every day, even if it was just a quick text conversation. He often came by my classroom to sit in, or we met up after work and got a pastry at our favorite bakery.

But he'd been radio silent.

Volt had something going on in his life that he wasn't comfortable talking about. That was the only way to explain his peculiar behavior. I felt like I was talking to three different people when I had a single conversation with him. He was all over the place, jerking me around with his unpredictability.

One moment, he was hugging me and pulling out the chair for me at a restaurant, and then a few days later, he acted like he hated me. There was no possible guess I could make that would explain everything, so I just stopped thinking about it.

It was a waste of time anyway.

He would come back to me whenever he was ready to be himself again. And when that time came, I wouldn't ask him a million questions. I would just let him be—like always.

I got ready for my date and wore the dress Volt had once picked out for me. It was skintight and short, and I was afraid it was a little slutty for a first date. But this was what he recommended, and I trusted his taste. I wore matching pumps with a pink clutch. We were going to an Italian restaurant, so I hoped I wasn't overdressed.

I got to the restaurant first and was taken to a table near the window. I arrived at my chair and sat down before looking at the time. I was purposely late, as Natalie told me to be, and he wasn't there yet. I looked at my phone to see if I had any messages from him, but I didn't.

I grabbed the wine list and tried to decide what I should get. A pair of eyes settled on me, and I could feel their burn. It felt intrusive and inhospitable. Without even looking up, I knew someone was staring at me.

But I didn't know whom.

I looked up from my menu and stared at the next table over. It was next to the window just as mine was, and a white tablecloth and low burning candle decorated the surface.

A man sat there alone, directly facing me. He wore a gray collared shirt that fit his broad shoulders nicely. Despite the fact the fabric covered everything, his muscular arms were still defined. He had dark brown hair with matching eyes. His face was cleanly shaven, revealing his hard jaw and smooth lips.

And he stared at me.

Heat immediately rose up my throat and entered my mouth. When I looked up, I hadn't been expecting someone like that to be staring at me. He was easy on the eyes, and I'm sure he felt good on the body.

Damn, he was gorgeous.

I looked at my menu again just so I had something to do. If I put it down, my eyes would wander to him again.

Why can't he be my date?

I felt guilty for the thought the moment I had it. The guy coming to meet me was probably a nice person, and I felt like a jerk for checking out some other guy who was probably waiting for his supermodel girlfriend.

Minutes passed, and my date still hadn't arrived. Was I being stood up? That didn't make any sense since he was the one who asked me out. And he knew what I looked like. It wasn't like he saw me then left.

I felt the man's gaze still glued to my face, and I wanted to take a peek and see if he was looking. But then I wouldn't be able to keep up my poker face of indifference.

Eventually, the waiter came over and asked if my date was coming. "Will he be here shortly?"

"Uh, I think so…"

After a dirty look, he walked away.

Now he was thirty minutes late, and it didn't seem like he was going to show.

How embarrassing.

My phone lit up with a message from the dating app, and I quickly read it. It was from my date. *Hey, are you still coming? I have a seat by the window at Le Chance.*

Le Chance? I peeked at the menu on the table and read the name of the restaurant. Le Chancet.

Shit, I got the wrong restaurant.

I was just about to type back when someone fell into the seat across from me.

The man sitting at the next table came face-to-face with me. He was even more beautiful up close. He had a nice

270

complexion that brought up his hazelnut eyes, and there was a kindness to him I hadn't expected. "I was waiting for a blind date, but she didn't show."

My first instinct was to tell him I was on a date myself but went to the wrong restaurant. But instead, I said something else. "Me too." I felt bad ditching the guy I was supposed to be on a date with, but something told me it would be a mistake to leave this opportunity. It was very rare when I saw a man I was truly attracted to. The first time it ever happened was when I looked at Volt.

And now it happened again.

"If you ask me, your date missed out."

Good-looking and sweet. What a deadly combination. I moved my lips to speak, but I didn't have any words to actually say. Finally, I found something to share. "That's nice of you to say. Your date missed out too."

"My friend arranged everything because he thought we would hit it off. I guess he was wrong."

"Sometimes things don't work out."

He stared at me for nearly a minute, examining every feature of my face like he was trying to memorize it. "Can I be your date tonight? And you be mine?" He grabbed a menu and handed it to me.

My heart was slamming against my ribs so painfully I was certain he could hear every beat. My mouth was parched and my fingertips felt numb. I never wanted to do online dating. Organic meetings like this were the kind I craved. I wanted something natural, to have the kind of chemistry that exploded the second we were in the same room together. I wanted a love story that was more authentic, more genuine.

I wanted something like this.

Chapter Fourteen

Volt

I took a step back.

My feelings for Taylor were undeniable. They were there, constantly bubbling under the surface. When I wasn't with her, she was all I thought about. And when I was with her, I did stupid shit like call her baby.

I was out of control.

I didn't exactly know what I felt for her. Did I love her? Did I just like her? Did I want a relationship with her?

I didn't have a clue.

But I knew I didn't want to feel this way. I wanted to go back to what my life was before. My chest was empty of all feeling, and I just went through the motions. I was detached from all human emotion.

And I liked it that way.

Whatever this was with Taylor was bad news. If we became anything more than friends, it would end in disaster. Just like my last relationship, she would break my heart and humiliate me at the same time. I didn't trust anyone, and I would never trust anyone again.

Even Taylor.

The best way to get rid of these feelings was to avoid her. After enough space, these emotions would go away, and we could go back to being friends. She could start dating someone new, and I wouldn't give a damn. I would screw an endless line of beautiful women and not think about her.

It was a great plan.

But by the end of the first week, I was going through withdrawals. I hadn't spoken to Taylor, and I missed her voice. Every time I saw a funny meme online, I wanted to show it to her but realized I couldn't. I wanted to tell her about the progress I was making with Clay, but I couldn't do that either.

I felt alone.

I stayed home every night after work and found myself staring at my phone. I wanted her name to pop up on the screen because I knew I wouldn't have the strength to ignore her call. It was an excuse to talk to her, an excuse for me to be weak.

But she never did.

Now I was worried over why she hadn't called me. Did she know how I felt about her? Did she pick up on all the signs? Or did I just annoy her? I hoped I just pushed her away.

I needed to push her away.

Because I would never be a boyfriend again—not even hers.

***

"What's up with you?" Jared handed me a beer before he plopped down on the couch beside me.

"Nothing. You?"

"You seem weird lately. Like, weirder than usual."

"I'm not weird. You're weird."

Derek walked in from the kitchen and sat on the other couch. "You guys are both weird."

"What's up with Taylor?" Jared asked me.

"Why the hell would I know?" I asked defensively. "She's not my girlfriend."

Jared gave me a strange look. "I never said she was, man."

"Good." I took a drink of my beer and focused on the game. "Because I'm not."

"She said she would pick up a pizza on the way," Derek said. "But Natalie isn't coming."

"Why isn't Natalie coming?" Jared asked.

Derek finished chewing a handful of chips before he spoke. "She said she was—"

"Whoa, hold on." I held up my hand. "Taylor is coming?"

"Yeah," Derek said. "Tayz. Why?"

"Shit." I set my beer down and tried to get the hell out of there. "I've got to go."

"But you just got here," Jared argued. "And why isn't Natalie coming?"

I walked around the couch and grabbed my keys.

"I guess she has a date or something," Derek said. "Looks like she's finally gotten over you."

"A date?" Jared asked in surprise.

Derek shrugged. "That's what Tayz said."

"I'm outta here." I headed to the door.

Derek turned to me. "Why, again?"

"I've got somewhere to be." Right when I reached for the door, it flew open. Taylor stood on the other side with two pizza boxes in her hand. "Sorry about that. I didn't mean to kick your door in."

I stared at her blankly, hating the fact I loved the way her hair fell over one shoulder. She wore some mascara today, and it made her eyes prettier than usual. I couldn't stop myself from memorizing the look, wanting to picture it when I made her come in my fantasies.

Shit, this was bad.

"It's all good," Derek said. "If you're bringing food, you can do whatever you want."

Taylor chuckled then walked around me. "Hey, Volt. How are you?" She spoke to me like the silence over the past two weeks was perfectly normal.

"Good. You?"

"Good. I changed the exam, and the kids did great. Maybe your suggestion was for the best." She set the pizzas on the counter. "Do you have any paper plates?"

"In the cupboard," Derek barked.

She grabbed a handful then scooped a few slices onto her plate.

Now that Taylor was there, I couldn't just walk out. It would be obvious she was the reason why I left, and that would invite unnecessary questions.

She grabbed a beer and sat on the couch next to Derek. She didn't pay any particular attention to me, which was a relief but also a frustration. She didn't think it was strange that I hadn't called her in a while? But wasn't it worse that it bothered me when she didn't call when I actually wanted her to?

This kind of psychology was hurting my head.

"So, Natalie has a date?" Jared asked.

I headed back to the couch and sat down, forcing myself not to look at Taylor. She wore dark blue shorts with a pink top. She normally wore dresses, and I loved seeing her in this new outfit. Her legs were to die for.

I hated myself for noticing.

"Yeah, she's been seeing this guy for a while," Taylor said. "She seems into him."

"Wow," Derek said in surprise. "Good for her."

Jared remained silent, his eyes glued to the TV.

"Yeah," Taylor said. "They like to spend time together, and she talks about him all the time. I think he'll be around for a while."

"Who is the guy?" Derek asked.

"His name is Peter," Taylor said. "They met when we were out one night. I don't know much more about him."

"I just hope he's a cool guy," Derek said.

"I think so," Taylor said. "He makes her happy."

Jared drank his beer.

I felt awkward not sitting next to Taylor and talking to her like I usually did. In fact, it was so strange I felt out of place. I was on a different planet with different people. Without her as my anchor, I drifted away to a place I didn't enjoy.

***

"Say what you want, but that game was totally rigged." Derek cleared the pizza boxes and shoved them into his garbage can.

"You're just a sore loser," Jared jabbed.

"Whatever," Derek said. "Those calls were bullshit, and we all know it."

"It's just a game," I said. "No reason to get worked up."

"Just a game?" Derek asked incredulously. "That's it. Get out of my house."

"I should get going anyway. Have work tomorrow." And I needed an excuse to get out of there without talking to Taylor...even though I wanted to talk to her.

What the hell was wrong with me?

"I should get going too." Taylor grabbed her purse and tossed her plate in the garbage on the way to the door. "Thanks for inviting me over."

"No problem," Derek said. "See you later."

Jared walked to Taylor with his arms across his chest. "So...is Natalie serious with this guy?"

Why did he care?

Taylor shrugged. "Not sure. But she wants to keep seeing him." Suspicion settled in her eyes. I recognized it because I'd seen it so many times myself. "I guess that answers your question."

Jared suddenly walked into the bathroom, not saying anything more.

What was that about?

"Alright. I'll see you later." Taylor walked past me and headed to the door.

I walked out with her because I had no choice. "Bye."

Once we were outside and the door was shut behind us, I expected her to interrogate me about the change in our relationship. One moment, we were inseparable. And now, we were distant.

"Good game, huh?" she asked as we walked down the hall.

That was the last thing I expected her to say. "Pretty tense."

"I love sports, but they're so heartbreaking at the same time. Kinda makes me hate them."

"I know what you mean."

We got into the elevator and slowly rode it down to the lobby.

I expected her questions, her concern. But it never came.

"How's it going with Clay?"

"It's okay," I said. "He's really behind. We meet every single day after school, and I still don't think that's enough."

"There's always the weekend."

"Nah. I'm not giving up my weekends too."

She pulled out her phone and read a text message. A smile stretched her lips from ear to ear. She typed a response then shoved her phone back into her purse.

I saw everything in the reflection of the doors.

The doors opened, and we walked through the lobby to the sidewalk outside. Her apartment was in the opposite direction from mine, and we were about to part ways.

"I'll see you later, Volt. Have a good week." She immediately turned around and walked away.

What the hell?

Did she not miss me?

She didn't think my distance was weird?

She didn't expect me to walk her home?

What was going on?

How could she not care?

"Taylor."

She turned around, gripping her purse on her shoulder. "What's up?"

I had her full attention, and I tried to think of something to say. There were a million things I wanted to share with her. She was the only person I could talk to, and I wished I could tell her about these strange feelings I had for her. She

281

would be able to help me figure everything out and what I should do about it. But she was the one person I couldn't tell. "Want me to walk you home?"

"Nah. I got it." She turned around and kept walking.

I stood there and watched her go, counting every step as she walked away and left me behind.

What was wrong with me?

***

I worked with Clay for an hour, and we were still on the vocabulary section of the SAT. Since he couldn't read, he couldn't complete the subject. So I had him read every sentence in the SAT prep book and work out every vocabulary word. When he recognized words he'd already seen before, he was able to remember them and spit them out easily.

But we still had a long way to go.

I was dreading the math section. Absolutely dreading it. Most kids struggled with math in some capacity, and that was perfectly fine. But I suspected he couldn't do much more than add and subtract.

Poor kid.

He rubbed his temple at the end of the session. "Fuck, my brain hurts."

"What did I say about cussing?"

He rolled his eyes.

"You're just making it worse."

"Sorry…" He grabbed his backpack and put all his stuff away. His stomach rumbled loudly under the table, and we could both hear it.

"Better run home and get some dinner."

"Yeah…" He got out of the chair and shouldered his backpack. "I'll see you later, Volt."

"Alright, kid. Good work today."

He waved and walked out.

I closed up the office because I was the last one in the building. I used to leave just after lunch, but since I'd taken on Clay, I had to stick around. It cramped my style, but it was temporary. Clay needed help, and I knew I was his only hope for some form of a better life.

I left the building and started walking to my apartment. After I passed a few blocks, I saw a familiar bike leaning against the wall in an alleyway. It was gray and rusty—and the chain was about to fall off.

Clay must be around here somewhere.

I stopped and peeked down into the alleyway, and that's when I saw something I'll never forget.

Clay pulled out a Styrofoam container directly from the dumpster and opened the lid. He examined soggy fries and leftover chicken inside, and after a few seconds of deliberation, he began to eat it.

My heart broke.

"Clay." I entered the alleyway and snatched the box out of his hand.

He stepped back and tried to brush it off. "I was looking for food for my dog."

"No, you weren't." I tossed it into the dumpster. "Don't lie to me. You're wasting your time."

He crossed his arms over his chest, putting up his walls to protect himself from my judgment.

"Why are you eating out of a dumpster?"

He shrugged.

"I asked you a question."

"I was hungry. Obviously."

"Do you have anything to eat at home?"

He shrugged again. "Not really."

"Your dad doesn't make you anything?"

He shook his head. "No. There's no food in the house."

The blood drained from my body as the depression hit. I knew Clay wasn't well-off, but I didn't realize things were this bad. Maybe that bruise on his face was exactly what I thought it was. "Does he hit you?"

"No." He blurted it out without hesitation. "He doesn't hit me. We're fine." He took a step back, his head bowed.

"Clay, are you lying to me?"

"No."

"What did I say about lying?"

"I'm not lying," he argued. "Don't call social services. You're wasting your time."

Now I was even more confused. How did he know about social services? Why would he lie and say he's not being hit if he is? I'd never been in this position before, and I didn't know what to do. "Come on. Let's get you something to eat."

"I don't need your charity." He walked to his bike, keeping his back to me.

"It's not charity." I followed behind him and grabbed him by the shoulder. "I'm only trying to help you."

He looked up into my face, inexplicable rage marked into every feature. "Maybe you grew up rich, but not everyone is so lucky. You don't need to pity me or look down on me. I can take care of myself."

"I'm sure you can, Clay. But when a door opens, walk through it."

"What?"

"Just come with me." I released his shoulder and headed to the sidewalk.

"I don't have a lock for my bike."

"No one will see it. And if it's gone, I'll loan you mine. I never use it."

***

I got him the most fattening and delicious meal I could find.

We went to Mega Shake and ordered burgers and fries. It was much better than any leftovers he could find in an alleyway.

Just thinking about it made me sick.

He was apprehensive to eat at first, but once he took the first bite, he couldn't help himself. He devoured the entire thing in less than five minutes. Grease and dressing were all over his fingers, and he licked it off.

Thankfully, I told him to wash his hands before he ate.

"Pretty good, huh?"

He nodded, still sucking his fingers.

"You want more?"

He shook his head. "No. I'm pretty stuffed."

His stomach was probably smaller than a walnut at this point. "If you ever need anything, you can always ask me, Clay." I wasn't going to let this kid eat out of a garbage can. I wouldn't let any kid resort to that.

He wiped his hands with a napkin.

"I mean it, Clay."

"I heard you, Volt."

The more I helped him, the more he resented me. I understood he wanted to make his own way in life, and he was embarrassed about being so far down on the economic ladder, but he shouldn't feel so ashamed.

I opened my wallet and set a twenty-dollar bill on the table. "That's for lunch tomorrow."

He eyed it without taking it.

"I'll give you more every day."

"What am I supposed to do with it?"

"Buy lunch at school. What do you normally do?"

"Nothing…"

"They don't have a lunch program there?"

"I dunno. Everyone makes fun of the kids who are on it… I'd rather not eat."

How was he functioning right now? No wonder he couldn't pay attention in school. He was malnourished and starving all the time. "Take the money and buy lunch."

"I'm not taking your money. I couldn't use it anyway."

"Why not?"

"They use lunch cards. You load it with money at the office and then use a card."

Even schools were going digital. "Then I'll take care of that tomorrow."

"I don't want your money." He shoved the twenty back to me. "I'm fine without it."

I shoved it back. "I'm not taking it, Clay. You may as well keep it."

He eyed it for a long time before he pocketed it.

"I'll pay for the card and leave it at the office. Pick it up at lunchtime."

"You don't need to do that," he whispered.

"I know I don't, Clay. I'm doing it because I want to."

He stared at his empty tray, his mind somewhere else. "This is the first time I've felt full since... I can't even remember the last time."

I didn't know my heart could break that many times in a row. "You'll never be hungry again. I promise."

"I'm not your problem, Volt. You don't need to make me your problem. I'm just some poor kid that will die in a ditch someday. No one will remember me, and no one will even notice when I'm gone."

It was one of the rare times I was speechless. No one had ever floored me with their words. The misery in his voice was difficult to listen to. It made me want to do anything in my power to make him happy, even rip off my own arm. "That's not what's in your future, Clay."

"It's not?" he asked sarcastically.

"No. You're going to go to college and make something of yourself. You're going to have a happy life with a beautiful girl and some kids one day. You're going to live happily ever after. This moment, right now, is going to be forgotten. Not you, Clay."

***

Taylor was always in my dreams.

I expected her to be naked and on all fours, but that wasn't the case. Sometimes, she was lying next to me on the couch, her long hair resting on my arm. Sometimes, we walked through a meadow holding hands. Sometimes, she laughed—just laughed.

What did that mean?

The more I pushed her away, the more I obsessed over her. Her absence only reminded me how much I needed her. The loneliness was worse than ever before, and I wasn't sure who I was anymore.

I wanted to tell her about Clay. This was the first situation I couldn't handle on my own, and there was no one better to ask than a great teacher. Actually, there was no one better to ask—period.

I showed up at her classroom at the end of the day and checked my appearance before I walked inside. I wore a navy blue suit with a colored tie, and I worried I didn't look my best. I never cared what women thought of my appearance before because they always seemed impressed no matter what I was wearing, but now I couldn't stand the idea of looking anything less than the perfect man—at least for her.

Pushing her away made me value our friendship even more. It was an amazing sensation, to be this close to someone without feeling pain. I hadn't had a relationship like that in...a long time. I didn't want to lose that. Actually, I couldn't afford to.

I walked inside with the intention of being normal. Taylor was just my friend and nothing more. These feelings would go away if I bottled them down hard enough.

Taylor was wiping down the whiteboard when I stepped inside. She wore a loose bright blue dress with a pink cardigan. Flamingo earrings hung from her lobes, and the heels she wore were safari themed.

She looked cute as hell.

I used to think her clothing was strange and a little dorky, but now I loved it. She stood out in the crowd, being unnaturally beautiful and unique. She didn't care what anyone thought of her, and I loved that about her. Actually, I preferred these outfits to the skintight stuff I told her to wear to bars and clubs.

Because it was who she was.

She set the eraser on the edge then turned to the desk. That's when she noticed me. "Oh, hey." She rested her hand against her chest and released a sigh of relief. "You scared me for a second." She chuckled at her own reaction.

I could do this.

It's just like old times.

She's just my friend. My gorgeous and amazing friend…but just my friend.

Think clearly.

"You should be James Bond with moves like that," she said with a laugh.

I came closer to her desk, trying to think of something witty to say in response. My eyes focused on those rosy cheeks, and I imagined my fingers running across her smooth skin until they rested on her lips. Then that image changed, and I was kissing her against the desk, hiking her up until she was sitting on it with her legs around my waist. "I miss you."

Fuck.

Goddammit.

What the hell is wrong with me?

I hadn't blinked since I uttered those words, and now the room fell quiet in intensity. I didn't expect her to say anything back. What could she possibly say to that? I came here determined to resume our friendship, but instead, I ruined it.

Like an idiot.

Her eyes softened as she examined me, seeing the sincerity in my eyes as well as everywhere else. Her lips parted slightly, reminding me of the gentle kisses we once shared. "I miss you too."

Liquid softness spread across my heart, giving me the greatest amount of pleasure I'd ever known. I never expected her to say those words, so I wasn't prepared for how they would make me feel. Cloud Nine was a real place, and I just landed.

"I just assumed you had a lot on your mind and needed some space." She stood at her desk and watched me with affectionate eyes. They were bright like usual, containing the secrets of the world deep inside.

I never needed space from her—just these ridiculous feelings. "I've just had some stuff going on..." Now I was even more convinced that these emotions were here to stay. All I could think about was the enchanting tone of her voice, the way her hair fell around her face like she was about to walk into a photo shoot, and the hypnotic way her eyes fell on me. I kept picturing her in my bed, but not naked and wet. She wore one of my t-shirts and a pair of boxers. Her lips were red and puckered from kissing me like she loved me. And I was just watching her sleep.

"You want to talk about it?" She sat in the chair behind her desk.

I couldn't tell her what was really going on. If I did, it would just make things awkward...or at least more awkward. And if I told her how I felt and she felt the same way, it would be a moot point—because I couldn't offer her anything. Maybe these feelings were real and not superficial, but that didn't mean I wanted a commitment. Right now, I was just focused on making them go away.

I pulled up a chair and sat across from her. "I caught Clay eating out of a dumpster."

It took her a second to react, and when she did, she wasn't shocked—just heartbroken. "Oh, no..."

"I gave him some money to pay for food at school, but he said they run on a card system. So I loaded one with enough cash to last him until he graduates. And I bring food to our lessons now so I know he gets dinner."

"That's so sweet of you, Volt."

No, it wasn't. I wasn't doing it for any kind of recognition. I wasn't doing it because it made me feel good. I was doing it because…I cared about this kid. "I asked if his dad hits him, but he said no. I feel like he's lying."

"Why would he lie?"

"That's the thing…I don't know. There is no reason. If you were in an abusive household, wouldn't you want to be taken out?"

"I would think so," she whispered.

"I haven't seen any bruises lately so…maybe he's telling the truth."

"I hope so."

"But if this kid isn't getting food, and he has to hide the fact he's being tutored…I can only assume the worst." Two things were weighing me down at the moment. The first one was my feelings for Taylor. They didn't die down during our time apart, and they definitely flared up when we were together. The second thing was Clay. I worried about him constantly, fearing what went down when he was home with his father. No kid should have to struggle like this, and my heart kept breaking over and over. I wasn't an emotional guy, but Clay brought out the worst in me.

"Wait until he trusts you. Then ask him again."

"Kids like Clay don't trust anyone. That's how they survive."

"But you've gone above and beyond for him," she whispered. "You aren't just another grown-up. He knows you care about him."

I hoped he realized that. Because I suspected I was the only person who did care about him.

"I'd like to meet him...if there's ever a time."

"You would?"

She nodded. "He doesn't have a mom in his life, right?"

I shook my head. "Not that I know of. It sounds like just the dad is in the picture."

"Every boy needs a mom...no matter how strong they are."

I could attest to that. Growing up, I was a momma's boy. And frankly, I was still a momma's boy. "I'll give him some more time to get used to me before I bring in someone else. He's very timid around people, like if he draws too much attention to himself, he's going to be punished in some way."

"Volt, this is heartbreaking." She ran her fingers through her hair and sighed. "How do you do it?"

"I don't know..." I really didn't have an answer to that.

"Well, if he's a sophomore now, he's almost done with school. You can get him a decent score on the SAT and help him get out of his situation. In a few years, he'll be in a better place, and this will seem like a distant nightmare."

"True." I just hoped I could get him a good score on the exam. If his grades reflected his skill level, then I could only assume he was failing everything. Then the score would carry even more weight.

Taylor stared at me, sympathy glowing in her stunning eyes. "How are you? Besides all of that?"

Miserable.

Confused.

Lost.

"Good. You?"

"All the kids did great on the exam, but now I'm worried that might get me into trouble."

"How so?"

"Well, they all got As. And that's suspicious."

It was.

"It makes it look like the test was too easy...which it was. And now I'm afraid when they move on, they won't be prepared. I'm afraid the kids will talk about me in the hallway and say how easy I am. The other teachers won't respect me, and when the principal realizes that, he'll start to reevaluate me."

All of those were valid points. "But it'll get the parents off your back."

"Frankly, the parents are the least of my problems right now."

"The principal has to deal with parents all day long. Trust me on that. The less often he sees parents about you, the more he's going to like you. Maybe this test was too easy, but you can make the next one a little more challenging. The parents won't be as alarmed because they know you're fair."

"I didn't realize teaching was so political..."

The sky was infinite in that regard. "It's just as political as anything else you hear about."

"Great..."

"But again, when you're tenured, you have a lot more freedom to run your classroom how you want. Just don't sleep with any of the kids and you're good."

She narrowed her eyes on me.

I chuckled. "I'm glad that's not your thing."

"That's not even funny to joke about."

In my short teaching career, I'd never come across anything like that, thankfully. If it happened to one of my students, I would be livid. If it happened to Clay, I'd see red. And if it happened to my own son or daughter...I'd be on trial for murder. "Yeah, you're probably right."

She closed her folder and shoved her papers inside her bag. "Have plans tonight?"

I was hoping to spend every free hour with her. "No. You?"

"Nope."

I wanted to invite her back to my place in the hope she would make another move on me. This time, I wouldn't turn her down, and I would enjoy every second of those beautiful lips against mine. But I knew that was wishful thinking. Even if she did come on to me, I would have to turn her down because I knew that wasn't what she truly wanted...but it was fun to imagine. "Can I take you out to dinner?" I immediately hated myself for wording it that way.

Taylor didn't seem to notice anything. "I think I should take you out to dinner—and for a drink."

There's nothing I wanted more. "I'd love that."

***

I forced myself not to stare at her too much over dinner. My eyes naturally wandered to her face, particularly her lips, and I needed to get a hold of myself before I freaked her out. I was coming to realize I was obsessed with her.

And I'd never been this obsessed with a woman.

"Have you moved on from the Drew incident?" She seemed to be in better spirits than she was three weeks ago. She was smiling just the way she used to, and that bubbling sense of life was bright in her eyes.

"Yeah. I'm over it."

"Good." I sipped my wine and returned to my new favorite hobby—staring. "He's an idiot for letting a woman like you go." I hated myself for the stupid shit I was blurting out, but I could never stop myself in time.

She smiled before she took her drink. "I actually started dating again."

My heart fell into my stomach quicker than the snap of a finger, and the nausea immediately followed it. My fingers were so tense I almost shattered the glass in my hand. I wanted to flip over the table and throw a tantrum, but I managed to restrain myself. "Oh…"

"It's actually a funny story."

Like ha-ha funny? Or blow my brains out funny?

"I started online dating—"

"Why the hell are you doing that?" I exploded like an active volcano. My anger had been building since she mentioned dating, and now I couldn't hold everything back. I didn't want her to date anyone, especially random strangers she met online. "Only losers do online dating. You're so much better than that, Taylor. I would never date someone who lowered herself to that level."

Taylor held her glass near her face but didn't take a drink. Her narrowed eyes showed her irritation as well as her unease. I could feel her pulling away without her actually moving.

Fuck. I'm an asshole.

She finally took a drink to mask the tension. Her eyes drifted away, growing more uncomfortable by the minute.

"I'm sorry I said all of that. I didn't mean it. I just..." *Don't want you to date anyone but me. I want to take you home right this second and kiss you like no man ever has before. I want you to be mine forever. And I want to be yours.* "I've had too much to drink."

Taylor took another drink before she set her glass down. "It's okay. I know you've had a stressful day."

Only Taylor could forgive me for being such an asshole. "That's not an excuse."

"Really, it's fine. Let's just move on."

The tension fell on the table all over again. I was determined to sabotage this relationship every chance I got.

I tried pushing her away and I succeeded, but not in the way I wanted. "So...did you meet anyone online you like?" I only asked the question to be polite. I wasn't sure if I could tolerate her answer.

"Uh..." She wrapped her fingers around the stem of her glass and stared at it. "No. I haven't met anyone." She took a long drink of her wine, finishing it off. "Natalie told me to give it a try, but I didn't come across anyone I liked."

What a relief. "Maybe it's too soon to date anyway. Take your time. There's no rush."

"Yeah...maybe." She poured herself another glass of wine.

Our natural chemistry still hadn't returned, and I spoiled the entire evening when I lost my temper. I got upset when I thought she was dating, but I had no right to be upset. I wanted her, but I didn't want to have her. So why would I have any right to be pissed?

At least she hadn't met anyone she liked.

I still had time to figure this out.

Chapter Fifteen

Taylor

Sage walked me to my door at the end of the night. His hand was wrapped in mine, and he pulled me close to him, wanting our bodies to be as close to one another as possible.

Without warning, he dug one hand into my hair and pulled me closer. He rubbed his nose against mine in the sexiest way imaginable before he leaned in and gave me a fiery kiss.

It started off slow and gentle before it escalated into something deadly. I was panting into his mouth and gripping his biceps so I wouldn't float away on my high. His kiss was almost as good as the one I had with Volt, and I suspected it would soon surpass it.

"Can I come inside?" he breathed into my mouth.

It was our second date, but we had a connection from the beginning. He was charming, funny, and oh-so-sweet. I loved everything about him. He made Drew look like a troll.

I wanted to invite him inside.

But I remembered everything that happened with Drew. We moved way too fast, and as a result, I got my heart broken. I thought Sage was different, and that's why I wanted to make sure I didn't sabotage it with a hasty decision. "I would love that…but maybe we should get to know each other better."

Instead of being disappointed, he gave me a gentle kiss. "Whatever you want, sweetheart."

Now I liked him even more.

He pulled me in for a hug and held me that way for a long time. "Never knew I would be happy about being stood up."

"Me neither."

He kissed me on the temple as he pulled away. "Are you free on Friday?"

"Yeah."

"Have dinner with me."

He didn't need to ask twice. "I'd love to."

"Great. I'll see you then." He gave me a kiss good-bye before he walked away.

I watched him go until he turned down the hall, treasuring the sight of his nice ass the entire way.

I walked inside and immediately called Natalie.

"How'd it go?" She insisted that I call the second the date ended.

"Great. Really great."

"You managed to say no to a sleepover?"

"Yeah…and it was hard."

"Good for you. I'm sure that wasn't easy."

I plopped down into the chair and realized I already missed him. "I really like him, Nat."

"I can tell."

"I think this could go somewhere. And he seems to really like me too."

"Why wouldn't he?" she asked. "You're perfect."

I rolled my eyes.

"When is Volt gonna meet him?"

I held back the laugh that tried to escape my throat. "Never. I'm not telling Volt about this."

"Why not? I thought he was your best friend."

I remembered that awful conversation we had just a few days ago. "I started to tell him the story, and I began with the blind date part and he flipped out on me...more than I thought he would."

"Really? Why is that guy so judgmental when it comes to you?"

"I don't have a clue."

"Well, he's going to find out eventually."

"I know he will. But at least I don't have to tell him." *And deal with his shit afterward.*

"Gotcha."

"Well, I should go. I need to call Sara and tell her everything I just told you."

"You called me first? Aww."

"But she's not going to know that."

"Or maybe you did call her first, but you're just playing me..."

"Hmm... I guess you'll never know."

She laughed. "Such a player."

Chapter Sixteen

Volt

Derek ran down the court and dribbled the ball past me.

I faked to the right then darted to the left, stealing the ball right from underneath his fingers. I charged down the court and made a slam dunk into the net.

It was nothing but air.

"Traveling!" Derek yelled.

"Was not traveling," I argued.

"You so were," Derek argued.

"I thought it was clean," Jared said.

"Oh, shut up." Derek rolled his eyes then retrieved the ball.

"I'm done." Jared wiped his face with his t-shirt, removing the sweat and dirt.

"I think I'm done too." I sat on the bench and downed my water bottle. It was an unusually hot day in the city for this time of year.

"If anyone asks, I won." Derek spun the ball on his finger for a second before he lost his balance and dropped it.

"We weren't keeping score." I squirted water in my face to cool off.

"Well, I was," Derek said.

He was a sore loser, so I let it go.

Jared sat beside me on the bench. "So...is Natalie still seeing that guy?"

The question came out of thin air, and it was so jarring, I actually looked at him. Did he suddenly have a thing for Natalie? Because he hadn't noticed her once for the past five years. Why did he notice her now?

"Yeah," Derek answered. "She and Taylor went on a double date last night."

Say what?

"They did?" Jared asked. "How did it go?"

Wait, hold on. Taylor told me she wasn't seeing anyone.

"Natalie likes her date, but I guess Taylor is totally enamored by this guy she met," Derek said. "They were both on blind dates that didn't show up, so they hooked up instead."

Hooked up? "How long has this been going on?"

Derek shrugged. "I don't know. Two weeks?"

Fuck.

Jared watched me. "You okay, man? You look sick."

I ignored his question. Taylor was already dating someone while I sat around and tried to figure out what the hell I wanted. Now that I knew she was already being wooed by some other guy the second she got out of a relationship, I realized how much time I had wasted. I could have swooped in before anyone else had a chance.

I had the perfect opportunity.

But I blew it because I was too stubborn and stupid.

I wasn't ready to be in a relationship, not after the way I was betrayed. But I couldn't let Taylor walk away. I couldn't lose out on the chance to be with someone I was so fond of. She was my best friend, the only person who had stepped into my inner circle so fluidly. She was special.

I couldn't let her go.

I had to do something before it was too late.

***

I didn't stop to shower and change my clothes. I went exactly as I was, in a sweaty t-shirt and basketball shorts. My palms were covered with dirt, and lines of sweat streaked down my forearms.

But I didn't have time to mess around.

I knocked on her door but didn't get an answer. So I rang the doorbell a few times and became the most obnoxious person on the planet. She still didn't answer, so I rang the doorbell once more for good measure.

I had to accept the fact she wasn't home.

Now I didn't know what to do.

It was getting late so she should head home soon. She wasn't out with me, so she must be out with whoever this dreamy guy was.

Or she might be staying at his place.

The thought made me sick.

I paced in front of her door so I had something to do. It was impossible for me to stand still for even a second. My heart was pounding painfully in my chest, and I could hardly catch my breath.

I had to fix this.

If I just told her how I felt from the beginning, I wouldn't be in this situation. When I kissed her on my bed, there was more chemistry there than the damn periodic table. It was an explosion of feeling. There was no way she didn't feel it too.

I knew she was attracted to me when we first met, and once romance was off the table, we became friends. So, I did have a chance. If I offered to give her more than just one night, she might take it.

But I was an ass to her.

Would she ever want to be with me after I insulted her? Would she want to be with me after I waited so long to figure out how I felt? Would she want me after I spent most of my life as a manwhore?

Was I good enough for her?

The elevator opened, and voices echoed down the hallway. I knew exactly whom they belonged to without even seeing them. Taylor and her date headed right my way, whispering to one another like longtime lovers.

Fuck.

Taylor spotted me by the door, and she immediately dropped the guy's hand.

I didn't look at her. I looked at him.

He was my height with dark brown hair. He clearly hit the gym several times a week, and he dressed to impress. Confidence radiated from his body in waves. I could feel his immediate dislike for me the second he laid eyes on me, some stranger standing outside Taylor's door.

I didn't like him.

I didn't like the fact he was good-looking.

I didn't like the fact he wasn't afraid of me.

I didn't like the fact he grabbed Taylor's hand again when she purposely dropped it.

And I didn't like the fact he was a threat.

Taylor immediately came to me, concern written all over her face. "Volt? Is everything okay?"

"Yeah, I'm fine. I just…wanted to talk."

"About?" she asked.

311

"Can we talk inside?" *Away from this asshole.*

"Uh…" She glanced at her date before she turned back to me. "I'm kind of on a date right now. Can it wait?"

"No." It couldn't wait another second.

"Um, alright." She turned to her date and lowered her voice. "I'm sorry about this. Can I call you tomorrow?"

A scowl was still on his face. "Are you going to introduce me?"

"Oh, I'm sorry." Taylor turned to me. "Sage, this is my friend, Volt. Volt, this is my friend, Sage."

She didn't call him her boyfriend—and that was music to my ears.

He extended his hand to shake mine. "Nice to meet you." He gripped my hand firmly, threatening me.

I did the same back to him. "You too."

We both pulled our hands away quickly.

Sage turned to Taylor and gave her a kiss. "Call me tomorrow."

"I will." She kissed him back.

And I wanted to die.

Sage walked down the hallway and didn't look back until he got into the elevator. The doors closed, and he was finally hidden from view.

Taylor got the door unlocked and walked inside.

I followed behind her. "Look, I—"

"I'm sorry I didn't tell you about him." She tossed her clutch on the table. "But when I brought up the online dating thing, you got hostile with me. And when I was dating Drew, you were an ass about him every step of the way. I just didn't want to deal with it." She blurted everything out a million miles an hour until she was out of breath.

Her face was contorted with stress, and somehow, I thought she looked beautiful. I always thought she looked beautiful. "You had every right to feel that way, Taylor. I was an ass. I don't blame you." It hit me in that moment how much I didn't deserve her. This guy wanted her the moment he saw her, but it took me four months to figure out she was a piece of treasure sitting right in front of me. She wanted me, but I didn't want her.

What kind of man was I?

I used to think her dresses and earrings were strange. I used to think she was a little ditzy. I didn't appreciate her, not until long after we met. She was always a good friend to me, and I knew I wasn't the best to her.

I didn't deserve her.

"What did you want to talk about?" She crossed her arms over her chest.

My plan was to come here and tell her the truth. I was going to confess all my feelings and ask her for a chance. But I realized that plan wasn't going to work. The second I saw the two of them together, I knew she liked him.

She didn't like me.

I was setting myself up for failure.

For heartbreak.

I took too long to figure everything out.

There was only one thing I could do. I could try to get her to want me again. I could be the kind of man she wanted me to be. I could sweep her off her feet and convince her to be mine without actually saying a word.

I could chase her—and chase her hard.

And maybe she would leave Sage and pick me over him.

Maybe.

"Volt?"

I could be the man she deserved—if I tried hard enough. That's how much I wanted her. I was willing to open old wounds to make this work. I was willing to get hurt again just for a chance.

I was willing to do anything.

"I had a hard day with Clay…wanted someone to talk to." I felt like a dick for using him as an excuse. If there was one thing Taylor was a sucker for, it was helpless kids.

"Oh, no. What happened?" She dropped her hands to her sides and came to me, her hands immediately reaching for my biceps.

When she touched me like that, I couldn't breathe.

I wanted to grip her around the waist and pull her into me.

I stared at her face and loved the concern in her eyes. I loved it when she looked at me that way, like I was the center of her world—at least for a moment. "He hasn't been focusing lately. Seems distracted." I couldn't think of a complex lie on the spot, so I just said something vague.

"Maybe something is going on at home."

"Maybe…"

She walked into her kitchen and made two cups of tea. "Sit down."

I took a seat at the kitchen table, looking directly at her. My tea emitted steam that wafted into the air. Instead of taking a drink, I kept my attention on her. I wished the table weren't separating us. I wish nothing was keeping us apart. I wish I didn't have to compete with Sage.

I wish I could call her mine.

As of tomorrow, I would be competing in a game I'd never played before. I would be giving my all to win over a woman I could've had long ago. But I had to convince her to be with me, not ask her to.

And I had to win.

The story continues in *Spark*, Book 2 of the Electric Series.

Available Now.

Dear Reader,

Thank you for reading Charge. I hope you enjoyed reading it as much as I enjoyed writing it. If you could leave a short review, it would help me so much! Those reviews are the best kind of support you can give an author. Thank you!

Wishing you love,

E. L. Todd

Want To Stalk Me?

Subscribe to my newsletter for updates on new releases, giveaways, and for my comical monthly newsletter. You'll get all the dirt you need to know. Sign up today.

www.eltoddbooks.com

Facebook:

https://www.facebook.com/ELTodd42

Twitter:

@E_L_Todd

Now you have no reason not to stalk me. You better get on that.

I know I'm lucky enough to have super fans, you know, the kind that would dive off a cliff for you. They have my back through and through. They love my books, and they love spreading the word. Their biggest goal is to see me on the New York Times bestsellers list, and they'll stop at nothing to make it happen. While it's a lot of work, it's also a lot of fun. What better way to make friendships than to connect with people who love the same thing you do?

Are you one of these super fans?

If so, send a request to join the Facebook group. It's closed, so you'll have a hard time finding it without the link. Here it is:

https://www.facebook.com/groups/1192326920784373

Hope to see you there, ELITE!

Printed in Great Britain
by Amazon